VIRAGO
MODERN CLASSICS
287

*Kate O'Brien*

Born in Limerick in 1897, Kate O'Brien lost her mother when she was only five, and was given a boarding-school education in a convent before studying at University College, Dublin. She worked as a journalist in London and Manchester, and for a year as a governess in Spain, a period which was to exert a profound influence on her thinking and writing. Her marriage, at twenty-six, to a Dutch journalist soon ended and she never remarried. Kate O'Brien's original success was as a playwright but the publication of *Without My Cloak* (1931) won her rapid acclaim as a novelist. This was followed by eight further novels, two of which, *Mary Lavelle* (1936) and *The Land of Spices* (1942) were condemned for their 'immorality' by the Irish Censorship Board. Kate O'Brien dramatised three of her novels and *That Lady* (1946) was made into a film. Noted also for her travel books, an autobiography and a study of St Teresa of Avila, Kate O'Brien was honoured by the Irish and British literary establishments. She died in 1974.

# THE LAND OF SPICES

Kate
O'Brien

*With a new Introduction by*
*Clare Boylan*

Virago

A *Virago* Book

Published by Virago Press Limited 1988

Reprinted 1991, 1993, 1995, 1996

This edition published by Virago Press in 2000

Reprinted 2001, 2002, 2003

A CIP catalogue record for this book
is available from the British Library

ISBN 0 86068 826 7

Printed and bound in Great Britain by
Clays Ltd, St Ives plc

Virago Press
An imprint of
Time Warner Books UK
Brettenham House
Lancaster Place
London WC2E 7EN

www.virago.co.uk

# CONTENTS

# INTRODUCTION

Kate O'Brien has always been something of an enigma. A subtle and persuasive feminist, she could still dismiss any woman who fell short of her standards as 'a repetitious old bundle' or 'a vain tulip of a woman'. High-minded and serious, she once confessed to a liking for dance music, quoting Masefield: 'Don't despise dance music. It's the music hearts break to.'

It is the breaking of hearts, and the role of heartbreak in the moulding of character, that motivates *The Land of Spices*. Mère Marie-Hélène Archer, Reverend Mother to the Irish convent of a French order, is a formidable Englishwoman who has sealed up her heart to devote herself to the 'impersonal and active service of God'. Once a radiant and hopeful young girl, she turned her back on life to punish her beloved father for what she saw as an unforgivable act of treachery. Young Anna Murphy has her whole life before her, but before she begins to live it, she too must suffer a possibly fatal blow to her emotions.

Like many of her novels, *The Land of Spices* is set in O'Brien's native Limerick, disguised as the imaginary Mellick. It was, in the 1930s, a limited, self-satisfied place, prosperous, nationalistic and rigidly Catholic. It is interesting to think that the novel is set in the same county and covers much the same period as *Angela's Ashes*, but whereas Frank McCourt's memoir is a searing study of poverty and prejudice in the Limerick slums, the children in O'Brien's novel come from the newly emerged Catholic upper middle classes, the prosperous business and professional groups. O'Brien was one of the few Irish rural writers to write about the middle classes and her preoccupations are of the Jane Austen school, snobbery and property and the struggle for intelligent girls to pursue their own destiny.

In *The Land of Spices* it is Anna Murphy who must overcome the petty aspirations of her family. At six years of age she becomes the youngest-ever boarder at the convent of *La Compagnie de la Sainte Famille*. Timid and inquisitive, she is noticed by the Reverend Mother, who responds to the spiritual and intellectual hunger of the small, intelligent girl. Anna is ready to be shaped by the sophisticated curriculum of the French order and Mère Marie-Hélène, who has reached the limits of her patience with the self-satisfied parochialism of her Irish nuns and clergy, now finds a new purpose in her vocation.

The reissue of *The Land of Spices* is particularly timely in a period when convent life has all but disappeared. This is no routine Catholic schooldays lark but a serious study of the politics and power of an all-female hierarchy. O'Brien exquisitely evokes the harem atmosphere of convent life, the beauty and the silence, the bickering and the cruelties and their lasting influence on the lives of young girls. The nuns are not figures of fun but professional women, stubborn and ambitious (and among the few of their sex in their time with authority and autonomy). The girls are impressionable and irrepressible, but along with the tug of life on their romantic sensibilities, there are the assaults on the spirit of a life of stillness and commitment, vividly described in this passage where girls, soon to leave school, hear the sounds of distant bathers and boaters as they walk in the convent grounds.

> ... the trees of the convent spread their wide and tranquillising arms, and the great house stood deep-based in reproachful calm, secure in its rule, secure in Christ against the brief assaults of evening or of roses. Girls about to leave, awaiting life, felt this dismissal by the spirit of the house of the unanswered, lovely conflict implicit in the hour ...

The author creates a beautiful balance between the relative worldliness of the governing nuns and the as yet untouched spirits of the girls. Beautifully balanced also is the contained emotional interplay of the characters. There is not a trace of sentimentality. There are to be no grand romantic resolutions. Anna never really develops any real affection for her mentor. In fact she lacks conventional childish appeal. At six, she is captivating in her solemnity but as she grows older her watchfulness and guardedness make her seem aloof and even charmless. O'Brien, who herself once said, 'I am entirely against the promotion of a sense of humour as a philosophy of life,' would almost certainly have shared Anna's disapproval of her adolescent companions' hysteria. Yet the emotions and vulnerabilities are revealed like a play of shadow and light: in the young girl who hardens with each hurt, in the older woman whose dulled emotions begin to show colour like an old painting restored. Merely by having her heart unlocked, Mère Marie-Hélène is able to forgive and progress. Anna's emotions never get unlocked, but a small epiphany at the book's ending makes a shaft of light that will guide her towards her true future. If novels can be music, then this is a novel with perfect pitch.

*The Land of Spices* is O'Brien's most autobiographical work. Her own mother died of cancer in 1903 when she was six and her father thought that life would be less lonely for her if she joined her older sisters at Laurel Hill boarding school, a convent of a French order, The Faithful Companions of Jesus. This convent was the model for the order of the *Compagnie de la Sainte Famille*, even down to the English Reverend Mother, who was considered something of a cold fish, but who won Kate's immediate allegiance by telling her that they had to order a special small chair for her and had asked for three to be sent on approval so that she could choose one for herself. The school was viewed with suspicion locally because the children were taught languages other than Irish and both nuns and pupils drank real coffee. Like Anna, Kate O'Brien won a university scholarship and was pressured by her family into taking a 'decent' job in a bank instead. She went to college, got her degree, and was outraged when a waggish uncle sent a letter of congratulation which ended: 'I wonder what the next step will be – M.A. or Ma?'

Exposed to both religious and French influences at an impressionable age, she emerged both high-minded and broad-minded. *The Land of Spices* reflects O'Brien's own ideal of moral perfectionism. Her books offer a cynical view of romance, almost as if love were a childish resolution to life's more serious quest. When Tom and Angèle fall in love in *The Last of Summer*, the serious-minded Jo sees it as 'a trick of the senses and of their passing needs' and reflected that 'she was inclined to see human love as a mistake anyhow'.

But O'Brien was as contemptuous of prudery as of senti-mentality. Long before other women writers tackled such sub-jects she wrote about homosexuality and sexual disease and must have enjoyed shocking the narrow sensibilities of her era when she had the blunt Mrs Cusack in *The Last of Summer* declare of her moody barmaid: ''Twill be an ease to me, I can tell you, when that one's periods are concluded and done with.'

Even more shocking to her Irish public was her outspoken-ness in regard to the smug insularity of her own country. Mère Marie-Hélène, exasperated by complaints about the foreign cooking produced by the Normandy kitchen nun who is a superb chef, considers: 'How odd were these Irish, who be-lieved themselves implacably at war in the spirit with England, yet hugged as their own her dreariest daily habits, and could only distrust the grace and good sense of Latin Catholic life!'

Later, after a failed conflict with a spiteful and petty-minded Irish nun, the Reverend Mother decides:

The Irish liked themselves, and throve on their own psycho-logical chaos. It had been shown to be politically useless for an alien temperament to wrestle with them. Wrong-headed, vengeful, even by the long view stupid they might often seem, and apparently defeated – but on their own ground in some mystically arrogant wild way they were perpetual vic-tors. ... They were an ancient, martyred race, and of great importance to themselves ...

# INTRODUCTION

Kate O'Brien frequently employed an outsider's view to show up the less likeable facets of Irish life. French Angèle in *The Last of Summer* is dismayed by the 'cold fanaticism' of a display of Irish dancing. Old Miss Robertson, Anna's suffragette friend in *The Land of Spices*, disapproves when a bishop expounds the virtues of the nationalist youth movement 'Sinn Fein' by telling her, 'It means "ourselves", you know.' To which the spirited Miss Robertson replies, 'It's a very unattractive motto to give to young people.'

Kate O'Brien did not see these broadsides as an attack on her people but, like her feminism, as a crusade against those who would inhibit their development. The authorities understood this only too well and extracted vengeance by banning her work. Ostensibly, there was no bar on freedom of speech in Ireland, so *The Land of Spices* – one of her finest and most moral works – was banned for lewdness on the basis of a single line where an act of intimacy is described with such delicacy as to seem almost Victorian: 'She saw [them],' O'Brien wrote, 'in the embrace of love.'

It was not the first time the author had fallen victim to a censor. When her first novel, *Without My Cloak*, came out, it was a source of great pride to her Aunt Fan, who was a nun in the Presentation Convent. Fan begged Kate's sister Nance for a copy, but Nance said it was not suitable reading for nuns. But she continued to plead and Nance gave her a copy, with certain pages pinned together and the warning: 'if you don't remove the pins you should be all right.' The elderly nun left the pins in place and thoroughly enjoyed the novel.

The author was greatly amused by the latter incident, which she recounted with relish in her memoir *Presentation Parlour*, but she was distressed and wounded by the official censorship, which affected her sales and effectively made her an outsider in her own country.

And yet, in many ways, O'Brien *was* an outsider. 'To possess without being possessed,' she once wrote, 'is the gift an exile can take from a known place.'

'To possess without being possessed' might also have been a

motif for her own life. A celebrated public figure, her private life remained extremely private. After a brief attempt at conventional marriage, she confronted her lesbianism, but so little is known of her relationships that survivors of her own family still debate as to whether Kate could really have been gay. Although she described herself as a Catholic-Agnostic, long years of convent life (and the fact that two of her favourite aunts were nuns) left her with a yearning for a life of perfection. She would probably have shared the rationalist Dr Curran's approval of religious practice in *The Ante-Room*: 'Religion exacts a soul of every man.' One of her acquaintances once said: 'What she really wanted most in life was to be a Reverend Mother.'

It may have been this private aspiration that thwarted her more public one. Kate O'Brien fell just short of being a great writer. Too polemical to let her books ever fully take flight, she was also too intellectually arrogant. She must have been an editor's nightmare. Large chunks of untranslated French and German punctuate *The Land of Spices*, yet this elegantly wrought novel is very close to a work of art. There is an enviable precision with ordinary emotions, as when little Anna is visited by her mother at boarding school: 'Anna stared contentedly up into a face which was, as it happened, pretty, but which was for her beyond qualification. It was Mother, and through it shone the images of fixity, the things that always were, and did not have to be mastered.' And the author accepted, as all great artists do, the role of the flawed in the scheme of perfection. Attempting to understand Pilar, a beautiful but frivolous South American student, Anna Murphy suddenly comes to a point of revelation, perceiving her as 'a motive in art'. By this understanding of how ordinary beauty is transformed by contemplation, Anna is herself saved from ordinariness. It is a wonderful moment in a book that is as delicate and as practical as a china cup.

*Clare Boylan 1999*

# BOOK ONE

## Rosary Sunday

## The First Chapter

## THE HOLY HABIT

"My child, what do you demand?"
"The holy habit of religion, my Lord . . ."

THE chapel was warm, although it was early October. Reverend Mother hoped that no one would faint, but from where she stood beside the Bishop at the top of the sanctuary steps, she could hear a hysterical fuss towards the back of the school benches: *Schwärmerei* for Eileen O'Doherty, who was at that moment receiving the veil of the *Compagnie de la Sainte Famille*.

Three postulants were being received. Two had already knelt as Eileen knelt, and waited for her now in *prie-dieux* placed outside the communion rail. Their heads were bowed into their hands. They were dressed as brides, in white silk and lace veils. All three had been educated at *Sainte Famille*, all were young; but for the school, alert and feverish, the dramatic day was Eileen's. She was beautiful, she had played hockey like a goddess, she had never spoken or looked unkindly; three Junes ago, when she was about to leave, the school had been all but unmanageable with *Schwärmerei*. Then she entered the world, was presented at the English Court, and admired, it was said, by the Queen herself, the beautiful Alexandra. She had danced through a London season, and returned to decorate Irish society for a year. Now here she was, back in the school chapel, asking the Bishop to admit her as a candidate for the religious life. Girls who had adored her from First Preparatory desks two years ago—members of the First Eleven now, or even *enfants de Marie*—giggled and sobbed into their hot gloved hands, and counted up the hearts that must be bleeding for Eileen to-day, in London

3

clubs, and in the messroom of the garrison. It was almost a certainty that Rosita Maloney would faint before the ceremony ended.

The Bishop blessed the folded habit, girdle and veil. The chaplain made the responses to the Latin prayers. As Reverend Mother stood in outward composure, but consciously struggling, as she would to the end of her life, to keep her hands in repose, she looked down at the beautiful bride-postulant and a reflection of dry pity escaped across her prayers.

"She had to come back to this—I wonder why? I wonder why she has refused the sunny, ordinary life her face was made for? But after all, she'll find it here. Plenty of sunny ordinariness."

Reverend Mother did not think highly of to-day's three postulants, and of Eileen O'Doherty, who brought her large *dot* to the Order, she thought least. But she reflected now, in correction of a passing uncharitableness, that all had good characters, good health and a true desire to serve God in obedience to the rules of the *Compagnie de la Sainte Famille*.

Received and blessed, with the folded serge garments lying on her opened hands, the white-robed girl rose from the altar-steps and withdrew with grace to join her less comely companions. Reverend Mother's eyes passed from her and fell by chance on the left-hand corner of the first of the School benches, near the communion rail. She almost smiled at what she saw there.

The little new girl, six years old and small for her age, was crouched down on her haunches and was leaning out over the lower rung of her pew; her chin was cupped in her hands and there was an expression of busy attention on her face. She watched the three brides genuflect in unison, and turn to walk with bowed heads and swishing trains down the centre aisle, between the murmurings of the School and their moved relatives. She leant out over her barrier to see the last train swirl to beyond her view over the red carpet, and then resumed her first position, chin still in her hands, to observe

4

the movements of the Bishop as, assisted by chaplain and acolytes, he vested himself to say Mass.

"At least there is no *Schwärmerei* in that face," Reverend Mother thought amusedly. "Anna Murphy isn't going to faint. Indeed, she looks as if she is memorising the whole affair, for critical purposes." But when she left the sanctuary and came to kneel in her own *prie-dieu* at the left-hand side of the chancel and close beside the little new girl, she leant over to her and touched her shoulder.

"You must try to kneel up straight, Anna. It isn't respectful to stick your head out through the bars," she said. "And now sit down until Mass begins."

Anna obeyed her immediately, and, clutching a hymn-book, began to turn its pages with care.

The organ wheezed far away at the back of the nuns' tribune, and the choir overhead, supported unsteadily by the girls in the chancel, began the hymn held dedicate at *Sainte Famille* to such occasions as the present:

> "Not for the consolations
> Outflowing from Thy love . . ."

Reverend Mother reflected as she listened that if Saint Teresa of Avila did in fact write the words now being chanted so untidily, there would be little doubt that her wisdom would have forbidden their devotional misuse by girls—but traditions were traditions, she thought wearily, and who was she to be so boldly sure of what Teresa would have thought? "Not for the joy that waits me . . ." if prayerfulness was stirred in her by such perilous assertion of the love of God, who was to know what instant of pure devotion, perfect praise, they might not light in some fresher, holier, more innocent heart?

"I have grown to be a coward and a snob in Thy service," she prayed repentantly. "Teach me to be otherwise before it is too late. Teach me to escape from the carpings of my small judgment, and to see Thy creatures sometimes with a vestige of Thy everlasting love. Make me humble, Lord; make me do Thy work from my heart, not always with this petty, miserable brain. Compel me to understand that there are a million ways of finding the favour of Thy mercy. Lord, give me charity. Give me the grace to find Thy image in us all . . ."

But as she prayed for herself and found momentary relief from the dryness of her own sensibility in an appeal against it, conscience reminded her that all her prayer to-day should be for the three new lives being dedicated to a work she knew to be so hard. Yet, dutifully though she turned her mind from her own need of help to theirs, thoughts of office and government crowded into it, so that the three novices were lost almost immediately in anxieties covering a whole community of nuns and a school of sixty girls.

The little new girl pulled her sleeve.

"I can't find this hymn, Reverend Mother." She held out the open hymn-book.

"It isn't in that book, Anna. But you can't read that small print, can you?"

"Yes, I can."

"And long words?"

"Fairly long ones."

The hymn was over. By now the three brides would have taken off their white silk and lace, and, bullied by Mother Mary Martin—poor old *Sœur Amélie*, tears pouring down her face—would have fulfilled her traditional duty of cutting off their hair. Now they were dressed in the black serge, the white coif and the leather girdle that, God willing, would be their fashion until death. The Bishop was waiting to begin Mass. It was time they reappeared and knelt in their *prie-dieux* of honour again.

As Reverend Mother thought this she saw them appear at the chapel door, Margaret first, Linda next, and Eileen bringing up the rear—tall and beautiful, looking pale in her white coif. As she reached the middle of the chancel there was a thud and a groan in one of the school benches. Someone was carried out then, on Sister Matthew's strong shoulders:

6

Rosita Maloney, in what she honestly believed was a "dead faint." Reverend Mother glanced without particular interest in the direction of the scuffling and giggling. "Be quiet, Madeleine," she heard someone whisper violently. "Reverend Mother is absolutely glaring at us."

The novices took their places and the Bishop began to say Mass.

The "Reception" breakfast was laid in the Long Parlour. The three new novices partook of it in the company of the Bishop, the chaplain, their parents and members of their families. It was the last time in life that they would sit down as guests at the same table with "people in the world." Reverend Mother, Mother Assistant, Mother Scholastic, and other important members of the community moved about the great oval table and waited on their guests. There were three white-iced "Reception" cakes, each bearing one of the three newly conferred religious names: Sister Angela, Sister Martin, Sister Imelda. (Eileen O'Doherty had chosen Blessed Imelda as her patroness, and now Rosita Maloney was fermenting a cult of that innocuous saint throughout the school.)

There were white flowers on the table, bitter-smelling white chrysanthemums and feathery Michælmas. Sunlight lay temperately on the convent lawns and golden elm-trees, but did not reach the westward windows, so that the parlour was cold. But voices fell warmly on each other, and tears, which had been wet and even desolate at moments in the chapel, were for now no more than a guarded brightness in a parent's eyes. There was a good French smell of coffee. At every footfall in the room the chandeliers tinkled prettily.

" . . . and such a beautiful little address you gave us, my Lord," Mrs. O'Doherty was saying. "So spiritual, I thought—didn't you, Frank? I always do say that your Lordship's sermons are really spiritual."

Mrs. O'Doherty was a woman whose stupidity might even be described as unusual, and the Bishop, of an intelligence wide and impatient, would normally not have wasted nervous energy in hearing anything she had to say; but he was invariably touched by the spectacle of youth, full of vows and prayers, making assault on the long, hidden life of perfection, and the gentle thoughts induced thereby made him temporarily inclined to attempt patience, even when a fool spoke.

"I'm glad of that," he said, "since, after all, they are sermons."

Reverend Mother smiled as she replenished Father Conroy's cup.

"You certainly gave them an encouraging send-off," my Lord," said Mr. McMahon, the father of Linda, now Sister Martin. "I've always thought I admired my daughter's character"—he smiled at her very lovingly; he was making a great effort to be bright at this farewell feast—"but your beautiful eulogy . . ."

"Oh Daddy, I know," said the young novice. "I'm afraid that most of what you said about us made me feel an awful hypocrite, my Lord," she added shyly.

"When I see a good thing being attempted, Mr. McMahon," said the Bishop—"and that's not very often—I like to praise the attempt. When people decide to give up the pride of life instead of planning to snatch it, I don't want to make heavy weather. I like to rejoice, since God rejoices. Time will test these three good girls, and whoever likes can start moralising then. But to-day we witnessed purity of intention, and when you see that, you know that for the moment God is glorified. A rare event."

The Bishop lifted his coffee-cup and drained it. Mrs. O'Doherty could never see much fault in him—since he was a Bishop and she was a snob—but the rapidity of his speech did always seem uncouth to her. Now, however, not having caught a word of what he had said, she very tolerantly gave a sigh of deep appreciation.

"In any case," said Father Conroy, "time enough for them to start hearing about their bad characters when the Mistress

8

of Novices gets a clutch on them! Isn't that so, Margaret?—
oh, I beg your pardon—isn't that so, Sister Angela?"

Sister Angela was a fat little thing and a giggler. She
giggled now.

"How long do you think it will be, Reverend Mother,
before they go to the novitiate?" Mr. McMahon asked, with
bright courage.

"I think that we shall be able to arrange for them to be
accompanied to Bruges within a fortnight, Mr. McMahon,"
Reverend Mother said.

"Ah! So soon?"

"I think so."

"It seems a shame," said Father Conroy, with pointed
playfulness, "it seems a shame that our own Irish girls have to
go off to do their religious training in a barbarous place like
that!"

Reverend Mother smiled as she replaced a dish on a side
table.

"Bruges is not a 'barbarous' place, Father Conroy—and our
novitiate there is one of the most beautiful religious houses in
northern Europe."

"No doubt, Reverend Mother—but it isn't Irish. Is it,
now?"

"No; it isn't Irish."

Father Conroy seemed to think he had won some point or
other.

"That is all I meant," he said generously.

Mrs. O'Doherty did not know Bruges, but she had spent
her honeymoon at the Italian lakes and twice since then had
spent a fretful and dyspeptic week in Paris. Also she was a
*Sainte Famille* "old girl," and considered that even in these
days of social disintegration the Order's French tradition
conferred a *"cachet,"* a *"je ne sais quoi"*—as she said now across
the table to young Sister Angela's mother, who was *not* an
"old girl"; who was, in fact, as Mrs. O'Doherty knew, a very
common woman, a daughter and sister of tradesmen. However, this was an occasion for tact, so Mrs. O'Doherty talked

of foreign parts, and in order to put the other lady at her ease, asked her for her opinions on Paris and Milan, though knowing that of course she could not have been in either place.

The Bishop talked across the ladies' talk to Mr. McMahon, about the Irish language and its possible revival. Major O'Doherty complimented Mother Bonaventure on the singing of the school during Mass.

"A perfect rendering of the *Benedictus*, Mother—perfect! And I flatter myself I know what I'm talking about."

Mother Bonaventure knew that the sopranos had been flat throughout the rendering, but she helped the major to roast apples and to cream whipped with sherry, and agreed with him that he knew what he was talking about.

"*Bruges La Morte*," said Mrs. O'Doherty, "how delightful for my darling Eileen—and your sweet—er—Margaret, is it not?—to be setting off for such a storied spot!"

Reverend Mother stood apart by the side-table.

Her memory had taken a curiously desolate plunge across many years.

She was forty-three now. It was twenty-five years since she had taken final vows in the chapel at *Sainte Fontaine* in Bruges, and thence gone out to her work as the Order directed. To Vienna, to Turin, to Cracow, then back to Brussels, to the *Place des Ormes*, where she had been child and girl and had received the habit, even as these three received it to-day, in her school chapel. For eleven years she had worked at *Place des Ormes*, as Mother Scholastic, and afterwards as Assistant to Mother General. She had been well content there, and looked forward to the long passage of the years, and to lying at last in the dusty cemetery by the orchard, where many of the names on the little black crosses were those of nuns who had taught her or worked with her.

But in her fortieth year she had been posted to this Irish house, as Assistant to its old French Reverend Mother, and two years ago, upon the latter's death, had been appointed to her office.

She had not accounted herself especially happy in her time of novitiate at *Sainte Fontaine*. There had been difficulties and fears, peculiar to her character and situation; but she had been glad at last to take her vows, and depart, asking God's grace, from a place of struggle, grief and self-doubt, to lose herself in work and in the encompassing of her complete dedication.

But now, as these deft Irish voices flowed together, forgetting her—she forgot them. She was momentarily a ghost where she stood and a ghost also where her memory revisited; divided within herself as lately too often she was.

She saw the wide cloister of *Sainte Fontaine;* she walked from the chapel door on its eastern side along the rain-pooled flags of the path towards the holy well in the middle of the square. A statue of Our Lady protected this well, and was itself protected within a niche of scalloped stone. The statue was of ancient wood; a holy woman had brought it from far across the Burgundian Empire to set above the miraculous waters which had restored sight to the eyes of her son. At that time, the fifteenth century, the house was an Augustinian monastery; but in the succeeding five hundred years its fortunes varied. It lost its monks during the religious wars of the Netherlands; it was stormed by the Sea Beggars; and used as a barracks by Alexander Farnese. It was an orphanage later, then the palace of a cardinal; often it was empty; it had been a hospital in many wars; in the mid-nineteenth century it was for a time a seminary for the training of priests for the African mission. But during the uncertain months of 1871, when the *Commune* raged in France, a shrewd Mother General accepted from a wealthy "old girl" the gift of *Sainte Fontaine* and transferred the novitiate of the Order there from Chartres.

Reverend Mother had often thought, when she was a novice at *Sainte Fontaine*, that the broken history of the ancient house had given to its stones a character which could only be suggested by the perhaps too emotional word "bitterness." There was an austerity over *Sainte Fontaine* that almost spoke aloud distrust of life, discomfort in it. It was old and graceful, but with the grace of hardened asceticism, not of mellowness. Its noble architecture, rigorous garden and almost empty rooms had taught the young novice more categorically even than did the Early Fathers those lessons of elimination, detachment and forgoing for which, as it happened, her hurt spirit craved somewhat hysterically at that time.

The lesson of the place had been deep, not tender. In later life she had wondered sometimes to hear other nuns of the Order speak sentimentally of their novitiate days at *Sainte Fontaine*. Had she been capable of sentimental speech, that would have been given, she knew, in torrents, to Brussels, and to the Convent there, where she had been a child and happy, and a girl and perilously unhappy.

But at this moment, whipped thereto by Father Conroy's little nationalistic commonplace, her exasperated spirit had fled defensively to the sheltering cold and pride of *Sainte Fontaine*. The masses of pale stone and dark brown roof; the orderly dark shrubs of the cloister garden; *Sœur Evangèle* in clogs and in apron of sacking, bent before Our Lady to haul a bucket from the cold depths of the well. Westward, where the cloister opened, an infinite-seeming view, beyond stripped apple-trees, of Flemish plain and pearly Flemish sky; from a window in the eastern wing, the voice of a novice reading aloud to her companions: *"Si l'homme donne tout ce qu'il possède, ce n'est rien. S'il fait une grande pénitence, c'est peu encore. Et s'il embrasse toutes les sciences, il est encore loin . . ."* The clang of the broken chapel bell, assenting.

That is my music, Reverend Mother thought. I have not loved it, but I think I have a little understood its terms. *"C'est peu encore."* And yet it should be possible, in all humility, to live by them, rather than too crankily to understand them. *Sœur Evangèle*, for instance. She died as she knelt in the rain in the kitchen garden, planting potatoes, and *Mère Générale* had read the news in her study in *Place des Ormes*. "Do you remember her?" she had asked her Mother Assistant. "Do you remember the beauty and ceaselessness of her work in the kitchen garden and how formidably silent she was as she went about it—but how, in the evenings at community recreation, she would talk of her day's events with such uncanny shrewdness and power to entertain?" Yes, Mother Assistant had remembered. "Listening to her," *Mère Générale* went on, "I sometimes thought that the Holy Spirit must have once celebrated a special Pentecost for *Sœur Evangèle*—she had all the gifts and fruits." That was true enough, Reverend Mother reflected now, but the lay sister in the kitchen garden had been especially blessed in not weighing her graces; she lived by her own nature; she was born an anchorite, a holy sceptic, who knew only one good, *le bon Dieu*.

That is how a nun should be, Reverend Mother reflected sadly—through sheer understanding of the sole perfection, tolerant and unself-conscious. So, compunctiously, she turned again to Father Conroy, whose crudities she always found fatiguing in themselves, and whose good qualities she resented because they made her too sharply aware of her own incongruity as Superior of an Irish convent.

"Let me give you another cup of tea, Father," she said. And when she brought his cup to him again she braced herself in contrition, so as to seem to plead with him. "I can't have you thinking that these children are going to derive anything but good from their years at *Sainte Fontaine*," she said gently.

Father Conroy was a country boy, fresh from Maynooth. His work as chaplain to *Sainte Famille* was made somewhat difficult for him by the enigmatic foreignness which he apprehended in this Reverend Mother. "A cold English fish," he called her angrily in his heart, and her English speech always alarmed him so much that in self-defence he became pugnacious.

"Oh, of course they'll learn to *parley-voo*, Reverend Mother! But is that so very important nowadays?"

"Perhaps not, Father. But since they have chosen to be nuns, can it hurt them to make contact with Christian culture, or to visit the fountain-head of their own Order?"

"We had nuns in Ireland before there were any in Belgium, Reverend Mother!"

She smiled.

"Had you? Certainly Ireland helped in impressing Christianity on Europe. So why should the Irish not go back now, and reclaim for Ireland some of the cultivated thing it planted?"

"Aha! You see! You have this notion that you can 'cultivate' us! But we are a very ancient race, you know!"

There were too many answers to this absurdity; Reverend Mother dismissed them all, and contented herself with smiling politely as she withdrew again to her post by the coffee-pots.

Linda McMahon's brother had a snapshot camera, and hinted politely that the light was very suitable for an experiment, so the younger guests, brothers and little sisters of the novices, were released with them through the French windows of the parlour, to amuse themselves with amateur photography and with shy jokes about the new garb and new status of the three. Major and Mrs. O'Doherty walked a little apart on the gravel, one on each side of their daughter. Mrs. O'Doherty fingered the black serge of the new habit uneasily; the Major looked at the beautiful girl out of a misty sadness.

Within the Long Parlour the Bishop, a forthright and progressive man, found it opportune to express himself clearly to Mr. McMahon on the subject of the Irish Language Revival. The latter, an orthodox Home Ruler and Irish Party man, was opposed to it, but he knew that the Bishop's views carried weight through the country, and he was interested to hear them. The Bishop also thought it well that they should be made known to this influential Dublin lawyer.

"You are shortsighted, Mr. McMahon, in regarding the language question as unimportant. In my view—and I don't know a word of it yet!—it is a key question. Because what we most need here is the establishment of the national character, and so to educate the people that they do not merely feel the

ancient national grievance, but see why it *is* a grievance, see its
cultural and historic reality——"

"That may be long-sighted, my Lord, but surely in the
wrong direction?"

The Bishop laughed.

"Not at all, you trimmer! If people are to progress, you
must educate them from their own roots upwards . . ."

"You see, Reverend Mother?" said Father Conroy
triumphantly. "That's what I meant, you see, about our
girls going off to Bruges . . ."

Reverend Mother smiled at him.

"Was it, Father? I don't see the connection."

The young priest looked dumbfounded at her stupidity.
She could almost hear his inward groan that an Irish school
should be under such crass Sassenach authority. But the
Bishop tackled her briskly.

"Nevertheless, there will be a connection, Reverend
Mother—one of these days. Irish national life is bound up
with its religion, and it may well be that educational work will
become difficult here soon for those Orders which adhere too
closely to a foreign tradition."

"The *Compagnie de la Sainte Famille* was founded by a
Frenchwoman, my Lord—but that was one hundred and
twenty years ago. Our nuns work among Maoris now, and
with Canadian Indians; we educate in Portugal and Poland
and England and Scotland; we are in Chicago and in Paraguay
and in Mexico City. And I think myself that we are of some
modest use in Ireland. You see, our nuns *are not* a nation, and
our business is not with national matters. We are a religious
Order."

"But you are not contemplatives, Reverend Mother—you
are educationists, with power in your hands."

"Certainly, my Lord—and it is our rule to adapt the
secular side of our curriculum to the needs we find in our
different foundations."

"Well then, if our need here is for a truly national
education . . ."

Reverend Mother smiled.

"When Ireland decides what she means by that, my Lord, the *Compagnie de la Sainte Famille* will try to provide it."

"With nuns trained on the continong?" said Father Conroy.

"With nuns acquainted with the spirit of the Order they joined, Father Conroy. Would it surprise you, my Lord, to learn that already some members of our community have asked and received permission to study your national language, and that very soon they will be taking regular classes under an enthusiastic lady revivalist from Dublin?"

The Bishop looked surprised. Reverend Mother indicated a tall, black-browed nun who stood near his chair. Mother Mary Andrew bent forward, frowning and eager.

"Yes, my Lord, that is so, I'm glad to say. I have persuaded Mother Joseph and Mother Agatha to study with me—I have very strong views on the matter . . ."

This nun came from Tyrone, had an unpleasant accent and was too pedantic for the Bishop's liking. He was a just man, and this unexpected progressiveness of the cold, enigmatic English Reverend Mother impressed him against his will. He turned to her with a rather too surprised graciousness.

"But that is enlightened of you, Reverend Mother!"

"Hardly that, my Lord."

"I've been convinced for a long time," said Mother Mary Andrew determinedly.

"Faith and you have, Mother Mary Andrew," said Mother Eugenia, who was old and outspoken. "With the result that you have myself ready to sing my *Nunc Dimittis* from this dark, unhappy nation!" (Mother Eugenia was the Mother Assistant.) She was the daughter of an earl, and oddly snobbish about that fact. She liked pupils and their parents to know that she had been Lady Eugenia Fitzmichael in the world, and she could not bear the "upstart educational pretensions," as she called them, of the vigorous young Mother Mary Andrew, whom she sometimes referred to as "that linen-draper person from Tyrone." The two, subject to Reverend Mother, were the school's intellectual directors, the younger being energetic in the busy general office of Mother Scholastic, and the old nun lecturing rather too well for her green audiences on Church and European history. Reverend Mother found them difficult yoke-fellows to drive, the more so as she knew she was generally in suppressed sympathy with the erratic and preposterous Mother Eugenia.

Mother Mary Andrew allowed herself to look as if she thought this *Nunc Dimittis* would be a national benefit.

"If it is true, my Lord, that you don't know a word of your native language, I have a real crow over you," said Reverend Mother. "Because Mother Mary Andrew has taught me to make the sign of the cross in Erse!"

"You'll be telling me next that you are a Branch Secretary of the Gaelic League, I believe!" said the Bishop.

"And calling the poor language Erse, if you please!" said Father Conroy. "Ah, glory be to God, Reverend Mother, will you ever make head or tail of us at all at all?"

The nun bit her lip and said nothing. She was undergoing a visitation very strange to her—a visitation of hatred; she desired to pray against it, but under the ugly weight of feeling, could not reach the outer barrier of prayer.

## The Second Chapter

# VOCATION

WHEN she was eighteen Helen Archer had, for a reason admitted to no other human being, turned her back upon herself, upon talents, dreams, emotions—and undertaken the impersonal and active service of God. Her rash decision had rewarded her. Spiritually, by an increasing faith in God, which gave her power to keep her life serenely at His disposal; practically, with professional success, for she became a most intelligent and capable member of the Order. From the beginning, chilled more than she knew by the shock which drove her to the purest form of life that could be found, and hardened in all her defences against herself by the sympathetic bleakness of *Sainte Fontaine*, she grew into that kind of nun who will never have to trouble about the vow of poverty, because poverty is attractive to her fastidiousness; who has looked chastity in the eyes with exaggerated searching, and finding in it the perverse seduction she needed at a moment of flight from life, accepts it once and for all with proud relief; but who will have to wrestle with obedience. Not that she does not understand its place in the ideal, or that specific acts of submission trouble her. But because it is a persistently intellectual sacrifice; it is always an idea. She found only cerebral difficulties in religious life. And this great strength was her weakness.

As a young nun teaching in Vienna and in Northern Italy, she had found it difficult sometimes to affect compromise between the persistences of native character and her own passion for the negation of temperament. She struggled for adjustment, simply out of reasonableness, and because she knew that to be a useful teacher of the young one must not be either an enigma or a machine; but it never occurred to her youthful arrogance that there was hysteria in her need to struggle, or that her dislike of the soft temperaments of the south was in fact an unresolved panic. The vows taken at *Sainte Fontaine* when she was twenty had finally, she believed, sealed up girlhood and its pain, and the resolute young woman, gladly dedicated to God, did not pause to review herself as a continuous life, or to ask if the present is not inevitably the delicate vessel of the past.

In the convent outside Cracow, in the pride, touchiness and bigotry of Polish life, she had found much to dislike, but there was a cold moodiness, physical and spiritual, to which her mind responded more freely than to charm. But, recalled to Brussels, to the *Place des Ormes*, when still under thirty, she discovered, on her own austere terms, happiness. This surprised her. She had dreaded the possible recall, and when it came toyed with her right to plead against it, but decided instead on the discipline of unarguing obedience.

She had dreaded return to a place where everything, big and little, was fixed in the hurtful, clear light of remembrance. Once, for a long time, all of life hung bright and potent always over the space that lay between *Place des Ormes*, No. 21, her school, and *Rue Saint Isidore*, No. 4, her father's house, ten minutes' walk. A little stretch of leafy, high-perched, shabby suburb. An unremarkable and informal example, repeated in a thousand European towns, of unpretentious, civilised routine; a little girl's world of everyday sounds and smells— tasks, pleasures and impressions hardly seen, hardly felt as they came in their time, so natural were they. But because, as it happened, they were happy, because they were the container of a deeply dreaming, cloudless growth, and were to be also the setting, the frozen witnesses, of its too sudden injury, its crippling and panic—they were remembered, held rigid, with a powerfulness of light and shadow their reality had not known, and which hurt too much the eyes of memory.

So she had feared to come back to the suburb of childhood; and this fear was not merely a tenderness towards herself, but also prompted her to think that the revisiting of her own heart which it would impose would be no more than watch-fully admonitory. For what was done at eighteen was done and if it were indeed as stupid as it was understandable, only prayer now, the constant, humble prayer of maturity, could repair the contempt, the cold, wild judgments, the silly self-defence and self-dramatisation of an ignorant girl. And no uneasy return to the physical scene of her blind distress could make her life-long prayer—for patience, for understanding—more insistent or repentant than it was.

She had learnt something of life between her eighteenth and her thirtieth years. In theory and at a remove. In meditation and self-examination; in reading the fathers of the Church; in learning to grapple with human material, as its teacher. And as, shrewdly enough, she took the measure of the forces which she had fled from, she endeavoured to teach herself, as well as she could, a belated mercy towards humanity in general, which did not, or could not, flee before itself. She saw, suspecting her own sentimentality withal, the courage required by the vulgar who undertake to live; she even saw, regretfully, the courage of the outright sinner. And, free in her meditations on God's will, and His hopes for humanity, she admitted that human love—such love, for instance, as she would have protested she felt for her father when she was young—must almost always offend the heavenly lover by its fatuous egotism. To stand still and eventually understand was, she saw, an elementary duty of love. To run away, to take cover, to hate in blindness, and luxuriously to seek vengeance in an unexplained cutting-off, in a seizure upon high and proud antithesis—that was stupidity masquerading offensively before the good God. She saw that—with the long view of the years; even became detached enough to plead with herself that the girl who had been such a fool was only eighteen, and absolutely innocent; that she had worshipped as perfect the author of her disillusion, and that the blow had been agonising pain, would indeed always leave her limping, no matter how she strove with wisdom. What had happened, in fact, *had* happened; and so ordinary life had lost a young woman of gifts and rippling sensibilities, and the *Compagnie de la Saint Famille* had gained a successful, over-disciplined nun.

Success developed especially from the effect upon her of the return to Brussels, from the humiliation and bewilderment which she underwent in her first months there. For she found her father living in *Rue St. Isidore*, a stone's throw from her convent, as he had always lived in her knowledge of·him; civilised, gentle, industrious, unexacting—beloved of all his neighbours, particularly of the poor and humble among them. Although he was fifty-five at that date, her eyes could discover almost no impairment of his physical beauty, which was always marked, and further marked by the carelessness with which he wore it. There was no change in his love for her. Her decision to be a nun had distressed him as she had never seen anything do, even her mother's death; but he had given in, though angrily, to her unexplained relentlessness. When she left Brussels for the novitiate at *Sainte Fontaine*, he had kissed her—not knowing how she trembled now in revulsion from his once dear kisses—and begged her to reconsider her intention well in the period of probation still ahead. Eleven years lay between that parting and her return, as Mother Scholastic, to the *Place des Ormes*.

Then, in reunion with him, in the observations drawn from many gentle interviews in the convent parlour and garden, she had undergone in secret a salutary humiliation, a bewilderment never entirely to be dispersed, and by its impingement on her rigidity beneficial—the debates, the anxieties it raised stretching her soul, activating her as no other spiritual exercise had done—so that from an efficient, accomplished nun she was subtilised into an exceptional one. The sharpened understanding induced by her unsuspecting father roused all the Protestant in her—she was a grandchild of English rectories—forced her to sessions of private judgment and compelled her to apply her Augustinian and Jesuitical doctrines of sin and grace to immediate instances, and be patient if theology did not seem to have the answer pat—the answer that rang true.

For she had been horrified at eighteen; she had been hurled by dynamic shock into the wildest regions of austerity, for ever out of reach of all that beauty of human life that she had inordinately believed in—trained most delicately and lovingly in that belief by the one who was to be its unwitting destroyer. And the years had ignored that proud, ascetic storm, that vibrant flight and sacrifice, and had been gently unrevealing, non-committal, as they flowed past her father. They kept the secret of sin and grace. They allowed him to be visibly happy, guiltless and good—who was guilty and evil, theology said. They suggested that perhaps she had made a fool of herself at eighteen. They instructed her, as she studied her father's candid, intelligent face in the sunny parlour of *Place des Ormes*, that a soul should not take upon itself the impertinence of being frightened for another soul; that God is alone with each creature.

The wind, in fact, was taken out of her sails. And the gradual effect of this, coming when her character was sufficiently formalised, when the habits of exacting virtue were strong, was to make of her suspect and disused sensibility a delicate instrument, a responsive ally to judgment. In fact, an experience which she had mishandled rewarded her at long remove, and by giving her diffidence to enrich intelligence and discipline, made her wise; made her gentler than her proud face revealed.

Often henceforward she pondered *Saint Augustine—dicta* swallowed with cold non-comprehension at *Sainte Fontaine: Nous savons que la grâce n'est pas donnée à tous les hommes*. She had hardly listened to the *Père Directeur* as he minced the theological refinements arising from this assertion, because for herself she had liked the dangerous arrogance of it, and had heard it ring like true coin in her soul. *La nature n'a plus de grâces suffisantes qu'autant qu'il plaît à Dieu de lui en donner*. But it had pleased God to endow her father with every grace by the world so-called; it had pleased God to have him wise, modest and good in all his reported encounters with fellow-creatures; and, most oddly, it had pleased God that this versatile and gifted scholar should be at his best, at his richest and least resistible, as exponent and apologist of English religious poetry of the seventeenth century. Donne, Herbert, Cowley, Vaughan, Traherne and Bishop King. These were his field and his passion; his austere and ill-rewarded labours on them were the enduring satisfaction of his life. What manner of ironist then was God?

The question stayed, at the centre of the nun's strong faith.

Her recall from Cracow to Brussels was no random idea, nor was it related to her being regarded in the Order as native of the latter city. But it happened that during *Mère Marie-Hélène's* early professed years the government of *La Compagnie de la Sainte Famille* underwent a change. Founded at Rouen in 1775 by a pious disillusioned aristocrat, the widowed *Marquise de Gravons St. Roche*, the Order's mother-house was thereafter for more than a century the ancient *Hôtel de Gravons* in that city. But when the religious Orders were expelled from France in 1882 *Mère Générale* surprised proud daughter-houses in Salzburg, Warsaw, Gloucestershire and elsewhere, by transferring the venerable portrait and relics of *Mère Marie-Félice de Gravons St. Roche* to an unassuming sixty-year-old foundation in a suburb of Brussels, and establishing the Government of the Order there.

This decision was sentimental and arbitrary. Brussels was nearer than other places to France, to Rouen; the French spoken by the community at *Place des Ormes* was meticulously the French of France; and *Mère Générale*, herself a daughter of Artois, liked the rains, the skies and the flat lands of the north.

To *Place des Ormes*, therefore, the promising nuns of the Order were usually summoned henceforward, within the first decade of their profession; to go through Staff College, as it were; to be under the Field Marshal's eye. And so it fell out that *Mère Marie-Hélène*, the young English Mother Scholastic at Cracow, was in her turn recalled to what for her was home.

The office of Mother Scholastic in the schools of the Order of *Sainte Famille* is an onerous one. Its holder is responsible for time-tables, routine and discipline throughout the school;

she is the meter-out of justice, the chief censor of behaviour, the arbitrator between pupil and teacher, the moral director and the gateway to the more detached and august authority of the Reverend Mother. She spends her entire day in active contact with her charges. Though she takes her share in teaching, she is usually elected to office because of qualifications of character and health rather than for intellectual ability. *Mère Marie-Hélène* taught English literature and, having been nurtured on it from the mists of babyhood, taught it well with originality and accuracy, and from the vantage point of high taste bestowed on her by her father. But, naturally enough, the accidental felicities of her knowledge were wasted on the giggling hordes of Polish, Italian and Belgian maidenhood who passed through her hands. What was not wasted on them, however, was her formidable character.

In confidential reports to *Mère Générale* the Reverend Mother at Cracow referred frequently to the young *Mère Marie-Hélène*. "This nun shapes well." "*Mère Marie-Hélène* has the qualities needed for command." "It is fortunate that with much beauty *Mère Marie-Hélène* possesses also detachment and authority. We have apparently none of the customary follies among the pupils which her appearance might suggest as likely." "*Mère Marie-Hélène* is very English, one supposes." "I do not think that *Mère Marie-Hélène* is 'a born nun,' but she is making herself into a very good one." "*Mère Marie-Hélène* should one day, by God's grace, be a useful servant of the Order, but I sometimes doubt if she proposes to make an assault, however humble, on saintliness. She is afraid of love, even the love of God. This makes one sad for her, for she has very high standards." "*Mère Marie-Hélène* is a valuable nun."

Such observations, scattered through the letters of four years, were not wasted on the General of the Order, and in due time *Mère Marie-Hélène* was directing the routine of her former school in a suburb of Brussels.

She found it enlarged, and more aristocratic now, with

young boarders who carried some of the noblest names in France. Houses to left and right of the original building had been acquired, and in the smallest house at the end *Mère Générale* had her study, her conference room, her oratory and her little herb garden. She lived apart from the school but shared the community life of her nuns, and watched them, studied them.

She watched *Mère Marie-Hélène*.

In a short time she had made up her mind about her. Mother Assistant-General was too old, and in fact too mad, to fulfil the secretarial duties of her office, so *Mère Marie-Hélène* was transferred to work in Mother General's study, as assistant to Mother Assistant. And when the latter died, she was elected to her office.

Friendship, tacit and clipped to the formality essential between a young nun and the General of her Order, flowered delicately through the official association. *Mère Générale* was a fat, plain woman and looked like a character strayed from *La Celestina*, but in fact there was no grossness in her; her religious feeling was deep and her devotion to work as unflagging as it was unspectacular; she rarely seemed either busy or anxious, but generally was both; a good-humoured manner concealed unblinking powers of observation, but as she did not often pronounce opinion or judgment on human beings, her shrewdness was not generally appreciated. This made her popular in office; Reverend Mothers and Mothers Provincial were not afraid of her, in council or in private interview, and although they were right in knowing that they need not be afraid, they were wrong in the premises which led them to this knowledge. She was, in fact, the right woman in the right place, and for the furtherance, as she understood it, of God's glory, she made free and perpetual use of the iron hand in the velvet glove. She ruled the thirty houses of the Order scattered over the globe, its eighteen hundred nuns, with cheerful, concealed astuteness, and on the principles of cold sanctity.

Being her secretary was not a sinecure; but besides being

arduous work, its exaction of hour-to-hour submissiveness and adaptability to another was a novel experience for one who, during four years and in two important houses, had held the authoritarian and independent-seeming office of Mother Scholastic.

When *Mère Marie-Hélène* came to her new duties her spirit was still moving uncertainly amid the clouds and emotions of return—to violent memory, to her father and to re-examination of the long cast out. Some trouble escaped, perhaps, into her disciplined face.

One morning *Mère Générale* examined a confidential report from Pondicherry on the lax-seeming conduct of a young member of the community there. She discussed it with her Assistant, seeming frankly to desire a moral judgment from her. Convention would have demanded, from this subordinate, an expression of pious anxiety, tinged with shock.

*Mère Marie-Hélène* looked troubled, but was unable to offer an opinion on the suspected offence.

"How old are you?" Mother General asked her.

"I am twenty-nine, *Mère Générale*."

"So young? Yet already you don't know right from wrong."

*Mère Marie-Hélène*, startled by this unconventional comment, decided that she had misheard it, and made no reply.

On another occasion *Mère Marie-Hélène* made a suggestion of policy for the South American province which impressed Mother General. She adopted and drafted it into a despatch to the Provincial House in Paraguay.

"You would have made a useful early Jesuit," she said amusedly to her secretary. "A Father Lainez to St. Ignatius."

"Truly, Mother General, I don't believe I could have managed the Council of Trent!" They laughed. "In any case, I'd rather have worked under Saint Teresa."

"An emotionally directed preference, I suspect, my daughter! Beware. The *Way of Perfection* is a more dangerous inspiration than the *Spiritual Exercises*—since we are not contemplatives."

# VOCATION

*Mère Marie-Hélène* acquiesced in silence, and went on with her work. It was the first time in her religious life that its emotional danger had had to be even so lightly indicated.

But her heart which had been frozen was in fact expanding again and growing warm; she was finding that life automatically had a quality which, in adolescence, had intoxicated her and which afterwards, in rage, she had dismissed as mirage, illusion or, at best, a lacquer spread on evil. It was none of these things, she admitted grudgingly now; it did not have a place in the moral category, deeply though it impinged on morality. But on the morality of saint and sinner alike, she saw, and to be used by each in accordance with his power and necessity. Sensibility must react to it, for better or worse, it seemed; and doctrines of grace piled up on the consequences of reaction.

"Your father likes sometimes," said *Mère Générale* on another occasion, "your father likes to present himself as the new materialist—advance model. Of course he is nothing of the sort. My own good Catholic father was, Heaven rest him, two-thirds materialist, though he never knew it! But your father is an older and more complicated thing—he is a pagan. I told him the other day that he is hopelessly out of date—a museum piece."

They were sitting in May sunshine in the little grey-green herb garden. *Mère Marie-Hélène* was made uneasy by this joke.

"He has devoted his whole life to a few very Christian poets," she said. "Rigidly Protestant ones, too, for the most part."

"Not his whole life. He reads Greek and Latin. And he grows more admirably Socratic in his habit of life with every day. But, as I tell him, the Church long ago took over all that was best of that philosophy—and he is an anachronism! He is very patient with an interfering old woman."

*Mère Marie-Hélène* looked away into the sunshine, towards the flowering orchard.

"What fruit there will be!" she said. "I hope we have no frosts this month."

27

Mother General did not heed this. She leant forward and patted the thin shoulder of her lieutenant.

"God is love, my daughter," she said softly. "And He is served by love. Don't take it on yourself to quarrel with that complicated fact."

Yes, there was the rub. She had decided that He was equity, detachment, justice, purity—anything good that was not love. Anything good that was cold and had definition —of which love, it seemed, had none.

One day her father said to her, in perfect innocence:

"I have never understood, Helen, why you became a nun. And, as you know"—he smiled at her—"I have never really forgiven you for it. When you sprang it on me I remember thinking—for in those days I knew you very well—that the proposition was somehow like an infection working in you— something unnecessary, and which could have been avoided. It seemed to me to outrage your character, as an illness might, or a nervous breakdown. Indeed, it seemed so much a thing *forced* on you that I was certain that, however long it invalided you, it would have passed before the taking of final vows. Well—I was wrong. But when you returned from Cracow last year—somehow, in eleven years, I had forgotten those last unreal weeks, and I—I expected to find my little daughter again, dreamy and impressionable, and perhaps too excitable."

"Then you didn't like the Helen who came back?"

"Oh, I think that when you came into this room I can hardly have failed to feel proud of your beauty. But——"

"But what, Father?"

"In that first interview, child, I thought that I had never seen anyone so—lonely. I did not know how to bear the— the horrible impression. You see—forgive me for saying this—your loneliness, your isolation, made you seem as if—well, 'merciless' was the word I kept thinking of, Helen. And I couldn't bear it. I—I couldn't see why our beautiful, happy child, your mother's and mine, should be like that— lonely and merciless."

"Father—I don't think I've ever felt really merciless——"

"I have not known you so, except in your decision to leave me and be a nun. But do you know, that day I thought that you were unfit for your work——"

She started.

He smiled at her pride.

"Yes, my dear. I thought of the young and the weak and the sentimental whose follies you would have to judge—and more than once I resented your dangerous choice of life. Of course, in any case, you know how I always suspect people who *look* their part——"

She drew away; her eyes were very unhappy.

"Don't look like that. The cruel impression of that first meeting hurt me more then than it can possibly hurt you now to hear of it. Because you can allow for my jealous resentment against your 'vocation,' and my general lack of sympathy with the ideal of the religious life. In spite of years of neighbourliness with the nuns here—since I first brought you to school on a Monday morning of January, 1868! So long ago, Helen! Such a mistake, had I but known!" He laughed to kill reproach, but her eyes were still unhappy. She looked about the room with defensive appraisal.

"It wasn't a mistake," she said almost sulkily. "I've always been happy here, Father—I can't tell you how happy. And safe." She dropped her voice on the last words.

"I know that," he said gently, although the sentiment still wounded him. "And return to it has been good for you. Lately you don't seem to me to be lonely—or merciless—any more."

Tears swam into her eyes, surprising them both; but she looked at him through them and gave him words he drank gratefully.

"I'm glad! Since seeing you again I *have* been different, Father! I know that. I haven't felt so lonely or so—merciless! It has made a great difference, coming back to you, and to things I knew when I was a child. These foolish tears!"

She laughed as she dried them.

"You used to shed them often when you were a little girl, Helen. They troubled your mother sometimes, but I approved of them. You remember I was always bored by stiff upper lips!"

The two had other conversations in this vein, the irony of which was the nun's locked secret. Clearly her father was innocent of all conception of offence against her, and would never—unless she yielded it—discover in his own life the clue to that infection of "mercilessness" in her which had distressed him. This almost *naïveté* in a man so observant and sensitive touched her sometimes to a faintly cynical amusement, but mainly to tenderness.

Thus, as has been said, by admission of this feeling; by the blurring of outlines it induced, the debates on sin and grace, the uneasy allowing of private judgment, she became humble, uncertain and more gentle than was generally perceived.

*The Third Chapter*

# IN THE PARLOUR

DINNER drew to an end in the school refectory; there was a noise of sixty girls talking, and chopping apples and pears with bright silver knives. Overhead the stridency was violent, but to those who partook of it it was a part of the customary Sunday atmosphere of pleasure and tension, an atmosphere which often by nightfall would have grown overcharged to a point of storm.

The room was lofty and lighted by four large windows; its four long tables were set in oblong, so that if a child came to school young enough to begin at Preparatory Table, she worked her way round the oblong—north to Junior, east to Latin, and finally south and up on to the dais to Foundress's Table, where she sat in honour during her last year under a copy of the portrait of *Mère Marie-Félice de Gravons St. Roche*.

Anna Murphy sat at the extreme south-west corner of Preparatory Table; a small hassock placed on her chair raised her to the level of the other children; Mother Josephine sat beside her, at the foot of the table, and peeled her fruit while also controlling the manners and conversation of the nine small girls who sat at the "little ones' end" of Preparatory Table. *La politesse* was a speciality of *Sainte Famille* education, and table manners were therefore tackled thoroughly at Preparatory Table, in particular at the "little ones' end."

Anna ate biscuits whilst she waited for her fruit.

"We all know you write beautifully, Gertie—but that is a knife you have in your hand now!"

"Oh, Mother Josephine, it slips when I hold it the other way!"

"It is extremely vulgar to hold a knife as if it were a pen. Molly, will you try to remember that you have neighbours at table. Poor Diana is in real danger from your elbow. Anyone would think you were a Hottentot."

Hottentot, thought Anna. Hottentot. "Anyone would think you were a Hottentot."

"Oh, Mother Josephine, this pear is just like a turnip! I can't peel it the way you say!"

Anna studied her companions attentively. She envied them their knives and forks and the excitement they were making with them.

"Begin on your pear now, Anna; I'll peel you an apple while you eat it. Hurry up." Mother Josephine smiled and turned her attention to the other little girls.

"Are you going home for the afternoon, Cynthia?"

"Yes, Mother. And I have permission not to be back for Benediction!"

"Really?"

"In honour of Daddy's birthday."

"You'll have to be in for Marks, though," said Molly. "Oh, I think I'll have terrible marks to-night. How many marks for politeness have you given me, Mother Josephine?"

"You'll see to-night—and I hope they'll make *some* impression on your dreadful manners."

"Ooh! That sounds bad!"

"I'm going to the parlour to-day," said Anna.

"Yes, pet, any minute now," said Gertie. "Isn't she a duck? Oh, Mother Josephine, isn't Anna a duck?"

"What a silly expression!" said Mother Josephine.

Anna, being three years younger than the youngest children in the school, was at once a curiosity and a reminder of home and nursery life to all these little girls. They fussed over her perpetually, to tease, to love or to dominate.

"Mother Josephine—do you know it is Second Prep's turn for reciting after Marks to-night?"

"Yes, Denise. I'm looking forward to hearing you. I hope you've all got nice pieces."

"Oh, rubbish, as usual," said Molly. "Mother Felicita's old rubbish!"

# IN THE PARLOUR

"Now, Molly—do you want another mark for politeness?"

" 'It was a summer's evening,
        Old Kaspar's work was done . . .' As
if anyone cared!" said Molly.

"We'll hear you to-night, thank you," said Mother Josephine. "No need to forestall the pleasure!"

Molly grinned.

"Well, all I can say is I'm sorry for you, Mother. Anyway, I have only the three first verses to say, so my troubles will be over in a jiffy after we start. I'm going to say my bit so fast that I bet no one will understand a word!"

When Molly's attention was not turned on to her, Anna found her very interesting; she had surprising ideas, like this of saying her poetry too fast to be understood. But in direct contact her face alarmed Anna. It made her think of doors banging, or candles going out on a windy night. It seemed a very large, variable face.

"I thought we'd have tipsy cake in honour of the receptions," said Cynthia.

"We're having it for supper," said Gertie. "*Sœur Antoine* told me."

"Three cheers! Did you like the reception, Mother Josephine? Did you cry?"

"Why should I cry, Denise? I thought it a very beautiful ceremony."

"Did *you* look pretty on your reception day, Mother Josephine?"

"Nonsense, child, of course not. One isn't thinking about looks on that occasion, I hope."

"I expect you looked sweet!" said Molly, who liked Mother Josephine. The young nun frowned shyly.

"You're a silly little girl, Molly."

Anna thought that Molly was right, and not silly, but her mouth was full of apple, so she said nothing—only stared admiringly at Mother Josephine's pink face.

33

When Mother Mary Andrew struck the gong on Foundress's Table, silence fell; then everyone stood up, with scraping of chairs.

"*An nom du Père et du Fils et du Saint-Esprit, ainsi soit-il . . .*" Grace was said in French, according to *Sainte Famille* tradition. Already the strange sounds fell familiarly on Anna's ears. Several times a day they danced, like a bright, nonsense refrain, across this cavernous foreign life which was so resoundingly big and hard to apprehend, a life of giants. "*Ainsi soit-il*"—there it was again—a very bright sound, like a bugle in a street.

Sister Maria was at the refectory door. Vibrations ran through the girls.

Me to the parlour? No, me. What do you bet? Who do you want, Sister Maria?

"Silence, if you please, young ladies."

It was practically impossible to disobey Mother Mary Andrew's voice. Sister Maria went up on the dais and whispered in her ear. Then Mother Mary Andrew called the names of girls whose relatives awaited them in the parlour.

"And go downstairs like ladies, if you please. Letitia, will you take Anna Murphy and see her safely to St. Anthony's Parlour?"

A fat girl, wearing the blue Child of Mary ribbon, descended from Foundress's Table, and took Anna's hand. The two set off from the refectory in the rear of six or seven girls who were straining under the exhortation to "go downstairs like ladies."

Anna went confidently with her hand in Letitia's.

Letitia did not laugh and call her "an old cripple" because she brought her two feet on to each step of the deep, shining stairs as she descended. Molly said she was a cripple for that; she knew she wasn't, but she often wondered how she would ever manage to go down these stairs the way she should.

"You're going to see your mother, Anna. Are you glad?"

"Yes. And Charlie."

"Is Charlie coming to-day?" Anna nodded.

"How old is he?"

"He's four."

"Oh, a baby—not like you."

"He isn't exactly a baby; he has trousers. Some long blue trousers, like a sailor."

"Very nice. Are you fond of Charlie?"

"Oh yes. I haven't seen him since I came to school."

"Then you must be very anxious to see him to-day."

Anna paused and looked up at Letitia.

"I'm not anxious," she said.

Letitia laughed at her.

"How do you mean? You're not anxious to see your little brother Charlie?"

"No. I want to see him, but I'm not anxious."

Letitia gave a roar of laughter.

"You're a funny little old codger, that's what you are," she said, and she picked her up in her arms. "Come on! Your mother will think you're lost."

Anna liked being carried by Letitia, who was soft and warm, although her brooch and her Child of Mary medal were bumpy. It was a relief to get up on her arm, away from the smell of the shiny, polished stairs. It was a relief to get back towards babyhood, leeward from the storms of huge impressions.

They galloped down the stately Visitors' Corridor, Anna side-saddle on Letitia's bosom, and the chandeliers ringing. They halted outside St. Anthony's, and Letitia pushed the little girl through the door.

Mrs. Murphy jumped from her chair by the window; Charlie stumbled forward with her. He had on his sailor trousers.

"My pet, my baby girl!"

The smell and feeling of her mother's face and neck and veil made up a perfect sensation for Anna; they brought back the life-size world; they were what she was, they didn't have to be considered and guessed at. She hugged them, hugged them. She was delighted. She kicked as she hugged her mother.

But the chute from alert to abandon was very sudden; it made her feel too gay; it made her feel frightened, glancing back at the new life among giants. She began to cry. She cried loudly:

"Oh Mammy, Mammy, Mammy!"

Charlie began to cry.

Mrs. Murphy sat down and, with Anna on her lap, put an arm round Charlie. She cried too, and she dried her children's eyes and her own with a little handkerchief.

All this made Anna feel relaxed and confident. In her new life, which she felt to be too big in every way but after which her interest strained without pause, much astonishment was made about tears, and Anna was told that she shed too many, and that grown-up people shed none. And it was true that in this place she had so far seen no tears spilt by anyone over nine. She hadn't felt bold enough to say that her mother often cried and her father sometimes; the vivid present made her unsure about the past. But now she was back in it. She was delighted. She smiled at Charlie's sweet round face and put her arm about his neck.

"Oh Charlie, how are Nellie and Buck?"

"Buck's shinier than Nellie."

"He was, before."

Nellie and Buck were a bantam cock and hen.

"We brought you almond toffee," said Charlie.

"Oh, we've brought you lots of things, my pet."

"We brought your new combinations," said Charlie. "Delia sewed your name on."

Mrs. Murphy laughed.

"I wonder if you'll be cold here this winter, with these little sleeves and socks, my baby?"

Anna was so much younger than the other children in the school that she was allowed to have short puffed sleeves to her school dresses of black cashmere, and to wear short white socks instead of black stockings.

# IN THE PARLOUR

"How are you getting on, my darling? Have you had a happy week?"

Mrs. Murphy had visited her daughter four times in the three weeks since she had brought her to be a boarder at her own old school, and these first sights of the little girl in her new environment pressed with a vague discomfort on a heart which she believed to be unusually tender and maternal. The child seemed smaller than at home; her face was very white. "Your arms are like little twigs," said Maud Murphy and stroked her daughter's elbow. Poor little Nan! If only Harry weren't——she frowned and brushed the frown away into a sweet smile.

Anna stared contentedly up into a face which was, as it happened, pretty, but which was for her beyond qualification. It was Mother, and through it shone the images of fixity, the things that always were, and did not have to be mastered.

"Sister Simeon has a red beard, like the tinkers," she said. "When she goes to feed the hens she sings 'Kyrie Eleison' at the gate. That's how they know it's their dinner!"

"Poor Sister Simeon! Is she still alive? You must never mention her beard to her, Anna. You know that, don't you?"

"Is this the drawing-room?"

Charlie looked round the little bare parlour.

"Nuns don't have a drawing-room, Charlie. There are a lot of parlours—this is an enormous place. You'd be very surprised at all there is."

The door opened and a chubby young nun with a spotted face came in. Maud Murphy stood up and embraced her, receiving a nun's kiss, a touch of greeting on each cheek.

"Oh, Ella! This is lovely! I asked Sister Maria, but I was afraid you might be in retreat or something."

Mother Agatha, *née* Ella O'Byrne, had been the bosom friend at school of Maud Murphy, *née* Condon. The two were still sympathetic.

"Reverend Mother gave me permission, as it is Rosary Sunday—and, of course, to-day is a special day for the community. We had three postulants received this

37

morning! Didn't Anna tell you about our beautiful
ceremony?"

Anna shook her head.

"Not yet," she said.

"Isn't she a Solomon?" said Mother Agatha. "Really,
Maud, anyone less like you than that child! Now, Charlie—
he is just you all over again! Aren't you, pet? Aren't you
just like your mummy?"

Charlie was climbing on to the window-seat and did not
look round. Mother Agatha drew a chair close to her friend's
and they plunged into talk.

"You're looking very much better, Maud. It must be all
the prayers I'm saying for you!"

Anna leant against the window seat near Charlie. She felt
very peaceful. Charlie and she were always peaceful together.
She had two other brothers, Harry and Tom, but they were
big. They were nine and seven and a half; she and Charlie
liked being together.

"Did Joe drive you here?"

"Yes."

"Where's the trap?"

"Along the roads. He said Princess was too fresh to stand
for a bit. He'll come back. He wants to see you."

"I hope he'll come soon. Over there—do you see,
Charlie? Over beyond that holly hedge, we play rounders.
Not on Sundays, though."

"What's 'rounders'?"

Anna told him about rounders.

" . . . It reminded me of my own happy day, of course.
The Bishop spoke beautifully—a little too fast, I thought,
though. They sang 'Not for the consolations——'"

"Oh, my favourite hymn, Ella!"

"I know. I thought of you. The novices looked very nice
—of course Eileen O'Doherty looked an absolute picture!
You may know her—her family, I mean; she's long after our
time! The eldest sister, Maeve O'Doherty, came to school
here in our last year, Maud. She's married in Malay now.

They're Major O'Doherty's children—of Cappadown. A fine, soldierly figure he looked in the chapel this morning—an ideal type of man, really!"

"I know old Major O'Doherty. Was his daughter received?"

"Yes, his youngest. You'd have to marvel at the strength of that vocation. Because if ever a girl seemed to have everything—everything the heart could desire! And there she is, giving it all up to God! The world at her feet, you might say!"

Maud sighed.

"Perhaps she is better off. The world isn't much catch, Ella."

"I know that indeed, my dear." Mother Agatha's manner was very sympathetic. "Often, Maud, when I think of all your trials, dear, I wonder if perhaps they aren't a part of your Purgatory here below—because you didn't follow your true vocation, it may be——"

Maud drew aside with a gentle suggestion of vanity in her movement.

"Oh, as to that—I don't think I was cut out for a nun, you know."

"Perhaps not." Mother Agatha smiled out of the generous automatic admiration of years. Maud had always been the admired and she the admirer. "Perhaps not. You were always so gay and pretty. But God is good, and He'll reward you, never fear. He sees your sacrifice, Maud. No cross, no crown."

Conversation about Maud's cross was always euphemistic; Mother Agatha understood that marriage did not suit her friend, and that Harry Murphy was in some unspecified way a monster, as life-companion for a woman of delicate and religious sensibilities. But since there was a thing called "duty" which confessors had to insist upon with Catholic wives, Maud's cross must be carried, it seemed. Besides, Harry Murphy drank now. Mother Agatha had no patience with him, but she loved and prayed for Maud.

No cross, no crown. He sees your sacrifice. Anna leant contentedly on the window-ledge; the women's talk flowed in dark shapes that interested her. The brilliant symbols, Cross and Crown, wound variously, in pursuit of each other, in escape, through velvet darkness; the deep word "sacrifice," the solemn "He," marked time. It was grandiose, it made her dreamy, and it was familiar. Grandmother said that too—no cross, no crown. It was a musical thing to say.

"Can you read, Charlie?"

"I don't know yet, really!"

"I can."

"Joe says there's no hurry."

"Ah, you'll have to. Don't mind Joe. I'll teach you."

"I'll teach myself. I won't go to school."

"Won't you? I think everyone does; Harry and Tom said like you, but look, they had to go."

Harry and Tom had been sent to the preparatory school for Clongowes.

"Joe says school is no good to you," said Charlie.

"It takes your mind off things," said Anna, who had heard her grandmother say this and lately thought she knew what it meant.

" . . . and I'm sure you're grateful to me, dear, for persuading you to send her here. The way things were going, Maud, it was far the best plan."

"I expect so. The house is lonely with the three of them suddenly gone, but of course Harry is nearly ten; he'd have had to go to school soon anyway."

"And it was your bounden duty to get that creature out of your house, dear. Fancy such a woman being a nursery governess! In charge of little innocent children, God help them!"

"Sh, Ella!" Maud glanced towards the window seat and dropped her voice. "It's only fair to say that I know nothing against her. Only, Harry is hopeless—oh, don't let's think of such disgusting things, Ella! This dear little parlour—I wish I were at school again! I wish I were in Anna's shoes!"

"Ah, the happiest days! Little did we know the trials life had in store for you. Well, His ways are wonderful, my darling—His Will be done!"

"He's been drinking practically every night this week," said Maud with resignation.

Anna was puzzled. She had thought Mother Agatha was talking about God—but what did God drink, and how did her mother know when He drank it? However, the curious remark, and the sun outside, and Charlie's gee-upping of a pony he thought he was riding, reminded her of pleasant days at home.

"Did you go down to Mr. Moriarty for lemonade any time, Charlie?"

"No. They won't let me go on the road on my donkey by myself. And Miss Cross is gone—did you know?"

"Yes. She told me she was going to be a governess in England. Much better than being with us, she said."

"She cried when she went," said Charlie. "I wish she was here. She could race my donkey up the well-field."

"She could race Harry——"

"No, she couldn't."

"Yes, she could."

"I play with Jamesy Meagher in the yard now," said Charlie.

"But he's a common boy."

"I know. He called the donkey a dirty bugger."

"Is a 'dirty bugger' a common thing?"

"Yes. Joe says Jamesy is no class."

Mrs. Murphy opened one of the parcels on the table.

"Look, darling—marshmallows! Would you like to have some now, with Charlie?"

Anna went and leant against her mother; Charlie climbed off the window seat and came too.

"Which will I have first, pink or white?"

"I'll have pink, all pink," said Charlie.

"Oh, no, Charlie, that's not fair. You can't have all pink," said Mother Agatha, who was very fond of sweets and sometimes thought wistfully of schoolday orgies of them.

"I want all pink," said Charlie, and clutched three sweets of that colour.

Anna was unperturbed, eating steadily. She had no intention of letting Charlie have all the pink marshmallows.

Mother Mary Andrew came in. As Mother Scholastic she thought it her duty to report to Mrs. Murphy on the adjustment to school life of her little daughter.

Maud Murphy and Mother Agatha had been at school with Mother Scholastic, but were three years her junior; they had disliked her because her father was a draper, and because she was bossy and "clever." Nowadays the latter, captaining Mother Agatha, who taught sewing and elementary pianoforte and took charge in dormitories and playgrounds, thought little of her capabilities; and regarded Maud Murphy as the same fool she had always been.

"How do you do, Maud?"

"How do you do, Mother Scholastic?"

"Sit down again, won't you?"

"Where are you going to sit, Mother? Oh, Anna darling—don't spill the sweets, there's a good child!"

"Charlie's pulling them."

"Who's telling tales?" said Mother Agatha.

"It's true; it's not a tale," said Anna. "Let go, Charlie."

The children pushed and pulled each other towards the window seat again.

"Well, Maud, you see she's quite happy."

"Yes, Mother; she's a bit white, of course."

"She was as white as chalk when she came, my dear girl. It's an experiment for us, of course, having a child who is so much more of a baby than anyone else. She is difficult to fit in——"

"But everyone's devoted to her," put in Mother Agatha. "She's the pet of the whole school, I need hardly say."

Mother Scholastic detested the habitual gush of Mother Agatha's speech.

"I trust that is not so," she said, frowning. "We have

precious little time for pets at *Sainte Famille*. But some of the younger ones do of course find her a distraction. It will be easier when she is able to follow some of the Second Preparatory."

"She was very fond of lessons at home, with Miss Cross."

"You can tell that indeed, Maud darling—some of the nuns who teach her now tell us she is amazing! Quite a little prodigy, they say!"

Mother Scholastic frowned again.

"She is hardly that, Mother Agatha. But she reads unusually easily for her age, I must say, which is often a good sign of intelligence. I hope she will be bright. At any rate, I think she will be better at her books than you were, Maud. But that wouldn't be hard for her—now would it?"

Mother Scholastic gave a sarcastic laugh, and Maud Murphy felt dislike of long ago stir in her lazy nerves; felt a chill of pity for her little daughter. This induced a weak half-wish that her children need not have been scattered from each other so young and placed at the mercy of such flints as this dark-browed nun. But if one lived five miles from a town; if—men being as they are—it was impossible to keep a governess in the house; if a husband drank all night and sneered at his wife all day, how else were children to be educated, and protected? It was hard this way, very hard on a mother's tender feelings—but what did he care for her feelings? What did he care for anyone but himself?

So pity became self-pity, and in dramatisation of her commonplace ineptitude Maud Murphy evaded the brief ordeal of a natural pang.

"Oh, here's Joe! Here's Princess! Doesn't she look lovely! Oh, I'm going out to see Joe!"

A round trap, pneumatic-tyred, came smartly up the curve of the drive and on to the gravel front. The bay pony shone; her harness jingled.

"Go steadily, children—yes, run out to see Joe, darling."

"The hall door is open, I believe," said Mother Mary Andrew.

"I'll see them out, Maud darling—I'll be back to you in a minute. Wait, Charlie, you naughty boy! You'll fall down the steps!"

Mrs. Murphy felt at a loss when alone with Mother Mary Andrew.

"I think Anna needs iron, Maud. You should send her some Parrish's Food. And not too many sweets." She looked contemptuously at the parcels on the table. "She is a good child, I think—but a bit spoilt, a bit of a cry-baby. We'll get her out of that."

"Oh, I don't think she's spoilt—really——"

"Well, I do, Maud. But I expected that. She promises well at her lessons—she has them alone, of course—and reports show that she is bright. When will she be seven?"

"On the 5th April, Mother."

"Oh—and now we are at the beginning of October. Well, since she shows understanding of her Catechism, we might let her make her first Confession before Lent. But that can be settled with Father Conroy a little later."

"She's only a baby—there's no hurry."

"We have no babies here, my dear Maud—you must try to remember that Anna is *at school* now."

Mother Mary Andrew rose as Mother Agatha came back into the room. She shook hands with Mrs. Murphy and made her departure briskly.

Mother Agatha caught sight of the tears in Maud's eyes.

"Don't mind her, darling; her bark is worse than her bite. But she always does get a bit funny if anyone is made an exception of, or anything like that—and, of course, Anna is a terrible pet—and she doesn't approve of pets, as you know!"

Maud dabbed at her eyes.

"I always loathed her! She never could open her mouth without snubbing someone! I was a lunatic to send the child here, Ella! Oh, why did you persuade me to do such a cruel thing?"

Ella set herself to the familiar task of soothing Maud.

44

The way to do this was to remind her of her daily martyrdom and to induce a sweet self-pity.

Out on the gravel Joe lifted Anna on to the shaft, and she leant against Princess's shoulder, and pulled her mane.

"So there you are, Miss Anna, as large as life! As big as a house you're growing on us! Whoa up there, Princess, till we have a chat, the lot of us!"

"Joe, Joe—I want to be up there, too!"

Charlie was lifted on to the shaft beside Anna.

"Joe, I'm delighted you came to see me! Is Princess very fresh?"

"Yerrah, wouldn't you know by the fly eye of her? But 'tis only the way she knew we were coming here to see you! Why wouldn't she be fresh in the name of God!"

Joe had bow legs, and a hard black hat with a square top. He was clean and red and small. Anna beamed into the shiny criss-crosses of his face.

"Is that really why she's fresh, Joe—because you were coming to see me?"

"The divil another reason then! She's a thought-reader, that auld pony. Charlie and I think that 'tis the way that she does be talking about you to herself sometimes, and she in the stable. Isn't that the truth, Princess?"

Anna climbed from the shaft on to the pony's back; so did Charlie.

"Are they killing you out with praying and learning, my little girleen?" asked Joe.

"I like praying," said Anna. "I'm in the front row and I can see everything. It is very interesting in chapel, Joe."

Joe cackled with laughter.

"Do you hear that, Charlie? Do you hear what she's after saying? We must take her home out of this, the two of us, or 'tis a holy nun they'll have made her into on us in the changing of the moon, God save us all!"

"Tell her about the pony you saw for me at Ennis Fair, Joe."

"Ah, you'd be talking! The very mount for him, if I have

my way to have him blooded this season! A little butty-made chestnut with just enough action, and no harm in him. Ten hands high, and two white stockings——"

A man on horseback came up the shadowy curve of the avenue and across the sunlit ground, his mount's hoofs scattering it.

"It's Daddy! It's Daddy!"

The children bounded excitedly on Princess's back, and had to be lifted down by Joe. Harry Murphy dismounted. "How's my little love?" he shouted, and swung Anna high in his arms. "How's my mouse and my grouse and my little old woman?" He gave her a great hug. He thought her a sweet child, and every now and then when he remembered that she was shut up in a boarding school at the age of six, it made him furiously angry, violently tender. Just now, "riding the land," as he called his Sunday inspection of cattle and ditches, he had remembered her absence from his daily life, and had turned back to the road and ridden three miles to have a look at her.

Anna preferred her mother's embrace to her father's, but she loved the excitement and racy violence he stirred up. She liked being held near his face when he laughed; his teeth were shiny, and his mouth smelt deliciously.

She stroked his hard face.

> "Dance her up and up," he sang,
> "Dance her up on high!
>  Dance her up and up
>  And she'll come down by and by!"

Anna flew from the air to his hands, back and forth in time to the singing.

> "She's the flower of the flock,
>  She's the rose of the garden,
>  She's her Mammy's pet,
>  And she's Daddy's darling!
>  Dance her up and up——"

Charlie hopped about his father's legs; Joe held the Master's mount and smiled admiringly.

Anna always loved the first moment of this familiar commotion, then grew a little sick, and anxious for it to stop; but to-day, as it violently scattered the surrounding scene, so grave and strange and holy, and set in its place, like magic, the grassy paddock at home, she liked it very much and bore the sick sensation without her usual resistance.

Her father stopped the song as abruptly as he had begun it. He hooked her up on his arm; and stroked her straight-hanging hair.

"Rats' tails," he said lovingly. "Why haven't I got a curly-headed daughter? Look at Charlie now, with his fancy curls! Are you ashamed of your rats' tails, my mouse?"

This was an old joke, hitherto harmless. But the observations of Mother Agatha and Sister Maria in the dormitory, and their plans to tight-plait or crimp her hair in preparation for certain approaching feast-days, had made her understand that the rats' tails Daddy made fun of were a deformity; and she was coming to understand, from a study of other girls, that her hair was ugly-looking, and that she herself was ugly-looking. She had cried three times over this discovery since coming to school, but had had to pretend that she was crying because she did not like her pudding, or had toothache. Now, at this mention of her ugly hair when she had been feeling so happy, she cried again. Over-excited, she cried with frantic abandon.

Her father was aghast. He held her tight against his chest. "There, there, my little pet!" He glared at Joe. "What's happened her, Joe? Was she upset before I came? Were any of you unkind to her?"

"Yerrah, no, sir! 'Tis the way she's too excited, the little crather! Hush there now, Miss Anna, let you! Look at poor Charlie, here, and he frightened out of his life to hear you bawling like a baby! Hush up let you now, Miss Anna—before you have us all upset!"

Harry Murphy stroked the huddled head.

"My little old woman! Don't cry."

He couldn't bear distress in his children, and he was confident, in his brief, casual way, that he was never its cause. When they cried he looked round in whirling rage for their enemy. He did not think of tears rising from hidden wells of personality; there was always an instant reason for them, a shaft sped by the world. Roughly his idea was effective if not precise; at any rate his instinctive protectiveness when they cried made his children fond of him.

He raged now, and his heart found the enemy, as he soothed and dandled her. Her mother, her grandmother, Mother Agatha, Father Doolin, the whole pious Cabal who disapproved of him, trembled for his example to his family, and scattered them in babyhood to holy prison-houses where his drunkard's breath could not contaminate them. He raged as he hugged his daughter, tramping the wide gravel sweep.

"Aren't you happy in this old hole, my little love? I'll take you home out of it, so help me! I'll take you home this instant, if I like! I will not have my little girleen crying! I'll tell that one all over again what I think of this arrangement!" he went on, unheard. "Herself and her sainted mother and her parish priest! A pack of Sankey-Moodys—that's what I'm married to, by God! . . ."

He stared past the lawns and fields to the placid lake. He did not admit to himself that his rage was a brief squib; he did not look straight at the fact that it was his wife's money, his mother-in-law's, which paid for this schooling he resented; but he knew that he would not take Anna home. He loved her, but he had sold her to the Cabal. He would sell her again, he would do many things he was ashamed of, for the sake of some peace and quiet now in Castle Tory. For the sake of the whisky decanter, and the comfort of being labelled a drunkard and a coarse, unfeeling brute. It was, after all, the easiest way with women, whom he needed but could not understand. They did not like what men liked, and the only way for a man to get on with his likings was to hand them the virtues, be dirt under their feet. It was a sell-

48

out, but it secured a kind of peace they would not befoul themselves by sharing. So he would not take his little weeping daughter home, because he had sold his authority over her, and was, in fact, the disgraceful reason she was here. But he felt lonely as well as angry while he comforted her. He remembered her contentment at home; he remembered how it used to amuse him, as he schooled colts in the paddock, to thunder by the high tarred paling, and interrupt the lesson going on under the chestnut-tree at the edge of the lawn. The boys were distracted, watching the horses; Miss Cross's eyes would wander too; but Anna was absurdly grave at her book. "Bluestocking" Miss Cross called her; and so, in her honour, they had christened the blue roan filly. But Miss Cross was sacked now and "Bluestocking" had brought in three hundred guineas at Doncaster; Anna was a schoolgirl, and there were no more lessons under the chestnut-tree.

"Stop crying, my little lamb! I should have brought you some sweets, damn it! Did they bring you any? Did that ruffian of a Charlie bring you any sweets? Sh, sh, my pet. Will I buy you a pony, Nan? Charlie tells me there was one at Ennis Fair for him—and I let it slip, it seems! But I'll be getting him one—so will I get one for you, Anna? Would you like a fat, cream one like you saw in the circus? Is that what she'd like, do you think, Charlie? A rotten old no-good of a circus pony?"

Charlie was delighted.

"That's what we must do, Charlie. Look out for a fat circus pony for her, that'll spell out her name, and stand up on a drum! Would you like an old freak of a pony like that, my little mouse?"

Anna's tears were over now. She leant luxuriously against her father's shoulder, smiling at him and at Charlie. Her face was dirty and her eyes were wet. She had forgotten her deformity of straight hair, and been made to feel, by this man's random, rash facility, that she was very precious, and quite safe. She was not a prisoner; home was still real and near her, and any time she felt it must be so, her daddy would take her back there and let her stay. She had needed to know this, needed just this violent assertion of it—but no more. Sure of Castle Tory and its defensiveness, she preferred on the whole to stay where she was; for her new life interested her deeply, and she was more acceptive of its ordeals than her gusts of tears suggested to lookers-on. She, in a sense, understood her own weeping, and did not really allow it to impinge upon curiosity, which here was stretched and gratified from minute to minute in ways unheard of in Castle Tory.

"I don't want a pony, thank you, Daddy."

Harry and Charlie laughed together. This was a familiar joke, that Anna did not care very much about ponies. Except Princess, whom she said was more like a person than a pony.

"Well, of all the comic little daughters! Did you hear her, Charlie?—'I don't want a pony, thank you, Daddy.' What are you to make of a girl like that?"

Anna enjoyed their wonder, and suddenly wriggled down to be with Charlie again. They all turned back towards Joe and the horses, and saw Mrs. Murphy descending the great stone steps of the house. Mother Agatha was with her. The two paused when they saw Harry; then the nun gave her friend a kiss and withdrew.

"Aha! Good riddance," said Harry Murphy.

Maud frowned her please-not-before-the-children frown; then, catching sight of Anna's tear-stains, herself forgot her own rule.

"I might have known you'd upset her! Really, Harry, what possessed you to come to-day?"

"To see the child—or is that forbidden? And at least I do come to see her—not darling, darling Mother Agatha. God save us!"

He had been thinking as she descended the steps that she was pretty and sweet, but he had been unable to resist a jibe at Mother Agatha. So he had brought to Maud's face the martyr look, compact of all the iron piety of the Cabal. Thus, though he had thought she was looking pretty and she had been touched by his having ridden unannounced to visit his daughter—these reactions were wasted now.

Joe, who was tactful, sought to distract the children by making Princess whinny for an apple. The Master had had a couple all right, and that was no way at all to be speaking to the Mistress. It was a show, so it was, the way these two couldn't agree for one blessed minute of the day. Joe lived alone in a little white hovel at the gate of Castle Tory.

Maud hissed at her husband under cover of the whinny.

"Well, at least you might try to be sober when you see her!"

"Ah, for God's sake, woman!"

Harry strode to his horse.

"Come on and mount us, Nan."

He snatched Anna under his left arm and, holding her, swung to the saddle. It always frightened her when he did this, but she liked the excitement of not betraying her fear.

Charlie shouted jealously:

"Me, Daddy, me!"

"Oh, you can mount me at home, old chap. I'm still allowed *your* company." He flung this sentence towards Maud. "Good-bye now, Nan, and don't overdo the learning, if you please! Here, Joe, take her down. God bless you, pet."

"I hate that 'mounting' trick, Harry—it's dangerous."

"So's sneezing," said Harry, and rode away, scattering the gravel.

Anna went and took her mother's hand. She had forgotten that they talked to each other differently from the way they talked to her. She had forgotten that their voices could be like flat pieces of wood banging together. She had forgotten this redness on the tops of her mother's cheeks. The whinny of Princess had not deadened her perception. She did not understand the cruel crisping of the air, but she remembered it, she knew it. She took a tight grip of her mother's hand.

Maud was touched, in her vanity as well as in her remorseful heart. It is dreadful of us to behave like this before the children, she thought compunctiously. But also: she feels like *me*, she thought; she is ashamed of him, and hurt for me.

This was untrue. Anna was feeling personal anxiety before grown-up conduct; she was confused and remembering old confusion. She was not expressing reassurance; she was in need of it. She trembled in her need.

Maud knelt and put her arms around her, the red spots fading from her cheeks as her eyes smiled.

"We must be going now, my darling—but I'm going to write to Reverend Mother to ask her if you may come home next Sunday for the whole long day. You'll like that, won't you?" Anna nodded. "Joe will be here with the trap at nine o'clock—won't you, Joe?"

"I will that, ma'am. On the very dot, Miss Anna."

"Me, too," said Charlie. "I'll come too."

"We'll have a lovely day," said Maud. "Granny will be staying with us, and we'll have the dogs all washed and nice— and perhaps there'll be pheasants for dinner!"

"With their tails on?"

"Of course. So now—won't that be grand? Good-bye, my little pet. Kiss Charlie. That's right. Now kiss me."

Maud got up from her knees.

"Good-bye, Joe," said Anna, and gave Joe a kiss.

They all got into the trap and drove away. Anna blew kisses to them, and they to her, until the elm-trees hid them.

# The Fourth Chapter

## A LETTER

On Sundays, when midday recreation ended, Reverend Mother usually left the Community Room and withdrew to her study which adjoined it. Unless some urgent summons to the parlour claimed her she guarded thus a sabbatical hour of peace until the Benediction bell rang.

To-day she entered the little room in alarm at her desire for it, dismayed by her passionate intention.

She went to her orderly desk, took pen and paper, made the sign of the Cross, and composed herself to write.

She had known, perhaps, from the beginning of her four years in Irish exile, that this hour would come.

Obedience, because it was very difficult for her, had been the fetish, the mania of her religious life. She had exacted of herself, in vanity maybe, a perfection of military obedience; sometimes as a very young nun in Turin and Vienna, she had accused herself of enjoying the comedy of giving flawless obedience to commands which her intelligence told her were absurd. That was the point of the vow, she would tell herself ironically—for can there be obedience without conscious subjection of the brain?

But vanity lay in exaggeration of surrender—vanity and a wider danger. Possible waste of service. She was a nun in order to serve God—not her capricious self. Such powers as she had were to be stretched and exhausted for His glory, and by no means so as to prove something odd and gratifying about her soul to her waiting vanity. She existed to work at full stretch for the *Compagnie de la Sainte Famille*, not to play a long-drawn game of skill with her own sensibilities.

In short, she had come to the end of pretending to be a successful Superior of this Irish house.

It would have pleased her to have made a triumph of this office; in the first place because she knew she had been appointed to it by *Mère Générale* as to a supremely difficult test of her abilities, and secondly because she had secretly been surprised and shaken more than once by the hard reality of her difficulties. Only vanity, she had often suspected with shame, only vanity had sustained her effort to be patient and scrupulous in office. But there were two things which, she knew, more than others offended *Mère Générale:* misdirection of energy, which made her angry, and inability to admit personal failure, which aroused her surprised contempt. She would offend no longer, in these ways at least, against the trust imposed in her.

Ireland was impossible for her to work in. She quite simply had not the personal qualities it exacted.

She laid down her pen; her hands came together, wrung each other in an uncontrolled movement of distress, her long fingers twisting fiercely. When she noticed this she dropped them apart and laid them, dead still, on the table. Why can I *not* command my hands? she asked herself in anger.

Beyond her window, in a high-walled path which led to the gate of the convent cemetery, old *Sœur Amélie* said the Stations of the Cross, pausing in front of plaster images niched into the deep ivy.

*Sœur Amélie* was very fat. She was the cook, a *Normande* from the lost Mother House. She cooked in a great and simple manner; and was frequently grumbled at, alike by nuns and pupils of this Irish *Sainte Famille*, for serving incomparably more civilised food than they were used to. When she died, the Refectories would undergo a break with a tradition which perhaps was wasted on them. A Reverend Mother might be able for a time to insist upon French forms of menu, but she could not replace the talent of an old Frenchwoman, and, eventually, by the unspoken will of the majority, British ways of eating would be happily imposed. How odd were these Irish, who believed themselves implacably at war in the spirit with England, yet hugged as their own her dreariest daily habits, and could only distrust the grace and good sense of Latin Catholic life! The parochial conceit of a Father Conroy—her hands crisped together again—might caricature Ireland's conception of itself; these curates, appointed chaplains to the house, varied in intelligence, naturally; but all were unpromisingly straitened, it seemed to her, in an unwieldly, bad assertiveness; and this was intensified, she allowed, in the fulfilment of their duties at the convent, by their awkward desire to counteract the menace of her foreignness.

They would win. In the twenty-three years of her life as a professed nun she had seen in the Order the numerical balance of Irish, Irish-American, and Irish-Australian nuns shift from fifteen to sixty per cent. The European populations were not producing nuns; the Irish populations were. At *Sainte Fontaine* now the predominance of novices of Irish blood was causing *Mère Générale* to review the constitution of the Order with some anxiety in relation to the future. This inevitable shift of power from the French-speaking to the English-speaking element was already making itself apparent in the Council of Provinces, and in the voices of particular Mothers Provincial. The Order was rightly ambitious to be an educational force in the century just opening—but as to interpretation of that just desire, there would be struggle, it was clear, between the root and the branch—between Brussels and Illinois, Brussels and Queensland, Brussels and Ireland.

It was possible that the next *Mère Générale* might be appointed from the old guard, the European clique—possible, but not certain. She would be, if the present head of the Order had her way. And traditionally the influence of an ageing *Générale* was so strong on the Council of Provinces that the candidate whom she favoured for the succession had always hitherto been secure of election; moreover, dying, a *Générale* left her vote, and her written reasons for that vote, in an envelope which was unsealed by Mother Assistant General after her death. The nun named in this paper had always been appointed to office—but this was only a tradition, not a rule.

Weighing the politics of the Order in recent years, Reverend Mother had come to understand that she, in fact, was *Mère Générale's* horse for the succession. That explained her appointment to this Irish foundation, when she was also, *ex officio*, Mother Provincial of the English Province, that is, of the Order's five houses in the British Isles.

Dismissing her own merits and demerits as beside the point, she often smiled as she pondered the guile behind the selection of herself for supreme office. Taken as a cipher, she represented or could seem to represent, exactly that compromise which the times, say ten or fifteen years on, might be guessed to require. She imagined that *Mère Générale* reasoned somewhat as follows: Mother Mary Helen Archer (her whole name would be written in English for policy's sake) was *not* French, as all *Mère Générales* of the Order had hitherto been; neither was she Irish, which would have been intolerable to the old guard, and, in *Mère Générale's* private view, unsuitable; she would have worked in the European houses, but really learnt government in the difficult neutral ground of the English Province, whence so much new blood was flowing; she would be held to understand the Irish character and the constitution of a Community Room predominantly Irish; she might be hoped to have gained the respect and confidence of the increasingly powerful Irish element. But she *would not be Irish*. These facts, coupled with the overwhelming one that she was the choice of her predecessor in office, would be practically all that would be known of her by the majority of Reverend Mothers and Mothers Provincial scattered over the globe, who would record their votes by proxy or by cable.

But—*Mère Générale* loved the Order as she had found it and as she proposed, quixotically, to have it remain. She loved its stiff, polite and predominantly pious tradition. It may be that she foresaw somewhat the twentieth century assault of "progress," guessed at new fevers of theory and experiment, in nationalism, in education, in social science, which, threatening the institutions of the Church with extinction, might force them in self-defence to unpredictable adaptations and vulgarities. Perhaps she foresaw that the awkward, finicky, *bourgeois* instrument forged by an eighteenth-century lady for the pious training of girls throughout the world would soon be made to seem, by the nimble and expeditious, a derelict thing, an absurd and deplorable curio. Wrongly or rightly, *Mère Générale* would hold these theorists to be short-sighted fools, and would desire *La Compagnie de la Sainte Famille* to hold to its prim, Christian way, as long as possible, amid the lures of progress. "*La pudeur et la politesse, mes Enfants.*" Already *Mère Générale* had seen some forward-marchers smile at those two amusing words—and had expressed herself aghast at the risks which she saw the informed preparing to take with human nature.

But she could fight, and so could her Order. And she knew in what hands tradition might be safe. She knew that the English nun who had worked with her in her study in *Place des Ormes* for eleven years might seem on paper to be a perfect compromise between old and new, and might even in many ways be able and willing to effect the compromise she suggested—but that her heart was passionate and ruthless for the stiff spirit of Rouen. Because she was sure of this, *Mère Générale* had laid a difficult authority on her favourite lieutenant; had deprived the Mother House of her diplomatic and executive abilities; and for herself had sacrificed a companionship which might have consoled the painful years of decline. The Order and the future must be secured.

*Sœur Amélie* passed the window, crossing from the seventh station to the eighth. Reverend Mother smiled at her and received her smile.

*Sœur Amélie* would die, as since 1882 she had lived, in exile from everything she understood. There were amusing *sotto voce* stories in the Community Room of *Sœur Amélie*'s temperament: of tears that flowed from her three days on end, so that even the *madeleines* for the chaplain's tea were salty; of her having once bombarded Mother Eugenia with a quick-fire round of potatoes, knocking her coif askew and injuring her eye; of a dangerous day of melancholy when she went alone to the lake-shore—for her a long walk—and with her own hands drowned her beloved Persian cat. "*Je me sens seule,*" she repeated all that evening in the kitchen. "*Je me sens si seule, et je songe à ma mère.*"

Reverend Mother had not known her then. By the time she came to Ireland, *Sœur Amélie* was old and quiet—an old lay-sister who liked to talk in French, of France. The French and Belgian members of the community were thinning out; where twenty-five years ago they had been forty, with only twenty of other nationalities in the house, now they were nine—five ageing lay-sisters and four choir nuns. *Sœur Amélie* had a devotion to the graves of these dead compatriots; she often prayed beside them, and decorated them for feast-days and anniversaries. She said that it was sad not to lie in French earth.

Reverend Mother once suggested in a letter to *Mère Générale* that *Sœur Amélie,* who never dreamt of such a favour, might perhaps be recalled to Belgium for her old age. But—"I have no Normandy to call her back to, my daughter," wrote *Mère Générale,* "so why trouble her with another foreign land? Any grave that is not Norman will seem, from this side, an alien grave to her. But when she comes to her Irish resting-place, she will rest well. No, let her be. She has made her good sacrifice to God; let her finish it, and be rewarded."

Reverend Mother recalled that letter now, and she felt a pang, of pity for the old nun beyond the window, of doubt of herself. But how was she ever to know how much was selfishness and how much wisdom in what she had decided to do?

She picked up her pen again, and wrote the date on the notepaper.

"*Dimanche du rosaire,* 1904."

There was a knock at the door.

Mother Eugenia entered. As Mother Assistant she had

some rights in the room, which was the administrative office.

"Forgive me for disturbing you, Reverend Mother, but Sister Maria tells me the De La Poles are in the Long Parlour. I thought you might wish to see them."

This was Mother Eugenia's way of announcing that, subject to holy obedience, she proposed to see the De La Poles herself. She dearly liked a chance to breathe the air of her own lost world, and although Lady de la Pole was nobody, just an "old girl" who had made good use of her training in *la politesse*, Sir Arthur was a fifth baronet, and even an acquaintance of her nephew, Lord Drumcartan.

"No, Mother Eugenia, I don't wish to see them. But perhaps they would like it if you looked in?"

"Well, perhaps one of us had better."

"I fear they'll be depressed by the state of Barbara's fingernails. She continues to bite them, in spite of all Mother Mary Andrew's preventives."

"She's a thoroughly stupid child, that one! But then, they both are, God help them! I really think I must ask poor Jane de la Pole to let us have the dentist put a band on Ursula's teeth. She has no control at all over her saliva as things are. It's disgusting!"

"I agree. Do get permission to have it attended to."

"All the reception guests are returning for Benediction, I hear?"

"The parents and relations are. I have arranged for them to have tea in the Children of Mary's Parlour afterwards— privately. I do not wish any members of the community to be present, other than the three novices. The *dépense* sisters will look after them!"

Mother Eugenia smiled. This Reverend Mother was severe on sociability, and she counted herself lucky to have annexed permission to see the De La Poles, after the unavoidable hospitality of the morning. It was a bit unfortunate, Mother Eugenia thought, for an Englishwoman to insist on such parlour rigidity in an Irish convent. The priests didn't like it, for one thing. However, she, Mother Eugenia, knew how to get her own way. It didn't occur to her that her superior chose deliberately sometimes to indulge her old age.

"I hear from Mother Mary Andrew that Mother Agatha is in the parlour with Maud Murphy?"

"Yes, I granted permission in honour of Rosary Sunday."

Reverend Mother did not add that certain sarcasms of Mother Eugenia and Mother Mary Andrew against Mother Agatha at recreation the evening before had disposed her to some indulgence of the latter. She could not tolerate sarcasm, which was, as she well knew, the ever-ready weapon of intelligent nuns, in community room and schoolroom. She crushed it at all encounters by blank refusal to understand it, and by immediate, sometimes perverse, indulgence of its victim. She sought no favour from those she governed, and believed that she was feared rather than liked in this house, but some of the humble and the stupid were often happily surprised by her support of them—for she was, they knew, one of the "clever" nuns, yet she did not seem to find them as stupid as they were known to be.

"That little girl of Maud's is promising," said Mother Eugenia.

Reverend Mother listened to her Assistant's opinions on personality, for though arbitrary she was shrewd. She herself had not yet had time, in the overworked weeks since term began, to form opinions on the new pupils.

"I'm glad to hear that. She appears to have foolish parents."

"Well, the man that could marry Maud Condon would need to be foolish, God help him!"

"She's a pretty woman."

"Aye—and she was a pretty girl. And if she was, she expected to be taken through life on a *brancard*, God help her!"

"I gather that isn't happening?"

Mother Eugenia laughed.

"Faith it isn't! Look at poor old *Amélie* outside," she said. "What a size she's grown! I wonder where in this world will we find a coffin to fit her?"

"I hope we won't need to find one yet. I'm proud of her Norman cooking."

"Ah sure I know you are—and you're welcome. I've nothing against *Amélie*, much as she dislikes me, but I could do with an odd plate of bacon and cabbage, *à la* County Kerry!"

"But you get it, don't you?"

"I get it, *rouennais*-ed, Reverend Mother! Well, well! Never mind."

Reverend Mother knew that her Assistant's eyes were on the sheet of notepaper on which she had begun to write. That she had written the date in French revealed that she was almost certainly about to write to *Place des Ormes*, to *Mère Générale*. Mother Assistant would wonder why. Yesterday morning the convent's hebdomadal report had been despatched as usual, drafted by her, and accompanied by her superior's usual covering letter. To-morrow morning an additional report—of to-day's reception—would be written and posted. Reverend Mother never departed from routine, and except to her father, to whom she wrote a letter in English once a month, did not write private letters.

"If you *are* to see the de la Poles, Mother Eugenia——"

"Yes, I'll be off. You wish me to speak about Ursula's teeth?"

"If you please."

Mother Eugenia withdrew.

Once again Reverend Mother made the sign of the Cross, and sought to assemble her thoughts.

What she had to write now could not be accurately written she believed; at least not by her, who had forgone alike the sweets and the schooling of self-expression. That she was maimed, that she was sick here in this deepening exile where she could not pitch a tent; that, misunderstood, she was becoming incapable of understanding; that, branded alien, her spirit took the brand; that invalidishly she dreaded now the restoration in her of a loneliness and mercilessness which once had made her father shudder; that without the help of human encouragement she was undone; that God had withheld the grace for this too arid phase of her vocation; that she was not good enough; that she was too vain to endure sustained distrust; that she was ill and foolish and self-pitying, perhaps no more a problem than any woman at a precarious age; that she was not the nun she had desired to be, and must have mercy shown her; that she was at the end of self-control, hated Ireland, hated being hated; that she must feel the dew of grace again, feel it tenderly in her heart —at home, under skies that loved her.

Would *Mère Générale* believe that this graceless outburst was, whatever else it was, the very truth? Would she understand that a vocation was in danger, that the bonds of a really strong control were perilously frayed? Would she insist on the full rigour of obedience and was there no other cure but discipline for so indecent a self-pity?

She could only entrust her own confusion to the holiest wisdom that she knew.

She thought of the bare study where what she had to write would be read: the brass crucifix on the white wall; autumn sibilations of elm-trees in the square; beyond, smoky, downward view of Brussels roofs. She was confused and ashamed. But peace dwelt in that room that she remembered; her tangled words, if she could find them, would be unravelled gently in that holy place.

Tears swam into her eyes. She began to write, ignoring them. She wrote very fast.

*Dimanche du Rosaire,* 1904.

*Ma Mère,—*

*Pour la première fois de ma vie j'ose écrire une lettre qui me touche personnellement. Je prends courage en réfléchissant que c'est vous seule, ma sainte et sage directrice, qui lirez ce qui suivra.*

*Je suis dans mon droit, ma Mère, en vous priant, fort humblement et avec tout mon respect, de me déplacer de mon poste ici et de m'envoyer n'importe ou remplir n'importe quelle humble et rude tâche pour la gloire de Dieu et pour La Compagnie de la Sainte Famille.*

# A LETTER

*Vous avez toujours reçu de moi des renseignements précis et absolu sur l'esprit et sur les travaux de cette maison, et vous comprendrez donc facilement, ma Mère, que la requête que je vous adresse ici n'est due à aucune difficulté de nature extérieure; ma seule difficulté prend sa source dans mon âme même, et elle grossit de jour en jour.*

*Je suis trop seule ici; je suis en train de devenir très dure, voire cynique. Je n'arrive point à comprendre le caractère irlandais, et je n'ai pas le courage d'accepter la tâche de finir ici ma carrière religieuse en travaillant pour Dieu dans une matière qui ne m'est pas familière. Je ne suis pas la personne que l'heure et la situation exigent ici, ma mère. On ne m'aime pas—cela a peu d'importance—mais on me redoute, ce qui est grave. Et je ne sais comment trouver la clef qu'il faut pour ouvrir la confiance mutuelle.*

*À l'heure qu'il est je vois déferler sur ce pays une vague d'idées nationales et scolaires qui ne sera pas à résister, mais en face de laquelle mon attitude sera, je le sais bien, ou neutre ou inquiète—ce qui épaissira encore davantage les ombres qui s'élèvent entre moi et ce pays mystérieux où je me sens découragée, défaite.*

*Je reconnais que c'est moi qui ai tort. Je ne connais que trop bien les défauts de ma nature, l'amertume, le dédain, la sécheresse, qui ont failli me terrasser dans ma jeunesse. Pendant les heureuses années de mon travail à la Place des Ormes, sous l'abri de votre sainte charité, j'ai cru avoir évité, même éliminé, ces grands dangers. Mais ici, seule, à l'étranger, ils se sont accrus. Je ne peux plus trouver les forces chrétiennes qui me sont essentielles pour sauver mon âme, pour servir Dieu.*

*Je mets ma confiance en vous. Je ne puis m'expliquer. Ne parlons pas, chère Mère, de "grâce efficace," puisqu'il me manque depuis long-temps le modeste "pouvoir prochain." Je prie Dieu, je me confesse, je me mortifie; je vous assure que je n'écris cette lettre qu'après des hésitations de plus d'un an. Mais tout ce que je fais ici est un gaspillage d'efforts, puisque je reste incomprise, et sans comprendre cette Irlande pourtant si belle et si mystérieuse. Laissez-moi quitter un travail humiliant, qui m'échappe et me défait. Laissez-moi retrouver ailleurs mon courage et mon humble capacité pour ce plein service de Dieu auquel je suis dédiée.*

*Je voudrais pouvoir vous parler de vive voix, mais je répète que je mets ma confiance en vous, en votre sainte sagesse.*

*Veuillez bien, ma Mère, recevoir l'expression de mon respect le plus profond.*

*Votre fille obéissante en Jésus-Christ,*
*Marie-Hélène Archer.*

Reverend Mother's hand shook as she blotted and folded this letter. She placed it in an envelope which she addressed and sealed, then she put it in a pigeon-hole of her desk.

She dried her eyes. She looked about her study and out past the stations of the Cross to the cemetery gate; she did not move again until the Benediction bell rang.

## The Fifth Chapter

## MARKS

"I TREMBLE to think of Reverend Mother's disappointment when she reads these marks. One might have expected children of *nice* feeling to make a special effort to have good marks to-night—when three of your former companions have set you such a beautiful example, receiving the habit. The 'politeness' marks of some of you"—Mother Mary Andrew tapped the big black book on the table—"the 'politeness' marks of some of you are nothing short of a disgrace to *Sainte Famille*——"

The *salle d'études*, commonly called the *salle* and pronounced "sal" by the school, was a vast room on the first floor. It was elaborately corniced and had spacious fireplaces, one of which was filled with a French porcelain stove. It had eight windows—one to the left of the stove, five down its length, and two embrasured on either side of the other fireplace. The walls were broken by bookshelves and racks for music portfolios, and hung with steel engravings of Roman and Greek excavations. Rows of mahogany desks and benches ran lengthwise through the room, one tier close to the windows, the other near the inner wall, with a wide aisle of polished floor between. Ornamental brass gaseliers hung from the ceiling in two symmetrical lines; palms and maidenhair ferns stood on pedestals in the windows. There was a flower-decked altar to St. Joseph near the French stove, and over the other mantelpiece a lamp of red glass was kept perpetually alight under a coloured print of Carlo Dolci's "Holy Family."

Every child had a desk in this room, which was the centre of the school's life. In the wide aisle between the desks the girls assembled many times a day in two graded lines; to be lectured by Mother Mary Andrew, to go to chapel or the refectory, to sit in a demure "hairpin" for Reverend Mother's "deportment" class or for the chaplain's weekly lecture on Christian doctrine. This long, polished pool of space between the desks was the stage for much drama and tension. Rosita Maloney called it "Old McWhirter's stamping ground." Mother Mary Andrew was "Old McWhirter."

She controlled her stamping ground and, at this moment, the demurely seated "hairpin" of girls—graded from little to big, with the seniors and Children of Mary occupying the head of the curve—from her table set in front of the stove. Her left hand fidgeted with the knob of a shiny table bell.

Waiting for Marks on Sunday evening was a strain on everyone. What her own marks were was hidden from each girl until, her name called by Reverend Mother, she stood up in her place, bowed politely, heard the week's record of her behaviour read aloud, bowed again and sat down. But the most complacent grew uneasy when they saw such a flush on Mother Mary Andrew's cheek as she wore to-night, whereas the customarily unlucky regarded their guilt as already proclaimed by the big hand twitching in bad temper round the bell.

This hour of Sunday evening was dangerous; some girls felt a delicious danger in it. The Sabbath atmosphere of interacting festivity and ordeal approached its climax before Marks. The *salle* often seemed a little too warm at that hour, with gaseliers lighted and curtains drawn; the tables wore their Sunday coverings of royal blue face-cloth, with richly embroidered hems; Mother Mary Andrew was self-conscious in her Sunday habit, and everybody was dramatised for better or worse, in Sunday dresses and by best gloves, worn ceremoniously, for Marks. Pretty girls became excitingly pretty in the brightened atmosphere; plain girls looked red and strained; those who had been "in the parlour" had sweets to scatter surreptitiously along the "hairpin"; those who had been out with their parents for the afternoon might flaunt a flower in the white collar of a black dress, or jingle a forbidden

66

bracelet; someone might have drenched herself in her mother's scent; all such brought back a flutter of gossip and comedy. Others had been worked upon by more restricted pleasures—glimpsing male visitors as they strolled under the elm-trees; "mooning" from windows at the lovely, sentimental view of lawns and lake and darkly flowing hills; or reading "Misunderstood" or "Sarasinesca."

And to-day there had been a reception. To-day Eileen O'Doherty had had her lovely hair cut off, had broken uncounted hearts, and given herself to *Sainte Famille*. Moreover, there would be tipsy cake for supper, *Sœur Amélie's* famous tipsy cake, which would assuredly make some people tipsy, and lead to unguessable excitements at night recreation, it was to be hoped.

So the air was winey and nervous; giggling might become exquisitely uncontrollable; some of the little ones, who had to recite, might start crying, and any minute old Mary Andrew might realise that Cecilia Hooley was wearing a carnation in her hair. If only the blessed old Marks were over! God knows how many marks for silence I'll have lost! Dolly, guess who you missed by going home to-day—Adrian de la Pole—looking heavenly! He's an absolute god——

Mother Mary Andrew struck her bell.

"Silence, young ladies! I will not tolerate this whispering across the room. Mabel Johnson, will you please sit up, and make some attempt to look like a lady—if possible?"

The nun screwed her eyes up suspiciously under her thick brows.

"There seem some vacancies. Or is it that you are huddling together unbecomingly? Is everyone present?"

There was an uneasy murmur and an attempt to look crowded. This was helped by the entrance of Letitia Doyle through the swing door at the far end of the room. She ambled modestly forward, through the lines, and placed a battered-looking glass paper-weight on the table in front of Mother Mary Andrew, who now seemed mollified.

"Ah, Letitia—I had forgotten you had taken the paper-weight. You have been rather a long time, I may say."

"I'm sorry, Mother," said Letitia, and withdrew to her place. She was fat, but even so when she was seated it was clear that the ranks were not complete.

Mother Mary Andrew glared about.

"I presume that, since you had the paper-weight, there was nobody else out there, Letitia?"

"No, Mother."

To take the paper-weight was a ritual and a euphemism. At *Sainte Famille* a lay sister took charge in cloakrooms at fixed hours—during forty minutes after breakfast, for ten minutes before dinner, for thirty minutes after midday recreation, and so on. At other times young ladies were only permitted to enter the cloakrooms one at a time. Thus an object had been chosen which was unlikely to be duplicated— a glass-topped paper-weight enclosing a coloured picture of the Taj Mahal. This object lay, when not in use, on Mother Scholastic's table in the *salle*, and a girl, who wished to go to the lavatory during the hours of study or sewing, approached and asked the nun in charge if she might take the paper-weight. If it were there, she took it and went through the swing door and along the corridor to the lavatories; if it were not in its place the nun said "After so-and-so," and when so-and-so had returned it, she came again to the table and collected it. While it was in her possession it proved her unique right to go to the lavatory.

The system did not work perfectly; girls at music practice or scattered in classrooms or in the parlour were outside the jurisdiction of the paper-weight, so there was not as much modest solitude and silence always in the cloakrooms as was desired; but the arrangement was adhered to as a useful half-measure, and it gave an esoteric, unembarrassing character to the business of "leaving the room." But the odd phrase, "take the paper-weight," trailed curiously in the memories of *Sainte Famille* "old girls," embarrassing them, making them smile, having only one inescapable meaning. And in later life views of the Taj Mahal stirred curious associations sometimes.

Now, with the paper-weight in its place and still some gaps in the "hairpin," Mother Mary Andrew knew that she must leap to the war-path.

She stood up, the better to trace absentees. She was very tall and her eyebrows bristled with anger.

"Aha!" she snapped. "Madeleine Anderson and Rosita Maloney are missing! I might have known!"

As she spoke the large swing door which Letitia had opened and closed "like a lady" burst open, and two girls pushed each other half-way through it, then with a wild burst of laughter pushed each other out again, and let the door slam to. Giggles and thuds could be heard on the landing— the sacred, carpeted landing of the grand staircase. A *frisson* of pleasure went through the school, though one or two Children of Mary looked demurely shocked.

Mother Mary Andrew's big finger forced a shrill peal from the table bell.

"Silence, young ladies! Angela, would you be so good as to go to that door and open it wide, hold it open."

A Child of Mary detached herself from the head of the "hairpin" and did as she was bid. Rosita Maloney and Madeleine Anderson flung themselves past her. They were out of breath and could not stop giggling; Rosita's curly forelock hung over her eye, and Madeleine's white collar was falling off. They dashed for their desks and flung them open.

"Come here at once. Leave your desks."

Mother Mary Andrew's voice was cold and full of County Tyrone.

The two shambled forward, knowing themselves heroines.

"All right—if *you* don't mind our not having gloves on for Marks," murmured Rosita.

"I must find a pin for my collar," said Madeleine.

"Why were you missing from the classroom now, Rosita?"

"I—I had permission for extra piano practice."

"Who gave you that permission?"

"Mother Bonaventura."

"Mother Bonaventura did nothing of the kind. She knows

that such permission can only be granted by me. And in any case where is your music?"

"I—left it in St. Joseph's when I realised I was late for Marks."

"Indeed?" Mother Mary Andrew flicked her eye significantly over the music-racks. The *M* division seemed completely filled. Her glance returned to Rosita.

"I see. But why this zeal, Rosita? Have you forgotten that you are not at all strong? You fainted this morning, my poor child! Fainted outright during the Reception Mass. I felt extremely sorry for you. But I shall find a way to look after your health—which, I assure you, is now beginning to alarm me. And you, Madeleine—what special permission did you have, dear child?"

"I hadn't any, Mother. I just thought that Rosita might be late for Marks, and I went to fetch her. Sometimes, when she gets playing, you see——"

This was a characteristic Madeleine touch—she loved to take her modest impudence too far. The school shivered amusedly. Mother Mary Andrew was furious.

"Remarkable solicitude, my dear Madeleine! I hardly believed you had it in you! A charming nature—charming but foolish. And you both look foolish and disgusting now. Get yourselves in order instantly. I'll deal with this disgraceful matter later on, and get to the bottom of it, rest assured! Go to your desks, and get your gloves, deceitful, insubordinate girls. Silence, if you please, young ladies!"

Mother Mary Andrew glared again at the rest of the school. A little girl came in at the door near St. Joseph's altar and announced that Reverend Mother had left the Community Room and was on her way upstairs.

Rosita and Madeleine came plunging from their desks to their places in the line, still flushed and giggling, trying to smooth their hair and collars. Whispers ran about near them. What were you up to? I know. Did you see her? Their news entangled with the questions. My dear, I haven't let her out of my sight—I hid in the arbutus tree for *hours* while they were in Bishop's Walk. Major O'Doherty is marvellous looking—she gets her eyes from him. She saw us once, and she only laughed. And we just caught her now this minute vanishing into the Community Room. Oh, my heart is breaking! I'm mad about her. I won't sleep a wink to-night —I'll never sleep again—such fun as we had—I guessed what you were up to—there never were such eyes in all the world—Blessed Imelda, pray for me—*priez pour moi*—shut up, Rosita—*priez pour moi*——

Reverend Mother appeared at the door of the *salle*, which the little girl was holding open for her. She entered, accompanied by Mother Eugenia and followed by eight other members of the community.

The school stood up; Rosita and Madeleine stopped whispering.

Reverend Mother took her stand at the table, Mother Assistant at her right side, Mother Scholastic at her left. The other nuns took their places by the ranged chairs. Molly Redmond, excited by the coming ordeal of recitation, signalled to Mother Josephine, who frowned at her shyly, and raised a hand to implore orderly behaviour.

Reverend Mother said a prayer in French.

"*Je vous salue, Marie, pleine de grâce . . .*"

Anna Murphy, with a little chair specially bought for her, had her place at the extreme right bend of the "hairpin," very near the nuns. She listened with passion to the French prayer, and got ready to try to respond with the school.

"*Sainte Marie, Mère de Dieu . . .*" the soprano antistrophe delighted her; she murmured in imitation of it loudly and lovingly, "*—à l'heure de notre mort. Ainsi soit-il.*" She wished she knew exactly how to make those sounds.

The sign of the Cross then and another "*Ainsi soit-il.*"

Reverend Mother bowed to the school and sat down. The school bowed to Reverend Mother and sat down. The hush of ceremony relaxed a little. Anna pulled her chair forward out of line; Gertie Davoren, who was next to her, pulled her in again, but Anna could not see in all directions then, so she

71

once more drew herself forward. She thought that it would be ridiculous not to be able to see everything that happened at Marks. Gertie found this very funny, and signalled frustration among her friends. Giggling spread through the Second Preparatories, but Anna was unaware of the amusement she caused.

"I hope we have nothing but *good* marks to hear to-night, Mother Mary Andrew."

Reverend Mother glanced along the columns of the page open in front of her. Mother Mary Andrew looked like a thunderclap in her silent dismissal of this hope.

"Dear me!" said Reverend Mother. "Let us face this bad news then. Genevieve Ahern."

The Marks list was alphabetically arranged.

A red-haired girl stood up in her place and bowed. She seemed self-confident.

"Conduct, 20; Silence, 19; Politeness, 20; Exactitude, 10; Order, 10; Application, 10."

Genevieve bowed again and sat down.

"Well, at least that makes a good beginning. Those are beautiful marks, Genevieve."

"A pity that she had to spoil them by talkativeness," said Mother Mary Andrew, who was in a mood in which she could hear no praise of anyone.

"But she doesn't seem to have been *very* talkative," said Reverend Mother. "Madeleine Anderson."

Madeleine stood up, her collar apparently in order. Her neighbour pushed her in the back while she was bowing; she almost fell over. "Stop it, Dolly," she gasped.

Reverend Mother waited for composure.

"Conduct, 20; Silence, 13; Politeness, 17; Exactitude, 6; Order, 5; Application, 6."

Very bad marks for anyone; for a girl approaching sixteen, and in Junior Honours, disgraceful. She could hardly have done worse, short of losing a mark for conduct, and that was traditionally held to be impossible. A mark lost for conduct was tantamount to expulsion; no one remembered it ever to have happened. The school sometimes liked to surmise how it might come about. Perhaps if you *kicked* Reverend Mother? or used some absolutely filthy word? or committed sacrilege?

Madeleine looked pretty and stricken; her friend Rosita beamed across at her sympathetically, out of a desperate confidence that her own moment would be worse.

Reverend Mother's face was very severe.

"This is even worse than last week, Madeleine. You seem to have started the scholastic year in very bad spirit. I shall have a private word with you to-morrow. You may sit down."

Madeleine sat down.

"Good Lord. A private word," she whispered. "That'll kill me outright." Rosita leant back in her place so as to signal across unobserved. But Mother Mary Andrew was glaring at her, though she did not know it.

The ritual went on. Reverend Mother made her customary comments on the bad, the good and the middling. Occasionally she suggested to a girl to stand more erect, or to bow with less contortion. Occasionally she foiled the savageries of Mother Mary Andrew, or softened the too forthright or too snobbish comments of Mother Eugenia on the idiosyncrasies of this girl or that.

But, trying to listen to herself with particular detachment to-night, she realised even more acutely than usual the deadening effect upon those over-keyed children of her level English voice and speech; she could even hear now and then, very soft indeed, very cautious, someone's preposterous mimicry, and the hushed titters it elicited.

She knew, early she had come to know, that at best she was a respected symbol in this house, at worst an English-woman. This was what her nuns, or at least the more influential of them, felt about her—whether or not they admitted it; this was therefore inescapably what the children felt.

She did not altogether approve of Mother Eugenia's technique with her responsibilities; but she knew her to be a very holy old nun, much devoted to the house, and amusedly held in love by many generations of "old girls." Moreover, as Mother Assistant, her influence on the school was only accidental, and was manageable.

About Mother Mary Andrew her superior held much stronger and more anxious views. This nun was young, intelligent and self-opinionated; she was a very hard worker, and was, in Reverend Mother's opinion excessively endowed —in view of her office—with health and with authoritativeness. The narrow class distinctions of her time, clashing on her assertiveness, had made her shrilly snobbish—causing her sometimes to ask nervously: "When Adam delved and Eve span, who was then a gentleman?" (heedless of Mother Eugenia's aside: "None of the McWhirters!") and sometimes to tell elaborate, unnecessary tales of the grandeur of McWhirter family life. Another symptom of her status-uneasiness was her tendency to fasten on "victims" in the school, and her counter-balancing need of favourites. She was, in fact, erratic and cruel, and Reverend Mother, having no direct power of appointment or dismissal from office, had more than once reported uneasily, in confidence, to *Mère Générale*, upon that violence of character in Mother Mary Andrew which she found unsuitable for the duties required of her. But *Mère Générale* felt that intellectually Mother Mary Andrew was the right woman in the right place, and inclined to believe that mildness would come with a few years of authority. . Reverend Mother did not see it coming—but she sometimes thought lately that perhaps she herself was one of the causes that delayed it: her Englishness, an *enemy* quality, kept Mother Mary Andrew in a rigid state of watchfulness that did not help her temper; she being of what the latter called "ascendancy" class was another exasperation and finally, being these alien things, yet having authority over a proud Irishwoman, and having to be conceded an unrelaxed politeness—yes, Reverend Mother really believed that Mother Mary Andrew would be a very much better nun under any superior other than herself.

74

But chiefly she believed—and this made her sometimes miserable with bewilderment—that this random assembly of sixty young Irish girls was happy under the casual, mocking eye of Mother Eugenia, and in the ill-advised, splenetic neurotic storms and uncertainties of Mother Mary Andrew's rule. Happier than she, for ever dreaming an impossible justice, a celestial understanding, could have made them. The Irish liked themselves, and throve on their own psychological chaos. It had been shown to be politically useless for an alien temperament to wrestle with them. Wrongheaded, vengeful, even by the long view stupid they might often seem, and apparently defeated—but on their own ground in some mystically arrogant wild way they were perpetual victors. They did not see what others saw; they had no idea they should try to. They were an ancient, martyred race, and of great importance to themselves—that meagre handful of conceptions made a history, made a problem—and made them at once unconquerable and a little silly.

Well, such a view of them, held in all gentleness and with much admiration, could never be discussed with their most intelligent without a quarrel. For the word "silly" would start uproar. Useless to explain the "silly" aspects of England, Scotland, France or Greece. They would be conceded freely, but the original point would remain a prejudicial insult and a lie. About Ireland there was no appeal to the comparative method; no detachment was regarded as just. And this nun, who would as little forgo the latter in her thought as undertake to live without sleep, had come to believe therefore that she could not rule an Irish house.

Well, but to-day, she reminded herself, to-day you have made an end of the long anxiety; to-day you have arranged to rid them here, if you are allowed to, of your weary, introverted, inexpressive conscience. To-day you have given them up to that narrowing future of their own which you are leaving. You have given them up, in fact, to Mother Mary Andrew.

75

Meantime she read the marks. And she thought as she did so, as on so many former Sunday nights, that the little weekly record of each child was in fact more an index of the health, moral and physical, of the nuns who marked, than of the erring victim who heard it read against her name.

Each girl had routine weekly dealings with say ten of the choir nuns, and on Saturday night or Sunday morning each of these nuns had power to enter in pencil in the "rough" Mark Book the number of marks of which she wished to deprive a pupil. Naturally all the marks threatened in the course of a week were not deducted, and sometimes even the ruthless Mother Mary Andrew, making the final copy on Sunday afternoon, had been suspected of some clemency in manipulation. But most of the nuns who marked were interested enough to come, as now, to hear the reading—and Reverend Mother had learnt to pick up the waves of vengeance or benevolence or self-righteousness which ebbed and flowed from them as she read their judgments. No one would ever know —because she would think it unjust and invidious that they should—how infallibly her sympathy was with the children on these Sunday evenings, and against the nuns. The marking arrangement was a harmless and indeed, she thought, an attractively formal way of punishment, and she conceded freely that directors of youth had to have some system of control, and that this was as little cruel as any she knew—yet, it was a fact that in her nine years as a teaching nun, in Vienna, Turin and Cracow, she had never deducted a solitary mark from the maximum of any pupil. As the process was traditionally held to be confidential, and as she had always looked through the book on Saturday nights and sometimes debated fiercely with herself about the questionableness of her restraint—no one anywhere knew that she had never actually registered a mark. Least of all did any of her pupils suspect this clemency—though she had sometimes thought that one in a hundred of them might surely have had the acumen to observe that in her displeasures, which so much impressed them, she never even referred to the weapon of Sunday marks.

Yet she knew that such forbearance, which she could not help, was something for which the Irish temperament would never thank her. It preferred the loose equality of *quid pro quo*. And she perceived that this judgment might be better and warmer. There was something deadly in the detachment that could not come to the decisions of wrath. Yet, if once all, all had been too savagely, too idiotically decided, in blind judgment—so long ago, so singly—and yet how it had neutralised the heart!

"Rosita Maloney."

There was the sibilation which usually followed any pronouncement of Rosita's name. She had a following. She also had enemies, who thought her conceited and a "notice-box."

Pushed and pulled by giggling neighbours, she stood up.

"Try that bow again, Rosita," said Reverend Mother.

Rosita tried it, her hair falling into her eyes. She looked very pretty. Molly Redmond, who adored her, leant forward in awestruck delight.

"Conduct, 20; Silence, 12; Politeness, 15; Exactitude, 6; Order, 6; Application, 4."

A gasp ran round the hairpin. Molly Redmond's mouth and eyes made three dark O's of astonishment. Anna Murphy, impeded in her view of the scandalous heroine by the forward-leaning school, stepped out to the edge of the table where the mark book lay, and leant against the royal blue Sunday cloth.

Rosita bit her lip and hung her head. She loved the sensation she was causing, but also it alarmed her. Say she was expelled? There'd be no holding Daddy! He'd just quite simply murder her! Besides, to be expelled the very day her idol entered *Sainte Famille*—what a tragic thing to happen! Surely, surely—but there was no knowing where you were with that queer fish of a Reverend Mother! Not that anyone ever was expelled. Still——

Rosita was a very innocent girl, and believed herself to be unusually wicked.

Anna Murphy turned to contemplate the effect of Rosita's record on the nuns.

"They're terrible marks," she said detachedly to Mother Eugenia. She did not know what the changes meant that passed then over the nun's face, which seemed to her larger than life-size and like a piece of the bark of a tree. It had rough lumps on it, as trees often had. She thought that Mother Eugenia would feel like a tree against your legs, if you tried to climb her.

"Faith if they are let them be a warning to you, young lady," said the big face, and Anna decided that it was laughing, in a spread-out, unrecognisable way.

This interchange sent nervous giggles through the school, easing the situation for Rosita. Gertie Donovan grabbed Anna back to her place. "Of all the little busybodies," she whispered in fussy delight.

"'Out of the mouths of babes and sucklings,'" said Reverend Mother, knowing that to pronounce the last word was to risk a subterranean crisis of schoolgirl indecency, but refusing to suppress it, as she well knew Mother Mary Andrew thought she should. . . . Did you hear the word she said, Daisy? . . . Reverend Mother's just this minute said. . . . Do you know what it means? . . . Remind me to tell you. . . . Well, I never. . . . Babes and suck. . . . She *never* said? . . .

"Rosita, these are very bad marks indeed. I see that you think so yourself. But it is in your hands to alter them. And you promised your father that this year would *not* be wasted. Why are you making such a very bad start?"

"I—I don't know, Reverend Mother."

"It has been a difficult week for Rosita, Reverend Mother," said Mother Eugenia with ironic indulgence. She liked the girl and, within what she called "civilised" limits, enjoyed the follies of *Schwärmerei*. "After all, the beautiful beloved has only this morning renounced the world——"

The school laughed outright.

Reverend Mother did not like such jokes, but was unable to snub an old nun before sixty schoolgirls. Moreover, she told herself as she shrank from the situation, that it was this easy stride with human nature, this random willingness to take psychological risks—indeed this happy blindness to them, which perhaps best commanded the dark places of segregated life. Nevertheless she could not endorse such naturalness—for she was afraid—for the young—of many natural things.

She let the laughter die.

She's too stiff, that one, thought Mother Eugenia impatiently. And—how can she let that foolish old nun demoralise *my* charges in this way? thought Mother Mary Andrew.

"You and I must talk things over, Rosita. I shall send for you to-morrow. We cannot have you drifting into habits of foolishness. You may sit down."

When the marks had been read silk sashes were distributed to those girls who had lost no more than a total of four marks in the week, and none against politeness. These sashes would be worn in chapel for seven days—across the shoulder, right to left, like secular honours. Anna watched their disposal with delight—and Reverend Mother's ceremonial kiss on the cheek to each recipient. She was glad to see Letitia Doyle arrayed in the broad blue sash of the Seniors. The Junior sash was purple, the Preparatories, scarlet. They were lovely stiff sashes. Anna longed to run her hand up and down Letitia's.

At last the Second Preparatories had to stand up to recite their poem. Mother Felicita came forward to range them in a line in front of the table. She was a gentle, merry young nun, well named. Her intelligence was small, but the eight little girls to whom she taught English and history and sums liked her, and she liked them. She should have been married and had eight little girls of her own, but she did not know this, and was at peace with her proxies. When she had got them ready and tried to calm them, she sat near Anna, in Gertie Donovan's vacant place, to be ready to prompt and direct. When she nodded her head the eight little girls bowed and said in unison: "After Blenheim."

Anna had sat apart at word-making, while the Second

Preparatories rehearsed this poem, and she knew it by heart. She found it interesting because it did not sound as sad as it ought to be, and always made her feel that she did not quite understand it, although the words were perfectly easy.

Molly Redmond's performance was disappointing. She had said at dinner that she would go so fast that no one would understand her, but, although Mother Felicita did say "Slower, Molly," Anna understood her.

The poem went on its way. Anna leant out to hear it, her chin in her hands. It so filled her mind with query that she forgot all friendly anxiety that the class should get through it safely. Yet once, when Ursula de la Pole stumbled, she said the line for her, without noticing that she did so.

Reverend Mother's eyes fell on her. The look of pure attention on the small face amused the nun, as that morning in chapel it had done. And she thought gently that it was pathetic to be forced, when so small, to become one of a large, alien body, merely because parents had neither the sense nor the sensitiveness to keep a child at home. She reflected that the confusions created by parents for children are the most deep and dark of all, and that the relationship of parent and child is grievously important. She thought with sudden bitter sorrow of her father.

When the poem ended Reverend Mother's eyes were still on Anna. She heard the little girl's long "Ah!" of pleasure as she turned to say some words of congratulation to the reciters. But the child remained in her thought, and she addressed her at the end of her speech.

"You seem to know the poem, Anna. Perhaps you should have recited with the Second Preparatories?"

Anna was startled.

"Oh no, Reverend Mother. I'm not in their class."

"Stand up, Anna. Reverend Mother is speaking to you!" Mother Mary Andrew's voice was stern. Anna stood up.

Mother Felicita laid a kind hand on her arm.

"She has a very quick memory, Reverend Mother. She reads extraordinarily well, and teaches herself all kinds of things."

"A bookworm, that's what she is," said Mother Eugenia. "Praise God if a pupil with brains has arrived at *Sainte Famille* at last! Come here, young woman."

Anna went towards the big, gnarled hand, which drew her round the table, so that she stood, almost hidden, at Reverend Mother's knee.

"It's early days to give her swelled head," said Mother Mary Andrew. "Anna is a good girl so far, Reverend Mother, but I'm afraid she's a bit of a cry-baby."

Tears rose in Anna's eyes at mention of this failing. Reverend Mother stroked her hair, then folded her hands together in her lap.

"Have you taught yourself any poems, Anna?"

"Yes, Reverend Mother."

"Will you say one for me?"

Anna paused. Then she nodded her head.

The school strained forward, amused and sibilating. The gaslight gurgled in one gaselier.

"Peace," Anna said, and bowed.

> "My soul, there is a country
> Far beyond the stars,
> Where stands a wingéd sentry
> All skilful in the wars;
> There, above noise and danger
> Sweet Peace sits crowned with smiles,
> And One born in a manger
> Commands the beauteous files.
> He is thy gracious Friend . . ."

Reverend Mother heard, on the little voice, wild floods and cataracts of memory. Much more than memory. She heard a storm break in her hollow heart, which was not her own storm, for that was over, but was rather an assault, a senti-mental menacing appeal, from past and future and from nowhere, from the child's voice and from her father's and from the accident of these verses—full of echoes and prefigurings, filled with she knew not what of shifting words and images, forming remorse, forming tenderness and accusation. Father would like this child, the quiet surface of her mind was oddly saying, as she pursued the remembered poem along the gentle thread of the little voice. He would think he saw here that which he liked to see; he would be touched, loving this pure touch on the visionary lines; deducing foolishly, to reward his own pleasure and indulge it, he would talk of the chance in a million, as he called it, of the gleam of the spirit, the hint of grace, the brush of a wing unspread. But as she skimmed ironically thus over the odd revival, through an unknown child, of hints and symbolisings which he had allowed himself when she was small and learnt his favourite poems at his feet—she could not drown thereby, but only swelled the strong, irrational assault of sorrow, demanding to be faced. For she heard within it her father's accusation that she was merciless and heard him plead for "the young and the weak and the sentimental," but against him, sardonically, heard her own young nights of uncomforted sobbing, and saw and felt once more, within her own one far-away experience, the dark convulsions and intersections of the paths that lead innocence to knowledge and desire and dream to reality. She saw this baby in herself, herself in those tear-wet eyes. The foolish father and mother of this child, the cruel voice of Mother Mary Andrew, the aged vain forgetfulness of Mother Eugenia—all pressed around the little voice, as Reverend Mother listened . . .

> " . . . There grows the flower of peace,
> The rose that cannot wither,
> The—the——"

"Thy fortress and thy ease," said Reverend Mother. Anna nodded gratefully, and repeated the line.

> "Leave then thy foolish ranges,
> For none can thee secure
> But one who never changes—
> Thy God, thy life, thy cure."

82

Silence fell. The nuns were touched by the child's recitation.

"Thank you, Anna," Reverend Mother said. "It is a lovely poem."

"You *know* it," said Anna in wonder. "You prompted me."

"Yes, I know it. My father taught it to me when I was a little older than you are now."

"Did your father compose it?"

"No. A poet called Henry Vaughan composed it, nearly three hundred years ago. Where did you find it?"

"It's on Sister Stanislaus's screen. It's printed."

Sister Stanislaus mended shoes and did carpentry. In her workroom she had a screen on which she pasted Christmas cards and holy pictures.

"I'm very glad you learnt it, Anna. Thank you for saying it."

The little girl put out her hand impulsively, and Reverend Mother took it in hers.

"It was lucky you knew that bit 'Thy fortress and thy ease.' But I'd have got it all right, I think."

"I'm sure you would. Will you have another poem to say to me next Sunday?"

"May I? But where will I find as good a one? There aren't many on the screen. It's mostly little pictures."

"I'll find some for you that you can choose from. But I don't want to know in advance which one you are going to say."

"I see. I'd feel like that too."

Mother Eugenia laughed.

"You're a caution, Anna Murphy. A regular old woman."

Reverend Mother stood up, and as she made the sign of the Cross and said, with the school, the customary "Hail Mary" in French which ended Marks, she knew that she was smiling openly, and she could hear the scandalised mutterings of the school at this unorthodox behaviour. Whereat she only smiled the more.

But as she descended the staircase to the Community Room her face fell back into gravity. I am after all at once his daughter, she thought, and a victim of his—his personality. Therefore, from two angles, coward though I am, I know of sensitiveness, of what it can do and what it can suffer. Apart from that, I see the actualities of her life. I do not know what I am looking at to-night; my duty is to lead souls to the glory of God; He must direct me to a greater understanding of what this Glory is . . . she frowned, remembering the hard tone of Mother Mary Andrew's voice, and tears standing in Anna's eyes. The memory led her back into customary scruples and anxieties of government, but before she obeyed the bell for evening meditation, she went into her study, and with a perplexed, grave look on her face, she tore into many small pieces the letter which she had written that afternoon to *Mère Générale*.

# BOOK TWO

## *La Pudeur et la Politesse*

## The First Chapter

## SOME LESSONS

*Mère Martine* told Anna that the "t" in such phrases as *a-t-i*
and *a-t-elle* was inserted for "you-funny."

This surprised Anna.

"Is it funny?" she asked.

*Mère Martine* spoke and understood English very badly.

"Yes, so that is," she said. "You-funny."

Off and on for years Anna pondered this French joke, but
she could not see why the inserted "t" was funny.

However, *Mère Martine* herself was funny, and agreeable.
During her first two years at school Anna spent much time
in her company.

She was a lazy old nun, a bundle of shawls, with an
unusually beautiful, merry face and a deformed left foot, the
result of an accident in girlhood, and the probable reason
why anyone so naturally pleasure-loving had entered religion.
She was of French birth, but as her father was a diplomat she
had seen more of Athens, Rome and Vienna than of France
during her brief years in the world. It was in Austria that she
joined the *Compagnie de la Sainte Famille*. She was bi-lingual
in German and French, but now after thirty years in a house
of the English Province, her English was still outrageous, as
she well knew. It was vaguely held by the older gossips of
the Community that *Mère Martine* had been appointed to
Ireland for some unspecified reason of correction or censure—
but she had never seemed to be aware of that. She
had taken an immediate fancy to the beautiful Georgian
buildings with their dark woods and gleaming lake; she
took an equal fancy to the Irish character; and so settled
down to as pleasant a life as might be found in a valley
shaded on the one side by religious vows and on the other

by an inborn need to be a success with her fellow-creatures.

Anna often sat with her in St. Joseph's Grotto, whence there was a wide view over the lake. The old nun had a folding chair; Anna sat on an up-ended flower-pot and leant against St. Joseph's pedestal. On cold days she wore her garden coat and boots. *Mère Martine* was very comfortably arranged, and little Sister Martha often ran out from the kitchen with a hot cup of this or that for her, sent by *Sœur Amélie*, and an apple or a piece of brown sugar candy, with string through it, for Anna. The grotto smelt of wet geraniums; St. Joseph was dressed in brown, and the stem of the plaster lily in his hand was like green marzipan.

"Regard if we are not finely placed for the study," *Mère Martine* would say, and if the sun were shining and *Sœur Amélie's* soup had been as good as usual, she might strike up on her guitar, and sing "*Il était un bergère* . . ."

Thus, with enormous pleasure, Anna learnt, in Anglo-French, to read the face of a watch and find the points of the compass; she learnt how to spell and separate the words of the French Sign of the Cross and "Hail Mary"; she heard what Napoleon said to his marshals after Austerlitz: "The happiest day of my life, gentlemen? Why, the day of my First Communion." She also learnt that Cafferty, the gardener, quite simply "ignored" ow to cultivate azaleas. She heard that Mozart tried to run away from home to Italy when he was four; she learnt to understand the sad ballad of Andreas Hofer, and to chime in with *Mère Martine* and the guitar in the last bar: "*Adieu mein Land Tirol!*" She learnt the whole of "Au Clair de la Lune," and although she cried over it, *Mère Martine* did not object any more than Charlie would have objected.

Strolling out of the grotto sometimes—*Mère Martine* could walk very well in spite of her stick and her lame foot—the two would go by shrubby paths to watch Sister Simeon feed the chickens. "*Kyrie Eleison*" they would hear her singing, and would join in suddenly and loudly behind the ilex-tree to frighten her: "*Christe Eleison*," as loud as possible. And

Alexander would snap at them, and *Mère Martine* would call him "a beast to horrify."

Strolling back, they would visit *Jeanne*, the old donkey who pulled the garden cart, and if Anna had her gloves on she would find a thistle for *Jeanne*, and cut it with *Mère Martine's* knife. They would try to make *Jeanne* bray, as *Mère Martine* said that was good for the hygiene.

Back at the grotto they might agree in criticism of Sister Constantine's arrangement of flower-pots round the Saint, and make some alterations. Then there would be a little fuss in getting *Mère Martine* comfortable again in her shawls and cushions, and with her guitar at hand.

"Now to our labour! To-day we shall recount to us of *Maître Corbeau, sur un arbre perché* . . ."

But after a few lines, Anna was usually left to struggle alone on her flower-pot with *La Fontaine*. She was content with the dreaminess that fell over the grotto on warm afternoons of spring and summer. She liked to turn the pages of the book, and spell it out her own way.

Sometimes then *Mère Martine* said her rosary. Anna would hear the beads clicking through her fingers. But sometimes she sat and gazed with a little smile at the lake. "*Vogue, mon beau navire*," she would sing very gently, "*sur les flots endormis* . . ." She rarely got further; she fell a little asleep at "*endormis*."

At half-past three Reverend Mother usually came and walked alone, up and down, between the elm-trees of Bishop's Walk. Far away, at the other side of the lawn, she read in a book as she walked. Anna wondered if it were a prayer-book, or perhaps some poems her father had taught her. *Mère Martine* blinked sometimes towards the distant, pacing figure.

"*Une vraie religieuse*," she murmured once, "*une âme bien née. Regarde-la bien, mon petit.*"

"Don't you mean *ma petite?*" said Anna.

"No, *mon petit*. I mean *mon petit*."

Anna went on with her lesson, unassisted.

*Mère Martine's* old eyes turned dreamily back to the lake. "*Vogue, mon beau navire . . .*"

Anna stayed in the grotto until Letitia Doyle fetched her to *goûter* at four o'clock.

On Wednesdays the chaplain addressed the school for forty minutes on Christian Doctrine. This lecture took place at half-past five in the *salle d'études*, his hearers sitting as for Marks in a "hairpin," very orderly and with gloves on. It was an ordeal for a young man, when every mannerism was pounced upon and giggled at, week after week, by the school wags. Indeed, Reverend Mother thought it a questionable tradition that in this Irish house the chaplain was always so young. Elsewhere in the Order's convents he was usually an old and experienced priest, hardened to folly and indifferent to giggles. But here in this rural parish, the duties of chaplaincy fell *ex officio* on the second curate of the village, which meant a succession of nervous young men for budding feminine wits to lacerate.

The Wednesday lecture was made additionally painful for the chaplain by the ceremony which preceded it, of drinking tea in St. Antony's Parlour, waited on by Reverend Mother. This custom held throughout the Order, and was based on the supposed need of chaplain and Mother Superior to discuss such problems of spirit or character as might have struck either in dealing with the school. But as, week after week, year after year, Reverend Mother poured tea for, and offered buttered toast to a succession of shy or truculent young Irishmen, she smiled wryly to herself at the characteristically Latin idea which justified the stiff reflection. No Irish boy just out of college was going to be drawn into other than the most perfunctory generalisations on the character or spiritual difficulties of a pack of schoolgirls. Nor, indeed, did she blame the successive young chaplains for their negative resolution. Still, she had to obey custom, and torture them with her half-hour of politeness. But as she really believed in discipline, for herself and all human creatures, she thought it no harm that the curates should have to sit for one half-hour each week and make conversation with her, when she knew they really feared and disliked it.

Father Conroy was the third chaplain she had known in her four years in Ireland, and the one with whom she felt least sympathy.

The two were nervous and at sea with each other.

"Well, Reverend Mother—that's a nice hare your friend Joe Chamberlain is making of himself these days!"

"*My* friend, Father Conroy?"

"Oh well—he's English; that's all I meant."

"I come of a Liberal family, Father. I have never known *any* statesmen, but if you were to speak of Mr. Chamberlain's opponent, Mr. Asquith, as 'my friend,' I mightn't be so startled."

"Aha! So you think there is some good in Asquith, Reverend Mother? I'm surprised to hear that. Six of one and half a dozen of the other, if you ask me."

"Nothing of the kind, if you ask me," said Reverend Mother amiably.

"Well, well—we must agree to differ there. But Tariff Reform, God help us!"

"You ought to be delighted with Mr. Chamberlain's Tariff Reform, Father."

"I—delighted?"

"Because it is a pernicious, greedy conception, which will very likely cost the present Government its office. And then Home Rule will become a near possibility again, surely?"

"Yah, Home Rule. What good would that be to us, Reverend Mother?"

"It is difficult to say." She spoke with faint malice, but he did not see the mild joke. "In any case, what should a nun know of these matters?" she amended gently.

"Ah, that's the trouble," he said, and as he went on she conceded that there was real trouble, and some diffidence, in his voice and face. "Nuns shouldn't trouble themselves with these secular things, I suppose. And yet you know, Reverend Mother, a convent like this wields great influence—through its girls afterwards—in the world."

"We are very conscious of that, Father Conroy."

She realised wearily that he was circling, as usual, round the Irish hierarchy's distrust of an independent religious Order. It was a patent exasperation to the authoritarian Bishop that, short of grave scandal, he had no power to counsel or direct the *Compagnie de la Sainte Famille*. And this exceptional privilege of the Order increased the offence of its foreignness; in fact, Reverend Mother knew very well that, as far as his Lordship was to be reckoned with, the independence of this house was the sole safeguard of its peculiar tradition, which the Bishop called "exotic" and *démodé*, and which he would have overthrown without hesitation had he the power.

The Bishop had some of the weapons of an intellectual to his hand; but Father Conroy had only an untutored, unbridled nationalism. He disliked the spirit of *Sainte Famille*, Reverend Mother suspected, solely because it was governed by an Englishwoman. And as such an emotional and bad ellipsis of argument was distasteful to her in anyone, but incomprehensible in a consecrated priest, spiritual communication between the two was impossible.

"To be sure you are, Reverend Mother. And the young ladies of *Sainte Famille* are beautifully educated—we all know that. But times are changing here, and somehow——"

"Somehow what, Father Conroy?"

The cold English tone annoyed him.

"Somehow it's a bit of a pity, it seems to me, Reverend Mother, to be training Irish girls as suitable wives for English Majors and Colonial Governors!"

He spoke angrily because he was afraid of his own audacity.

"We educate our children in the Christian virtues and graces. If these appeal to English majors, why, so much the better for those gentlemen!"

"Our young girls must be educated *nationally* now, Reverend Mother—to be the wives of *Irishmen* and to meet the changing times!"

"We do what we can about that, Father. But if the 'changing times' you are so sure of are to have no place for Christian discipline and common politeness, I can only say I'm glad I shall not see very much of them."

She spoke very coldly, and offered the young man some cakes.

"No, thank you, Reverend Mother," he said. "It's a terror the way you won't see what I mean at all."

"I do see what you mean, Father—and I find you are rude, and officious. But you are, after all, very young."

He looked so startled and indignant that at once she was ashamed of herself, and distressed in her turn at the cruel enmity she felt towards him. As she sought a way of apology there was a knock on the parlour door.

Anna Murphy came in.

"Yes, Anna, that's right—come along. I told her to come to the parlour to you this evening, Father, as she appears now to understand her catechism well, and you may wish— after you've talked with her—to arrange her instructions for First Confession. She will be seven next month."

"On the 5th April," said Anna.

"Will you now?" said Father Conroy. "You're a small girl for that—aren't you, Anna?"

Anna drew near.

"Still, I'd like to make my First Confession, please," she said.

"Well, I expect we'll let you. On the 5th April you will have reached the age of reason, Anna—and even now you sound reasonable enough, God bless you!"

Reverend Mother smiled.

"Reasonableness is her *forte* at present, Father."

"Would you like a biscuit, Anna? May I give her one, Reverend Mother? Which kind will you have?"

"The one that's like a piece of orange, please."

Father Conroy handed her the yellow-sugared biscuit shaped like a piece of orange.

"Thank you, Father Conroy."

"Now Anna, we must prepare you for First Confession, so that you can make it about the 5th April. You know I come to hear the other girls' confessions every Saturday at half-past five. This Saturday I'll come at five—if I may, Reverend Mother?—and have a talk with you about Christian doctrine and what confession is. Then on this day week we could have another talk, I suppose, Reverend Mother? and when we have talked together about six times, I think you will be able to receive the Sacrament of Penance. You know it *is* a sacrament, don't you?"

Anna nodded.

"I'm doing that chapter now in Catechism. I had two questions about contrition to learn to-day."

"Oh, good girl. You're quite far on in your catechism. You've learnt the Ten Commandments then, and the explanations of them?"

"Well—yes."

The frowning uncertainty which entered her face made both nun and priest smile faintly.

"You mustn't worry if you don't completely understand them all," Father Conroy said. "You couldn't expect it yet. They cover a wide field."

"I can see that," said Anna. "Still——"

"Still—what?"

"Well, since they really are *commandments*, I think I should have a rough idea—and Mother Felicita too, I think she should. After all, she's *old*."

"And what's bothering yourself and Mother Felicita, may I ask?"

"We don't know what adultery is. Either of us. What is it?"

Reverend Mother sat very still, anxiety in her heart. The awkward, not to say loutish, young priest was in charge of this conversation. He was the spiritual director and Anna had rightly put her query to him. He must answer as his wit directed, but the child who questioned him was not easy to hoodwink, and the questing ease of her mind was, in

94

Reverend Mother's eyes a very delicate and cherishable thing. As she waited alert for the sequence of dialogue, one region of her heart were rapidly flooded with uneasy prayer. If this little child were told a lie, or made to suspect already by any clumsiness the sordid hush-hush of sexual troubles—the nun winced with anxiety, as she searched, without any clue, the broad, unsubtle face of the young priest.

"Are you sure Mother Felicita doesn't know the meaning of adultery?" Father Conroy asked Anna.

"Oh yes. She didn't exactly say so, but anyone could tell it muddles her."

The priest nodded.

"Well, of course, being a nun she wouldn't have to know, as it doesn't have anything to do with her, in her life. And until you are grown up it won't be any concern of yours."

"Still—it's in my catechism, after all——"

"Yes—and I'm going to tell you what it is. I was only explaining to you why Mother Felicita might happen not to understand about it. You see, it isn't everyone's business. But when you are grown up, left school, you will perhaps decide to be a nun and live entirely for the glory of God; or you may decide to live alone in the world, devoting yourself to work or study of some kind; or, very likely, you will feel that you do not want to live always alone, that you would like a husband and children. In that case you will choose some man who will also choose you; you'll choose each other by what is called 'falling in love'—which means you will find that you love each other more than you love other people. And so you'll receive together the sacrament of marriage—you've learnt about that?—and having promised in that sacrament to love each other always, you live together and have children. Well—if afterwards either of you should stop loving the other, and begin to let yourself love another person more than the one you had promised to love best always—that is adultery."

"I think it might be very easy to commit," Anna said.

"Why do you think that?"

"Well—how could you be sure of loving anyone best always?"

"You couldn't be *sure*, I suppose—on our own steam we can't be sure of anything. But marriage is a sacrament—which is, you know, a special way of receiving special grace from God. God helps us a very great deal in difficulties, as you'll discover when you grow up, young lady. Well, are you clear in your mind now about the sixth Commandment?"

"Oh yes. Thank you very much. Do you mind if I explain it to Mother Felicita?"

"Not at all. But after all, it has nothing to do with her."

"But she's *teaching* catechism. I think it'd be better if she understood—for another time."

"Perhaps. Well, off with you now and eat your sugar biscuit. And remember, on Saturday at five I'll examine you on the first two chapters of the catechism."

"I'll remember. Good-bye, Father Conroy. Good-bye, Reverend Mother."

Anna shook hands with the priest and bowed to Reverend Mother, who smiled at her as she withdrew.

The bell for Religious Instruction rang, and Father Conroy rose from his chair.

As the nun ascended the broad staircase with him on the way to the *salle d'études* she pondered in bitter humility. This priest whom she judged crude and unwise had just shown himself gentle and wise and a good, honest teacher. He had shown perfect understanding of innocence and intelligence, and had spoken to them out of peace and humour, and without a shadow of evasiveness in word or implication. She was ashamed of her earlier extreme severity with him; she felt very grateful to him for the guarded sensibility with which he had impressed her as he replied to the good sense of childhood. She racked her brain for a way of expressing friendliness and repentance. She decided that the only just course was to apologise for having sought to humiliate him.

"I hope you will forgive me for having spoken unjustly a few moments ago, Father. But I fear I lose my sense of proportion, and of justice, when I think people want to make a political weapon of the education of children."

But he thought he saw a further thrust at himself in this piece of self-explanation—and he was still rankling with dislike of her.

"To be sure, Reverend Mother. But isn't that exactly what you English have done all the same, all over the globe?"

"I was only speaking for myself," she answered wearily.

Genevieve Ahern opened the swing door of the *salle d'études* and, as the chaplain and Reverend Mother entered, the school stood up and bowed.

When Anna began her third year at school in September, 1906, she was eight and a half years old, and was pleased to find herself promoted to full status in Second Preparatory. In the two preceding terms she had followed many of its classes, but was still considered too young for the full schedule; now, however, after long apprenticeship, she was promoted at last to unprivileged school-girlhood, and was well content.

There would be no more of the liberal education of a free lance. No drives in the garden cart, with loads of dung or blowing leaves, and Cafferty to talk to; no dressing nuns' graves for feast-days; no mending of shoes with Sister Stanislaus behind the ever-changing and ever-enchanting screen; no fetching and carrying by kind Letitia Doyle, who was gone and lost into the world. No music of the guitar in St. Joseph's Grotto. *Vogue, mon beau navire.* . . .

Anna supposed that also there would be no more Sunday evening poems for Reverend Mother. In a way she would be glad of that; it was getting a bit awkward saying those poems always after Marks, made her feel silly. And some of the others teased her and said she was a "show-off," and "Reverend Mother's pet." The two years of choosing, discarding and learning her Sunday poems had filled her head with words and suggestions she liked. And now she found it very easy to remember poetry. She often said her favourites to herself in bed or in chapel. How sweet is the shepherd's sweet lot and Orpheus with his lute made trees, and the mountain-tops that freeze and Under the wide and starry sky, and the Night piece to Julia that Mother Eugenia said was a funny choice, and Fear no more the heat of the sun, and where the pools are bright and deep, where the grey trout lies asleep. That was called A Boy's Song, and she said it to Charlie once and tried to make him learn it, but he wouldn't. And at home the other day she found a very good one—The poplars are felled; farewell to their shade. Reverend Mother would have liked that one, which perhaps she did not know. Still, it was better not to say poems out loud by herself any more, and have people laughing at her and calling her "a pet." It was better to be a real Second Preparatory.

Molly Redmond, Gertie Davoren and their contemporaries were First Preparatories now, and Mother Felicita's class consisted of five new girls, five who had come to school during the past year, and Anna. The average age of this eleven was nine and a half, and Anna was nine months younger than its next youngest member; but her two years of solitary beginnings had been useful to her; also she liked acquiring knowledge, and her dominant characteristic still was impartial attentiveness to whatever she heard and saw, so she did not find the widened routine of lessons oppressive or beyond her power.

Mother Felicita, stupid and kind, said that she was "a little genius." Mother Mary Andrew, intelligent and unkind, said that she was nothing of the sort.

At *Sainte Famille* there was an attractive institution called Emulation Holiday. It was a recurrent reward for good class-work, and it had to be earned by a not impossible series of trials. The curious thing was that, reasonable as the conditions of victory were, it was rarely that more than fifteen or eighteen girls, out of a possible sixty, came through to it safely. But it was always the best of the school holidays, and it could be enjoyed at least once a term by the industrious or the fairly intelligent. On Emulation Day the few who were, presumably, to be emulated, sat together and apart from the rest for their meals, at Foundress's Table. These meals were of a very festive character, and were free of the everyday drawback, sustained at the other tables, of French conversation. For the rest, the pleasures of the day were planned with understanding. In summer there would be a picnic, or a steamboat expedition on the lake, with *Mère Martine* and her guitar for added grace; in winter, one of the smaller parlours, with fire and arm-chairs, was at the disposal of the elect. Toffee and caramels could be bought from the *dépense* Sister; story-books and even some magazines might be read, and there were bagatelle, chess and Happy Families to play. And always, winter or summer, after a supper of onion soup and tipsy cake and elderberry wine, the holiday-makers gathered again in their private parlour and—the fire piled high now, the lights turned out, and the curtains drawn to let moon, sky and lake shine inwards—Mother Eugenia came and took her place in the centre of the semi-circle and told ghost-stories. Banshee stories and stories of the headless coach, and "Who will answer my Mass?" and "I must return to Purgatory—pray for me, pray for my soul!" Sweet caramel in the mouth and bright logs crashing; the nun's voice deeper, softer than everyday. And long after normal bedtime, the shadowy climb, whispering, terrified, excited, giggling, a little sick, to the silent dormitories—past the Foundress's bust—like a death-mask under the moon; pouncing at each other going by it, for comfort and to freeze each other's blood. Who will answer my Mass? She nodded her head at me. That means you have a vocation. Pray for my soul. Sh, sh, be silent, children, everyone is asleep. *Priez pour moi, Mère Marie-Félice de Gravons St. Roche.* Good night, Mother Eugenia. I must return to Purgatory. Steady, Maud, that isn't your cubicle. Too much tipsy cake—ah, Emulation's over. Who will answer my Mass?

A day of pleasure no grown-up life contains. It was worth working for.

At *Sainte Famille* the whole school was set, according to class, a short written examination on every Sunday morning of term. The subjects of these examinations were normally in rotation: Christian Doctrine, Scripture History, English Literature, History, Geography and a mathematical subject. Class mistresses marked the papers, and the results were read aloud in the refectory and entered in a register. The maximum of marks was 100; 70 was Honours, 50 a pass. When in a series of six Sundays a girl had achieved 70 or more marks on three papers, and 50 or more on the remaining three, she was eligible to take the last fence for the Emulation holiday. This fence was a special examination in French, in which 70 marks had to be scored. A surprising number of possibles fell out at this test.

In her second term as a Second Preparatory Anna came through six Sunday examinations with the requisite Emulation marks. She was delighted, and so was Mother Felicita. The latter spoke with amused kindness to Mother Mary Andrew of her pupil's pleasure at the near prospect of being in the Emulation.

"And she deserves it," said Mother Felicita. "She is a real worker at her lessons."

Mother Mary Andrew had never "taken to" Anna, perhaps because her quick nerves sensed Reverend Mother's guarded interest in the child. Now if Mother Mary Andrew did not "take to" a pupil, the safest that might be wished for such a one was that she should remain unremarkable throughout her schooldays; for her to distinguish herself in any way was, if she were not "a favourite," tantamount to becoming "a victim."

"I'm glad to hear that," Mother Scholastic said coldly now. "But I presume you realise that the Second Preparatories are not usually eligible for the Emulation. Their standard of examination is babyish, after all—and we cannot make a farce of the reward."

Mother Felicita had moments of detesting Mother Mary Andrew, and this was one of them. She saw that she had made a tactical error in mentioning Anna's prospect of success, but she was determined that, short of cheating, the child should have her Emulation holiday. She said no more now, but she reflected on this passage of conversation throughout the day.

Mother Mary Andrew was capable of uttering a sudden *fiat*, banning the Second Preparatory class from the Emulation competition. Such a ban would be imposed quickly, and so timed that, if it ever did reach Reverend Mother's knowledge, it could not interfere with the gaining for Mother Scholastic of her immediate point; Anna Murphy would have been kept out of the approaching Emulation, and afterwards, by quick covering tactics, the ban could be removed, if necessary, and perhaps made to seem like the result of a misunderstanding. Mother Felicita was not endowed intellectually, but she was every inch feminine and she knew her Mother Scholastic. She thought of a plan to forestall the threatening *fiat*.

At evening recreation in the Community Room, the nuns sat, loosely grouped, about a large work-table, at the head of which was Reverend Mother, busy with embroidery, or with neat, amateur re-binding of old books or music. Most of the nuns occupied their hands at this time, but an oddity like Mother Eugenia or *Mère Martine* preferred to sit in talkative idleness, and give ironic advice to their industrious companions.

It was forty-five minutes during which Reverend Mother strove to promote lightness, and a reasonable freedom of speech. She approved, without commenting on it, of idleness at this hour, and would have encouraged it by sitting idle herself, were she not too much ashamed of the unconquerable restlessness of her hands. She particularly liked to see the older lay sisters get the more comfortable chairs, and that they should fold their hands in their laps.

It was perhaps during community recreation that the humbler and simpler nuns learnt, unconsciously, to like and trust their cold, calm Reverend Mother. Certainly at this hour she was deliberate in putting her personality at the disposal of the simple and diffident ones. She knew that her habit of making the lay sisters and novices lead recreation talk annoyed Mother Mary Andrew and Mother Bonaventure, and somewhat bored Mother Eugenia. But she did not care. She had strong views on the conduct of community life, and she liked lay sisters, who, she thought, managed very often to draw near to sainthood. Sometimes as she steered for her objective, the general pleasure, among the cross-tides about her, she wished she was Saint Teresa, or could, by wishing, inherit a fragment of the latter's power to amuse and exhilarate simultaneously the lowliest and the proudest of her daughters in Christ. She wished she had some of the Castilian's guile too—for she knew very well that the nuns used the veiling innocency of the hour of recreation to make points, to get her authority for personal manœuvres and, all-innocent-seeming, to score off each other. But she admitted to herself sometimes, with amusement, that she was by no means as lacking in wiliness as in the arts of entertainment.

On a certain Monday evening in Lent, Mother Felicita, seated near the end of the table, looked up from her darning of an altar cloth and said with a benevolent, girlish smile:

"I think you'll be delighted to hear, Reverend Mother, that little Anna Murphy will probably be in her first Emulation holiday on Wednesday."

Reverend Mother smiled, but warily. News of Anna always interested her so much that she resisted it for justice' sake, and veiled it in the name of good example. And still it worried and amused her to see that certain of the nuns were quite confident of her special concern for the child. She was doubly wary now, because she thought she felt purpose in Mother Felicita's casual observation.

"That is very nice. How pleased she must be! She's an industrious little ant."

"Oh, she's in heaven at the idea. She has only to get through the French test to-morrow morning—and I really think that will be all right."

"No Second Preparatory has ever been in the Emulation, as far as I know," said Mother Mary Andrew, and Reverend Mother grasped the situation at once.

"Well, it looks as if Anna is going to remove that precedent," she said lightly, and thought she saw a faint flush of pleasure rise on Mother Felicita's face.

"But those Second Preparatory examinations are only fooling, Reverend Mother!" said Mother Mary Andrew.

"It's a pity they wouldn't be Fellowship standard!" snorted Mother Eugenia.

"But these infants!" Mother Scholastic persisted. "I cannot think that you would approve, Reverend Mother, of lowering the prestige of the reward?"

Reverend Mother smiled as kindly as she could—out of pure guile—at the frowning nun.

" 'Prestige' is a solemn word," she said. "The Emulation is just a little gaiety arranged for children who work well. I don't think we need take it *too* ceremoniously, Mother Mary Andrew. And I really don't see why the poor Second Preparatories should be done out of it."

She spoke with as little outward sign of authority as she could—almost making a query of her last sentence. But she knew that what she said had settled the issue, and that Anna would take her French test in the morning. Somewhat dejected by this new glimpse of the temperamental unscrupulousness of Mother Mary Andrew, and touched by the bright pleasure in Mother Felicita's eyes, she turned her attention dutifully to the general conduct of Recreation.

"Well, Sister Simeon, what news of the incubator to-day?"

"Little that's good then, Reverend Mother! I don't know will that contraption be the death of me in the heel of the hunt!"

"For me, should I have been a chick," said *Mère Martine*, "that little lamp could please me for a shelter. I may care not for the suffocation of a hen."

"Nor I—come to think of it," said Mother Eugenia.

"No wonder, faith, and the hens that's in it now! Glory

be to God, Reverend Mother, what is the nation coming to, if even a hen won't attend to her duty like a Christian?"

"We must make a *novena* for them, Sister Simeon," said Mother Bonaventure.

The French test for the Emulation had by tradition to be severe, and Mother Felicita honourably set Anna a laborious one. She sat her in front of some sheets of foolscap and told her to write from memory and in full each of the four regular verb conjugations: *donner*, *finir*, *recevoir*, and *vendre*, the principal parts of each and, in order, the tenses derived from each principal part. She allotted her two hours for the task.

It was a heavy physical labour, but Anna knew how to conjugate regular verbs, and she set to work resolutely. At the end of two hours, a little tired from the sustained struggle to be tidy and systematic, and believing she had made no really bad mistake, she gave her foolscap sheets to Mother Felicita.

This was at midday. The results of the French tests would be announced during *goûter*, and those who had accomplished 70 per cent would spend the evening dreaming a little hysterically of the next day's Emulation. Those who had failed—there were always some—would withdraw to cry in the lavatory, or on the landing by the Foundress's bust, and their friends would put little holy pictures in their desks with "Cheer up" or "*Priez pour moi*" written on the backs.

Mother Mary Andrew did not customarily take *goûter* with the school. For that meal, in the interests of French conversation, *Mère Marie-Claire*, a lively tough nun not long out of *Sainte Fontaine*, sat in authority at Foundress's table. And as she taught all the senior French, it was fitting that she should strike the gong half-way through *goûter* and read the French test results.

There were some gasps of relief; there were some sad casualties—Cecilia Hooley being meanly served, everyone felt, with sixty-eight marks. But last on the list, sole representative of Second Preparatory, Anna Murphy sailed in safely with seventy-five. She was still the school baby, and the school cheered, and *Mère Marie-Claire* smiled down at her and said: "*Mes félicitations, Anna; que ça continue, ma petite.*" So Anna felt happy and spent a happy evening.

That night she said her prayers well; she tried to be polite at supper, kept her elbows in and attended to her neighbour. At night recreation the others wanted to play "Puss-in-the-corner," so she did not ask for "*Meunier, tu dors.*" In the dormitory she brushed her teeth with care, although she was very sleepy. She did not break silence once in the dressing-room, and as she went back between the rows of stiff white damasked curtains to her own cubicle, felt as peaceful as if she were in bed. Where the pools are bright and deep, she said to herself, where the grey trout lies asleep, up the river and o'er the lea . . . but when she passed Our Lady's alcove she did not forget the convention of pausing to say a good-night "Hail Mary." Monica Honan, a Child of Mary, was doing so at the same time, and Anna was careful to imitate her attitude before the statue.

As she stood there imagining herself into the importance of Monica Honan, as she stood there in her red dressing-gown and slippers, with her sponge-basket in her hands and her straight hair in a plait, Mother Mary Andrew came to the alcove and tapped her shoulder.

"I wish to speak to you, Anna."

Anna was too sleepy to be surprised.

"Yes, Mother Mary Andrew."

The nun sat down at a little table near the alcove where, under a dimmed light, she was accustomed to sit on guard, correcting exercises or reading her Office, until silence and sleep filled the dormitory. Quiet was already descending on the cubicles, and only the lowered alcove light burnt in the vast, shadowed room, so Mother Mary Andrew spoke softly.

"There has been a mistake about your French test, Anna, and you will *not* be in the Emulation to-morrow."

Anna stared at her. What had been said drifted slowly into her sleepy brain.

"A mistake?"

"Yes. A very foolish mistake—of your own making." Mother Mary Andrew opened the drawer of the table and produced the foolscap sheets of Anna's French conjugations. She laid them down and the child saw on the front page, in Mother Felicita's marking, a big blue-pencil 75/100 V.G.—but crossed through now by a red pencil, and replaced by a big red O. She could only stare at first. She felt very frightened.

"You—you've put a nought," she said at last.

"Yes, Anna—because that is what it merits."

"All my verbs? Oh, why did you? They're not all wrong! They couldn't be?"

"Certainly they're not all wrong. But in one conjugation you made a mistake so silly as to show that you have no understanding of what you are doing, and so cannot receive marks like an intelligent schoolgirl."

"But—I got 75. Mother Felicita gave me——"

"Mother Felicita is very kind to you, far too kind—and she evidently thinks that your getting the other conjugations right excuses the absurdity of your conjugating of *finir*. However, I disagree with her, and have told her that you are clearly too young for examinations, and for Emulation holidays!"

"But *finir*—I—I know it! *Finir, finissant, fini, je finis, je finis*. Oh, what did I do? What did I do?"

Anna wailed this question. There were uneasy stirrings in cubicles near by. Some listening girls had been tortured by Mother Mary Andrew in their time, and felt frightened now for the child they could not help.

"Be quiet, you insolent little girl! Look and see for yourself what you did."

Anna looked. She had written the present participle of *finir* as *finant*. The error had been logically carried through the subsidiary parts of the verb which derived from the present participle, so that she had written *Je finais, que je fine*, and *que je fine*. Beside the initial mistake Mother Felicita had put a gentle blue cross of protest, and had written "Anna!

Anna!" in the margin. And her pencil streaked through the derivative errors.

But all this blue reasonableness had now been slashed with red.

Anna was completely bewildered. She saw the foolishness of her mistake, which really was only foolishness, because she knew quite well about *finissant* and *que je finisse*. But Mother Felicita had taken away twenty-five marks for it—and there were no other mistakes. She was sorry to have been so silly as to write *finant*, but she could not understand why she might have *no* marks, and no Emulation.

"I only made that one mistake," she said shakily. "That's why I got seventy-five."

"You dare to call it *one* mistake?"

"It is only one mistake. How silly." Anna's courage flowed back for a second. "Because you see, when I put *finant* I had to put the others. It would have been sillier even if I didn't. Oh, don't you see?"

"How dare you try to instruct me, miss?"

"Oh, I'm sorry, Mother Mary Andrew! Please, please let me have my marks! Oh, it was only that one word! It isn't fair! Mother Felicita——"

She was crying wildly, her head down on the foolscap sheets. She knew that she was in the grip of omnipotence, that there was no Emulation, and that she only wanted to be at home, with Charlie.

There were twistings, mutterings, behind some curtains. Mother Mary Andrew took Anna's shoulder in her enormous hand and shook her.

"Be quiet, you impertinent child! Everything you say proves that you are only a baby and unfit for an Emulation holiday—even if this paper did not show it conclusively!"

The words were hissed in a half-whisper. Anna wailed out loud in reply:

"Go away, go away! I'm going home! I'm going to run away! If my Daddy were here—oh, Daddy!—oh, oh!"

Mother Mary Andrew shook her again and hissed at her to be quiet. Then she half dragged, half carried her to her cubicle and pushed her inside.

"Get yourself to bed at once, miss—I'll wait here until I know you're undressed and in bed. And don't forget an Act of Contrition, if you please!"

She began to pace up and down the aisle outside the cubicles, uttering hisses for silence to the uneasy occupants.

Anna sank in a heap in her dark cubicle, on the strip of carpet. She did not cry out loud any more, but she was choking and shaking with tears. She had never before been the victim of an injustice which she could see; she had never been shaken and dragged, and arbitrarily refused a pleasure she had won and been promised. She had never been flung into a dark place, crying, and left to find her nightdress in the dark, and go to bed crying.

Molly Redmond was in the next cubicle. She ran her hand down under the stiff white curtain, and groped on the floor for Anna. When she found her shoulder she thrust her head under the curtain too, risking its starchy rattle. She dared not speak, but she stretched more than half-way out of her bed and caressed the sobbing child, but Anna did not seem to feel her, and just shivered and choked where she lay. In terror Molly slipped her whole self under the curtain and bending over Anna picked her up and seated her on the bed. She found her nightdress under the pillow, and keeping an arm around her, kissing the hot, wet face, but silent as death, she undressed her. As she pulled the nightdress over Anna's head, Mother Mary Andrew entered the cubicle and gripped her by the shoulders.

"How dare you leave your bed and enter another. Insubordination *and* immodesty! I suppose you know that I could give you a mark for conduct now, or have you expelled! Let go of that nightdress and return to your bed at once!"

She dragged Molly away from Anna with violence.

"She was lying on the floor—she couldn't undress herself."

"No excuses, Molly Redmond! For an action like this there *are* none."

"Oh, she's only a baby—and she *deserves* the Emulation——"

"So you've been listening to what wasn't your concern! I might have known—coming from your sort of home. There are some things which unfortunately no education can eliminate."

Mother Mary Andrew pushed the girl out of the cubicle and round into her own. Molly fought under the terrible grip of her hand.

"How dare you say that about my home? How dare you insult me in this way?" she sobbed.

Mother Mary Andrew flung her into the cubicle and stood on guard outside the curtain until she thought her two victims were asleep. Then she withdrew to her own sleeping place, afar in the shadow of the inner dormitory.

Then Molly slipped back again under the curtain. Anna was huddled in a twitching, choking heap on the quilt—her nightdress only half on, as she had been left. Molly got her second arm into it, and buttoned her up. She put her day-clothes on the chair and picked the little girl up to settle her in bed.

Anna's arm went round her then, and she awoke and gave a wail which Molly hushed against her shoulder. But the shaking of the small body distressed her very much. She was twelve years old, and the sobbing burden in her arms made her feel grown up and brave and tender.

"I want to go home. I want Charlie," Anna was saying.

Molly got into her bed with her and rocked her to sleep in her arms.

## The Second Chapter

# MOLLY REDMOND

ANNA never learnt that Mother Mary Andrew's injustice to her about the verb *finir* almost caused a change of *personnel* at *Sainte Famille*. She forgot it soon—superficially; but she was never to unlearn the contempt it taught her—her first contempt for a fellow-creature.

Reverend Mother asked Mother Felicita why Anna had failed in her French test. She was told the story; she sent for the unlucky foolscap sheets and examined the blue markings and the red. Her deductions therefrom made her so angry and so troubled that she allowed seven days to pass before she demanded an explanation, a possible defence, of Mother Mary Andrew.

The two women confronted each other in Reverend Mother's study. Proud and rigid both, and more emotionally mettled for the issue than either perceived. In all they said clipped in by the peculiar etiquette of their situation; bound, Mother Mary Andrew, by the fixed euphemisms of veneration for a superior, and Reverend Mother by her inability really to assault the self-respect of another.

It was, nevertheless, for all their outward care, a bitter interview between enemies. Mother Mary Andrew based her explanation on two planes: the first a theory—which Reverend Mother felt to be suspect and trumped-up—of the danger and absurdity of encouraging an infant to regard study as a mere matter of parrot performances; and the second, a specific accusation that Anna Murphy was no more than a very quick echo, was growing dangerously sure of herself, and needed the shocks of real severity to counteract the unwise encouragement and indulgence of Mother Felicita—and others.

Reverend Mother noted the daring innuendo of the last two words, and conceded that truth and an unadmitted explanation lay somewhere in their shadow. But she could find no acceptable defence of her arbitrariness in anything Mother Mary Andrew said, and there was a minute of very painful silence in the little room when the latter ceased speaking.

"I am sorry," Reverend Mother said at last, "but I cannot see or concede any of your arguments. I am still compelled to view your action about this examination paper as an impulse of vindictiveness towards Mother Felicita, and towards a defenceless pupil. I am therefore compelled to censure you, and I tell you now frankly that had I the power I would, on the evidence of this episode, withdraw you from the office of Mother Scholastic. However, I have not such authority. But I shall write my version and view of what has taken place to *Mère Générale*, and shall make in my letter such comment as I am entitled to. The letter will go in Saturday's post. You, of course, may also write exactly as you wish to *Mère Générale*, and seal your letter."

"I shall do so."

"That is all, then. Thank you, Mother Mary Andrew."

*Mère Générale* took, however, the line Reverend Mother knew to be characteristic. She disapproved on principle of correction by retrogressive or negative device, and did not command the removal elsewhere or the degradation from office of Mother Mary Andrew. She was shocked by the cruelty and egotism the episode revealed, but observed that Mother Scholastic was young and mettlesome, and that the proper course was to work her hard and reprimand her freely and forcibly when authoritarianism took her into danger. There was much wisdom and gentle scepticism in the letter, and no reproof to Reverend Mother—but the latter saw that her proud inability to seem to clash with Mother Scholastic had been perceived, and that she was suspected of nursing her own temperament. In fact, she surmised ruefully, Mother Mary Andrew is being left here as much for the good of my soul as her own. So be it, she thought, and accepted the ruling of the old far-away nun, who could surprise and occasionally hurt her, but whom alone on earth perhaps she trusted.

What passed in Mother Mary Andrew's sealed correspondence with Brussels was hidden from her, but letters of a certain bulkiness came and went during many months, and Mother Scholastic was stiff, polite and subdued for a considerable time.

Meantime school terms ebbed and flowed and carried Anna Murphy with them through many sorts of weather. But the storms were mostly external—either observed, or shared with her class or the school. They were never her own. She was a very detached child in the years before puberty—even, though no one suspected it, she was cold-hearted. She was contented, and loved the occupations of school, but its personages did not fully engage her attention once she had begun full-time lessons. This was partly because of the shock to her confidence which had been inflicted by Mother Mary Andrew and the verb *finir*—a shock which made her both defensive and cunning. But also—and this was perhaps only an outcome of defensiveness—she developed a need, a love of reading, which made her unsociable and absent-minded towards other children as it grew. She was, for many of her early years, the kind of reader who will gratefully read anything rather than not read. Words, their shapes and lengths, their possibilities of breaking into other words, or into pairs and groups of letters, became her constant amusement between her eighth and thirteenth years. As other children played with paper dolls or marbles she liked to play private games with words. Also she liked to worry over the colours of words. She liked to shut her eyes and wonder why "yellow" was dove-grey, and why "black" was flaming orange. She tried in vain to turn them to other colours. Long words were like striped ribbons—"constitution," for instance, was scarlet, white, blue, black across its flashing syllables. The best long words broke up into groups of three letters, leaving no tail; the next best went in twos; words of eleven letters were ugly-looking, disappointing.

The school library was guarded by a Child of Mary, and story-books were doled out on Sundays for a few hours, and on holidays. Anna might only range through the shelves reserved for children under twelve, and she read their contents steadily, many of the volumes twice and three times—notably *The Cuckoo Clock*, *Helen's Babies* and *Three Men in a Boat*. During her tenth year she had a passion for comic writing, and she believed that nothing could ever be written that could be funnier than *Helen's Babies*.

A bookcase called the Reference Library was always open and free to any reader at any time. *Mère Martine*, who sometimes took charge of evening study in the *salle*, was amused to watch Anna, who in these years remained small for her age, perpetually climbing up and down to reach the Reference Library.

"Hold, *mon petit*," she used to say. "It is a damage of the greatest to be a *femme savante*." And Mother Eugenia, waiting by the door one day while the seniors assembled in line to follow her to a classroom, bent over Anna's desk near by and discovered that she was reading *The Confessions of Saint Augustine*.

"Praise be to God!" she exclaimed, and then: "Excuse me a minute, child, till I look at your book."

Anna handed it to her.

"It's from the Reference Library, Mother Eugenia," she said.

The old nun looked at the title-page and the *imprimatur*, and gave the volume back to Anna.

"Bowdlerised," she said with a smile, and Anna wondered what that meant. "Let you get on now with your study of the Fathers—and pardon my flippant interruption, if you please"; and, ironically affectionate, she pushed Anna's head right down against the pages of the book.

Anna read some of Miss Strickland's *Lives of the Queens of England* from the Reference Library, and many of

Macaulay's *Essays*. She read—with devotion—the *Roger de Coverley Papers*, and also a little volume by Washington Irving called *Bracebridge Hall*. She read *The Four Georges* and Lingard's *History of England*, and *The Rape of the Lock* and *Irish Penny Readings* and a great deal of *Paradise Lost*, and with tears and tender memorisings, *The Lays of the Scottish Cavaliers*. She also read Father Lacordaire's *Sermons*.

This random and uncritical hobby developed her already nimble memory, and gave her a larger vocabulary than her classmates. It made her somewhat unpopular, and stressed her detachment. By absorbing much of the free time devoted by others to casual friendliness, and also by making her formidable and annoying in class, her reading held her back somewhat from normal friendships. Moreover, she never felt inclined to substitute anyone else for Charlie. As long as Joe could bring Charlie to see her once a week, or come to fetch her home sometimes for a whole Sunday; as long as the bright, solid wedges of holiday in Castle Tory were safely fixed in memory and ahead, she was content with her own impersonal interest in school-life, and did not perceive that she was different from others in having no "special friend."

One Sunday evening in May she came back from home only in time for supper, having had late leave in honour of Charlie's birthday.

It was Charlie's tenth birthday, and years before he should have been sent to the nuns' preparatory school for Clongowes, but although Harry and Tom were full Clongownians now—the former *Victor Ludorum* of Lower Line—Charlie had so far half achieved his resolve not to go to school, for he was let off with desultory attendance at Lissanmoher National School in the company of common boys like Jimmy Meagher. He was also supposed to study Latin and French with the curate, Father Hogan, but, according to what he told Anna, those lessons were chiefly in hurley-swinging and in target practice with a rifle. Anna marvelled at this victory of his will, and he thought well of it himself, and wondered how long it might hold. It did not occur to either child that such luck was attributable to any cause other than Charlie's decisiveness of character.

Since his nature was so gentle, this faith was surprising, but it contented the children. They were very peaceful friends and they never quarrelled. They had cousins with whom they fought, and occasionally during holidays there was trouble with the big brothers. But mostly at home they were left together unmolested, and that suited them very well.

They enjoyed this long, sunny birthday. Although the saddle Daddy had promised him had not come—was "on order," Daddy said—he liked the battledore and shuttlecock Anna had bought for him through Sister Thomas, the shopping sister; also there were a bow and arrows from Granny, and he had a new blazer, striped red and white. And Joe gave him a ferret and a tin of nut toffee. Dinner was chosen by Charlie—duck and peas and ham, and *Charlotte russe* and apple-pie, and dessert with the Crown Derby fruit plates and pink sweets in silver dishes. Daddy insisted on Charlie's having a glass of wine with him, but that made Mother angry, and she said: "It would have been more to the point to have got him the saddle you promised so freely." Daddy said nothing to that, but dropped back in his chair and seemed to go to sleep during dessert.

The rest of the day was in the garden and in the yard and in the kitchen—the peaceful day of accord and leisure Anna and Charlie usually had together. And tea under the chestnut tree with Mother and Father Doolin—Mother drying her eyes over some sadness as they ran up to her, and saying something about "it's much too late for legal separation." Mrs. Rorke herself brought out the cake from the kitchen, and it had "God bless Master Charlie" written in pink icing on white. After tea everyone, including Father Doolin, got into the trap to drive with her to *Sainte Famille*.

"Where's Daddy?" Anna asked. "I haven't said good-bye to him."

"He's busy upstairs, darling. Come on, you mustn't be late."

Joe let Charlie drive Princess all the way, except through the gates of *Sainte Famille*, which were an invention of Satan, he said.

It was a happy day, like all Charlie's birthdays. Anna kissed her mother and Joe, shook hands with Father Doolin, and hugged her little brother tight. Then she ran back into school-life, feeling exhilarated and full fed of secure affection for Charlie and for Castle Tory.

Marks had passed off without abnormal fuss, it seemed. (Norrie O'Dowd had written down Anna's for her. She had lost three for silence, one for order and one for exactitude. No scarlet sash to wear in chapel therefore—but she seldom gained one, as her marks for silence were always bad.) Nevertheless, the mood of the school, particularly of the Juniors and the First Preparatories, Anna's class, was palpably feverish. During supper it became clear that news of some unusual kind was going round, or about to go round, in whispers. Funny things *did* happen sometimes on Sunday night, if a great many girls had been out, or in the parlour. Anna guessed that she would hear whatever was going at night recreation; and eating buttered currant bread and drinking milk she dreamt contentedly back over her own day. But she looked about the refectory as she munched, and it occurred to her that Molly Redmond seemed different from usual—red-cheeked, and as if troubled, as if she had no friends.

This was so unusual as to hold Anna's eyes in wonder. Molly Redmond was nearly fifteen now and in Junior Honours. She was in Mother Eugenia's view the cleverest girl in the school, and in Anna's the prettiest. She was rich and gay, and what Mother Mary Andrew called "insubordinate," but there were occasional hints thrown out, as much by some of the nuns as by the school, about her "unfortunate" upbringing, and the "class" she came from. Anna, at twelve, was rather belatedly beginning to grasp the principles of school snobbery, but she was still not very clear about them. During these cool years of emergence from babyhood she felt more affection for the remote and dashing and friendly Molly than for anyone else at *Sainte Famille*. She did not altogether realise that this feeling dated from a night of grief when, through the medium of the verb *finir*, she could be said to have suffered the first bruise on intellectual innocence—but this admiration was, naturally, founded on memory of the older girl's brave kindness to her then. And as she stared now across the refectory to where the others sat at a corner of Latin Table, some speculative sadness trailed over the reminiscent peace of Charlie's birthday.

Night Recreation was usually taken out of doors in the summer term. The school was divided for playtime into three "Recreations." Girls of the senior classes belonged to First Recreation; those of Honours Junior, Second Junior and First Preparatory to Second Recreation; and Second Preparatories formed a small band with the courtesy title of Third Recreation. At midday these groups played, on their own playgrounds, the orthodox games: hockey, basket-ball, tennis. But after supper they danced or took whatever exercise they felt inclined for, in winter—and in summer they loafed at their ease, or sewed, or played desultory rounders, under the great trees. A nun took charge of each group or "recreation," and kept its members within sight and loosely in order.

Mother Agatha was mistress of Second Recreation during this summer term. She was fussy and incompetent, and, particularly out of doors, it was easy to hoodwink her, to enjoy *tête-à-têtes* with one's special friend, or to talk in little groups on forbidden topics.

On this Sunday evening of May the sky, open and infinite, renewed its glory in the radiant breast of the lake; the hills had the dark bloom of grapes, and seemed to breathe and sigh; the impassioned, flaming garden, held in as it was by conventual order and design, seemed for that all the more at breaking point, most feverishly poised—oblated. The perfume of wallflowers was palpable, troubling the air. Fuchsia and sweet geranium foamed along the terrace; and pleasure-cries, the distant songs of bathers and of boaters, rang sadly to the children from the far shore of the water.

But the trees of the convent spread their wide and tranquillising arms, and the great house stood deep-based in reproachful calm, secure in its rule, secure in Christ against the brief assaults of evening or of roses. Girls about to leave, awaiting life, felt this dismissal by the spirit of the house of the unanswered, lovely conflict implicit in the hour; heard the same victory in the voices, beyond the lawn, of nuns taking recreation in Bishop's Walk. And so decided perhaps, tearfully, but in some outlet of relief and holding each other's hands, that *Mère Marie-Félice Gravons de Saint Roche* was calling them.

Younger children also felt this assault from all that lay before their senses—but less conclusively, more naturally. It excited them, made imperative an immediate expression, in no matter what irrelevant direction, of excitement. So that it was impossible this evening for Mother Agatha to gather them into a safe and docile ring. They spread away from her, sitting on the shallow steps above their playground, sitting under the chestnut tree, sitting in forbidden twos on the low window-sills of the playrooms.

Anna walked by the holly hedge with Norrie O'Dowd and Katey Sheehan. These two were thirteen and therefore might sit for Intermediate Preparatory in June. They were foretelling their own results now on the points of holly leaves. "Honours, Pass, Fail; Honours, Pass, Fail." Anna was still ineligible for the public examination—she was twelve—so she did "Nun, Married, Old Maid" on her holly leaf.

She noticed that Molly Redmond was sitting alone with Mother Agatha at the other side of the playground; this was even more odd than her air of trouble noted at supper. Someone always had to be dutiful and hang round the mistress at recreation—but that person was *never* Molly Redmond.

"Is Molly in a row, or something?" she asked Norrie O'Dowd.

"I don't know. Why? Her marks were all right, I think."

"Ursula de la Pole is 'black-out' with her," said Katey. "Jenny Meldon told me during night prayers that Ursula heard something in the parlour to-day—and she can't be friends with Molly any more."

"Well, that's no great loss," said Norrie. "Ursula de la Pole is nothing but a stuck-up notice-box."

"But what did she hear?" asked Anna.

"I don't know. Jennie said she'd find out at Rec."

Ursula de la Pole stood nearby, under the chestnut tree, with a group of girls around her. She was tall and thin, and had bright, coppery hair. She still wore a wire band on her teeth, which made her spit when she laughed, and she was still bad at her lessons. But she was a social power in Second Rec., as was her elder sister Barbara in First. She was snobbish and self-confident, and could be amusing sometimes. Although seeming brainless, she could twist and turn the intelligent Mother Mary Andrew in any necessary direction. She and Molly Redmond had had, from Second Preparatory days, a cat-and-mouse attraction for each other—for Ursula liked wealth, audacity and a well-bred air, which Molly had, and Molly liked Ursula's undeveloped suggestion of glamour, her impudence and her worldly knowledge. It was a friendship of violent quarrels and giggling reconciliations, and was more an expression of frivolity in each than of heart. Molly did Ursula's algebra, and Ursula collected postcards of Gladys Cooper for Molly; they shared a passion for the King of Spain.

"It's something about Molly's father and mother, Jenny says," said Katey Sheehan.

Anna stirred uneasily. Questions of people's fathers and mothers often made serious trouble, and lately she was not sure how her own parents would stand up to the tests of Second Rec. To-day, in spite of the all-covering happiness of being with Charlie for his birthday, she had noted with anxiety that Daddy did not wear spats on Sunday, or stand up every time Mother did—which Colette Bermingham said were the two proofs of being a gentleman. Also, it was probable that a gentleman wouldn't fall asleep at dessert, in the middle of the day.

In fact long ago Ursula de la Pole had been much impressed to learn that Anna's home was called Castle Tory, and often since then her letters, laid in the post-basket on Mother Mary Andrew's table, had excited awe among her friends. "Anna Murphy lives in a castle. Did you know?" The de la Poles, generous before such a correct address, had said patronisingly that that was only natural, since Anna was a lady. "Her *grandmother* was at *Sainte Famille*, you know—not just her mother!"

Anna had been relieved by this judgment when it was pronounced, and glad that there was no fault to be found with Castle Tory. And being sealed as a lady by the de la Poles saved her from the closer assaults of the snobs.

But of late, from reading the novels of Florence Montgomery and Rosa Mulholland, she saw that the life lived in Castle Tory was not castle life, nor was it even as grand as that led by quite ordinary children of "Misters" and "Missuses" in those books. Mother didn't wear a teagown in the afternoon, and she didn't ring a bell if coal had to be put on the fire, and dinner was at two o'clock, and there was no such lovely thing as "schoolroom tea." Besides, you simply couldn't call Delia a "parlourmaid," and Mrs. Rorke wasn't exactly a cook either—she was always out with the chickens, or milking a cow. And as for Daddy—well, he just didn't wear spats, the fact had to be faced. And Castle Tory was really only a house, Anna told herself with anxious love—and hadn't even a conservatory.

In fact Castle Tory was a solid stone farm-house of good design, built in 1850 by Anna's great-grandfather who was lucky enough to hold his land, and eventually to be able to buy it, from a reasonable landlord. It was placed felicitously in the shelter of an old ruined tower from which it took its name, and its owners, the Murphys, were gentlemen farmers, or "squireens," with a traditional *flair* for the breeding of bloodstock. Anna's mother, *née* Condon, was the daughter of a successful country-town ironmonger and timber merchant. So lately, from her reading and from observation of school troubles, Anna had begun to fear that the true facts about her pedigree and her address could not possibly satisfy the de la Poles.

But Molly Redmond—surely she had all the requisite splendours? She lived in a place called Monkstown, near Dublin, and her home was called Rosedene, and had a tennis court *and* a croquet lawn. And she was always grumbling because she couldn't have a bath every day at school, and she had bangles and *eau-de-Cologne* hidden in her desk, and her petticoats were pleated and made of *moiré* silk, and were bought at Switzer's. She had been to London twice for Christmas, and always spent the summer holidays at a place called Knocke. Her mother often sent her angel cake, and sometimes truffles from Mitchell's, and her father had lately come to see her in a motor car, a *Mercédès*, she said it was.

Besides, one day when Colette Bermingham asked her very coolly: "What *is* your father, Molly?" she said he was a turf commissioner. This was a calling no one had ever heard of, and it appeared to be very grand indeed. Norrie O'Dowd thought it was something at Dublin Castle, but the de la Poles said it had to do with the Curragh, they thought, and was an important thing to be. So what could be wrong with Molly's father and mother?

Jenny Meldon came over to them, arm-in-arm with Colette Bermingham.

"Isn't it awful about Molly Redmond?" said Colette.

"But what has happened?" Anna asked.

"Ursula says she'll have to leave——"

"Be expelled?"

"Well, no—but just be asked to leave. Her father and mother—you know. Do you know what her father really is?"

Norrie, Katey, and Anna looked grave, all fearing that their own fathers and mothers were not proof against a de la Pole inquisition.

"No," they said together, uneasily.

"He's a bookie," she whispered vigorously.

Anna winced. She did not know what a bookie was, but it sounded peculiar, and she feared that Jennie's whisper must have carried across to where Molly sat. She did not dare to look in that direction now.

"What's a bookie?" asked Katey Sheehan.

"Ursula says he's a man who takes your money at the races, when you bet—and that he stands on a chair on the racecourse, and shouts and roars. She says it's an *impossible* thing to be. Worse than having a public-house, even."

Norrie O'Dowd winced. Her father was in the wine and spirit trade, though he didn't have a public-house.

"But she *said* he is a turf commissioner," said Katey.

"Well, he may be that too—I don't know—but anyway, he *is* a bookie—and it all came out in the *Irish Times* the other day——"

"Oh, it's simply terrible," said Colette, in giggles of nervousness. "He is in the Law Courts, of all things!—he won't pay for a fur coat Mrs. Redmond ordered, Ursula says—and—but really, one oughtn't to say—ought one, Jenny?"

"Considering Ursula says that Lady de la Pole says she'll remove her and Barbara unless Molly is removed——"

"What was in the *Irish Times?*" Anna asked very anxiously.

"It said that someone said in the Four Courts that Mrs. Redmond ordered the fur coat when she was under the influence—you know—drunk!"

Jenny's eyes danced with horror and delight. The three younger girls huddled together.

"You mean—it said *in the papers* that Molly's mother was *drunk?*"

"Oh, much worse. It let out, you see, that Mr. Redmond is just a very common man—a bookie. That's what Ursula says her mother is so wild about——".

"But isn't it worse to be drunk?" asked Anna.

"It's more of a *sin*," said Colette.

"Yes—but being a bookie is *common*. And Lady de la Pole can't bear there being such a common girl at school with Barbara and Ursula."

"Oh, but wait till you hear this—Lady de la Pole told Mother Eugenia—Barbara and Ursula heard it all, and I must say I think it was exciting for them—Lady de la Pole told old Eugenia that Sir Arthur heard some men talking about the case in the Kildare Street Club—and these men knew Mr. Redmond—he does their bets for them, or whatever it is —and they said that Mr. Redmond is sick of it all—the way Mrs. Redmond drinks, I mean—and that he said to one of them that it was high time he had a legal separation."

The three children to whom this was news, both in fact and in abstract, fell apart now, terribly shocked.

"No, Colette," said Jenny. "Ursula said that Sir Arthur said that Mr. Redmond said that he was going to have a legal separation—even if it *was* a bit late. I heard that distinctly."

Anna's heart was bursting. She saw her mother again as she was this very afternoon under the chestnut tree, saw her drying her sad eyes and heard her say to Father Doolin: "It's too late now for a legal separation." She had wondered then only for a second what she meant. Now she stared in alarm at the phrase as it issued in Colette's violent whisper. "Drunk" too—that was a word which once or twice in the last year had sought admittance to her emotional understanding, and been thrown back by her defences of dreaminess and reluctance. During the Easter holidays she had heard Joe say to Mrs. Rorke, neither knowing she was near them, "and the Master, poor man, as drunk as the divil himself." Jamesy Meagher, too, once told Charlie that Daddy was a drunkard. Charlie didn't exactly know what that was at the time, but he blackened Jamesy's two eyes for him all the same.

But Molly Redmond's mother was drunk when she bought

a fur coat, and her father wanted a legal separation. Two very frightening, shocking things—so bad that Ursula de la Pole couldn't speak to Molly, and Molly would have to leave *Sainte Famille*, Lady de la Pole said. But they were both in *her* family; both these things were known, and mentioned, in Castle Tory.

A girl called Alice Randolph came away from Ursula's group and put her arm round Colette's neck.

"What is a legal separation?" Katey Sheehan was asking timidly.

"It's when married people get permission not to live together any more."

"But do they have to have *permission* for that?"

"Of course they do. Marriage is a sacrament."

"It says somewhere that when people are married they are one flesh," whispered Jenny. "What does that mean?"

Norrie O'Dowd had some literary talent.

"I think it's only a figure of speech," she said.

"Do you, Norrie?" said Alice Randolph with a curious smile. "Listen—do your father and mother sleep in the same bed?"

Norrie's cheeks reddened.

"Yes," she said slowly. And then: "Shut up, Alice Randolph," she added as she turned and walked away.

"No need to be insulted, Norrie," said Alice blandly, "so do mine."

Anna turned away too, not to follow Norrie, but taking an uneasy line of her own about the playground.

Alice Randolph spoke softly to Colette.

"Do you know what it means, Colette—about being one flesh?"

Mother Agatha clapped her hands suddenly and commanded a game of rounders.

"No more of this foolish huddling together," she said. "I can't imagine what you're all whispering about! Come along now, young ladies—a nice, quick game."

Most of the Rec. came round her, reluctantly—only

Ursula and one or two of her friends remaining under the chestnut tree as if they had not heard. Molly Redmond stood near Mother Agatha—lonely and at a loss. It seemed very strange to see her unsure of herself.

"I'll be captain of one side," said Mother Agatha, "and you, Anna Murphy, you're very good at rounders, you be captain of the other. Come on, young ladies—you must stop supporting that tree—we're choosing sides. Quickly, Anna. You choose your first man."

Anna looked around the Rec. and at Molly, usually its restless queen, standing apart from it.

"Molly Redmond," she chose.

Molly smiled at her, a good attempt at the friendly, mocking smile which she gave the "little ones," and crossed to her side.

The choosing went on, and as it came near an end, Ursula and her last adherent strolled over lazily, submitting themselves in boredom for selection.

It was Anna's turn to choose between the two, who alone were left. Ursula was a good runner, and always quickly snapped up by a rounders captain.

"Agnes Moran," Anna chose, and the heavy, lazy girl crossed to join her side, which groaned at the captain's folly.

Anna's choosing of Molly first for her side had been an impulse of love and sympathy, which Molly's smile had suggested she understood; but her rejection of Ursula was not an expression of chivalry, but only diplomatic, for she saw that it would be awkward to have the two on the same side. But as Molly glanced quickly at her again, as if searching her thoughts, Anna felt uneasy. She feared she was accidentally suggesting that she had enough courage to defend the underdog, but in truth she felt that she had not. She reflected uncomfortably that if she were socially secure, like Ursula, she would spring to fight for Molly now—but since, after all, Castle Tory was only a house, since Daddy never wore spats, and got drunk sometimes, since Mother this very day

had spoken of that awful thing, "a legal separation"—oh,
how could anyone so shakily placed as she take up the
cudgels for a *common* person? On the other hand, if what
had just been said showed one to be flying false colours; if
one was actually getting away with the very drawbacks which
were about to ruin Molly—Anna felt guilty and anxious
indeed as she called for lumbering Agnes Moran, and saw
the sneer of astonishment and enmity which flashed to her at
once from Ursula de la Pole.

The latter was chosen by Mother Agatha, and the game
began.

Anna's side went in and she batted first. On an easy
long stroke she got to second den, and Molly followed her to
bat.

Ursula de la Pole could field, but Molly knew how to drive
a ball on a long twist. Inspirited by the general nervousness
and catching for one second Ursula's contemptuous eye, she
sent a fast and savage shot straight down her line.

Ursula flew like a possessed thing to field it; it was a lovely
stroke, and gave Anna easy time to get the whole way home
and make a run. It also stirred Molly to try for third
den in one without getting "burnt"; this was always a
difficult thing to do, and was usually only attempted as an
insult to bad fielding. As Ursula sped for the ball she saw
her enemy's arrogant intention. Frenziedly she fielded, and
hurled herself back, turning quite superbly without losing a
second, to run within aiming distance of Molly. She hurled
the ball with precision. It struck Molly's shoulder as the
latter's hand touched the beech-tree trunk which was third
den. Ursula tripped in her onrush after the ball, and fell
headlong and flat at Molly's feet.

"Burnt! Burnt!" yelled Ursula's side.

"Oh no! She's in!" yelled Molly's.

During the community's evening recreation, Reverend
Mother and one or two other nuns had left Bishop's Walk
and gone with Sister Simeon to the poultry yard, to admire

some chickens which she thought well of, in their "foster-mother." Sister Simeon had, with the years, grown devoted to incubation, and she tended now to despise the natural ways of hens.

Returning from the inspection which it had delighted the old lay sister to conduct, the nuns decided to rejoin their companions, not by the shrubberies and the Lawn Field, but by Rosary Walk and the playgrounds.

"Since the Lord gives you such success, Sister Simeon," Reverend Mother said, praising her gently, "we must take it that He approves of your methods. But myself I feel, very cruelly perhaps, that chickens, like the rest of us, should take Nature's chances."

"And leave us without a pullet to our name; is it, Reverend Mother, in the heel of the hunt?"

Reverend Mother was preoccupied, although she played her part in the Recreation talk.

Just after Marks, while she was writing a postscript to her monthly letter to her father, Mother Eugenia had come to her study, and gossiped.

She had been in the parlour with Lady de la Pole. She was amused by the latter's agitation, but also sympathetic; she had seen the *Irish Times* cutting about the Redmond lawsuit, and she thought that, from the point of view of the de la Poles and the school, it constituted a situation.

Reverend Mother disagreed.

"We knew who Molly was when we accepted her. We also knew, from Mr. Redmond's own lips, of her mother's occasional—weakness. That, you may remember, was the reason why he sent the child to school when she was only eight."

"To be sure. Being a turf commissioner is embarrassing, I suppose, but I quite see we can't all be dukes. Only getting yourself into the papers is another thing—being written about as a *bookie* who won't pay for his drunken wife's fur coat."

"He pays full fees for his daughter, Mother Eugenia—

which, may I be so crude as to point out, is twice as much as Sir Arthur de la Pole does for his."

"*Touchée*. But you have to pay, you know, for being the first generation to get into a school like this. Praise be to God, I often wonder what my poor father would have said if he found that his daughters were at school with his bookie's children!"

"Was *Sainte Famille* exclusively peerage then, in your day?"

"Faith, no. Many's the common article was squeezed in even then. But we did draw the line at shopkeepers—and as for *bookies!* But jokes apart, my dear Reverend Mother— Lady de la Pole is in a state. She says—and I agree with her —that this Redmond thing is most unsavoury, and that it is very unfortunate that Ursula has always been so friendly with Molly, and that she must consult Sir Arthur again, but she really thinks of removing her girls."

Reverend Mother smiled.

"So be it. At the risk of being mistaken for a shopkeeper, I must mention that, as between losing two de la Poles and one Redmond, the school accounts will not register any difference."

"You're a hard nut to crack, Reverend Mother. But don't you see it isn't the two silly de la Poles that matter, but the effect of their removal on people like them, people of their class? Of course, if you really want to settle down to being a National School——"

"I very much want us to be a National School, in the exact sense of the word. I only wish my community would seek to understand it." They both smiled, with caution. "Seriously though, I agree that 'the Redmond thing' is unsavoury, but the unsavouriness is Molly's trouble, *not* Ursula de la Pole's! It's a very unfortunate state of affairs for any child to have to endure through her parents. Poor Mr. Redmond! He's such a kind, affectionate man."

"Then why in God's name doesn't he pay for the fur coat, and keep out of the papers?"

"Oh—one can get maddened. I imagine——"

"Jane de la Pole tells me that her husband heard at the Kildare Street Club that Mr. Redmond is going to have a legal separation, if you please!"

"It might be the best thing——"

"But a man of that class, Reverend Mother? To have the impudence to make such a show of himself! As Jane said—and she doesn't often speak sense—it really does take breeding to live down that kind of thing! But praise be—if we're going to have the bookies going in for it!"

Reverend Mother laughed outright.

"I don't think I need point out to you the irony of that line of attack, Mother Eugenia, because I know that you do in fact put the laws of God before the assumptions of privilege. And in any case, since when have *you* allowed breeding to Jane de la Pole?"

"On my deathbed I'll deny it to the poor, climbing fool, and may God forgive me! But what are we to do with this Redmond scandal?"

"Close our eyes to it, say our prayers, and let the de la Poles go. One Molly Redmond is worth six of them to any school—and if she weren't—still, let the de la Poles go."

"Well, I'm old enough to call you a caution to your face, I suppose. But there'll be trouble in the school, believe me."

"When is there not, about one thing or another? It will pass, Mother Eugenia."

"Aye, child—you're right. And so will the de la Poles—and the Fitzmichaels."

Reverend Mother was touched.

"The Redmonds too," she conceded with a smile.

But although she would not make a mountain of a vulgar little molehill, she was sorry for the sordid gossip that must by now inevitably be sweeping through the school—and she was very much troubled for its victim. And ascending Rosary Walk she pondered on how best to protect Molly in the coming weeks, and how to guard the school against its own *nostalgie de la boue*.

As she turned into the open by the great chestnut-tree, she saw at once, by the disposition of figures on Second Recreation Playground, that the batting had begun, and was at its climax. She stood, unobserved, with her nuns under the chestnut-tree.

Molly leant against a beech-tree trunk, her rigid body proclaiming her right to be there, "in den." Ursula, dirty and bedraggled as if from a fall, stood facing her some feet away. Fielders nearby looked uneasy, and many of the batting side, including Anna Murphy, Reverend Mother noticed, had crossed the home-line, the better to hear whatever was going forward. Mother Agatha, the ball in her hand, looked on from some distance up the field, with an irritated expression on her spotty face.

"I 'burnt you,' " said Ursula.

"Not you!" said Molly. "I was 'in.' "

"That's a lie!"

"But honestly, Ursula, she *was* 'in,' " said a fielder.

"Shut up," said Ursula. "I 'burnt' you, Molly Redmond. Are you going to admit it and get out of that 'den'?"

"Who on earth do you think you're talking to?"

"I'm talking to a *bookie's* daughter—I'm ashamed to say!"

Molly's face was as white now as the death-mask of the Foundress. She closed her eyes and spoke through her teeth.

"I'd hit you—only I'm too strong, and you've just had a fall, trying to field me."

"Trying to field you! As if you could play any game, you cheat!"

"I am *not* a cheat!"

Mother Agatha rang her little pocket-bell and called out nervously:

"What is going on down there, young ladies? No quarrelling, if you please! Do let's get on with the game."

Neither Molly nor Ursula heard her. The girls around stood fascinated.

"You *are* a cheat—but you can't help it, of course. All bookies are cheats, my mother says! But at least you'd think he'd pay for the fur coats your mother buys when she gets—drunk."

The nuns with Reverend Mother stirred uneasily, but she did not move.

Molly had no answer now. She covered her white face with her hands, but held her body straight and untrembling by pressure of her spine against the beech-tree. Reverend Mother thought that she looked very beautiful and piteous then, almost as if crucified.

"Well, why doesn't he pay her bills? Does he even pay for her whisky? Will he pay for his legal separation?"

Anna, drawing nearer, understood that Molly could not take her hands from her face while these things were being said, and it struck her that perhaps she was the only one in Second Rec. who was in a position to understand the true painfulness of this quarrel. She could see how startled the others were. And she thought, like Reverend Mother but more vaguely, that Molly looked very beautiful, so stiff and hard against the tree. Also, her nerves remembered painfully a great kindness of four years ago.

With a great last effort she came and stood between Ursula and Molly.

"Don't, Ursula," she said very shakily. "What you're saying is private, I think."

"Private! It's in the *Irish Times!*"

Anna could not answer this. She felt she had made a bad beginning.

"Oh well—people get drunk, you know. My Daddy does. Honestly."

Ursula was staring at her as if she were some kind of worm. She could hear Molly sobbing now behind her hands. She could hear Mother Agatha jingling towards them. "What is this fuss, young ladies?" She felt unnerved, she felt a fool and

very small. She turned with a cowardly wail to Molly, and
flung her arms about her waist. She spoke to her loudly,
through tears.

"He does—he gets drunk, really! And Castle Tory isn't a
castle at all! And Molly, listen! Mother said to-day it was
too late for a legal separation! I heard her! I know! Things
happen we don't know about! Oh Molly, don't mind Ursula!
Don't cry!"

Mother Agatha did not interfere now, because Reverend
Mother stood, as if by a miracle, in the strange group by the
beech-tree. Her eyes were very bright, and Mother Agatha
thought, with bewilderment, that she seemed as if pleased by
this appalling situation.

She laid her hand on Anna's head.

"Hush, don't cry," she said very gently. "And Molly, you
have nothing to cry for at this minute, my dear child."

Molly, taken from her own rigidity by the assault of
Anna, was bent above her now, in the sweet comfort and
escape of comforting her.

"It is you, Ursula, who have tears to shed for all this that I
have overheard, and you will shed them, my poor child—
believe me." The level English voice rang deeper and more
strongly than usual, and all the children listened with fast-
beating hearts. "For you are here at *Sainte Famille* to learn to
live among your fellows as a Christian and a lady, and that
cannot be learnt by any of us without tears and humiliations.
You have learnt a little about that just now—by your own
yielding to impulses of cruelty and vulgarity which far out-
strip our usual temptations. But you have so deeply
humiliated yourself before us all that I can for the moment
imagine no further punishment. I shall speak to you in
private for your own sake, of the details of your dreadful fit of
self-indulgence. For the moment, since I am sure you could
not bear to face your companions, I suggest that you return to
the house and go to bed—but on your way upstairs perhaps
you will go into the chapel and ask Our Lord to purify your
heart and your lips."

Reverend Mother paused. Ursula flung a wild look of misery at her, and then turned and went quickly, with bent head, towards the house.

Reverend Mother turned to Molly.

"I am very sorry for this," she said simply, and distinctly, for all to hear. "I can only ask you to be so generous as to forgive us all, and perhaps, out of love of *Sainte Famille*, you will do me the honour of not hurting your parents by telling them of this disgraceful episode. Will you do that for us, Molly, although you have been so terribly hurt?"

Molly bowed her head and sobbed, tears streaming.

"Oh yes, Reverend Mother—oh yes, of course."

The childen were surprised there had been no attempt to argue social codes, to preach equality, or to investigate once again what was so rawly exposed—but only grief for Ursula's dreadfulness and this plea for Molly's pardon. They listened in wonder.

"Good night now, children," Reverend Mother said. "Enjoy your rounders, all of you."

She moved away but turned again.

"Good night, Anna. No more crying."

As she rejoined the nuns, Sister Simeon saw tears in her eyes, although she was smiling. On the way back to Bishop's Walk, a verse from Vespers came into her head, and she spoke it aloud with pleasure.

"*Laudate pueri Dominum: laudate nomen Domini. Sit nomen Domini benedictum ex hoc nunc et usque in seculum.*"

The nuns took up the antiphon:

"*A solis ortu usque ad occasum . . .*"

*The Third Chapter*

## NEWS OF DEATH

*Quarant Ore* was usually celebrated at *Sainte Famille* during the last week of April, the tradition being that thus a particular blessing was laid on the work of the last term of the scholastic year; also at that time the garden and greenhouses had fresh beauties to give to the Altar of Repose.

The day preceding the forty-hour feast of the Blessed Sacrament was busy for Reverend Mother. Gardener, sacristan and choir mistress all particularly needed her attention, and the *dépense* and kitchen sisters had to be counselled, as the convent served lunch to the priests who celebrated and assisted at the Sung High Mass with which the Exposition began and ended. Also, Mother Assistant required her to endorse the time-tables of the two all-night vigils sustained in the chapel by the community, and Mother Scholastic required a like endorsement for the names of girls allowed to share this vigil. These two sets of arrangements involved debates on health and precedent; the latter also embraced argument as to whether a pupil's recent conduct merited the reward of rising in the night to keep guard for an hour before the Altar of Repose. To get up in the night during *Quarant Ore* was an adventure and a thrill most passionately desired by the school, but only children over fifteen were eligible for it, and they had to earn it with a period of good behaviour.

Such preoccupations prevented Reverend Mother one day from examining the midday post until late evening. She came to her study desk feeling a little tired, but content with the work of the afternoon. Dusk was advancing, but there was still enough daylight to work by. She laid her restless hands on the pile of letters, and allowed her eyes to fall for an indolent second on the pleasant pathway outside with its ivy-niched stations of the Cross and, beyond, through the gate, on the little black crosses of the convent cemetery.

"Perhaps I shall have to lie there after all," she thought resignedly. "Perhaps I shall never see Brussels again—or father."

She turned to the letters and sorted them.

There was only one for her. It was from Brussels, which pleased her, but she did not know the pale, illiterate handwriting of the envelope. She opened it. It contained two thin, large sheets of Belgian writing-paper, and, within their fold, one of her father's thick and well-filled envelopes, closed, and with the sole word "Helen," written on it in his hand, but not very strongly.

She laid this envelope on the desk and looked at it in suspicion and fear. Helen. Too tired to write more, yet making a great effort to have that one word look strong and normal.

She clenched her hands together.

"*Deus in adjutorium meum intende*," she said.

She unfolded the thin sheet of Belgian paper. It was addressed from home, from her father's house, *Rue Saint Isidore*, No. 4. It was from *Marie-Jeanne*.

Reverend Mother's first thought was that it was curious that this was the first time she remembered to have seen *Marie-Jeanne's* handwriting.

*Marie-Jeanne* was the *bonne à tout faire* at *Rue Saint Isidore*, No. 4. She had always been that, in Reverend Mother's memory, and indeed *Marie-Jeanne's* face was the first that she could find whenever she glanced back at the half-furled impressions of infancy. It was a young and round and rosy face in those first and in many later memories; and now *Marie-Jeanne* must be sixty-seven or sixty-eight; and all the long intervening years had been given to the service of *Rue Saint Isidore* No. 4.

Reverie descended for a minute, but at last Reverend Mother unfolded the first letter she had ever read of *Marie-Jeanne's*.

*Ma pauvre Chou-Chou,—*

*Monsieur s'affaiblit de plus en plus; il ne veut écrire l'adresse sur sa lettre, de peur qu'elle n'arrive pas. Nous avons deux Bonnes Sœurs ici à son chevet, le pauvre—mais il préfère que ce soit moi qui t'écrive, quoique j'aie peu d'instruction. Il n'aime pas les étrangères autour de lui, comme tu le sais bien, mais Monsieur le médecin dit que c'est grave. L'anémie pernicieuse, croit-il. Il dit que le temps est court maintenant, et que bientôt Monsieur rejoindra ta chère Maman. Il rit et bavarde avec moi entre les allées et venues des Bonnes Sœurs. Doux comme un ange, mon grand pauvre—comme tu sais, chérie, comme toujours. Nous causons longtemps le soir ces beaux jours lointains de ton enfance, et nous rions beaucoup en évoquant les gentilles petites façons de notre Chou-Chou. Il ne prie pas, et il ne veut pas voir de prêtre, ou belge ou anglais—et maintenant à la fin j'ose le gronder à cause de cela, pour la première fois de ma vie. Mais il ne fait que sourire, et certes en ce qui le concerne, je ne dois pas avoir de soucis. Sois sûre que le bon Dieu connaît un saint.*

*Hier, en goûtant sa soupe à l'oignon qu'il aime tant, il m'a dit: "Là où je vais, chère vieille, je ne trouverai pas ta soupe à l'oignon." Je répondis qu'on trouve tout ce qu'on désire au ciel. "Ça se peut," dit-il, "mais moi je suis en route pour les Champs-Elysées." Qu'est-ce qu'il voulait dire par cela, Chou-Chou—lui qui n'aimait pas beaucoup Paris?*

*Il ne te reverra pas—mais qu'est-ce ça fait, puisqu'il ne cesse pas de t'aimer avec tendresse, et de te visiter de ses plus douces souvenirs? Reviens néanmoins, chérie, avant que, moi aussi, je parte pour mon dernier voyage, parce que je voudrais apporter de tes nouvelles au ciel, aux chers parents. Monsieur t'embrasse, je le sais bien. Prie de tout ton cœur pour lui. Quand l'heure arrivera je serai à son chevet; je le lui ai promis. Il ne souffre pas; seulement il s'affaiblit rapidement.*

*Mon petit enfant, je t'embrasse toujours. Marie-Jeanne Picart.*

This letter did not really surprise Reverend Mother. Recently she had felt a suppressed but increasing tiredness in her father's faithful monthly letters; *Mère Générale* too, who often spoke of him and quoted from his conversation, had seemed now for many weeks to be preparing her for such news as this of *Marie-Jeanne's*.

She was not shocked. Her father was seventy-seven, and were he younger would have had small difficulty in composing himself to welcome death. Loud exclaiming against the natural and inevitable would have shocked him, he who had usually declined to be shocked by human behaviour. He would die, troubling *Marie-Jeanne* by his refusal of priest and prayer far more than her loyal love would permit her to betray; and although by theologian's terms he was no saint, whatever *Marie-Jeanne* might say, it was impossible to be sure that one so lovingly, so freely learned in the poetry of Christian metaphysics, who could say of himself half-mockingly: "I believe I *worship* George Herbert," would set out for the darkness about which he had never been arrogant, without some last and saving humility of surmise? He never had denied in life his need to keep about him what he called the decent, unpretentious rags of intellectual pride. "Such as they are, Helen, your formal and punctilio-loving God must let me keep them—since I truly haven't another thing to wear." But he could shed them and go naked to eternity if at the last that seemed to him the truest. The humiliation would not trouble him, for he was too well trained in thought to be ashamed of shedding error. So at the last it was impossible to guess if he would be consistent and ask passage for his Elysian Fields, or shamelessly set a last-minute sail for the Christian Heaven of his fathers, where he might talk with Donne and Bishop King.

That, however, would be his secret. And she, thank God, could pray for him—leaving all other offices, alas, to *Marie-Jeanne* and the *Bonnes Sœurs*.

She could not read his letter yet. She held it in her hands and thought of him writing it, wearily, awkwardly, in bed— to go with *Marie-Jeanne's*.

She thought of the two, perhaps now at this very hour, in the half-light, finding some peace from the nurses to talk together. "*Ces beaux jours lointains de ton enfance.*"

They rose before her, on a tide of sorrow. And it astonished her suddenly, platitude though it was, to consider that their dream-edged, physical setting of forty-five years ago, of her first memories, was still in actual, tangible existence; unaltered by any spiritual change or loss. Were she to go back now to say farewell to him, she would not have to contemplate his house with the questioning eyes of return—for a part of her had never left it, and its life was of the simple kind that does not change. A narrow, modest house, detached, like each of its neighbours, in a narrow, leafed-in garden. Guelder roses budding over the tall, squeaking, difficult, secretive gate. ("Everything that a gate should be," he used to say.) Small blue and yellow tiles coming loose on the path to the front door. The pale blue white-wash of the house, the faded grey-blue shutters; the screen of white iron arabesques over the glass panels of the door; the gentle bell, and *Marie-Jeanne's* cat among the flower-pots on the balcony.

Mere nothings, mere externals, but alive as much in her, she noticed now, as in their actual place—and drawing her in, for ever as once, to the sweet life of being his child, and pleasing and loving him.

Her mother had been a scholarly woman, and had always seemed old to Helen. Even when she died, in Helen's twelfth year, of pneumonia, and people said that she was thirty-two and six years younger than her husband, Helen still thought of her as old, and though she grieved for her death, could not feel that it was an outrage against the sense of life.

She saw now, had seen long since with bitter sympathy, that her mother's death seemed natural, and she herself seemed very old to a child, because she did not wish to live. She was broken inside; something was wrong which she must have understood only too well could not be put right—and she was content to die.

Nevertheless, whatever the private sorrow, Helen remembered the years while her mother still lived as mainly harmonious, and certainly never witnessed any misunderstanding or harshness between her parents. When Henry Archer was away from home—he often lectured in provincial universities, and in France and Holland; also he went on occasional journeys to England, to buy books, to do researches, or to see his publisher—the child thought her mother was more troubled and melancholy than at normal times. But she talked more freely then to Helen of England and of Cambridge, and the child sensed her perpetual loneliness for English life and English friends.

Helen had no clear memories of Cambridge. She knew that she was born there in 1861 and that her parents came to the Continent in 1864. She had some confused impressions of an apartment in Paris in that year, and later of life in a little grey house in Bonn. In the summer of 1866, when the garden was a neglected tangle of roses, guelder roses, and geraniums, the Archers had taken possession of *Rue Saint Isidore* No. 4 and of *Marie-Jeanne*.

Once Helen asked her mother why they had left Cambridge. She knew that her father had distinguished himself there, and had been made a Fellow of St. John's when he was only twenty-three.

"Why did he give up being a Fellow, after two years?"

"He had to, darling—to marry me. It was a mistake, probably—but I was only nineteen and did not understand the issue. And he was quite extraordinarily young for his age then—completely a scholar." Her mother smiled very tenderly. "My father loved him like a son, and thought nothing should stand in the way of our marriage. Besides, we had enough money between us—and Henry's books were going to bring him immediate fame. Still, it was a mistake—a sacrifice of him which we should *not* have made."

"But then—I wouldn't have been born?"

Her mother laughed.

"That would have been terrible, my darling. Still, he made a mistake in sacrificing his Fellowship."

"But you didn't leave Cambridge until I was three. Why did you?"

"Well, many of your father's ideas began to change about that time. When we were married he was very much a boy, far too young for his age. But when he did grow up he did it suddenly. He became rationalistic and sceptical—I'll tell you when you're a little older what those words mean, Helen, or perhaps Daddy will explain them himself. And he began, rather belatedly, to read the Greeks, and neglect his own work. Well, in general, things went wrong somewhat—and your father found he did not care for English life. It was thought best to live abroad for a while. Some day we'll go back, perhaps."

"Do you think so, Mother? I don't."

"Maybe not. I'd like to go back."

"I wouldn't. I like it in Belgium."

When Helen was seven she started to attend the day school at *Place des Ormes* nearby, up the curving leafy hill. Her mother had been received into the Catholic Church during the Archers' sojourn in Bonn, and through attending daily Mass at the convent chapel she became acquainted with some members of the *Place des Ormes* community, and found affection and kindness there which were to be precious to her for the remaining years of her life. Henry Archer also liked the nuns, and they arranged for him to give a lecture to the school each term on English literature. So when Helen began her education there, the entire household of *Rue Saint Isidore* was friendlily associated with the convent.

The Archers were not rich. For a reason unexplained to Helen, but which she guessed in later life, her maternal grandfather, cutting off association with his daughter and son-in-law when they left Cambridge, had also cut off the former's annuity of one hundred pounds a year. So they had only Henry Archer's inheritance of two hundred pounds a year, in addition to what he could earn. But in Brussels he earned a good deal as coach and tutor to university students, military cadets and the diplomatic corps. Also with lectures and with occasional advances for his learned works on the English poets of the early seventeenth century, he kept his household in modest dignity, and he collected a library that overflowed from room to room.

He and his wife devoted themselves with solicitous tenderness to their only child, but so real and quick-witted was their care that it was only when looking back to it from her experience of middle age that Helen could measure it with the gratitude it deserved. And then appreciation was touched with pain, for she saw in such success with her the reverse of a more important failure. They had injured each other in youth and ignorance, so, snatching some wisdom, they would salvage their child.

Certainly they made her happy, and saw her daily happiness. But what they did not see—or perhaps her mother did—was that, granted the thousand light subtleties of their love; granted the ease of open books and open minds, the free, simple traffic with kitchen and garden, with priest, ambassador and milk-boy; granted *Marie-Jeanne* and the cats and all the lovingly kept feasts of family life and of the Flemish calendar—the little girl they loved was happy not merely in all these things and in her natural love for father and mother, but because she found in her father an accidental delight which had no necessary spring in filial feeling, but rose from the privilege of intimacy with someone whom she found pleasing and satisfactory far beyond what was necessary in a father, or in any fellow-creature.

When she was only six and seven she often thought, as she walked up and down the garden path repeating after him: "Art thou poor, yet hast thou golden slumbers?"; as she heard him playing the harmonica with *Marie-Jeanne* and trying to learn her thousand Flemish songs that made him laugh and that he said, while mother frowned, were far too wicked to translate to a little girl; or as he sat her down in a straw-seated chair in *Sainte-Gudule*, and kneeling before her, told her carefully and lovingly of Charles V and the Order of the *Toison d'Or*, and of the Emperor's love of William the Silent, and of the day when, in that very church, in hope and pride he confided the Netherlands to Philip, his son—often at such times she thought, while listening to him with full attention, how lucky, lucky, lucky I am to know him like this, and to have him, of all people, for a daddy!

Before she became a pupil at *Place des Ormes*, her parents shared the giving of her first lessons—but always, until she left him to become a nun, her father continued to teach her English literature and history—and not as parents usually teach, at irregular hours and intervals, and either as a joke or in parental irritation, but with an exacting vigour, method and love which she received from no other teacher, and was never to observe again in her work among teachers.

He worked her very hard and he was often impatient, but he poured imaginative knowledge all about her; he gave her an individualistic, sunny access into life, and so, as she thought, into herself. He never punished her. He seemed to fear discipline, or at least to be uncertain of its forms, but he allowed it, without dispute, in the hands of those who believed in it.

"Punish her if you must, Catherine," she heard him say to her mother once, when neither knew she was listening, "but do not ask me to witness punishment of her or anyone."

Helen had been puzzled, looking out at them from the rustic summer-house, by the curious expression which flitted over her mother's face, when he said that. Almost as if she were secretly sneering. But the impression passed in the sustained tenor of family kindness.

In childhood she thought her father very beautiful. It always delighted her to come on the sight of him suddenly and realise, always with new pleasure, that he was different from other men, stronger and bigger, with curly, silky hair and eyes that shone like stars. And studying with him, or reciting poetry seated on his knee, she noticed that his face grew more beautiful as one drew nearer to it. This was not true of other faces, and she told him of it one evening, but he laughed at her impatiently.

He had many friends; most of his pupils sought his friendship, but unless they could be content with his austere and modest ways of entertainment and of pleasure they couldn't have it. Very early Anna learnt his passion for simplicity and quiet, and his need for long hours alone, in his study or the garden. Even if he were not working he often required, for many hours at a time, not to be spoken to by anyone save *Marie-Jeanne*. He liked also to sit in the *Café Flamand* at the bottom of the hill and talk with *Monsieur Robert* or with *Armand*. It was a very humble *café*, a *bistro*, and he said it was his second home. He liked Helen to come and find him there, and join the talk with *Monsieur Robert*—although her mother did not think it a suitable practice. However, as everyone in the neighbourhood knew "*la petite Anglaise*," and as her father was the friend of all, provided only they gave themselves no airs, she came to no harm on her emancipated expeditions down the hill to the *Café Flamand*. And her mother smiled and said: "Father is the Socrates of our suburb, darling. But I wonder what *rôle* he has in mind for you?"

Her mother died in the winter preceding Helen's twelfth birthday. There was a short illness which did not seem grave; then a night of hurrying messengers, night-lights and prayers. The little bell in the street when *Père Bernard* brought the Host; *Marie-Jeanne's* arms around her in the cold dawn; her father standing by the bedstead with bent head: "Good-bye, dear Catherine."

That was all.

Reverend Mother could remember that bereavement in its details now; could recall with love the warm grieving of *Marie-Jeanne;* could feel her father's pensive and uneasy sadness too, and the sustained quiet of the house. But in remembering herself of that time she could revive more clearly her own sense of remorse that grief should be so temperate than any remembrance of grief itself. She remembered feeling guiltily relieved, and shocked, to discover that life went on as before at *Rue Saint Isidore* when her mother was gone; she remembered her relief that rooms and habits remained as they had been. She had feared there would be changes, perhaps even a change of house, which she would have found insufferable, but might have thought correct, a gentle tribute to the lost one. But she was glad to see no thought of such sentimentality in her father's face. Yet she winced now, after many years, at realising again how little he had loved her mother, and how much, how bitterly at the end, her mother had loved him.

She had never known anyone refuse him love, or at least the response of good will. Yet now, at the end of so good, and so bad, a life, he lay dying in forgotten solitude, with only two stranger nuns to minister to him, and an old *Marie-Jeanne* to make him smile and give him courage.

But he would exclaim against her "with only." She could hear his protest: "What else could a sane man want, Helen, except to die quietly in his own quiet house, at seventy-seven? With two good strangers to keep the dreadfulness of decay out of sight, and with a faithful good cook to make the last broth, and pray me off. With debts all paid and work all done, and knowing that a few friends down the hill will mourn, and will come to the funeral—Helen, what possible other way would you ask me to die?"

That is what he would say, generously. Stressing to the end the contentment of his days—although in fact they had been strung with punishment, which he detested, and never meted out. For, in fairness it could be said that fate had punished him just before he was awake to it, by letting him give up his fellowship and marry her mother before he had discovered what in fact existence meant or held for him. Thereafter, she guessed, in his first pain and excitement of self-discovery he fell into some offence against society, some stupid sin, which made it necessary, or at least wise, for him to live in exile. There were repetitive small punishments in this: the married state, undertaken in darkness and gracefully upheld, to the world at least, in light; the penalisation in England, by chill silence or cold regrets, of his published work; the loss of background and early friends. And she too, in her turn, was to punish his sin. She, towards whom he was conscious of no iota of wrong or disillusion, was

144

to turn in terror from his love, and from all he had thought and implanted, and leave him to the lonely years, to the days of loss and decline—alone, with *Marie-Jeanne*. Alone with the old *bonne* now, waiting for death, and laughing with tenderness while he waited, over *"ces beaux jours lointains de ton enfance."*

The bell rang for Evening Meditation.

Reverend Mother rose, relieved by the obligation of obedience.

She folded *Marie-Jeanne's* letter and placed it with her father's in her desk.

"Not yet, Father," she said gently. "Not yet. There will be time."

But throughout that evening and that night there was no time, or she believed that there was none, to read his letter.

"When *Quarant Ore* has begun, I'll be ready to read his letter," she assured herself.

It was as if she had to keep a kind of vigil for it. And indeed she might be said to have knelt immobile and seeking grace, all night, before her memories of him. Wrestling with her unresolved grief and fear.

While she sat in silence at supper and listened to a young novice's bad reading of the Imitation; while she laughed and sewed at Recreation, and led the Community at Night Prayers in the darkened tribune of the chapel; even when alone at last in her cell, at her own *prie-dieu* and as she prepared herself for sleep—she managed to hold him at bay, and even half forget that he was dying, that any one of the passing hours might certainly be his hour.

But when she was in her narrow bed at last, in darkness, she was assaulted by the necessity once more at last to relive a scene which, since entering religion, she had not allowed her conscious mind to rest on. By facing it at last, and asking God's mercy for him and for her hard, uncomprehending self, she might somehow help his dying hours, and bridge, at least to the easing of her own heart, the years of pain

145

that left her now so far from him in his last hours of human need.

Some months after her mother's death, Reverend Mother at *Place des Ormes* had suggested to Henry Archer that it would be wise to allow Helen to become a boarder at the school. As it was necessary for him to be away from home often, and as he could not bear to impede *Marie-Jeanne's* legitimate freedom—she liked sometimes, for instance, to go home to Malines for a day and to come back drunk on the midnight train, and he wholly approved of these outings—he agreed to Reverend Mother's suggestion. But the separation was not a harsh one. Helen spent the whole of every Sunday at home, and often during the week was allowed to run down the curving, leafy street and spend an hour in the kitchen with *Marie-Jeanne*, or in the study or garden with her father. And he and *Marie-Jeanne* were also favourites at the convent, so that the gentle life of *Rue Saint Isidore* flowed all about the girl still, and was only enhanced, made clearer, by this slight lengthening of perspective.

The sense of companionship with her father deepened rapidly as she entered adolescence. She was considered a very pretty young girl, and she was happy and successful at school; also she loved the nuns, and was sincerely pious and believing. But she had no thought of taking the habit, and often laughed quite frankly over her lack of religious vocation. Indeed, on the contrary she sometimes thought, with real pleasure, that there was very much of her father in her. Beginning at this time, as she thought, to understand his terms, she often amused herself by thinking guiltily that she was, to some degree, "a pagan."

But his was a frugal, honourable paganism. She learnt many better things of him during girlhood than that he had, for her, a shattering charm. She learnt that he was an almost primly honest man, and that he was very kind in practical things. She learnt his mania for simple people—and though in later life she saw that this may have been a defence, a flight by one who had been hurt by the sophisticated and was afraid of them, may even have been, she thought with grief, an escape from the sterile, intellectualised devotion of her mother—yet it was to her a very sweet and pleasing characteristic. Sometimes in her religious life it occurred to her that it was probably his doing that she was more successful and at ease with lay-sisters than with choir nuns.

He took her on journeys of pleasure and instruction sometimes in vacation, and taught her how to travel, not at all as a young lady of her time and class should do, but as a person of frugal means who could not waste money on inessentials. He showed her how to be comfortable in third and fourth class carriages, and how to enjoy the chance food and chance company of journeys; he taught her to be unself-conscious, and to overcome the pudic suspicions and fears of young ladies in encounter with strange men.

Without mercy he fed and loaded her mind. She was free to read anything, but she had to read the works he prescribed and discussed with her. He took her all over Belgium and into Holland and the Rhineland in pursuit of art and architecture and history. He took her through Normandy one spring, through Brittany another. When she was sixteen he took her for eight weeks to Paris.

"This is going to be real work, Helen," he warned her. And it was. Often she jibbed during those weeks, and asked for mercy.

"What for?" he would say.

"Oh, to loaf a bit, Daddy."

"You haven't the right to, yet," he would say. "Wait till you've grown a soul to invite."

"Information won't give me a soul!"

"No—but it may manure one, my darling. Anyway, believe me, there's no defence like a full mind."

"Why should I need a defence?"

He laughed.

"Helen—I thought you were at least a *bit* of a theologian!"

But she was never afraid of him or afraid to resist him;

and she was never bored by his exactions. Sometimes, if her interest in some picture, building or poem did not satisfy him, or if she would not read some book which he impatiently desired her to read, he lost his temper without a blush and abused her extravagantly.

"You remind me of *Marie-Jeanne* now," she would say to him.

"Well, I could remind you of worse. *Marie-Jeanne* has a head on her shoulders."

Still, it puzzled her that the only people he ever abused were herself, *Marie-Jeanne* and *Monsieur Robert* of the *Café Flamand*. She asked him why that was—because he was quite maddeningly gracious and gentle with the ordinary run of acquaintances.

"Well, there's nothing to get abusive over with those others; who wants to fight about inessentials? I'm fond of you three, so you have the power to get me shouting."

She reflected sadly then that he had never shouted at her mother.

They walked miles each day in Paris, for economy's sake; they ate very well in *bistros*, talking with the *habitués* and taking down recipes at the dictation of *patronnes*, with which to infuriate *Marie-Jeanne* on their return to Brussels. They went, unflaggingly and as cheaply as they could, to theatres and concerts; once they went to a carefully chosen music-hall, but Helen did not really like it, and was troubled.

"I'm sorry, darling," he said. "That was a mistake. But you see, I'm terrified of your thinking I want you to be a prig."

This was the summer of 1877, the year of the death of Thiers, early days of the Constitution of the Third Republic; edgy, nervous days with Marshal MacMahon, monarchical and clerical, still in the Presidency, the statue of Strasburg crêpe-hung in the *Place de la Concorde*, and Gambetta bitterly rallying all true republicans. It was a lively and instructive time in Paris, with "much to be examined," Henry Archer said. And in the *bistros* they made friends with

148

artisans and clerks who were eager to talk politics. So occasionally Henry gave Helen a rest, leaving her for an evening with the family of their hotel-keeper in *Rue St. Jacques*, and went with his chance friends to political meetings or to spend some hours in informal *café* debate. Also, once or twice by day he allowed her to go shopping in charge of *Madame* of the hotel. But these separations were rare, and almost all their days in Paris were spent together. They went home in mid-September with no money left, but the richer by a great many second-hand books, a few modest purchases of clothes, some presents for *Marie-Jeanne* and a sense of great, reciprocal contentment.

"We'll do something cheap and boring next year—walk through the blessed old *Ardennes* perhaps—because the following summer you'll have left school; you'll be eighteen —and I think it will be time to tackle Italy. We must save up for that."

"Oh, Daddy!"

"But mind you, if you found Paris hard work—and you are looking thin on it, Helen—I dare not think of the trouble you'll give me in Italy."

They saved, happily and erratically, in the next two years, for that journey to Italy—which they were never to take.

Reverend Mother, trained to lie still in bed, composed as if to the restriction of a coffin, turned about now in sharp distress. She dreaded, almost madly, what lay in wait for the next movement of her thoughts, so she escaped a minute into the present, and prayed for him as he now was, prayed that the horny good love of *Marie-Jeanne's* old hands, so worn in work for him, would warm his dying hands in this dark hour and remind him, for as long as possible, of the human sympathy which he had always given, and needed, so abundantly. *Marie-Jeanne* would pray aloud, in her strong Flemish accent, her prayer of every occasion, which she had repeated over and over at her mistress's bedside, and repeated alike, all through life, when the pancakes went wrong or the stove smoked or her head ached after a day of pleasure at Malines: *"Que le nom du Seigneur soit béni. Que la volonté de Dieu, toujours juste, toujours aimable, soit exaltée pendant toute l'éternité."* Reverend Mother knew that while human sound could reach her father, that old prayer of *Marie-Jeanne's*, which he loved to pick up and shout with her whenever he heard her beginning it, would make him smile with love, and trap him into his old chanting. So maybe—she smiled in the darkness—maybe he would go with the Christian words on his lips, tricked into Heaven by *Marie-Jeanne*.

But that was what *Etienne Marot* had said. She winced from the name that was so famous now, and that she could never hear pronounced in all these years without pain.

One sunny day she was reading in the summer-house, and *Etienne* was lying in the grass at Henry Archer's feet, his English lesson over. And *Marie-Jeanne*, overtaken by some misfortune in the kitchen, began her clamorous prayer, which her father took up in loud plain chant: *"Que la volonté de Dieu, toujours juste, toujours aimable . . ."*

Etienne laughed and chanted too. And then:

"Take care," he said. "*Marie-Jeanne* will trick you into Heaven yet, on that."

"Ah, it isn't so easy," her father had said. "I honestly don't think God is as simple as *Marie-Jeanne* hopes."

*Etienne Marot*, world-renowned and getting old. Since she was fifty-one this year, he would be sixty; living in New York now, very wealthy, very civilised. Once or twice in an illustrated paper sent to some sick nun or child, Reverend Mother had come upon photographs of his strange, melancholy face. One of the greatest violinists in the world, people had said for many years; and later, perhaps the greatest of musical conductors.

But she had known him as an obscure young man from a Brussels slum, an artisan's son, put to all conceivable shifts to achieve his goal of musicianship. A worker of incredible endurance, her father said. Certainly a young man sure of where he was going, so sure that, to be ready for the world, long before he gave his first concert in Brussels, he came to Henry Archer for lessons in English.

Quick-witted, graceful, shabby, and with that indifference to non-essentials which her father always sought in friends; ravenously eager for any crumb of culture that his English tutor might bestow—and he was not stinted. And in return giving a world hitherto not open to Henry Archer—his world of music.

He became the friend of the house, even of *Marie-Jeanne*, who thought, and told him, that he was born too low to be on the level he was allowed with her master and young mistress, but that since *Monsieur* was mad and an angel, "*enfin, que la volonté de Dieu, si juste, si aimable . . .*"

*Marie-Jeanne* told Helen that there could be no doubt that *Monsieur* intended, later on, to marry her to *Monsieur Etienne*.

The *bonne* considered this an unwise plan on many counts since the young man was poor and low-born, and, she thought, a bit too sure of himself in a gentleman's house. However, she conceded his industry and that music was a very beautiful and satisfactory thing.

Helen thought nothing of this plan—and indeed did not believe in it. She had no intention of marrying anyone, for many years, and was sure that her father did not wish her to do so. Also, she could only laugh at the idea of his choosing a husband for her. Her father, so obsessed by the beauty of personal freedom, and the human obligation of non-interference! She said all this to *Marie-Jeanne*, who smiled and said that a father was a father, and knew his duty.

Helen was peculiarly happy just then. She had grown extremely attached to *Place des Ormes;* she worked well and her father became more than ever interested in her mental growth. He thought she showed some potentialities for scholarship, and talked of the possibility of her following the Modern History School in Brussels University. He explained that for her to do so would be unusual and perhaps embarrassing, but in spite of moments of panic, she was not daunted by his talk of the audacious step, and she began to look forward to her university studies as part of a wide, dreamy plan of life after her own heart.

She noticed beauty in her surroundings at this time. She was shy of the pleasure she took in the old slanting square, *Place des Ormes*, but in every weather and every light it pleased her. Its houses were shabbily baroque, grouped on three sides under elm-trees, behind wrought-iron gates. The stone fountain, shabby too, was ponderously beautiful. The cab that stood where the horse-tram stopped, on the west side, where the landscape fell towards Brussels, was nearly always there, for very few dwellers in *Place des Ormes* took cabs. Under rain or sun, and whether it was empty or mildly astir, Helen felt a significant melancholy in this square, in the stand-off shabbiness which even the trees expressed, and in the sharp descending curve of *Rue Saint Isidore*, so shabby and stand-offish too, with its smaller ancillary houses.

She admired much of Brussels, and had been enchanted by some of the places her father had taken her to visit; she thought and read very eagerly of what she would find in Italy, and *afterwards* Heaven knew where else under the sun —but again and again as her own suburb surprised her with undramatic variations of its character, she felt, as it were, an admonition in her heart, that beauty, the necessary root of the matter, was here in a particularly good, unassuming form. She sometimes thought, with a premonitory uneasiness not altogether welcome, that she would not feel again before any of the world's sights as sharp an æsthetic pleasure as these schoolday mornings and evenings gave her now in her own suburb.

One October afternoon she sat by the fountain with her father. They were waiting for the horse-tram to come up the hill, turn, get its breath, and take them down to Brussels, where they were meeting *Etienne* and would attend a concert. Helen was not feeling very much in the mood for *Etienne*, but she could not grudge him his right to take them to concerts. While they waited they bought ice-cream wafers from *Matteotti*, who was passing in his cart. And as they licked them up, her father talked of Siena to her, whence

*Matteotti* came. He described the great square of the town, and went on to generalise about accidents of design, of perfection and its oddness and elusiveness.

"I expect you'll think me mad," Helen said, "but you know I think that this square, all this round here, is just what you're saying—accidentally perfect."

He looked at her with attention.

"Are you saying that loosely? I mean, just the way a girl gushes, or do you mean anything?"

"Daddy, when do I gush? No, I mean that practically every day I think that this bit of Brussels is just one of those lucky things—perfect—and no one sees it, except me."

He gave the quick, unsteady laugh that meant he was more moved than amused.

"Heaven bless your impudence! Why do you think your parents chose to live here—when they had Europe to choose from?"

"Why, have you always liked it as much as I do, Daddy?"

He looked about him.

"Since one must live somewhere, I've always liked this place enough to live and die in. And that's saying something. I think, like you, that it's perfect. Some obscure man, or men, designed this central bit about 1680. I suspect they were Spaniards, or sons of Spaniards. Anyway, never mind—they did everything right, even to the spacing of the trees, even to leaving this side open to the west. And the next century, following on with our little streets, behaved with its customary good sense. So there it is. I'm glad we agree about it, Helen. I often wondered if you liked it."

"I don't believe I thought it out until just lately."

"Your mother and I would have preferred to live in this square—but a whole house would have been crazy, though they are cheap—they are let in apartments now, of course, but some of them weren't when we first came. But we thought you ought to have a house, and a back door and so on."

"I love our house. Still, *Sainte Famille* are lucky.

Fancy having five of those exquisite houses to live in!"

"Aye—but fancy having to be a nun to live in them!"

She did not answer; she smiled towards the convent, pondering the suggestion he had raised.

"You're not thinking you wouldn't mind *being* a nun—are you, Helen?" he asked her sharply. "If I thought that, I believe I'd turn tyrant and take you away from *Sainte Famille* right now."

"No, Daddy," she said. "I don't want to be a nun. I do think it is a very good life, but—I don't want it."

He smiled.

"Actually, you frightened me for a minute," he said.

The tram was ready to start, and they mounted it.

Helen was not sure that she was quite truthful in saying to her father that she did not want a nun's life—but at least such untruth as she suspected was directed as much to deceive herself as him. For she was sometimes afraid of her own erratic, moody understanding of the rightness of the religious life, visitations of which she turned from with emphasis again and again. And she was glad of what she had always known without his own brief expression of it—her father's horror of such a vocation for her. In sympathy with him, and in proud desire to be the daughter he desired and saw in her, she shared his horror, and felt safeguarded by his reliance on her, and his apparent need of her. Besides, instructed by him, steeped in his poets, she believed in human love, and felt in her English blood the rightness of compromise in the English mystics. And if love had somehow failed her father and mother, perhaps her love, and the development of her life on his principles of goodness, perhaps above all one day, her children would make up to him for whatever had gone wrong in a life which should have known completion in itself.

So, vaguely, she argued herself away from the threat of vocation. But perhaps her soul always knew that these arguments were beside the point, and that the issue was quite simple—that it lay between him and the only thing that measured up to him in her mind—the religious ideal. But all her *feelings* gave victory to him—and the other thing remained only an intellectual temptation, a shadow moving stealthily about her brain. And she was not afraid of it; it would pass, as her need and love of him could not. So it followed she would not be a nun, and when she said she did not want that life, she had spoken truly.

It was strange, after thirty-three years in religion, to lie in the dark in her cell and recall each foolish *nuance* of that adolescent flight towards life and her father, and away from God. Sharply indeed her course had been reversed. But perfection, or the sight of it, is nevertheless not to be won, as a child might know, by the clamour of egoism, the display of wounds, the reactions of vanity. It seemed indeed that spiritual victory can only be gained by those who have never lost it, who set out for purity already pure-intentioned. It was hardly fair to make the difficult thing impossibly difficult. "The land of spices, something understood." She remembered her mother smiling over that line one day not long before her death, and saying that whereas to her the image was odd and surprising, "yet your father accepts it with his whole imagination—only, at the same time, he happens to have no real use for it. Isn't that ironic?"

Helen had been puzzled.

"All I mean, darling," her mother went on, "is that religious understanding is really a gift, like a singing voice—and can be wasted."

Life among nuns had clarified this observation, and had made her ponder, sometimes amusedly, sometimes in sad longing, the poet's line.

Far off on the Grand Staircase a clock struck one. At half-past four the community rising bell would ring, as usual; and *Sœur Antoine* would knock on her door and call out: "*Loué soit Jésu*," and she would answer, as all these years, from childhood at *Place des Ormes*: "*Béni soit le Seigneur à jamais*." And another day, the first day of *Quarant' Ore*, would have begun.

But she could not seek sleep.

She struck a match and lighted a candle at her bedside. She felt that she must pray. She rose and put her black chapel cloak about her and knelt at her *prie-dieu*. She considered the Crucifix on the wall above her, and sought with her whole will to find the formal pattern of meditation.

But the past would not lie still.

And suddenly its last scene, the last scene of youth, of innocence, filled the austere dim cell.

It was June and brilliant weather. Helen's last term as a boarder at *Place des Ormes*. At the end of July she was going to Italy with her father and they would not return until mid-October, when his autumn classes, and her university studies, began. This brilliant prospect dissipated much of the sentimental melancholy she felt at giving up her schoolgirl life at *Sainte Famille*, yet she savoured the last term with particular affection.

One Saturday evening many of the girls who lived in Brussels had gone home for the week-end, and there was a pleasant sense of indolence through the convent. Helen, after having played some tennis, amused herself by helping *Mère Alphonsine* to arrange the flowers for the chapel. The next day was the Sunday within the Octave of *Corpus Christi* and *Mère Alphonsine* was dissatisfied with the colours of the roses *Sœur Josèphe* had sent in from the garden. She wanted more red ones, she said, and *Sœur Josèphe* said she couldn't have what wasn't there, and that she was never satisfied.

Helen said that unless *Marie-Jeanne* had taken them all to Malines that day, whither she had gone for her nephew's First Communion, there were red roses in the garden at *Rue Saint Isidore*. *Mère Alphonsine* commanded her to go and fetch them.

She went very happily, as she was, hatless and in tennis shoes. Glad of the sun and the lovely evening, and the chance of a word with Daddy, if he was at home.

The gate squeaked and let her in unwillingly, as usual. She never rang the front-door bell, even when *Marie-Jeanne* was at home to hear it; she always went straight through the garden to the ever-open kitchen door.

Her father's study was at the back of the house, above the kitchen. It had a long, wide balcony of wrought iron which ran full across the wall and ended in an iron staircase to the garden. This balcony made a pleasant, deep shade over the flagged space by the kitchen door, where *Marie-Jeanne* often sat to prepare vegetables, or to have a sleep. Traffic was free up and down these stairs; and Henry Archer was not formal about access to his study, even when he was working, even when he was having a silent and solitary mood.

Helen glanced in at the empty kitchen, scratched the cat behind the ears, and hoped that *Marie-Jeanne* wasn't getting too drunk at Malines. Then she ran up the iron stairs and along the balcony to the open window of her father's study.

She looked into the room.

Two people were there. But neither saw her; neither felt her shadow as it froze across the sun.

She turned and descended the stairs. She left the garden and went on down the curve of *Rue Saint Isidore.*

She had no objective and no knowledge of what she was doing. She did not see external things. She saw *Etienne* and her father, in the embrace of love.

Now in her dim and holy cell she could recall no more of the hours of that summer day. She did not know how long or where she walked, when she returned to *Sainte Famille,* or what she said of her lack of roses. She only remembered that later, after many days and very gradually, like an organism stirring again, distorted, after paralysis, her spirit moved and spoke again—unrecognisably.

She remembered her savage awareness of total change within, and the cunning which she used to hide it, and her delight in that cunning. She saw now that her self-control was like that of a mad woman, and that she might in fact have been mad. She slept hardly at all, for many nights.

She remembered the long, bright, summer nights. She remembered the discipline with which she wept in her moonlit cubicle, without movement, without sob, drinking the tears. She remembered how the picture of *Etienne* and her father, stamped on her brain, became luridly vivid in those nights, and would not leave the stretched canvas of her eyelids. She remembered how it changed, became dreadful, became vast or savage or gargoyled or insanely fantastical; how it became a temptation, a curiosity, a threat, and sometimes no more than piteous, no more than dreary, sad. She remembered how she prayed to be delivered from it, to be blind, to be stupefied—and how it still moved and glittered evilly, faceless, nameless, and then again most violently identified—and every night at last, such sleep as she found came only through struggle with this image, and was broken by its glare.

She was cunning. Her normal health was so good that she could walk and talk and half-sleep in a blasting trance like this for many days without its telling very remarkably in her face or her behaviour. And by the time her frenzy, of which she could not allow a hint to appear to any living soul, might have become incontinent, she had grown up, she thought; she had seen what it all meant and what she had to do to escape from it for ever.

Within those days of enclosed insanity, she saw and understood, with much cold, true sense and mercilessness, the whole concealed shape and flame of her father's life. She saw what must have happened in Cambridge, and the woe to her mother, and the waste of love. She saw the source of that sensitiveness and oddness which marked him off; she saw the real meaning—or so she thought—of many observations, many actions and many friendships. With an anguish her frame could hardly bear—and in which now, after many years, the accusing nun saw jealousy as clearly as more honourable passions—she surveyed the two years of friendship with Etienne. Ah, blind, blind, blind! And she who believed she was the centre of her father's heart, who felt his love for her as sweet and certain as her own for him, who held him for a saint—by his own rules—but still, a saint!

So that was the sort of thing that the most graceful life could hide! That was what lay around, under love, under beauty. That was the flesh they preached about, the extremity of what the sin of the flesh might be. Here, at home, in her father, in the best person she had known or hoped to know.

She had absolutely no one to turn to; and she was innocent —and jealous. And would have freely died rather than say one word in any place, even in the Confessional, which might have betrayed the nature of her desolation. And there was no one old enough and detached enough to see her crisis, or approach it without seeking the specific facts. *Mère Générale* was not in Brussels then, or even known to her. She was in Rouen, and not yet *Mère Générale*.

So alone the jealous, proud, fastidious and religious girl, just eighteen, steered herself through a brief, dark madness, and for ever away from what she saw as the devilry of human love. She did not have to harden her heart; as she came out of the first long convulsion of shock, and saw what she desired to do, she found to her pleasure that her heart was hard. She found, more specifically, that she hated her father. For many years she was to feel—without sign, without word— that hate.

It was a great defence, and made everything easy—even his shock and rage when she told him that she intended to be a nun. When she told him that she would not go to Italy, that she was sorry to disappoint him, but that she wished to enter the Order of *Sainte Famille* at the conclusion of the term.

The hatred held her up even against the contemptuous fury of *Marie-Jeanne*, and made her frozenly indifferent to the puzzled, half-pleased reaction of *Etienne* to the news her father seemed unable to hear.

She left him as she said; she entered the Convent on the

25th July, the Feast of Saint James. She did not heed the almost sacrilegious hatred in her heart; there would be time to work that out, and save her own soul—which now alone seemed the bearable use to make of life. She went into religion with a merciless heart. But her father, saying he would never forgive her, was dazed and sick with mercy for her, with sorrow and foreboding—and forgave her every day with every other thought and look and appeal.

But she could not bear him. She only desired to be out of sight of him, to be alone, and quit of all that he had stood for. And when, after she had left for Bruges, for her novitiate at *Sainte Fontaine*, he wrote one last despairing letter to her, and in his innocence told her that he was leaving Brussels for a little while, going to Vienna with *Etienne*, even then she felt no particular emotion—not even disgust. She turned indeed with a kind of delight to the life of loss and elimination.

But now he was dying; and she wished with her soul to reach him. There was no casuistry in her about sin, and she held him to be a sinner, one who had better have had a millstone about his neck; but she saw her own sin of arrogant judgment as the greater, in that it was her own, on which alone God sought her scorn. And she saw its insolence, not merely against God but against His creature.

"Father, forgive me," she prayed. "Father, forgive me— I know not what I did."

She repeated the prayer. In her weariness she did not know whether she addressed it to Heaven or to her earthly father, whom now again at the eleventh hour she beheld, and felt in her heart with sudden sweetness, as he had been to her in childhood. She saw him all good again now, all wise and fatherly; she saw him as he had triumphantly shown himself so many happy years to her watching innocence; and also, looking up to the merciful Crucifix, she tried to see him as, his weary flesh forsaken, armed only with his humble, unexpecting spirit, he might appear to one who had borne all the sins of the world.

The faraway clock struck two.

She bowed her head into her hands, and began the Penitential Psalms. She offered them humbly for her father's waiting soul.

*"Domine, ne in furore . . ."*

She was still at prayer when *Sœur Antoine* passed by and cried *"Loué soit Jésu!"*

She was not alone again until three o'clock in the afternoon.

She came to her study desk exhausted but composed. Having accomplished and directed all the duties of the day, and the last the most exhausting, to sit in the Long Parlour and converse for more than an hour with the four priests who were her guests for lunch and who, pleased with what they had eaten and with the convent's excellent coffee, felt no desire to shorten a comfortable hour of leisure—yet, even this duty ended, she had returned to the chapel, to see the completed beauty of the Altar of Repose, and to make sure that the great feast was on its way in traditional hush and splendour.

She knelt awhile under the shadow of the Tribune.

The golden monstrance shone, like a fixed sun, against cloth of gold. Flowers stood in waves of red and purple, and blazing candles pressed about the Host like sentinels.

Like sentinels too the two young nuns who knelt on guard inside the rails; and almost as still, in their white veils, the Children of Mary who knelt without, below the step.

The silence was immeasurably peaceful.

Reverend Mother bent her head into her hands.

"He is at peace now," she said peacefully. "He is at peace. Oh God, forgive us both."

She made the sign of the Cross, genuflected and left the chapel. So she came at last to her desk and was alone.

She opened his letter.

# THE LAND OF SPICES

"Brussels, Rue Saint Isidore No. 4.
"18th April, 1912.

"MY DEAREST HELEN,—

"This is the last letter I shall ever write to you, and it makes me happy that its chief message is nothing different from that which I know my first contained—my tender love and pride.

"I may be gone when you read this—I have an idea that my days are numbered on the fingers of *Marie-Jeanne's* right hand. But if that is so, you will guess how easy death can be—since I write well enough, do I not? And my heart is light. I have in fact no pain—which is far more than I deserve. But I have always been given more than I deserved —and do not yet know, even on this last bed, whom to thank for that.

"Do not grieve at my flippancy, I beg you. At least I am sure that if your God is there and acts according to your theology, I have a chance of meeting you again, and gladly acknowledging your rightness. For your God will hear your prayers, Helen—and I know that you will pray for me.

"But—if we do not meet again—remember that I have loved you tenderly, and that, against my will, I have been proud of your successful, heroic life. I wished another kind of life for you, and even now, after thirty-three years of resignation, I still wonder, and so does *Marie-Jeanne*, why you turned away so sharply from that life. But you have been very patient with that monotonous wonder—and, I hope, will only smile to see it raised again in my very last letter.

"I have instructed my lawyer, Charles Rodier—you remember his father?—to let you see my will. It is a very simple document. I leave my annuity of £200 to *Marie-Jeanne* and her heirs, without condition. She does not know this. I hope she will not get dangerously drunk when they tell her. Certain books I bequeath to St. John's College, Cambridge; certain other belongings and small sums from my savings I bequeath to friends in Brussels, to Armand at the *café*, etc. This house, its contents, and my savings, subject to funeral expenses, to the Order of *Sainte Famille* without condition. My affairs are in order; there should be no delay or difficulty in execution of the will. I trust her wealth will not make *Marie-Jeanne* unhappy; I have asked Rodier to look after it for her, as I do not trust those nephews in Malines. She will be lonely without this house, etc. I wish you were in Brussels to comfort her. But '*que la volonté de Dieu, si juste, si aimable* . . .' Do you remember that, Helen?

"Well, no more postponing. I must face this curious moment, my dear child. I must say farewell to you, forever. I do so from a full and grateful heart. All my life I have been proud of you and have seen in you a possible defence of my otherwise fruitless life. I thank you for all that you have been, my darling, and I wish you the deep spiritual happiness which you deserve and I am so wretchedly unable to understand.

"The eleven years of your Irish exile have been the longest of my life. But in any case, I suppose that, if one dies old as I do, the last years seem very long. Still, it would have been good to have seen you again. Not that you are dim to my eyes, or to *Marie-Jeanne's*. But she and I, talking together, tend to see you from far off in the dear past, our own little girl, in your pinafore, with your long hair blowing about. You must forgive our sentimentality. We make each other happy with our stories of you, darling.

"And now indeed farewell. My road has been long and peaceful, and you were its chief joy. The end is easy, and as I close my eyes for the last time I shall think of you and send my love.

"Your devoted father,
"HENRY ARCHER."

In spite of his boast the writing was bad.

She fingered the pages of the letter dreamily. She would read it and reread it. There would be time. "The end is easy and as I close my eyes . . ." She knew that now he

163

had done so, that the easy end had come and gone. She felt so peaceful in that realisation that she smiled, as often in girlhood she had done over his letters, at their characteristic ease and innocence. Innocence—to the very end—of all the woe and pain that lay between them. Thank God. Thank God at least for that.

She sat and dreamt of him, half sleepy from her passionate vigil of the night, half puzzled by its onslaught, and the cold peace it left in her now.

A lay-sister came to her with a telegram.

Before she opened it she knew what it would tell her.

It was from Brussels, from *Mère Générale*.

*"Chère enfant il est mort en paix à quatre heures du matin, assisté de Marie-Jeanne et des infirmières aucune souffrance il parlait de vous jusqu'au dernier moment courage et bonnes prières."*

*The Fourth Chapter*

## CHAPLAIN'S CONCERT

ONE of the anomalies about the annual Chaplain's Concert
was that whereas, listening to Mother Mary Andrew's threats
at rehearsal, and appraising the tension in all performers, one
might think that a hitch was a major offence, deserving a mark
for conduct perhaps—yet, on the night, it was almost *de
rigueur* that a few things should go wrong, and any girl who
broke down in a song, knocked a wig askew, or got outright
hysterics during a big scene, became at once a heroine with
high entertainment value, raising a most gratifying laugh from
a rather nervous audience, breaking the ice, and as a rule
even being let off Mother Mary Andrew's wrath at the end
of the day.

Anna Murphy noticed this every year, but it did not
prevent her from getting as nervously excited as everyone
else a day or two before the concert.

This always took place at the end of the autumn term, about
three days before the Christmas break-up. In November,
for Foundress's Day, the concert had its first, and very formal,
try-out. The audience then was the community and a large
number of "old girls," many of whom returned to stay in
the house for the re-union. And although this might have
been an informal celebration, somehow by tradition it was
not, but, on the contrary was a full-dress parade of "*la pudeur
et la politesse.*" Everything had to go smoothly for Foundress's Concert, and therefore somehow, by hook or by
crook, comedy and disaster were kept to the wings, and the
result was that, the first anxieties allayed, everyone was a
little bored—the school sitting very decorously, in white
silk dresses and scratchy white silk gloves; the old girls,
watchful and shy of each other, in carefully chosen

165

dinner-gowns; even the benevolent lay-sisters, amused on their perilous perch on desks at the back and willing to enjoy anything, were unable to escape some boredom, at Foundress's Concert. Indeed, Reverend Mother, seated in a very grand chair in the front row, and with the more loyal and important of the married "old girls" to left and right of her, marvelled often at the self-control of the children, ranged along the walls of the *salle* to left and right, and could only conclude that youth was illimitably interested in its own events—even in such a programme as the traditional one of *Sainte Famille*—a bit of everything, in every language, or on every musical instrument which was taught in the school; and affording chances of self-expression to all, from Senior to Second Preparatory. Also she thought gently that youth, on the whole, is patient and well-mannered. For herself, she knew with compunction that her chief interest in Foundress's Concert was in observation of the social comedy of the "old girls"—which often indeed touched and saddened more than it amused her. But there was—to make a saint smile, she pleaded for herself—the perennial tussle for precedence between Lady de la Pole, a punctilious "old girl" who loved this yearly chance to show her contemporaries where she had got to, and Madame O'Hea, who, daughter of a Lord Chief Justice and wife of The O'Hea, was more arrogant with, in her own view, incomparably more right. But Lady de la Pole, although never quite sure of herself, could not see why the wife of a fifth baronet should have to concede social importance to the wife of anything so absurd as a "The"— and calling herself Madame too—for all the world like a dressmaker! Reverend Mother sometimes wondered why the fires of antagonism, blazing across her chair from these two poised and smiling ladies, did not scorch her.

However, none of this grown-up, bitter comedy infected Chaplain's Concert.

Only priests were invited to it—usually about twenty-five or thirty priests. The chaplain, of course, and the parish priest and senior curate of the village; parish priests and curates from neighbouring villages; Jesuits and Cistercians from nearby colleges, one or two Franciscans, and any ex-chaplains who were within driving distance of the convent. It was probable that at least to the younger of the priests the function was alarming and even unattractive—but most of the invited came, sheepish and friendly. And whether or not they enjoyed the evening, it is certain that the young ladies of *Sainte Famille* did so.

However, the preparations for it were as uneasy as for an *auto da fé*.

The concert took place in the *salle*. This was an awkward arrangement, but the tradition of *Sainte Famille* was to keep theatrical effort as amateur as possible, so that no young lady should be encouraged to think of herself as a gifted actress. No platform was erected and there was no drop-curtain. Performers took their stand on a red carpet in the middle of the *salle* and did what they could with the rôles assigned to them. They made their exits and entrances upstage, through the barrier of three pianos arranged as a kind of wall. The concert was begun and concluded by the execution of a piece of music by six young ladies, seated at three pianos. Music was not well taught at *Sainte Famille*, as the six-handed performance of "*Dichter und Bauer*" or "*Si j'étais Roi*" gave proof. If any girl played a musical instrument well, or played any composition worth listening to, that was entirely accidental. However, the three pianos made "wings" for the actors, and covered their exits from the *salle* to *extempore* dressing-rooms.

The morning of Concert Day was mad and stormy in the *salle*.

Lay-sisters were laying the red drugget; Mother Bonaventure, seated at one of the three pianos, was rehearsing Madge Willis in a song; people were moving desks and tramping about with pots of flowering plants. And almost all the girls, falling over each other and delighting in the nervy confusion, which, for its sheer stimulation, they sought to increase, muttered or chanted unexpected words, often in foreign languages—their parts for to-night. Some of them carried pots of hydrangeas in one hand and a tattered manuscript of "*Wallensteins Tod*" in the other. For the Seniors, coached deliriously by *Mère Martine*, were to entertain their guests with scenes from the fifth act of that tragedy.

Mother Mary Andrew, riding the whirlwind, also rehearsed Una Madden in her Irish recitation. This was a rendering into Gaelic, by Mother Mary Andrew herself, of "*Who Fears to Speak of Ninety-Eight?*" In 1912 a great many of the rich *bourgeoisie* did fear, or dislike, to speak of it—but mentioned in Irish it would not make much impression, and in any case, this timidity was not true of the younger priests. Though whether their linguistic appreciation of Una Madden's performance would equal their emotional no one might hastily gauge. However, study of the Irish language, though not compulsory, was a living part of the *Sainte Famille* curriculum now, thanks to the brains and energy of Mother Mary Andrew, and in to-night's programme Gaelic studies would be represented by Una Madden's recitation, an "action song" called "*An Maidrin Ruadh*" by the little ones, an eight-hand Irish reel, and, to conclude the concert, a three-part choral rendering by the whole school of "Faith of Our Fathers" in Irish—"*A Creidh-eamh Athara.*" It could not so glibly be said now that *Sainte Famille* trained its girls to be the wives of British majors and colonial governors; for at least there was a choice of cultures offered to them. But ignoring the jibes and exaggerations launched by partisans alike of old and new ideas, and approving the theory, if not the execution so far, of the optional revival of the Irish language in Irish education—Reverend Mother still regarded that as a local incident, and not as the mission of her Order. She still held out as strongly as ever for the European and polite tradition initiated one hundred and fifty years ago at Rouen—indifferent alike to the future needs of Gaelic Leaguer or British officer. She still thought it necessary to train girls, for their own sakes and for the glory of God, to be Christians and to be civilised.

Anna Murphy and Norrie O'Dowd, captaining some little ones, were decorating gaseliers with the silk flags and garlands of tradition.

" 'Bless thee, Bottom, bless thee; thou art translated,' " Norrie was chanting from her gaselier. They were standing on desks.

"Oh, we know that scene, Norrie—it's Katey Sheehan I want to rehearse with. Where on earth is she?"

" 'What angel wakes me from my flowery bed?' " Katey yelled from afar off, where she was heaving desks against the wall. But Anna could not summon courage to sing the bit for which that was her cue.

"Go on," said Norrie—" 'The finch, the sparrow and the lark——' "

"I can't sing it, Norrie."

"You'll have to to-night."

Anna looked uneasy.

"I think I'll talk it," she said cautiously. "It was awful when I sang it on Foundress's Day."

Pilar O'Farrell was seated, comfortable and high, on the desks against the wall where the lay-sisters would perch to-night. She was eating caramels, and throwing them to others. She came from Lima and was non-co-operative, but generous.

"I'd think it dreadful to have to play a part called Bottom, Anna," she said. "How do you face it?"

Anna secretly thought it dreadful herself, though she was flattered in a way at having been given the part. (The Juniors were playing Act III, Scene 1, of *The Midsummer Night's Dream*.)

"It's just his name," she said anxiously.

"Of course, but surely a joke was intended? And, if I may say so, you spoil it. You are so thin, Anna."

"Pilar, my dear, your caramels are lovely," said Bernardette Delane, helping herself to a few, "but you admit you've no brains. Old Eugenia has, however, and she cast Bottom very well. You see, the whole point of him is his very foolish conceit."

Bernardette was in Middle Grade, the class between Honours Junior and Senior. She was clever and pretty, but somewhat unpopular. She liked to hang round the Honours Juniors and tease them. Also she was rather keen on Pilar O'Farrell.

There was a time when Anna would have wept at this attack—but of late, to her secret pleasure, she was growing hardened to such jibes, especially when they came from Bernardette Delane.

"Ah, shut up, Bernardette," said Norrie, who did think Anna conceited, but liked her, and disliked Bernardette. "We all know what's wrong with you—you're mad that you haven't a part to-night."

"Mad! That I haven't to make a fool of myself before a lot of priests! As a matter of fact, if I wanted to, I'd have been playing *Wallenstein*."

Everyone laughed. Molly Redmond, head of the school, brilliant and beautiful, was playing *Wallenstein*.

"I hardly think so," said Pilar, who sometimes seemed rather grown-up for fifteen. "Have a caramel."

Anna, weaving artificial roses through a gaselier, thought with pleasure of last night's rehearsal of *Wallensteins Tod*. " . . . *schnell geht der Wolkenzug, die Mondessichel wankt, und durch die Nacht zuckt ungewisse Helle*."

Anna was fourteen now, would be fifteen in four months. The long years she had spent under school discipline and the accidental training given to her naturally good memory by the years of learning "Reverend Mother's poems" still gave her an advantage at her lessons which exasperated girls who knew themselves to be as intelligent as she but were less well adjusted to the *Sainte Famille* system of teaching. Having had to spend three years grinding over the First Preparatory course before she was allowed to take the examination, her boredom with it had seemed insolent to those who came to it fresh each year; and this boredom drove her into bouts of fevered reading, which made her even more exasperating.

Moreover the bitter lesson taught her when she was eight by Mother Mary Andrew and the verb *finir* made her into a careful, alert examinee who was not going to fall twice into such a trap. Now in Honours Junior, and second time round, she enjoyed her lessons, and, although she worried over recurrent charges of "conceit" and "cockiness," she tried to make a point of seeming to ignore them. She did not know that this defence increased the impression of vanity. When her Rec. played Stool of Repentance sometimes at night, it hurt very much to have to hear when she sat on the stool that somebody said she thought she was Julius Cæsar, or that somebody said "*Sainte Famille, c'est moi,*" or that somebody said she was "intoxicated with the exuberance of her verbosity." But she accepted that it was a cruel game, and always played cruelly at *Sainte Famille;* so she learnt not to weep as her attackers wanted her to, and in her turn she endeavoured to give as good as she got.

But the trouble really lay in her continued detachment from the personalities of school. She was genuinely more interested in books and her own thoughts than in people. She underwent, as it happened, none of the emotional phases common to those around her; she could discover as yet no stimulus at all in the other sex or in jokes about it; and she could only look on in mystification at the storms of *Schwärmerei* for nuns or senior girls which swept the school like epidemics. She simply did not feel these things. Sometimes those who disliked her called her "Reverend Mother's pet," and addressed her humorously as "my dear child" in what they conceived to be an English accent; but this immovable general idea puzzled her. She did not like Reverend Mother very much, she thought her stiff and old-fashioned, and she always felt nervous when she was around. She did not see why, just because she had been in the school since she was six, she should be made into such a fool as "Reverend Mother's pet." Good Lord, it seemed to her that you might as well call her Mother Mary Andrew's pet—and Heaven knew she wasn't that! In fact, her emotions were all, or

almost all, at home with Charlie and Castle Tory—and the
few she found at school arose from words, words read or
spoken or sung—as Madge Willis was singing at that
moment, " . . . *die letzten roten Astern trag herbei* . . ."
or as last night she was moved by *Wallenstein,* by tall and
clear-voiced Molly, saying so distinctly—" . . . *Gut' Nacht,
Gordon! Ich denke einen langen Schlaf zu tun* . . ." No
*Schwärmerei* for Molly, but a private, grateful pleasure for
Molly's power to widen out the night by saying these things
so that they rang in your head. But her heart was at home
with Charlie, always loving towards him, and lately troubled
now and then. For she could see that there were anxieties
at Castle Tory, anxieties she did not often try to formulate,
because she could not bring herself to judgment, and still
needed very much—since she was lonely at school—to feel
her parents as her protectors and as the source of warm
safety. And as this grew less and less possible she became
not merely uneasy for herself but very uneasy for Charlie,
who although thirteen now was still going to Lissanmoher
National School with common boys, and spoke with a
dreadful accent, and told her things about Daddy being drunk
and about Mother crying—told them to her almost as if they
were not horrible events. She feared for Charlie, and worried
about shadows she did not yet see clearly; and although she
loved him more than anyone on earth, she was often happy
to be at school, safe from anxieties she could not define.
There were escapes at school—but at Castle Tory life too
often now came menacingly near, looking sad and intractable.
However, to-day she was not thinking in that vein—but
rather that term exams were over, that she would be going
home to Charlie in three days, and that it must be splendid
to be *Wallenstein* or Molly Redmond.

Colette Bermingham came giggling along, fresh from a
tussle with Mother Agatha about her costume for *Wallensteins
Tod;* she was playing *Gräfin Terzky* and *Mère Martine* wanted
her gown to be low-cut; Mother Agatha would not hear of
such a thing.

"She says it's a priests' entertainment—really the woman has a filthy mind."

Pilar O'Farrell laughed.

"And you are as pure as a baby," she said. "Have a caramel?"

"Where do you get all these caramels, Pilar? Why has everything in this silly school got to be in foreign languages? Poor old Madge can't even sing her solo in English! Do you hear her?"

"That's on account of the priests too," said Norrie. "*Vive la pudeur, mes enfants!*"

"Why, what's it say?" asked Pilar.

" 'And let us talk of love again,' " said Anna, " 'as once in May, as once in May.' "

"Dear, dear, how very indiscreet," said Colette.

"Anyway, it's nicer in German," said Anna.

"Perhaps for geniuses," said Bernardette. "How many languages can you make love in, Pilar?"

"Spanish is best," said Pilar dreamily.

Anna climbed down from her last gaselier.

"Have you made love often, Pilar?" she asked in straightforward wonder.

Pilar opened wide grey eyes at her.

"*Por Dios*, no!" she said.

"Anna Murphy, are you really such an innocent as you pretend?" Colette asked her, grinning.

"Not she!" said Bernardette.

Anna ignored Bernardette.

"What have I said that's innocent?" she asked Colette.

"Ask old McWhirter," said Colette.

Anna felt a fool; all these gigglers were older than she.

"I thought *you* were experts on the subject," she said coolly, and walked away with Katey Sheehan, who plunged into rehearsal at once—" 'I pray thee, gentle mortal, sing again . . .' "

Pilar O'Farrell gave the first enlivening turn to the concert. She had to recite—a Spanish poem. She held this ordeal to be absurd, as she was bored by poetry and no one but she knew a word of Castilian. Old Mother Philip, who had spent some years in Mexico City, was reputed to understand Spanish, and had the duty of "keeping up" Pilar's home tongue with her, but Pilar said that "Old Phil" didn't know a syllable of it, and everyone had the impression that the lessons were a sore ordeal for the nun. However, perhaps to soothe her own vanity, old Philip insisted that, as Spanish was "taught" in the school, there should be some Spanish in the concert programme. So Pilar, immensely bored, had to memorise some verses of *Noche Serena*, by *Fray Luis de León*.

"And anyway," she said to Colette, "since no one understands Spanish, she might have let me be amusing—just for my own benefit!"

"What's it about?"

"Oh my dear—an old fogy going on and on about the sky and the stars, and how lovely he imagines everything is up there! Absolute rot! You are all mighty lucky that it *is* in Spanish!"

At Foundress's Concert she got through it by gabbling and cutting, and with philosophic acceptance of the fact that the "old girls" were bores anyway, and that the whole evening was a bore. But Chaplain's Concert need not be boring, and Pilar resented in any case being marked down to bore an audience of men—even if they *were* priests.

She began politely and gravely:

"*Quando contemplo el cielo . . .*"

She did not notice the Chaplain's gentle smile. Father Quinn was his name and he sat in the chair of honour with Reverend Mother on the left hand, and the Abbot of Mohervin on his right.

Father Quinn was fat and small, and made up of nervous mannerisms which were the delight of the watchful, mimicking school. He hiccuped; he tapped his nose violently when in thought; he cleared his throat so loudly and suddenly sometimes, even during Mass, that the noise threw the whole school into exquisite agonies of giggling. He was the perfect butt, and Colette Bermingham and numerous rivals worked very hard at polishing and improving their imitations of him.

He smiled now at this contemplative Pilar O'Farrell.

She was looking brilliantly pretty. The School always thought that, to a girl, they were made to look ridiculous on occasions of festivity; and it is true that the massed white silk dresses of Foundress's Day and Prize Day were unbecoming in general and particular result. There was something countrified in their effect which always depressed Reverend Mother. But for Chaplain's Concert the white silk dresses were not worn. Instead the girls wore their Sunday black dresses, their prettiest white collars, white gloves—and, curious final touch, wide sashes, tied in great bows at the back, stiff silk sashes, uniformly of brilliant salmon pink.

They were a tradition—and no one knew why they were salmon-pink. There was a general feeling that they were diabolically ugly, and they were donned by the girls in a mood of hilarious ribaldry. But in truth their effect was miraculous. In the warmly lighted *salle* with its dark red curtains and dark green potted palms, against the black garb of nuns and priests, and worn on black, these flashing, swishing sashes were urbane and gay. They made graceful girls into sylphs; they made the little ones look merry and surprised with themselves; and they lent a mild sophistication even to the plain and the large.

They were accidentally lovely in effect.

The sash illumined Pilar's innocent exoticism.

Father Quinn knew no Spanish, but he did know something of the mind of Fray Luis de León, and he understood the poem's first line. From the weekly ordeal of Christian Doctrine Lecture, he knew Pilar to be frivolous and unmanageable—one of the real menaces to his courage in fact. So now he smiled and tapped his nose violently with his index finger.

At the end of the second verse Pilar stopped. She stared appealingly at Reverend Mother, who smiled encouragement.

" '*Morada de grandeza*," whispered Mother Philip from the back row. " '*Morada de grandeza*,' child!"

"Oh, I know it all right," said Pilar, "only"—she swept her grey eyes with solicitude up and down two rows of priests' faces—"I simply can't bear boring you like this!"

The audience was surprised and burst out laughing.

"You weren't boring me, Pilar," said Father Quinn.

"Well, any minute I would; there are reams of it."

"What's it about?" asked the Abbot.

"Contemplation of the heavens, my lord. You know the kind of thing."

The priests were delighted now, and thought her charming.

"Go on," they said. "Go on, like a good girl!"

"Can't we have a little more?" asked the Lord Abbot.

"Well, the last verse isn't bad," she said, and repeated it in her sweet, contented, unimaginative voice.

" '*O campos verdaderos!* . . .' "

She was loudly and obstreperously cheered as she withdrew. With her back to the delighted priests, she winked contentedly at her friend Colette; she knew she deserved well of the school, for she had set the ball rolling in the direction of frivolity. Chaplain's Concert would be all right now.

It was more than all right. It was feverishly amusing and crazy that year.

The children sat in two rows to right and left of the carpeted space which was the stage, and at right angles to the audience proper, which they always examined ruthlessly, searching for absurdity or thrill.

When Pilar got back to her seat she discovered that Colette had noticed what she had noticed, and so had Jennie Meldon, and so had Bernardette. Indeed, even Children of Mary, even Ursula de la Pole and Gertie Davoren were giggling with excitement.

The thing was that there was a Greek god in the audience. Nothing less, my dear! Have you ever seen anything like him? Who on earth is he? I shall die, I shall die of it! Oh, a priest, if you please! However, isn't it just our luck! Have you ever imagined a man could look like that? Oh, if that fat old Father Considine would only move out of the way! Look at him now! Look, look, Jenny! What on earth possessed him to become a priest? Broken heart, I bet! Oh, get back, Tessie, you can't lean out like that! Colette, I'm crazy about him! Oh, Pilar, he laughed like anything at you and your poem! Good Lord, you are a notice-box, Pilar! I bet you did it on purpose! No, I only saw him in the middle of the last verse—my dear, I very nearly broke down! I wouldn't blame you! What is his name? Is he a Jesuit, Gertie? He must be—he looks so civilised! Oh, he's lovely! Oh, it's just my luck to fall in love with a priest!

Every year there had perforce to be some novelty in the audience, to rejoice the sensation-mongers; sometimes it was only farce, as if an old priest fell asleep and snored during the play, or took snuff loudly; sometimes debate as to the relative good looks of Father This and Father That had to suffice for working up a commotion. But a Greek god, an out-and-outer, meant a perfect evening of intensely satisfactory insanity.

It was a game these adolescents played, a game deep-founded in the urgencies of growth, and one with which psychologists and educationalists made heavy weather, even before the science of psycho-analysis was developed. But in its normal expressions wisdom, perhaps somewhat bored with it, and only too well aware of its natural implications, preferred to ignore its central folly—knowing that to be at least theologically innocent—and to check its extremities of exuberance under the general accusation of bad manners and insubordination. As for its spring, its immediate victim, he can hardly have been aware of the traditional outlet of foolishness he provided—or if he did become conscious of some giggling fuss about him, it can have meant no more than an hour's discomfort or amusement, according to his temperament.

Anna, dressed as Bottom, and waiting in the wings, while

the eight-hand reel was danced, peered between the pianos
and said to Quince, who was Norrie O'Dowd, that she knew
that tall priest at the end of the second row, the young-
looking one.

"You mean that one they are all 'gone' on?"

"Are they? He was Harry's Greek master at Clongowes
until last term. He's been moved to Pallascrowe now, and
he came to see Mother one Sunday. He says Harry is very
good at Greek. I wish I learnt Greek!"

The news that the Greek god taught Greek at Pallascrowe
flew like the marvellous, amusing news it was, from mouth
to mouth of the infatuated; but when Anna, all cold and
innocent, sprang her second piece of information, that he
wasn't ordained yet but was only a scholastic, and was called
*Mr.* Farrahy, she became in crazy demand for a minute, so
that her entrance was held up, and she shot on the scene with
such force as to cannon violently into Quince. Thus their
opening gambit: "Are we all met? Pat, pat . . ." was
greeted with a roar which should have satisfied the
Fratellini.

Act III, Scene 1 of *The Midsummer Night's Dream*, which
in cold blood the school thought quite inane, went riotously
well to-night—partly because of its felicitous opening which
unnerved the players and drove them from folly to folly, and
partly because, infatuation for the Greek god now being fully
launched, the traditional application of every other word said
on the stage to the immediate emotional crisis engaged the
attention of the wits to left and right, and warmed up everything. Thus the opinion that "to bring in (God shield us) a
lion among ladies is a most dreadful thing" was clapped and
laughed at by the school with a gusto which startled the priests
into a rivalry of applause. And so throughout. The emotional antics of Pilar, Colette, Ursula and Bernardette—all
seeking to outshine each other in suppressed, but palpable,
extravagance of excitement—carried the innocent performance on at a pace of pleasure that, unexplained, infected the

whole *salle* and killed boredom. And Katey Sheehan, steady, reliable, dull Titania, had an immeasurable success. Every word of infatuation which she uttered was taken up with ecstasy by the side-lines.

"So is mine eye enthralled to thy shape," said Katey, and Pilar and Colette groaned and signalled their delight. All the imbecility, as they held it, of Anna in her ass's head, was swept out of the scene, and they just sang at the aptness of Titania.

"On the first view to say, to swear, I love thee." Oh, but that's so true. She says it well—but not the way I'd say it! Well done, Katey. Look at him now, Colette—no, no, not now—he's looking this way, I think. After all, he isn't a priest yet. You never could tell! Anyway, it would be worse if he were. Fancy that little fool Anna *knowing* him! Well—she's jolly well got to introduce me before supper. Bags I to take him in to supper, Ursula. I said it first. I'm getting next him at supper—you can take him in if you like.

"And I will purge thy mortal grossness so . . ."

How dare she! He hasn't any. He's a saint, I'm sorry to say. Mortal grossness. Did you hear that? What does it mean exactly? This is a lovely play, it turns out! Who'd have thought it? Poor old Anna—must be hot in that thing! Can't see *him* either!

"Hop in his walks and jambol in his eyes——"

This line induced exquisite giggling, which infected the whole audience, even to the puzzled lay-sisters on the desks at the back.

"Hop in his walks," cried Pilar, in convulsions of delight.

Act III, Scene 1 was concluded to wild and warm applause.

Hop in his walks, indeed! Oh, this'll be the death of me, Pilar!

During the little ones' French play, *La Belle au Bois Dormant*, most of the young ladies enamoured of the Greek god were absent from the *salle*, getting ready for *Wallensteins Tod*. Except Pilar, who did not learn German. She grew bored, even with contemplation of the glorious profile, when left alone to it, so, by the time the last act of Schiller's tragedy began, she was in ready mood to enliven it with noises off.

Perhaps the priests knew some German, or something of the Austrian hero victim of the Thirty Years War. If they did not, it is impossible to imagine what they made of this performance by the Seniors.

Most of the caste were in a completely irresponsible mood, set on looking as dashing as possible in extremely sketchy attempts at seventeenth-century costume—no trousers allowed—and on turning the play into a series of calamities and thrills. That was the frivolous intention of the wits—and to-night they were all in love, and positively ablaze with folly. Moreover, during their dressing, *Mère Martine*, always temperamental and frivolous, had been infected and gone mad, and she could now neither find her place in the prompt book, nor yield it up, even to the command of Mother Mary Andrew. And Molly Redmond, who liked her part of the great General and took it seriously, was in a passionate fury with everyone, and played for all she was worth, speaking fast and loud to cover the helpless giggles of *Thekla* and the *Gräfin*, cutting scenes that were clearly unplayable with these lunatics, giving cues, making other people's speeches—saving the whole field, in fact, with flying, furious intelligence, and enjoying herself tremendously.

Anna Murphy, seated far down the side-line, the better to follow this play she liked so much, was made very angry at first by the clowning of Ursula, Bernardette and their satellites, but soon she began to take a devoted interest in Molly's battle, single-handed, against their wrecking tactics. Anna liked serious things to be serious, and she admired very much to-night's grim and bright-eyed and rapid-spoken *Wallenstein*. And indeed Molly's rage gave her stature and soldierliness, and lifted her performance over the surrounding farce of tilted wigs, stuck swords and snorting giggles.

> ". . . *weg ist er über Wünsch und Furcht, gehört*
> *Nicht mehr den trüglich wankenden Planeten—*
> *O ihm ist wohl! . . .*"

Anna listened in delight, perceiving in the words, beyond her present recognition, a vista of wide, starry melancholy, a measured, mournful panorama of she knew not what, of evocations, intimations, images—the floating, formal beauty of suggestive words. Very sad, very shapely on the air. So that Colette's crown, falling off at that moment, and rolling straight to the Lord Abbot's feet, was not funny at all—however much Pilar O'Farrell might laugh.

Reverend Mother was also pleased by Molly's fight for the reality of what she was doing, and was somewhat bored by the guying of the others. For she, like Anna, liked serious things to be serious, and had perforce remained sufficiently unsophisticated for it to be a pleasure to her to hear good verse spoken aloud once in a while, even by a schoolgirl. And she liked Molly's voice and her ringing sympathy with Schiller's lines. So, although she knew that the harmless, traditional mood of folly which was *de rigueur* at this concert must not be taken pompously or resented, yet she felt bored with all the giggling—and somewhat ashamed of the school.

And thinking thus, she ran her eyes over the side-lines, and they fell on Anna Murphy, bent forward in her seat, her hands tight-locked about her knees, her mouth a little open, and her eyes fixed in ravished attention upon *Wallenstein*.

" . . . *Das Schöne ist doch weg, das kommt nicht wieder . . .*"

Reverend Mother smiled contentedly. Here at least was one other listener as humourless as she; here was another who actually welcomed the sound of someone spouting Schiller. Her eyes stayed gratefully on the fourteen-year-old child whom she had watched with particular caution from afar since she was six, and whom she did not really know, but continued to like, by guess and surmise. She had thought it better not to seek to know her; and perhaps she would never seek to lessen the distance that could always stay between nun and pupil—but unsentimental as she thought she might claim to be, she held it as odd, and comforting, that her eyes rarely fell on Anna without being satisfied by the mood, the state of mind, they saw in her.

Reverend Mother turned away dutifully.

"It really seems to be Anna's *rôle* in life to cheer me up," she thought, mocking herself, "to reassure me."

However, Wallenstein once "off," and his tragic fate assured, burlesque carried all before it.

A girl called Maudie Honan had the part of a *Kammerdiener* and at a significant moment had to rush on the scene excitedly crying *"Hilfe! Mörder!"* She was very bad at this, and anxious to do it correctly. However, to-night *Mère Martine*, aided by Pilar O'Farrell, took measures to ensure naturalistic acting, and at the moment of her entrance, without forewarning her, they gave Maudie Honan a very violent push in the back. To their delight she shot on to the scene in effective disarray, and they waited for a convincing cry of *"Hilfe! Mörder!"* It did not come. Maudie Honan, having overshot her mark and scattered the other players, gathered herself up, withdrew to her correct position, said *"Hilfe! Mörder!"* in a modest tone, and then went off into helpless laughter.

There was no more to be done with *Wallensteins Tod.* The last scene went from bad to worse, and Colette Bermingham said afterwards that she had never in her life enjoyed anything so much as her own playing of the *Gräfin's* last minutes on earth. She certainly gave the bewildered priests something to puzzle over. They had no idea what her contortions indicated, or even whether she should or should not, in her part, be laughing as she was, but when she lay finally with exaggerated grace along the drugget, she planted her last line with enough effect to delight and annoy Pilar. With her eyes rolled tragically in the direction of the end of the second row of priests, Colette spoke clearly for the first time throughout the play.

*"In wenig Augenblicken ist mein Schicksal Erfüllt,"* she said, and closed her eyes.

All the wits were generously ravished by this.

"Oh Colette, what does it mean?" Pilar implored in giggles from the side-line.

*Wallensteins Tod* was applauded for several minutes by the very good-natured priests.

When "*A Chreidheamh Athara*" had at last been sung, the girls advanced, looking orderly and civilised again in their black dresses and bright sashes, to shake hands with Father Quinn and the Lord Abbot, and thereafter to "mingle with their guests," according to the counsels of Reverend Mother's Politeness Lesson. That was one of the occasions when a public display of "*la pudeur et la politesse*" was called for, if not always perfectly produced. The older girls were expected to try themselves out as hostesses, to make conversation, to look after the shy and the silent and tactfully to assist the move from the *salle* to the refectory, for supper.

Outwardly this phase was executed with grace and credit. The children formed demure groups round the priests and were joked and congratulated about their performances in the programme; the brainier girls tackled the Jesuits, as a rule; the devout inclined towards whatever priest had directed the school's last retreat; the head girl had to make herself particularly agreeable to the Chaplain, and, with Reverend Mother's assistance, to any very venerable guest, such as the Lord Abbot of Mohervin.

All this fell out according to custom now, but on a concealed current of hilarity. The wits had by no means yet squeezed the evening dry of folly.

Anna was furtively pushed and edged by some of these until she stood before the Greek god; she was under oath to speak to him, and to introduce Colette and Ursula to his notice.

"How are you, Mr. Farrahy?" she said nervously. "I'm Anna Murphy. You know, Harry Murphy's sister—you taught him Greek at Clongowes."

The young scholastic nodded nervously.

"Oh yes, Harry Murphy, of course. So you are his sister?"

"Oh Mr. Farrahy—this is Colette Bermingham and Ursula de la Pole. They want to speak to you."

Anna vanished from his sight into the crowd as suddenly as she had appeared, and rejoined Norrie O'Dowd who was talking to Father Conroy. She went with them to the refectory, and took her place for supper beside the ex-chaplain to whom she had made her First Confession, and whom she remembered as a very kind, nice man.

For this supper-party the girls sat where they chose, with their guests scattered amongst them—the only formality being that the Chaplain sat at the centre of Foundress's Table, under the portrait of *Mère Marie Félice de Gravons St. Roche,* and struck the gong and kept order, in Mother Mary Andrew's place. This was great fun, as Father Quinn was supposed to be comic over it, and of course he only became more nervous than ever. What do you bet he taps his nose with the gong-stick?

The refectory was softly lighted by fairy lights hooded in coloured glass, and laid along the tables amid flowers and fruit. As people edged about, choosing places, Colette and Ursula, content that they had secured their prey, stood politely by two chairs, reserving his between them, while he stood a little aside, finishing a conversation which Mother Bonaventure, of all talkative bores, had engaged him in. They smiled tolerantly towards where Father Quinn, at the daised table, was doing his best to be funny. Both were wondering where Pilar was.

The gong was purposefully struck at last, and the Lord Abbot said grace in Latin. When Colette and Ursula turned at its conclusion to invite Mr. Farrahy to be seated, they saw him about five feet away, with his back to them, docilely taking a seat at Latin Table, while Pilar smiled at him and slid into the neighbouring chair.

"Reverend Mother thought it might be better to spread people out this way," Pilar was saying very politely.

"Of course," said Mr. Farrahy. "Whatever Reverend Mother wishes."

Without loss of a second, Colette and Ursula circuited round Latin Table, to the two places facing Pilar and the

Greek god. They seized the young Preparatories who were just about to occupy them.

"You are to go over there and sit with Father Hartigan," said Ursula.

"Reverend Mother thought it might be better that way," said Colette.

Pilar laughed appreciatively as the Preparatories departed.

There was no resentment felt—indeed Pilar's move was appreciated by her friends—and the three girls settled down to idolise their unconscious victim.

The convent's very potent elderberry wine was not served at this light supper, but only tea or coffee. However, there was always tipsy cake, and a great deal of it was eaten, and it was always very strongly laced with wine. There can be no doubt that the light-headed became a degree intoxicated as they ate.

The climactic general pleasure would be when Father Hartigan sang. Everybody knew that, and some of those priests who were *habitués* of this party entered mischievously into the universal conspiracy of approach to this moment.

Reverend Mother did not care for the annual rapture of Father Hartigan's song, but, as Mother Eugenia said to her: "You'll ruin the party for the poor man if you *don't* let him sing—and in any case, you and I are not supposed to know that the performance is a classical joke."

All of this was true; but Reverend Mother suspected Mother Eugenia of herself profoundly enjoying the farce. For her own part she thought that it would be better once and for all to hurt Father Hartigan by letting him go home with his song unsung, than tacitly to allow this ecstasy of baiting, but the unmentioned tradition dated from before her day, and was as precious to its victim as to the school. Moreover, this party was allowed the maximum of *laisser aller* conformable with courtesy—and certainly no one had yet come within miles of hurting Father Hartigan's feelings. That was clear from the delight and anticipation with which he returned year by year to his ordeal.

Mr. Farrahy, strange to his surroundings and discouraged, as young Jesuits are, in the practice of conviviality, may have wondered why his director at the House of Studies had bidden him attend this curious party—as evenings of hilarity in mixed company have no place in the Ignatian scheme. But the Rector of Pallascrowe admired the community of *Sainte Famille;* Jesuits usually directed the Retreats alike of the school and of the community, and it was a part of mutual friendliness that three or four members of the Society should attend this re-union each year. However, Mr. Farrahy had not been warned that he might be surrounded by so many gracious and mad-seeming young ladies—and he felt uneasy and suspected a joke somewhere. Father Mallon, an old Jesuit who knew the convent well, sat not very far off across the table, so Mr. Farrahy kept his eye on him for guidance, and meantime did his best to tranquillise the absurd excitement that he felt about him in his hostesses.

He need not have troubled. He was a dull young man—and could never be of emotional danger to any spirited person. And it is probable that his adorers sensed this quickly, and became therefore all the more mad and free in their enjoyment of this extemporised excitement. For all they wanted of him was his profile, his smile and some polite submission to the rules of their undeclared game. He was a symbol, and the less he interfered by trying to be anything else, so much the better.

They plied him with coffee and tipsy-cake. They were faintly disillusioned by his vigorous appetite, not realising the dullness of meals in a Jesuit house of studies, or that their hilarious concert had been long and perhaps trying to the audience.

They talked to him as women of the world addressing, say, a lieutenant of hussars.

"It must be frightfully boring for you to be stuck in Pallas-crowe—after Clongowes! You're so far from Dublin now!"

"Oh, I didn't see much of Dublin—and Clongowes is a quiet spot, you know."

"I always wish my brother was there," said Ursula untruthfully. "He's at Beaumont. You see, as he's going to be a baronet, my father thought that perhaps he'd *better* go to England!"

Pilar and Colette winked at each other. If that was Ursula's line to-night, they could show her how to spin it.

"What are you doing for Christmas, Mr. Farrahy?"

The young man stared at Pilar in bewilderment.

"I'm going to Paris," she went on. "I'm meeting my mother there."

This was true, but might just as well not have been, so long as it amused Pilar to say it.

"You know Paris well, Mr. Farrahy?" asked Colette.

"I've never been abroad at all," said Mr. Farrahy. "Yes, thank you, Sister—I'd love more tipsy-cake."

"You'll be staying at the *Crillon*, as usual, I suppose?" Colette asked Pilar.

"Oh the *Meurice*, if Mother's feeling tired," said Pilar.

The O'Farrells were rich, but they did not stay at these hotels. The *Continental* was their category—for all it mattered to Mr. Farrahy, or to his tipsy adorers.

"I expect we'll go to Scotland—deer-stalking, don't you know—if Father can get out of attending the Castle functions," said Colette.

"Deer-stalking—at Christmas!" said Ursula, exquisitely amused.

"Oh, Father deer-stalks just exactly whenever he likes," said Colette.

"Why not?" said Pilar.

But the supper singing had begun—Father Conroy was tuning up for "The Minstrel Boy." However, as he sang moderately well, it was difficult to be amused; the next item, however, was a duet between Father Feeney and Father O'Rourke—called "Watchman, What of the Night?" These two priests took their singing seriously—but no perfection of headnotes could remove the out-and-out absurdity of Father O'Rourke's extremely red face. Indeed, the business of singing stressed it very effectively, so that even the Children of Mary could hardly stand it when he came to "bright shall its glory be!"

But at last Father Hartigan sang—and even the Chaplain, announcing the item playfully, seemed to feel excited, because he gave the loudest hiccup in the school's memory—thus heaping pleasure on the moment.

Father Hartigan always sang "My Dark Rosaleen," a song with beautiful, strange words, and an awkward, uneven musical setting. He was a fat, complacent man without a vestige of music in his loud voice. He sang all the verses, with a great variety of expression, facial as well as vocal. He sat back in his chair, and roared it all out, sometimes gazing at the ceiling, but more often sweeping his audience with his small, fervent eyes. But he cannot really have seen them, because had he done so, he would only have sung to them once—not on fifteen happy successive occasions.

The comedy was in the innocent pleasure which he took in the quite hellish noises he was making; people like Molly Redmond and Ursula and Anna, who had now heard him sing his song many times said that he seemed to enjoy it more every year.

He cracked and banged around on notes that were not notes at all, and had only the wild, momentary order he inflicted. His neck swelled and his bald head glistened. The nuns stood polite and grave, careful to catch no eye; the children hugged themselves in an ecstasy of self-control—indeed they felt that by any noise or movement they might break their delight, or lose a drop of the honey of this absurdity.

"Woe and pain, pain and woe . . ." roared Father Hartigan —and Pilar was so happy in the sound he made that, as she told Colette afterwards, she practically fainted. Everywhere girls sat rigid; as the song advanced keeping their eyes mostly on their plates, or sometimes, as Pilar had to, burying their faces in their hands. Molly Redmond sat like a beautiful statue by the Lord Abbot, but her head was slightly bent, and anyone could tell she was in agony. Norrie O'Dowd's face was quite purple, and when the song was over she would probably have one of those awful fits of laughing that nothing could stop. As for Anna, she was in the line of Father Hartigan's eye, and although she believed in his blindness to surroundings when he sang, she had all the same in panic more than once to force her thoughts on to the Crucifixion. But it was impossible to keep them there. Oh, if he didn't stop soon—and really, if Norrie's face got any purpler. . . .

Mr. Farrahy sat in polite bewilderment. The singing of this priest seemed very appalling to him, but the atmosphere it created was difficult to assess. He could read no expression on Father Mallon's tired face, nor on those of the nuns standing by the side-tables. But the girls around him—he did not wish to stare at them overmuch—seemed oddly affected. Was there something which escaped him in the singing? Was it perhaps what was called traditional? Was it some offshoot of the Gaelic Revival, and should one be able to admire it?

When the song ended, the applause was frantic, and under its wild tempest laughter poured in glorious torrents up and down the rows of happy girls. For they were as forcefully happy in having once more got safely through the agonising comedy of Father Hartigan's song as if purged by great art or visited by brilliantly good news. And they had in fact carried through the odd triumph of forcing the philosophy of "*la pudeur et la politesse*" to contain a moment of sheer brutal delight in human fatuity. So they laughed in the most delicious relaxation of soul and in positive gratitude, and Father Hartigan, enchanted, mopping his brow, stood up and bowed again and again in acknowledgment of their delight.

Mr. Farrahy was very much puzzled. He began to peel a large pear, and he accepted more coffee from Mother Felicita.

"You enjoyed that song?" he asked Colette.

"Oh 'enjoyed' isn't the word!" said Colette, drying her eyes—" 'enjoyed' indeed!"

"I don't know what I'll do without Father Hartigan when I'm left school," said Pilar.

Bernardette Delane had been annoyed at the despatch with which Ursula, Colette and Pilar had walked off with the Greek god. Now as the "Dark Rosaleen" storm ebbed, she left her place by Father Rogers, another Jesuit, and came and bent very politely over Mr. Farrahy's left shoulder, ignoring the bright eye of Pilar, on his right.

"Mr. Farrahy, Father Rogers tells me that you sing very well indeed—and so the Chaplain hopes that you'll sing for us now perhaps?"

"Oh no—really, I'm afraid—you know—really, I don't think I have a suitable song——"

"Anything will do," said Bernardette, knowing her ruse was pleasing him. "And you know it's a sort of rule that all the priests do sing for us, if they can."

"Well, really it is very kind of you to want me to—but——"

Pilar could see that Bernardette was about to score a strong point with the Greek god. It seemed a pity.

"There's no rule really, Mr. Farrahy, and we'd hate to make you miserable——"

But Colette, usually Pilar's faithful man, yearned for a song from her hero.

"Please sing for us, Mr. Farrahy," she said. "Oh, please!"

But Father Mallon from down the table smiled the permission he saw the young scholastic waited for.

"Go on, Farrahy. Any old ballad will do. We are an easy audience!"

Mr. Farrahy was very pleased. He thought little of his staggering profile, but he was somewhat vain of his tenor voice, and this weakness having been noted by a Master of Novices, he was rarely allowed to sing. But the applause awarded Father Hartigan had irritated him, conscious as he was of his own talent. So he smiled on Bernardette.

"Well, since you ask me so graciously, young lady," he yielded.

Bernardette's eyes flashed triumph and Pilar acknowledged with a flick of her lashes that the trick was fairly won.

Mr. Farrahy had learnt no songs since he left his mother's drawing-room for the novitiate ten years ago, and he thought this feminine occasion required a drawing-room song. So, flustered, he broke into a song in which he had really liked his own voice when he was eighteen.

"Come into the garden, Maud," he carolled, and Father Mallon smiled at his *gaucherie*, and Father Rogers, a prim adherent of Ignatian niceties, looked irritated.

The young man sang it well, on a current of nostalgia for evenings of boyhood and home, his mother's graceful accompaniment and her praise of his tunefulness when the last note died away.

The adoring wits were ecstatic. It was their idea of a foolish, outmoded song—but that made its romantic folly all the more *à propos*—and, Heavens above, it was sentimental and it *suited* him. He couldn't possibly have heightened the fantasy of their infatuation more effectively than by singing this crazily blushful ballad.

> " . . . There has fallen a splendid tear
> From the passion-flower by the gate   . ."

His face was fair and undebauched, and he sang with his head lifted high as he leant back in his chair. He sang without thinking at all of the words of his song, but out of simple male pleasure in himself and the satisfactory, gentlemanly noise he was making.

And the girls who watched him, amused and compelled by their own nerves to keep themselves amused—for they were on the brimming edge of life, and had not simplified it, had no intention of simplifying it for themselves as he had done—took him, each of them, for a symbol, and his song for a reassurance. Soon, their nerves said, there would be a lover, and he would be beautiful and young like this, as easy as this, and his courtship would be just this of the song, Tennysonian and dewy and flattering, and there would be no catch anywhere, and none of the dark difficulties or failures that life at home and here and there on furtive report suggested. Men looked like this, like Mr. Farrahy, and love was a whisper of larkspur and lily. How absurd, how wildly sloppy—but oh, how it made you want to giggle, and what an angel he looked! My dear, an absolute angel!

When his song ended he received the murmuring, soft tribute he liked, reminiscent of his mother's, from the girls about him. The rest of the school clapped politely—for everything was an anticlimax to the majority once Father Hartigan had sung.

Presently Father Quinn made his last effort to be facetious with the gong, and the Lord Abbot said grace. Chaplain's concert was over. Reverend Mother led the priests down the broad staircase. Lay sisters came into the refectory to clear away the tables, and Mother Mary Andrew, tired and stern, formed the school into its lines, to go to bed.

But Ursula and Bernardette escaped somehow in the dim light, as if towards the cloakrooms. And, arm-in-arm, dreamy and tipsy, Pilar and Colette glided unnoticed down the carpeted Grand Staircase. Girls were absolutely forbidden to go to the hall with the priests or to see them off. Everyone wondered at the missing four, as the school climbed up to the dormitory. During hair-brushing in the dressing-room Mother Mary Andrew's wits returned. Just as she was beginning to look round in a suspicious manner, Ursula de la Pole sailed nonchalantly into the room with a polite excuse about wanting a prayer-book from her desk, and Bernardette Delane, who must have sneaked up the other way, emerged, correctly dressing-gowned, from her cubicle. Trust these two to play safe, thought the school. But "old McWhirter" soon saw that Pilar and Colette were missing. Looking like a murderer in Macbeth, as Jennie Meldon said, she deputed her authority to Sister Alicia, and left the dormitory.

The lights were out, except the lamp in Our Lady's alcove, when the school heard her return, driving her stray sheep before her. She was hissing fiercely about insubordination and immodesty, and Anna actually heard her threaten marks for conduct.

But Pilar and Colette were irrepressible, perhaps with the confidence that vacation in two days made serious punishment difficult. Their cubicles were near together and after McWhirter had stopped hissing at them and withdrawn to her own place, their neighbours could hear them giggling contentedly still.

"I just wanted to see how he looked in moonlight. Didn't you, Colette?"

"He told me he'd have sung again if I'd asked him."

"He's really ideal-looking! What's a mark for conduct matter, even—when you're in love!"

One of them even sang quite loudly for a second.

> "To faint in the light of the sun she loves,
>     To faint in his sight . . ."

But a Child of Mary called out: "Silence, please!"

"I don't care," said Pilar. "I'll be in Paris this day week!"

*The Fifth Chapter*

# SUMMER WITH CHARLIE

DOON POINT was a village in the west where the Murphys always spent the months of July and August—a holiday plan ranging back into the childhood of Grandfather Murphy. A furnished house, called a "lodge," was rented, and the family, with Delia and Mrs. Rorke—indeed everyone who mattered at Castle Tory except Joe—was transported by a long train journey to the Atlantic coast. Daddy usually spent only the first month at Doon Point, returning perhaps for one or two week-ends of August. The arrangement in its entirety was a beloved tradition of summer.

One of the first real shadows flung on childhood for Anna was when this tradition seemed insecure, when she became aware of doubt as to its continuance. She was very much shocked when in the summer of 1912 the lodge was taken only for July. And during the summer term of 1913, when she went home for Sunday afternoons, she and Charlie listened anxiously for the customary promises and hints about Doon Point—but they did not come. She was fifteen now and Charlie was thirteen, and both knew better than to precipitate trouble with their elders by direct questioning. Perhaps also they feared the reply they might be given. Indeed, so passionate was their desire for summer at Doon Point that, though each saw, at every meeting in May and June, the fixed anxiety in the other's eyes, and knew its cause, they had not the heart to speak of it together. And Anna developed a superstitious hope that if no doubt were uttered custom would somehow unfold the expected pattern.

And it did, though not quite perfectly.

When the Murphy children, Harry, Tom and Anna, returned from school at the end of term they were told that

194

they were going to Doon Point for August, to the usual lodge—but that this time they were Granny's guests, that business was bad just now for Daddy, and that they must all write and thank Granny very politely for being so kind as to give them this lovely summer holiday.

Anna did not care for Granny, who, although she seemed rich and was free with presents, exacted from children large measures of docility, piety, and reverence for herself. However, she wrote as directed; and indeed she *was* grateful, as she would have been to anyone who secured her Doon Point in August. But she perceived complications of sadness and anger behind such an arrangement; she felt it as a slur on the Murphys, a sign that the family was going downhill.

And one evening she was present during a crude piece of argument between her father and her mother.

"In any case," Daddy was saying, "we'll be well quit of each other in August. Because don't think I'm going next or near Doon Point this time, my girl! I've stood my share from that mother of yours, but I'm not going to stay in any house she pays for—by Christ I'm not!"

"Well really, Harry, I don't think she had meant to invite you. I believe her idea partly is to give me a rest from you."

"Indeed? And do you mean to tell me that one doesn't know that your whole life is one long, sweet rest from me— an unbroken, chaste, devotional retreat, by God!"

"Are you aware that your daughter is in the room?"

"Is she? Poor child. Poor Anna!"

Anna left the room.

Nevertheless, summer at Doon Point was summer multiplied, rendered imaginatively indestructible. And this time Anna held its days like a miser or a lover. For the fluke of Granny's kindness, and the crude airs of sadness and rancour at home made her accept uncertainty at last, and look ahead at facts sometimes with wider-opened, adolescent eyes.

And when she beheld Doon Point again on August 1st, when after the day's hot journey she stood by the sea-wall and smelt and heard and beheld again all of this unchanging,

unforgotten Paradise; when, astonished in joy as she had
known she would be, she gathered in the welcome of its
brilliant, evening innocence, she felt, in excess of her usual
delight, a sharp bright pain which reminded her not of former
arrivals like this, but of mornings of departure. For the first
time she felt that Doon Point too was subject to sadness—not
the brief disappointments and hurts of everyday which, she
knew, were everywhere—but the undefined yet increasingly
perceptible sadnesses of life beyond childhood, the changes
and shadows that darkened older faces, and made so much
uncertain that once was sure. She realised with a shock in
that first minute of arrival, and for no special reason other
than that she was now fifteen, and was more hurt than she
knew by the flight of childhood, that even all this joy and
beauty—so impervious-seeming from afar in winter and spring,
so wrapped apart in an isolation like that of dreams, and of
stories told and read—was a reality like other things, and, as
she had witnessed, as much a source of trouble and anger.

This perception slid into place, however, and was half
forgotten.

The summer days were happy, in spite of having to kow-
tow to Granny, and look actively grateful to her as often as
possible. Anna was in favour, because the school reports had
come before the family left Castle Tory, and hers was very
good.

"Really," said Mother, "she seems nearly as promising as
Harry. I can't imagine where these children get their brains!"

Granny bridled at that.

"I know you were never very bright at your books, my
dear Maud—but I was, I'd have you remember. However, in
this case, I can't help wishing that the brains hadn't skipped
poor Tom, and descended to Anna. After all, they're wasted
on a girl."

"Miss Robertson doesn't think so," said Anna.

"But she's a suffragette," said Harry.

Granny and Mother looked bewildered.

"Who are you talking about?" Granny asked sharply.

"Oh, an old fogey from England—she's staying at 'The Cliffs,'" said Harry.

Mother giggled.

"I believe that must be the lady Father Reilly was talking about—you know, the one who's been to prison, and wouldn't eat when she was there, or something. He says she wears the suffragettes' ribbon in her hat!"

"Poor misguided creature!" said Granny.

Anna assumed an expression of absent-mindedness. She knew that one false move would bring about a prohibition to speak again to Miss Robertson, and she intended to speak to her whenever she got a chance. She thought with pleasure now of the green, white and purple ribbon round the dusty panama hat. She hoped that perhaps Miss Robertson would give her a piece of ribbon. Not that she could wear it, but she'd like to show it to Norrie O'Dowd and tell her that she had a friend who was a friend of the lady who ran in front of the King's horse in the Derby, and was killed. She'd like to tell Norrie about hunger-striking and the Cat and Mouse Act —all the things Miss Robertson had told her that morning.

So now she kept quiet, and realised that her intervention about girls and brains had been a mistake.

Recently, Anna was becoming nervous about the shape her personal life might take, or have forced upon it. For, side by side with her reluctant realisation that the family was going downhill, began to stir an uneasy understanding that liberty— she hardly knew for what, but just liberty, the general principle—might be an expensive thing.

For instance, some trouble was having to be taken in order that Harry might be at liberty to justify his industry and success at school.

He had left Clongowes in June, and was going to do Classics and also study for the Bar at University College, Dublin. He had passed Matriculation, naturally, and when the Intermediate results were published in September there could be no doubt that, keeping to his record through school, he would be awarded every Exhibition and prize it was possible for him to win in Senior Honours, and perhaps even get some First Places in Ireland with bronze medals as he had done in Middle Grade.

But for practical purposes all that was nothing. The important thing was that in June he had sat for the County University Scholarship, worth seventy pounds a year for three years, and had won it. In addition he was going to sit in September for a University Entrance Scholarship, which would be of smaller monetary value, and would have to be re-won from year to year. But no doubt he would do all this necessary winning, and lose no chance of any other prize he could snatch by the way. Nevertheless, it seemed that it was going to be somewhat difficult to send him to the University, and in order to make it easier, Granny and Mother had conceived the plan of removing Tom from Clongowes which was, they said, wasted on his dullness, and sending him to a much cheaper school, St. Osbert's, which was famous for its Rugby football and where it seemed he might be taken very cheaply indeed, because of his talent for that game. And Charlie's neglected education being a worry to his elders, in this economical change-over his case was being examined. It was possible that a bargain might be struck at St. Osbert's which would rope him in; Granny wrote many letters this summer, and some of them, as the children knew, taking them to the post, went to the Rector of St. Osbert's.

Harry thought it a frightful come-down that his brothers should be sent to such a common school, but as the sacrifice was to aid his ambitions he did not protest. Tom was content to go anywhere where Rugby was appreciated. Charlie said he wouldn't mind St. Osbert's much—better than Clongowes anyway. But Anna felt sad over the plan for Charlie; sad over the bargaining about him, for he seemed to her to be easily the most valuable person in the family.

However, the main reflection from all these plans for Harry was that Harry could, perhaps, get what he wanted, his quite ordinary wish, only if an intricate combination of effort and calculation, his own and other people's, were brought to a correct resolution.

This made Anna nervous.

She did not think with awe of Harry, as she could see her Mother and even sometimes her Father did. She liked her rough, unpretentious brother Tom, and she loved Charlie with her whole heart. But she did not think Harry either very kind or very interesting. She would never have dreamt of saying such a thing, because he would have thought her insane, but she knew that Harry could do nothing intellectual that she could not do, given equality of age and teaching. She did not want to do the things he did, but was not awestruck before them. Having been nine years at school she was familiar with the jargon and the standards of the Intermediate Board Examinations and it was her private opinion that Molly Redmond, who also had taken Senior Honours in June, was incomparably more brilliant at her lessons than Harry would ever begin to be.

However she had no grudge against her eldest brother. Merely she was learning from his case that liberty to pursue life can be withheld or made difficult—and, from observation of Granny and talk with Miss Robertson, she saw now that whereas a boy and an eldest son may expect or command the sacrifices and co-operation of others to his ends, a girl can do no such thing. And that in fact if a girl sees liberty as the greatest of all desirables, she will have to spin it out of herself, as the spider its web—her self-made snare in which to catch Anna did not yet know what.

However, such anxieties as visited her in these reflections were for a faraway prospect. She was only fifteen and in June had taken Honours Junior. There were at least two years still, perhaps three, before she could have any liberty to tussle with. That was a long time, and half of her was glad it was. Only, she told herself cunningly, it was well to be warned, it was well to have noticed in time that liberty was precious; it was very well to have got to know a suffragette.

One morning she lay on a rock in the sun and waited for Charlie to come swimming with her. A little way off he was playing a racquets match. A racquets court had been made on the strand against the sea-wall, at a place where this was very deep.

Charlie played racquets beautifully. The boy he was playing against now was eighteen and very tall, but he was having to run all over the court after Charlie's drives. Anna had brought "Brigadier Gerard" with her to read—for about the sixth time—but she preferred to look about her and watch Charlie's play.

Almost the whole bright horseshoe of the little town—pink, blue and yellow houses—lay in front of her. The shining arc of yellow sand, the still-breasted sea, and the immaculate, lovely sky were between them the sole frame and vessel of whatever was desirable. The tide was very far out, but it had turned, and in about an hour there would be enough water at Kirwan's Rock—even enough for Charlie's swallow dive.

She would never be able to dive as he did—and of course it would be impossible to play racquets as well as he. She was a stronger swimmer, of course, but that was only because she was taller and didn't waste so much energy on fancy dives and racing strokes.

Granny said that Charlie was an ungentlemanly boy and that he had a very common accent. Well, so would anyone have who was sent to Lissanmoher National School and had only Jamesy Meagher to play with at home. Anna didn't think it fair of Granny—or Mother for that matter—to neglect Charlie's education, and then to make cutting remarks about him. But herself, although she was still somewhat at sea among *Sainte Famille* rulings on gentlemanliness, she thought Charlie had the best manners of her brothers. Harry was just stuck-up, and hardly ever knew what anyone was talking about; but Charlie was as peaceful as your shadow; although he never read or cared about books, he liked you to tell him things you were reading, and he simply never chucked a book out of your hand or thought it funny to try to make you cry or lose your temper. In fact, for a boy who rode and rode to hounds, so well, and was so particularly good at every game he tried, he was, Anna thought, surprisingly dreamy. She often wondered what he dreamt about; he sat for ages sometimes, just munching apples or doing nothing, while she read. But if she asked him, he smiled and said: "Oh, Snapper, I think." Snapper was his pony. Once she asked him what he'd like to be. He looked surprised.

"I don't want to be anything," he said. "I want to be like we are always. Don't you?"

She thought he had the nicest face it was possible to imagine; she envied him because his eyes, when he was excited—after riding Snapper, say—were exactly like sapphires. Sometimes his face pleased her so much that she did not know how to keep herself from hugging him. But she thought he wouldn't like that—because although she was inclined to regard him as a baby still, in fact he wasn't nearly so babyish as his modesty led people to believe. He said things that surprised her sometimes.

For instance once he said to her that he did not believe in hell, and that the more he thought of it the more impossible he saw hell to be, as an idea. Anna had long pondered the doctrine of hell with distaste and bewilderment, but she had never thought of Charlie's troubling his head with it. She said to him that she thought *as an idea* hell might be possible, but that we didn't have to believe that anyone had ever been condemned to it—so that although it was possible, perhaps in practice it didn't exist. But Charlie wouldn't have that. He said that struck him as too mean a dodge for God, and that just as an idea, no matter if it was never used, he thought hell impossible.

Although Anna really agreed with him she was surprised.

Another time he found her crying up in an appletree at home, and he knew why. Daddy had come in drunk, really drunk so that you couldn't miss it, at tea-time. He had knocked his tea-cup over, and then got cross about something, and for a second it looked as if he was going to hit Mother. He hadn't done so—he had gone off, cursing dreadfully—and Mother had cried. Charlie put his arms round Anna up in the tree.

"Don't cry," he said. Then after a silence he had started to say a lot of things that surprised her.

"Even if he does get drunk," he said, "you know that isn't the terrible thing they make out."

"Oh, Charlie, it is!"

"I don't think so. A thing isn't really terrible unless you've planned to do it against somebody else. You can't say that those drinks he has are any harm against anyone else."

"Yes they are. Look at Mother crying, and everything getting so funny here lately——"

"I know—it turns out that way, and he gets so that he makes Mother cry. But he doesn't *do* it for that. He doesn't mean it. Really he's good, Anna. I see him here all the time, and can't see that he means any harm to anyone."

"But all the money is going wrong and everything—you know what Granny says."

"Yes. It turns out wrong—being drunk. All I mean is, he isn't a *bad* man, Anna."

"Still, he ought to try——"

"I know. But Joe says whisky cheers you up like anything and he has terrible bad luck. You've no idea the bad luck he's had this year with the brood mares."

Anna was so much interested by Charlie's observant charitableness that she stopped crying, but she didn't altogether agree with his free-and-easy attitude to drunkenness, and she said so.

"I only mean that I don't see much harm in drunkenness in *itself*," he repeated.

She was sure that he talked to no one else in this hair-splitting fashion, except, she supposed, that in confession he might argue with the priest about hell and such points, or perhaps he turned over ideas sometimes with Joe, in the harness-room.

Once long ago, when she was thirteen and he was only eleven, she went blackberrying with Jamesy Meagher while Charlie was schooling a pony, and when he heard of it he asked her not to do it again.

"Jamesy is a low-down fellow," he said; "he has no right to give you any of his low-down talk."

"And what about you? You're always with him."

"Oh, I'm all right. I don't mind anything he says."

That seemed a long time ago, and since then, one way and another at school, she had heard a good deal of what Charlie would call "low-down talk," much of it ill-understood and of a kind that would never be mentioned between her and her brother. And he, thirteen now, wore still a shining face of innocence, and almost never spoke of anything more complicated than swimming, or riding, or the circus, or caramels. But these occasional signs that his observation was awake and ranged independently and kindly over his small field made Anna more than ever contented in his company, or perhaps explained to her why she had always felt so contented.

From where she lay she could see the Judge bending over a pool in the rocks. He collected seaweed and lived all the year round at Doon Point in a little house near the Murphys' lodge. His real name was Mr. Lawson—but everyone called him the Judge. He had once been a Civil Servant in India—perhaps a judge for all anyone knew. He was withered and small, and very kind to children. He lived alone—he was said to be a widower. Granny and Mother liked him very much and his manners were often held up to the Murphy boys as a good example. He grew the best carnations in all the neighbourhood of Doon Point, which was famous for carnations. He always wore one in his blazer button-hole.

Anna smiled friendlily now, thinking of his silly old sea-weed collection and the way he loved to march you round the frames and glass-cases, explaining it, and holding on to your arm so that it was black and blue. She hated "collections" on principle; people bored you with them. She thought that if the Judge knew they were going swimming he would come and watch them—he always liked to—and he would probably give Charlie a shilling for his swallow dive.

"Hallo, Anna."

A girl called Mabel Bassett had dropped down on the rock

beside her—a cheeky girl whom Anna did not know well or like. She had bathing things with her.

"Coming swimming?"

Anna did not want to swim with Mabel Bassett.

"No water yet," she said.

"There'll be enough by now. Come on—let's get up a crowd."

The idea was anathema to Anna who often devoted hours of thought and ingenuity to avoiding the "crowds" which people liked to "get up" at Doon Point.

"No, thanks," she said. "I'll wait for Charlie."

An almost vindictive look crossed Mabel's face.

"That baby! Why are you always with him?"

"He isn't a baby."

"Oh yes he is—believe you me, I know."

Anna stared at her in disgust. What could she—a Protestant—and a rather low-class kind of Protestant at that—know about Charlie?

"You should knock around more, you know," Mabel went on—"with the boys, I mean. People are beginning to think you are not 'all there,' the way you stick by yourself and with baby Charlie!"

"I don't mind if they do," said Anna.

"Oh very well, hoity-toity." Mabel got up and made to go on with her climb over the rocks to the road. "Anyway, Jimmy Manson and the McVieghs are waiting for me." She glanced around and. then giggled. "Only look out for yourself with the Judge, Miss Superior! He's sloping along in this direction."

Anna was taken off her guard.

"How do you mean?"

"Do you really not know about the Judge—and you always around with him, Anna Murphy?"

Anna was embarrassed. Sometimes the Judge had asked her to kiss him, and she hadn't liked it but she had thought it was her own evil imagination and things heard at school that made her so uncomfortable. After all, he was a very old man;

you might as well make a fuss about kissing Mother Eugenia. And you did that at the beginning and end of every term without minding in the least.

"Do you mean just because he kisses people?"

"No, I don't, Holy Innocent, and you don't either. Poor old Judge! If kissing was all he wanted! Well good-bye—but I don't believe you're as green as you look. Charlie is though. Good-bye again."

She went on her way.

A minute later Charlie came and dropped on the rock at Anna's side. He was hot and smiling. He had beaten Desmond O'Flynn twenty-one to nineteen.

"It was a lovely match," he said. "How about our swim?"

"Let's not go to Kirwan's Rock, Charlie. Mabel Bassett's on her way there with a 'crowd.' "

"Righto. We'll go at Devil's Point, only the diving isn't so good."

"I know. But we'll have peace."

Charlie looked away over the sea.

"What was that one, Mabel Bassett, saying to you?" he asked.

"Nothing much, why?"

"I thought you looked a bit funny." He leant over to pull up his blazer off the rock. "I have two bars of chocolate for us. I didn't come over till she'd gone because I didn't want to give her any of it."

This wiliness was very unlike Charlie.

"Why? Don't you like her?"

He shrugged.

"Protty-wotty, ring the bell!
Call the Soupers down to hell!" he said mildly.

"That's very bigoted of you," said Anna. "She can't help being a Protestant."

"I know she can't. Here, have your chocolate."

While they were eating it the Judge came over to them.

"Good morning, young Murphys."

"Good morning, Judge. Will you have some chocolate?"

"No thank you. Are you going swimming?"

"This minute," said Charlie. "We're going at the Point, though, for peace and quiet."

"You're quite right. How's the diving getting on, Charlie? May I come and watch you?"

"Yes, of course, Judge."

The three wound over the path together, climbing slowly. The Judge took Anna's bare arm and stroked it. As soon as she could she slipped ahead and tried to shake off her uneasy thoughts. It was going to be a heavenly long swim at the Point. She might even swim half-way to the Pier to-day. That dreadful Mabel Bassett! "Protty-wotty" was right. But why had Charlie his knife in her?

One afternoon Anna walked up the east cliffs with Charlie, who wanted to have his second swim at Black Creek, where mixed bathing was not allowed. Anna had swum for so long before dinner that she was willing to forgo another swim in order to walk to Black Creek with Charlie. When he vanished down the twisting slope which led to the bathing place, she stretched out on the springy turf of the cliff-top to wait for him. To her great pleasure Miss Robertson came by, and asked if she might sit on the rough stone bench and talk.

Anna felt greatly honoured, and sat up politely.

Miss Robertson was very thin and really, Anna thought, a bit saintly-looking. And she spoke in an English way, almost as if she would rather do anything on earth than speak—but she spoke quite a bit all the same, when she got going, and you really listened.

"What are you thinking about, Anna?"

"Well—only that you remind me of Reverend Mother at school, I think. Do you mind my saying that?"

"No, why should I?"

"It's the way you talk, really. But of course, she's a nun, and very Victorian—quite ridiculous about some things. I can't imagine what she'd think of you—you know, about your going to jail."

Miss Robertson laughed.

"Wouldn't she understand that?"

"Oh, I don't think so. A lady in jail!"

"You may be wrong about that, Anna. After all, a nun knows more than you or I about devotion to an idea, or an ideal. If your Reverend Mother had been in the world she might quite easily have gone to jail for the vote!"

Anna hoarded up this idea for the amusement of Norrie O'Dowd.

"It's hard to imagine it," she said politely, trying not to laugh. "She's very strict and—well, a bit enigmatic, we think. Anyway, she's all for "*la pudeur et la politesse*"—you know!"

"I know," said Miss Robertson. "And both are very good things. You don't seem much repressed by them. What are you going to be when you leave school?"

Anna hugged her knees and looked out anxiously over the bay. Whenever anyone asked that question—even this stranger, on whose lips it could have little menace—her heart thudded uneasily. She had no idea at all of what she wanted to be. She wanted time, and secrecy, and no interference and no advice. She knew already that her supply of the first two would be limited, and that she would be overwhelmed from all sides by the remaining two. She knew also that everything which she saw, or read about, which appeared to be done well seemed for an hour or a day the kind of thing to which she also must devote her life. As, when the canoes went out at evening from Doon Point to the long night of fishing and peril, she desired to be a leader of brave fishermen, the strongest and best; when she read in the papers of the Balkan War just ending, she saw herself as a brainier Venizelos, and when she thought about Captain Scott she dreamt of the tragic and splendid expeditions she would lead, over even more desolate and heart-breaking Antarcticas. She thought of herself sometimes as a very heroic doctor, sometimes as a conductor of symphony orchestras, and sometimes as a humble and handsome Canadian "Mountie." When her father quoted Tim Healy's witticisms at the Irish Bar, she foresaw that shafts of hers would one day hit more deeply and amazingly. When Father Hogan talked contemptuously of the Irish Party, and expounded the political doctrines of Arthur Griffith, she pondered the value to herself of a patriot's career; and when she talked with Miss Robertson she felt her own strong ability to out-Pankhurst Mrs. Pankhurst.

But underneath these foolish self-dramatisations she was both cunning and realistic. She knew quite well, with the older part of her mind that the roads ahead were hidden, that she had as yet no map, and that she was young and silly and very ignorant. However, others had been these things also, and got through. What you had to do was to play for time. You wanted none of the lives you saw about you, and at present saw no way to any other. But the thing was to keep your head, to be still and watchful, and walk into no traps. The thing was to have patience, and to build a high fence about the precious distant freehold, your own future, which you could as yet neither see nor attempt to describe. And meantime, though it would come and be a fact, how unreal it was, how it melted, dissolved and darkened, just as dreams did when you tried to hold them. How unreal—beside this, the bright sky and the seagulls, and the rattling suck of waves through the stones below, and having nothing to do, just waiting for Charlie.

"I don't think I want to be anything, Miss Robertson," she said politely.

Miss Robertson was disappointed.

"Oh but, Anna—that can't be true! Look at how vast the world is, and how much there is waiting to be done! So much good work needed everywhere, Anna!"

Anna nodded.

"When I think like that I get desperate, and I practically decide to be a nun," she said. She lay face downwards on the turf, and rubbed her cheek against it fretfully. She stared out over the blue water. "The thing is to be a *genius*," she said disconsolately. "And I haven't a chance in a million of that."

Miss Robertson smiled and did not say how very much smaller the chance was.

Soon Charlie came up the slope, rubbing his wet hair. The Bishop was walking with him, also rubbing his wet hair. Anna knew the Bishop, from his prize-giving and other visits to *Sainte Famille*. Miss Robertson knew him too. She had called on him, for permission to lecture in certain women's training colleges in his diocese. He had edited her lecture, and granted the permission.

Anna found the Bishop alarming. He sometimes walked into Mother Josephine's Latin class, snatched Livy or Horace from her hand and commanded anyone at random to translate. He was impatient and unnerving when he did this. She was surprised now to find him with Charlie. He was a very strong swimmer, and a faithful summer visitor at Doon Point. There was a dangerous thirty-foot dive at Black Creek which he was renowned for. It always annoyed Anna that she could not see this dive, not even if Charlie ever did it, simply because men could not be bothered to wear bathing costumes at Black Creek. She thought it silly of them to be so obstinate.

The Bishop smiled at Miss Robertson and at Anna.

"I've just discovered that this young fellow is your brother, Anna Murphy. He'll be trying to cut me out at the Thirty-Foot before I'm much older. He knows more about diving, Anna, than you do about the Samnite War."

Charlie smiled modestly. The Bishop evidently expected them to walk back to the village with him. They all moved on to the stony path.

"Well, Miss Robertson," said the Bishop, "I see you believe in catching 'em young! Or were you preaching to the converted?"

"To tell you the truth, my Lord, I couldn't be sure. The Irish are hard to pin down, I think."

The Bishop looked amused and pleased.

"It's not so much the Irish as the Catholic, I think, Miss Robertson," he said gently. "We really have a difficulty about causes and platforms which arises not so much from cynicism, as our detractors like to say, as from the peculiar nature of our faith."

"Yet you seem to feel no difficulty, my Lord, about the cause, the platform of nationalism."

"I personally feel none—but then, I believe it to be wrong that a nation fervently professing one Church should be subject to the rule of a nation professing an entirely other Church—so you see, for me, that platform is very closely allied to religion. And therefore I believe that, when such a state of things exists, education, for instance, should be very nationalistic indeed, even what is called narrowly so, until such a political anomaly is renounced, by the educational process."

"You must forgive me if I say I disagree with you, my Lord."

"Ah, you're not the only one, Miss Robertson. This child, for instance, is at school at *Sainte Famille*"—he touched Anna's head—"you may have heard of the school. It was a French foundation, and its tradition is certainly very Catholic—but it is, I contend, too European for present-day Irish requirements. Its detachment of spirit seems to me to stand in the way of nationalism."

"I like detachment of spirit," said Miss Robertson.

"If I may say so, you haven't adhered to it exclusively, Miss Robertson."

"Oh, that was an accident of time and place."

"I might say the same of nationalism," said the Bishop, "only I won't. And I want our schools to be patriotic."

Anna thought the Bishop was not being quite fair to *Sainte Famille;* she heard prejudice in his voice, and although he was a Bishop, she felt compelled to speak more accurately for her school to Miss Robertson.

"We learn a lot of Irish history at *Sainte Famille*," she said, "and we do a terrible lot of Irish language."

"Indeed? How very progressive!" said Miss Robertson politely.

"Yes, very," said the Bishop. "And Anna's a prize-winner

at it. Very good indeed, Mother Mary Andrew tells me. So perhaps, in spite of everything, these young people may save us yet. *Sinn Fein*, you know, Miss Robertson! It means ourselves."

They paused where the track forked towards the Bishop's lodge on the hill.

"It's an unattractive motto to give to young people," said Miss Robertson.

"No, no," said the Bishop, "not as we apply it. And noble deeds will be done in its name, I believe."

"I am sure they will, my Lord."

"Even so, you don't like it?" Miss Robertson smiled. "Ah, you're a hard nut to crack, Miss Robertson. But sure the English police discovered that before I did!" He laughed very charmingly. "Good evening now to the three of you."

He strode away from them.

Anna thought Charlie was looking bored, so she was glad Miss Robertson's hotel was not far off. Herself she had been interested, and irritated, by what the Bishop said. He was of course far more up to date and sensible than Reverend Mother—but somehow while he talked you felt fonder than you had thought you were of her. Anyway, he was often a bit unfair—and her worst enemy could never say she was.

"A brilliant, dangerous man, your Bishop," Miss Robertson said with a smile.

The children felt somewhat shocked. It was queer to call a bishop "dangerous." However, Miss Robertson was a Protestant, and might not know that.

When they shook hands with her outside "The Cliffs" Anna summoned up courage to ask if she might have a bit of green, white and purple ribbon.

Miss Robertson was delighted. She had a little reel of it in her bag, it turned out. And Charlie had a penknife, so Anna was given a fine long piece at once—almost a yard of it, she thought.

"Could I have a little piece, Miss Robertson?" Charlie asked.

Anna was surprised.

"But Charlie, it's for Votes for Women!"

"I know. I'd like Votes for Women. May I have a *little* piece, Miss Robertson?"

Miss Robertson gave him as long a piece as she had given Anna.

"Oh thank you very much, Miss Robertson."

The children said good evening and strolled on. They were silent a while.

"The Bishop dives very well," said Charlie. "What does that mean, Anna—detachment of spirit?"

"I think it means when you don't let the things that happen to be happening round you seem much more important than what happens to other people or in other times."

"Ah! I thought it might mean something about not being conceited."

"I suppose it does too, in a way."

"It sounded to me like something you'd expect a priest to be. Have you any money, Nan?"

"No. Why?"

"We could have got some coco-nut ice."

"You—don't want to be a priest, do you, Charlie?"

"No. Anyway, I don't learn Latin."

"But—do you *want* to be a priest?"

Anna's heart pounded in surprise and fear.

"No. Not really."

As they turned in at their own gate he spoke again.

"Would Granny notice, do you think, if I wore my Votes-for-Women ribbon as a tie?"

"No—she's getting very blind. It'd make a lovely tie, Charlie."

"That's what I thought. I like Miss Robertson, don't you?"

A German band played by the sea-wall every evening that summer. Some of the elders refused to put money in their tin box; they said that it was dangerous and disgraceful to have such people around the coast. But the children in Doon Point were passionately devoted to the band, and the more so because of the exciting farce with which their performance was brought to an end on many evenings.

There were five men in the band. One had a very small piano on wheels; there were two violinists, a 'cellist and a man who sometimes played a viola and sometimes a flute. They all wore yachting caps, and rather dirty white trousers. They all wore glasses too; they had pretty little iron music-stands, and their music was always blowing about the road.

They played "The Merry Widow," "The Blue Danube" and "*Wienerblut*"; they played and sang a repertory hotly disputed and loved by their audience; student songs, lullabies, love-songs and hymns—from "*Ach, du lieber Augustin*" to "*O du Selige.*" And sometimes the flautist sang alone: "*Ueber allen Gipfeln*" or "*Sah ein Knab'.*"

But best of all was "*Die Lorelei.*"

They sang it in harmony, and with orchestral effects of lapping water. These were so brilliant that, although some of the audience liked to join in the singing, with parodies—"I cannot think what is the matter, but I am feeling so sick . . ." the majority preferred simply to listen. Franz, the one with the little piano, was very clever, and you never knew from evening to evening what he might do to heighten the effect of lapping water. Charlie told Anna that he simply couldn't get over the way Franz played in "*Die Lorelei.*"

But there was a man in the village who could not bear the tune. He was a man called Mack, who hired and, sometimes, built canoes. He drank a good deal, but no one ever saw him get cross when he was drunk—except at the sound of "*Die Lorelei.*"

The band usually played it towards the end of their programme, and Mack was never to be seen until it was more or less due. Then he would come sloping along the edge of the crowd, saying nothing at first—just smiling bitterly. The children watched him with fear and delight; the Germans seemed not to know he was around. As they got ready to begin "*Die Lorelei*" he usually came well into view in the front of the crowd. Some public-spirited person, often the

Judge, would seek to engage him in conversation, and in the
first exchanges it always appeared as if the gambit succeeded,
for Mack was very polite and would answer attentively, and
seemed to remove his eyes from the musicians. And once or
twice the Judge, linking arms with Mack and cunningly
murmuring an invitation to "a drop of something at Mary
Jo's" almost got him away before the storm broke. But that
was only Mack's guile, or his reluctance to offend his friend
the Judge. He never intended to be diverted from this hate.
After the first affabilities he forgot the Judge and stood stock-
still, smiling terribly at the unfortunate Germans, so gallantly
singing and playing and creating the effects of lapping water.

Anna noticed that his control always gave away at the same
place—so that it became for her like watching a well-known
scene in a play.

Exactly at *"Der Gipfel des Berges funkelt im Abendsonnen-
schein,"*—Franz's best bit, really—Mack gave his first
appalling roar and kicked the 'cellist off his stool. Always the
'cellist got the first of it. Then, while the brave music and
singing still went on, he let them have it—knocking everything around. He was very strong.

"Bloody, dirty German spies! Spies and cut-throats, by the
Lord God Almighty! I'll have your lives, ye sods! I'll cut the
guts out o' ye, so help me Holy Jesus! You're spies, I say,
you're spies! Ye're not men at all, dirty little rats from
Germany—ye lowdown buggers! I'll have justice done—I'll
kick the daylights out o' ye—wan by wan! Come on, let ye—
Tralá, la-lá-là-là-lá! Dirty, filthy, skunking little sods—come
on here, let ye, till I knock the dirty stuffing out of ye! Jesus
and Mary! Is it to have the Kaiser's spies destroying this
country! Be the sweet and lovin' God . . .!"

Somehow the music went on a little while; cunning boys
grabbed the music-stands, and braver ones made grabs at
Mack who swung them benevolently aside. His quarrel was
solely with the Germans, who edged about, and sang
vociferously while the children scuffled around Mack in their
uncertain defence. But at last Sergeant Madden sneaked up

behind him—Mack was an awful fool really—and the handcuffs were clipped on in a twinkling.

"Come on let you now, in the name of God, and don't keep me all night," said the Sergeant.

And bellowing in astonished fury, shouting pious and terrible blasphemies and bad words, Mack was marched right through the village, all the children following him in excitement as if he were the Pied Piper. And when he came at last to the lock-up, he always gave the same deep, startled howl of grief, and turned for the last time to his followers:

"Spies, spies, I'm tellin' ye. Ye'll rue this day, and the wrong ye done me! Them lot is bloody spies, and your doom is comin' towards ye! Be the sweet and lovin' Lord Jesus!"

Sergeant Madden showed him into the barracks then and wiped his eyes for him, for tears always poured down his face when he saw the lock-up. But one evening Charlie caught hold of his chained hands just as he was being pushed into jail, and he said:

"Don't cry like that, Mack—don't be silly, sure you know as well as I do you'll be out in the morning."

And of course he was. All he ever needed, in Sergeant Madden's opinion, was a nice, quiet sleep, the poor, decent fellow.

It was great fun. But Anna, though she might have been ashamed to admit it, was not always in the mood for Mack. Just as her sense of humour was not ravished by the school's wrecking of *Wallensteins Tod*, so sometimes she desired the German music far more than the violent farce that silenced it. For often listening to it she was revisited, more gently, more bearably, by the pain of premonition which had startled her on the evening of arrival at Doon Point, and she was willing enough then to sit still, and, protected by the sentimentality of the sounds and the hour, to examine in peace the love and the faint anxiety she felt for all that lay about her.

So she was glad if it happened that Mack was sober, or away in a canoe, and the Germans could do *Lorelei* twice,

perhaps, and go on playing when the sun had disappeared
into the water, and the breeze was cold, and they had to peer
at the music. Many children went away then; nurses and
mothers called them from the doorsteps of lodges. Below
the sea-wall pools grew very brilliant between black rocks,
and the wet, ribbed strand shone more and more coldly, as
if it were silver. But Anna stayed, shivering, until the last
song was over, and Franz wheeled his piano homeward.
*Gute Nacht, Fräulein.* Charlie stayed too as a rule. He sat
on the flat wall with his knees drawn up to his chin, and he
sang all the time, though he didn't know the words of anything. Anna liked to hear him singing gently to himself and
to see his Votes-for-Women tie floating in the breeze.

There were only two days left of August, but the children
tried to ignore the signs of preparation for departure and to
behave as if the present was for ever.

Charlie went pollock-fishing after dinner on the great
headland of deep-pooled rocks to the west of the bay. Anna
did not care for pollock-fishing, and anyway could not go
with him because the pollock pools were a bathing-place for
men where women were not allowed. She said she would
finish *Spanish Gold*, and perhaps go to meet him at the edge
of the rocks, to help carry home his catch.

It was nearly four o'clock when she closed her book. Just
as she was leaving the house Granny called to her from
the drawing-room window. She said she knew Anna "would
love" to go over the fields for her, to Mrs. Harvey's dairy,
and pay the cream and butter bill, and say good-bye to Mrs.
Harvey on Granny's behalf.

Such requests from Granny were in fact commands, and
during this holiday, under the *duresse* of especial gratitude,
there was no question of rebellion. So Anna set out over the
fields for Mrs. Harvey's, and she was content enough, because
she decided that after she had left the dairy she would climb
up the inner slope of Coastguard Hill, and then have the
lovely walk back across the golf-links, all but blown into

the sea the whole way—and reach Charlie just when he was on his way back from his old pollock-fishing.

On the field-path between the village and the dairy, it was as if you were far inland. There was no sign at all of the sea, and a deep, brown stream ran by the track, tangled over by foxgloves, meadowsweet and pink and white mallows.

Anna liked the soft novelty of these things, so near to fierce rocks and waves and pungent seaweed. When she came to St. Enda's well in its little roofless chapel of stone, she laid Granny's money and the bill very carefully on the top step, and lent down over the dark, cold water for a blessed drink.

She was reminded of "The Boy's Song" as she went on by the little stream. "Where the pools are bright and deep, where the grey trout lies asleep." She remembered how she tried to make Charlie learn it, and she laughed at herself. I must have been a terrible bore to him with all my poems, she thought, but he never got cross with me, or told me to shut up. Her thoughts strayed over babyhood and early days at school. It was really rather sweet of Reverend Mother, she admitted, to let her learn a poem for her every week like that. I must have been an awful little prig. She felt the lines of some of them moving about in her memory now, and realised what pleasure, unperceived, unattended, all those shapely verses had made for her ever since, when half asleep, or bored in chapel, or just walking along as now. She wondered where Letitia Doyle was, and if she was married. She remembered Letitia had once said to her that she would very much like to be married. At the time Anna had thought that very natural, but now she understood it less. Letitia was kind—she would make a very nice, kind wife. Anna remembered sitting sometimes in St. Joseph's Grotto with *Mère Martine* and being half asleep when Letitia came and picked her up and took her into *goûter*.

"*Vogue, mon beau navire* . . ." What was that? *Mère Martine's* song? Ah yes! "*Vogue, mon beau navire, Sur les flots endormis* . . ." *Mère Martine* was getting old and silly now.

She certainly had a rather nice time those first years at school. All that fooling around with *Mère Martine*, and saying special poems and everything. She supposed that all that must be the root of the "Reverend Mother's pet" business. Certainly Reverend Mother had no pets nowadays that anyone could notice . . .

She paid Mrs. Harvey and said good-bye for Granny. But she made the speech as short as she could because Mrs. Harvey was, as everyone agreed, a wailer and a bore. The only interesting thing about her was the way her lamenting, tragic voice echoed and thundered through her cold, stone dairy. But that dramatic phenomenon had been observed often before, so Anna did not linger with it now.

She set off again across fields, towards the curve of Coastguard Hill which would take her up to the sea, to the majestic panorama—breakers and green cliff-heads and stretching rocks. She was going to take her ease over this walk, as it would be the last time this holiday that she'd walk down from Coastguard Hill, and Charlie wouldn't mind. He'd go home without her if he got tired or hungry—he'd understand when she explained about Mrs. Harvey, and then about not wanting to hurry down Coastguard Hill. "*Vogue, mon beau navire . . .*"

Charlie moved from pool to pool over the headland of rocks, but fishing was unsatisfactory, with bathers diving into all the pools. He moved off dreamily into solitude along the jagged, lonely edges of the headland. The tide ran very fiercely on this craggy breakwater. Charlie delighted in the green and creamy water, and in the founts of spray that drenched him. A little way out cormorants were busy, so he spun his line, but in fact he was more interested by the antic bobbings of seals and the greed of the gulls than by his chances of a pollock. It was a lovely day, and he decided that later on, when the pools were emptier, he'd go back to them and have a swim. Meantime, dropping down into solitude under great shelves of rock, he felt very happy, quite alone with the Atlantic. Except for those canoes out there. Marty Hourigan and his father in that one leading, I bet, thought Charlie. But they were too far off to identify, let alone to shout at.

He threw his line again. He wished one of the seals would land up on that flat bit of rock. They were great fun to watch. The tide was coming in now, he thought. Water washed more deeply each time over his bare feet. The rocks were weedy, so he moved with care. He noticed some beautiful seaweeds being swirled about in the breakers. It's a pity Anna isn't here, he thought—she's mad on seals. She thinks they'll land if you sing to them, or something. He began to sing the *Lorelei*, but he knew the seals couldn't hear him, against the breakers. That's a lovely bit of seaweed, that red and white bit, all frilly. I bet the Judge would like to see that. Where's my crab-hook—I'll hook it in off that rock for him. Steady. Yes, I've got it. Wait a jiffy.

He slipped and fell into the strongly running sea. But even as he did so he had no fear. He knew the current was powerful, but he was confident that, if he kept calm, he could use it to carry himself back to the rocks. He was not frightened, for he loved and understood the sea.

Anna knew by the empty quiet round the clubhouse that it must be after six o'clock, and so she did not look for Charlie. He would have got hungry and gone home.

She was hungry too; Delia would be furious at all the currant loaf she'd eat. Oh heavens! Only one day more! Oh Charlie, Charlie, what'll we *do* the day after to-morrow?

Passing the first lodges of the village she saw people sitting down to tea, and that made her even hungrier, so she ran down the slope. But as she came near the curve of the road she saw, over the sea-wall, that people, children she knew, and fishermen, were hurrying across the rocks to Devil's Point. She got an odd impression that they were frightened. She did not hear them talk or call out as they went. Then she saw, or half saw, below the rocks that two canoes were pulled in at the bathing ladder. There was something the matter then? A—a—drowning accident?

She paused. That was why they seemed frightened. Two years ago a woman was drowned and the fishermen brought her in like that—in the evening. A lovely evening like this.

Oh yes, they were crowding round. They seemed to be lifting something. Someone. Oh, poor thing! Oh, who was drowned?

They were coming up this way, to the steps and the opening in the wall. She could hear the fishermen saying "Hail Marys" now, and everyone answering. That meant that the poor drowned person was—dead. When they prayed, she prayed too. She felt very frightened for whoever it was. "Holy Mary, Mother of God, pray for us sinners now and at the hour of our death. Amen!"

She still could not see what they were carrying—she did not exactly want to see. She had never seen a dead person. Oh Lord, have mercy on the dead! Oh, the poor thing. Lord, Lord, have mercy.

She looked away from the burdened fishermen, at the crowd of children she knew, all looking so different, so frightened. She saw Mabel Bassett staring up at her—staring very queerly. Then she saw the Judge, and he saw her. He started to run when he saw her. He ran up the steps and to her. He looked almost ninety, Anna thought. His face was covered with tears. He caught hold of her very strongly, but he was shaking.

"No, Anna—come away. Come away quickly, child."

But her eyes had gone past him.

The fishermen had paused with their burden, below the steps.

She saw Charlie lying in their hands. She saw a great, dried wound in his head, and she saw his bare feet. She saw his beautiful, dead face and his bedraggled Votes-for-Women tie.

"Hail Mary, full of grace, the Lord is with thee . . ."

# BOOK THREE

## *June*

## The First Chapter

# IN REVEREND MOTHER'S STUDY

*Mère Générale* died on the last day of May, 1914.

Reverend Mother had foreseen this death for many weeks, and five days before it took place received a feebly written letter of farewell from the old nun.

*Place des Ormes, Bruxelles.*
*"le 21 mai 1914.*

*"Chère enfant,—*

*"Bientôt je vais partir pour toujours. D'une heure à l'autre j'attends l'appel du Seigneur. L'heure est bien sonnée, puisque j'approche de mes quatre-vingts ans et que je deviens inutile. Néanmoins une si longue vie n'a pas suffi pour purifier cette pauvre âme, et je me trouve à la fin assez mécontente de moi. Mais j'ai toujours confiance en Dieu, qui aura pitié de mes faiblesses, et je sais que mon séjour au Purgatoire sera raccourci par les généreuses prières de mes chères filles en Jésus-Christ, La Compagnie de la Sainte Famille.*

*"Je laisse tout en ordre. Il ne m'est pas permis, comme vous le savez, de parler de mes désirs pour la direction future de L'Ordre. Après ma mort vous lirez, comme toutes les Mères Supérieures et Mères Provinciales, mes désirs et mes conseils à cet égard. Du reste, que Dieu vous dirige toutes, mes chères filles.*

*"Je vois, à courte échéance, de grands dangers s'abattre sur le monde entier. Impossible de nier que l'Allemagne prend ses dispositions pour une guerre éventuelle et prochaine contre l'Entente Cordiale—et qu'est-ce que cela signifiera pour l'Europe, pour le monde, et pour l'Eglise de Jésus-Christ? Je ne peux que vous laisser ces lourdes questions à résoudre, en vous promettant que toutes mes prières et toutes mes souffrances pénitentielles seront offertes au ciel pour la cause de la chère Compagnie.*

*"Je n'ai plus la force d'écrire. Chère enfant, il n'y a que vous*

223

*au monde à laquelle je voudrais faire les adieux d'une amitié particu-*
*lière. Pendant toutes les années de séparation vous êtes restée très*
*proche de mon cœur, et vous savez que seulement le devoir m'a forcée*
*de me priver si longtemps de la consolation de votre présence et de*
*vos conseils. J'ai la plus grande confiance en vous, en vos qualités*
*de caractère, de jugement et de sainteté, et cette confiance rend*
*tranquilles et heureuses les quelques heures de vie humaine qui me*
*restent. Je vous embrasse en Jésus-Christ, et je vous quitte dans la*
*douce espérance de vous revoir avant longtemps au paradis, vous et*
*votre très cher père. Et comme je vais me moquer de lui, de mon*
*bon Socrate, à cette réunion!*

"*Priez pour moi—et que notre doux Sauveur vous protège et vous*
*égarde toujours.*

> "*Adieu, chère enfant,*
> "*Catherine Mandel,*
> "*C. de S. F.*"

This letter had roused many emotions and reflections.
But also, as she knew it was meant to, it had made Reverend
Mother smile, and recalled to her amusing moments in the
little study at *Place des Ormes*, where she and *Mère Générale*
had connived together delicately for the glory of God. "*Il
ne m'est pas permis, comme vous le savez, de parler de mes désirs,*"
and further on: "*J'ai la plus grande confiance en vous . . . et cette
confiance rend tranquilles et heureuses les heures qui me restent . . .*"
She could see the smile with which *Mère Générale* would
have re-read those sentences. They delivered their gently
illicit message. They told her that she had been commended,
in the customary sealed letter to the Council of the Order,
as its next *Mère Générale*.

She might not be elected. There was a powerful Irish
Reverend Mother in Chicago whose name would be put
forward by the Western Provinces; and the venerable and
holy Austrian Mother Provincial would also receive some
votes. But the former would almost certainly not appeal to
the Council, which was still far from ready to hand the Order
over to the twentieth century and to the English and Spanish

tongues; and European war clouds would militate against an Austrian appointment. So it was very likely that tradition would once again provide the politic line, and that she, a surprise and a dark horse, would be called to government at *Place des Ormes*.

Ten years ago she would have embraced any duty, however humble or exacting, which sent her back to Brussels; and now, were her father still living, there would have been an irrepressible human joy to set against the anxieties and doubts of assuming the highest office of her Order. But—her father was gone, and *Mère Générale* had gathered up her soul to go; and the clouds massing over Europe made her shrink even more doubtfully than she would have done in a normal time from responsibilities which war, if it came, would not fail to multiply heavily. And whatever was human in her had thrust at least one root into Irish soil. She would of course pull up that root, and go wherever God's Will and holy obedience directed, and do her best with duties for which she knew herself unworthy. But she would have been glad if such uprooting could have been delayed a little time.

At a moment of weak discouragement in her own life she had decided against an appeal for flight, because of a vibration of sympathy with a little child who by chance had repeated to her a poem which she in her time had repeated to her father. The sentimental whim had been guarded from over-nurture, and she had in fact compelled herself to let it stand unexamined; but she knew that her nerves had sensed some potentialities, some needs in the child which might not be interesting, might not be attractive, might not win her sympathy, but which she should be able to understand, and might conceivably desire to defend—from she knew not what! From the ignorant imperative, perhaps, or the rule of thumb—or from mercilessness, which her father, and so much more deeply than he knew, had taught her to hold in horror. "The young and the weak and the sentimental." Perhaps it was no more than that, at a significant moment, Anna Murphy had seemed the epitome of these.

Yet she had grown, through nine formative years, more simply and even perhaps more dully than many children. She was intelligent in the class-room and was the conventional child bookworm, reading without perceptible selectiveness, once an early devotion to poetic form had worn away. This love of reading—almost, apparently, for reading's sake—had given her an advantage at lessons which made her seem bored with the stumblings of classmates, and won her a reputation for conceit. She was not unpopular, but she appeared to rouse enmity in some schoolfellows; she made no violent friendships and appeared immune from *Schwärmerei* for older girls or for nuns; in religion it seemed as if periods of acute devotion alternated with periods of exaggerated coldness, but intellectually she seemed considerably interested, for she was keen on apologetics and Church history. Her tastes were literary and linguistic rather than scientific; she appeared to admire distinction in personalities and in achievements—yet for a growing child she gave an impression of detachment which was not very endearing. She was orderly, quick-witted and tenacious of her point of view; and in spite of a reputation for intelligence which she justified in performance, Reverend Mother sometimes wondered whether she wasn't just pedestrian and cautious.

Herself she had nothing against that; but Anna had originally quickened something of her father in her, something erratic, speculative and quick on the wing. And, oddly enough, through all the quiet, cold years, the child had never really lost her power to do so. Reverend Mother had watched her grow, a little sadly; she thought that, with the end of the period of the Sunday poems and the beginning of serious lessons, light had seemed to dim round Anna, or to draw inwards. Above all—and she tried in vain to accuse herself of sentimentality here—she thought that spontaneity went and cunning took its place after the episode of the first French test and the verb "*finir*." She held that occasion to have been one of evil revelation to Anna, and to mark the loss of innocence; and she knew that—as hysterically perhaps as if she were the child's mother—she would never forgive that blunder to Mother Mary Andrew.

But though Anna grew conventionally and warily thereafter, into the common stream and away from indulgent observation—Reverend Mother continued to watch her. And it pleased her to note accumulatively that, although in this observation she did not uncover great talents, noble characteristics, or flashing, precocious originality—she always found some unnamable thing she liked, which made her go on watching. Something which was not altogether seriousness, though that was in it; nor the poetic quality, though suggestively too that stirred; not courage, though its struggle was there, never quite beaten; nor honour, though the guileful child did not seem able to escape it—yet all these abstracts came to mind if, unwatched, one watched her. And that they did was enough for Reverend Mother, and made her feel a curious affection, and an anxious sympathy which nothing in the girl's steady progress seemed to justify.

All that was true until a year ago, when in June Anna went home for the summer vacation. She had taken Honours Junior in the Intermediate, and, as the September results were to show, had done very well, winning a double exhibition and three language prizes. She had distinguished herself in general through the school year, and had gone home happy and laden with book prizes. And she came back on September 6th, the opening day of the scholastic year, like everyone else. But meantime her thirteen-year-old brother had been drowned; she had seen him carried in from the sea in the arms of fishermen, and she had seen him buried.

This experience had "changed her very much," some of the nuns said, and so did her mother and grandmother. Reverend Mother let them say it, because she believed that the less foolish discussion of Anna now the better. But herself she did not accept the word "change" in psychology, and in the Anna of the three terms just sped she saw not change but violent disturbance of the individual that had hitherto been in no hurry to uncover itself, but had lain defensively still so long, so wisely young and content. She saw growth, too fiercely fertilised by a pain which she apprehended day after day as almost increasing in this troubled victim's mind. She saw a crisis sustained perilously long, and attempting in escape from itself to turn outward, in assault on circumstances, on plans and people and the practical future.

And all of this was still unresolved—indeed, was at present in some of its parts in external conflict—and Reverend Mother believed that she alone saw it fully, saw it with love.

And now on the morning of the first Saturday of June she sat alone at her desk with two cables in her hands. The one had come before breakfast, and had been read at once to the assembled community, the chapel bell tolling in accompaniment. It simply announced that *Mère Générale* Catherine Mandel of the *Compagnie de la Sainte Famille* had died at midnight in the Convent of *Place des Ormes*, in Brussels, fortified by all the rights of the Church. *Requiescat in Pace*. The other, delivered two hours later, was longer and was for herself alone. It told her that in the presence of the Chaplain of *Place des Ormes*, of her Confessor and of the lawyers of the Order, Mother Assistant had opened the late Mother General's sealed letter of farewell, copies of which would be sent at once to all Reverend Mothers and Mothers Provincial. In this letter she, Mother Mary Helen Archer, was strongly recommended to the Council for succession to the Generalship. During the last month of her life the late Mother General had accepted two other submitted nominations for this office—Mother Mary Patrick Duggan, *Sainte Famille*, Chicago, Mother Provincial of North America, and *Mutter Gertrud von Ammensbach, Sainte Famille*, Vienna, Mother Provincial of Austria. In view of the threatening state of world affairs, it was the late General's wish, the telegram went on, that the election should be as expeditious as was legitimate. The three names of candidates were being cabled therefore to all voters, in the hope that a decision might be effected within a month. The message concluded with a pious exhortation to wisdom and to the seeking of heavenly direction.

Reverend Mother knew at once that she would vote for the old Austrian saint in Vienna, whose cause had already been lost for her by international politics. And as to Mother Mary Patrick Duggan—the Order was not yet ready for American domination. It was almost certain therefore that she, the late General's choice, would assume her office. It meant that at the conclusion of this term she would leave Ireland, presumably for ever, and return to her beloved Brussels and to the graves and gentle shadows of her few human loves.

There were anxiety and division in her breast as she surveyed this prospect.

This would be a busy day for Reverend Mother. The convent was quiet in its mourning, but she would have much correspondence to deal with, the condolences of many important callers to accept, and detailed arrangements to make for the Solemn Requiem Mass to be upheld for *Mère Générale's* soul, on Tuesday. A great many invitations would have to be issued for that, and there was the delicate problem of deciding whom to invite, among many jealous priests, to preach the memorial sermon.

Yet Reverend Mother did not scruple to sit still and think about Anna Murphy, with these matters of organisation waiting for her thought. For she felt the girl to be an urgent problem now, and one apprehended solely by her—and she believed that the dead *Mère Générale* would understand and bless her anxiety.

She remembered an evening six months ago, an evening of December, when she had heard a very timid knock at the door of this little room and on replying had been surprised, and very glad, to see Anna enter.

No schoolgirl ever entered the nuns' Community Room for any reason, or knocked at or entered Reverend Mother's study without having received a specific command and appointment from the latter to do so. Often during the term, watching her from afar, and assembling with as little ostentation as possible information about her work, her health, her sleep, Reverend Mother had thought of sending for her to come and talk in this room. But she knew well that she was only a symbol, almost an out-of-date effigy in the eyes of youth, and she was sure that, unless Anna spoke first of her own overcharged heart, no one who was so rash as to speak to her of it could hope at all to help her. It did not seem that Anna, if she ever relaxed the guard she had placed over herself lately, would do so to her, the reserved, cold Reverend Mother. And so the latter had undertaken the difficult task of protection at long range, unsuspected, and by guesswork. Also by the forbidding of well-meant assaults by other people. For she was confident that a soul, left to itself, has good chances of recovering in some measure from any sickness—whereas rash manipulation may establish a deformity. Also she thought that there are some maladies which should be allowed to develop, perhaps—since what the cheerful call *mens sana* is not necessarily the best or richest condition of spirit for every phase of life. She could not help hoping that Anna's grief might, by Heaven's mercy, be such a malady. At any rate, she felt she had to gamble somewhat on leaving the child alone as long as possible, unless she herself moved out of the shadows and spoke, asked for something.

There she was then, entering Reverend Mother's study without appointment. A very surprising event.

The crude gaslight in the bare white-walled room fell on her without pity. She was averagely tall for her age, but had grown extremely thin during the autumn term; she was very pale and her face was long and hollow-cheeked. Reverend Mother noticed that her hands looked as if they had been violently scrubbed in cold water in preparation for this interview. Also, her hair was carefully brushed, but her black dress seemed dusty and as if she had outgrown it. Her eyes burnt very darkly.

Reverend Mother looked at her out of an anxious pity which she hoped was not hinted at in her face. She sought for a manner which would be leisurely, yet not seem too pointedly encouraging.

"Anna? Yes, come in, my dear child. You remember this room, don't you?" During the baby years, the years of the poems, Anna, by unprecedented exception, had been allowed to come to Reverend Mother's study sometimes, to read to her, or run little errands about the convent for her. "When were you last here, I wonder?"

Anna looked about the bare little room with remembrance in her eyes.

"I think it was once after I had a cold and I sat here a whole afternoon, Reverend Mother. You gave me a big plate of grapes."

"Did I? Would you like to sit down?"

Anna shook her head.

"No, thank you, Reverend Mother. I'm—I'm sorry I knocked without getting permission first, but——"

"But what?"

"If you say 'no' to what I'm going to ask you, no one else need know I asked it—need they?"

"I imagine not."

"I know I shouldn't bother you with it——"

"What is it, Anna?"

The question was put with all the gentleness the nun could summon into her voice—for she could hardly bear another moment the shy, struggling agony in the girl's face. And her tone fell luckily—with an unmistakable ring of solicitude and good will. Some quick movement of Anna's eyelashes suggested that she was surprised and encouraged. After another second of hesitation she raised her eyes to Reverend Mother's in direct appeal.

"Could it possibly be arranged, do you think, for me not to go home for Christmas? Just to stay here—or anything? Could it?"

Reverend Mother answered without a pause: "Most

certainly it could be arranged, Anna—if you really wanted it?"

Many thoughts and questions lay behind this simple answer, and she did not think that Anna would or should stay at the convent for the holidays—but that was unimportant compared with the necessity for coaxing her trust a little further now. Moreover, she accounted what she said to be justifiable, because if she could not persuade Anna to go home without greatly increasing her state of distress, unhesitatingly she would keep her in the convent for the holidays. But she was rewarded for her insight in having answered unfussily and assentingly by the almost brilliant look of relief that passed over the girl's face.

"Ah! Thank you, Reverend Mother."

"But, as you know, it is an odd request. Won't you tell me why you think you might want to stay here for Christmas?"

"Well—I suppose I ought to."

"Yes—I think so. Do sit down. When you were little you used to sit in that chair very often, helping me to seal letters, and tie up parcels. Do you remember? Your legs didn't reach half-way down the chair then."

"I remember, Reverend Mother. Your seal was a sword and a distaff."

"Yes—here it is. It was taken from the arms of the Foundress's family—and only Reverend Mothers of the Order may seal their letters with it."

Anna handled the seal gently, and smiled a little.

"Yes, that was why you wouldn't ever let me use it unless you were holding it too."

"I used to tell you that you'd have to be a Reverend Mother to do that. You said once, I remember, that perhaps you would be a Reverend Mother some day."

Anna laid the seal carefully back on its little tray.

"Why don't you want to go home for Christmas, Anna?"

Anna bent her head.

"I'm afraid—for one thing," she said very quickly.

"Of what are you afraid?"

"Of beginning—to dream of him again. Of Charlie."

She caught back her breath on the last word and swallowed it. It occurred to Reverend Mother that probably this was the first time since his death in August that Anna had attempted to speak his name to another person.

"And if you did dream of him again—of Charlie—would that be very hard to bear?"

"Oh! I—couldn't——"

"You have been sleeping very much better for the past five or six weeks, haven't you?"

"Oh, yes."

"And you are still taking hot milk last thing in bed, I hope?"

"Yes, Reverend Mother."

"For nearly eight weeks now you haven't walked in your sleep?"

Anna looked at her with faint wonder in her eyes.

"No, Reverend Mother," she said.

She is wondering how I know these things about her, Reverend Mother thought. I must be careful lest she thinks she is being watched, spied on.

But Anna was unsuspicious. She was in fact half dreamily groping back, under the influence of the steady voice, to the trust which it had established in her in babyhood, and which the years with their schoolgirl conventions had overlaid. When she held the old brass seal in her hands memory had given her one of those moments of restoration which can so lovingly and beneficially visit weariness; so that, for such a split second as can seem to re-establish a world, she was six years old and very happy talking with this tall, grand nun, and Charlie would be coming on Sunday. It was a full breath, a warm embrace, a sleep, a bath, a drink, a restitution—something at least that she had been unable to find or feel since the 29th August. And when it passed it left her different at least in this, that she felt less afraid to look back, less horrified of seeking the details, the trivial, the true position of the past.

She did not know this, but her nerves were picking it up for her as she answered Reverend Mother's voice and responded automatically to long-planted trust.

Reverend Mother clasped and unclasped her nervous hands. At the back of her mind she was praying for guidance, in its foreground wondering anxiously if the brusque kindness of Mother Eugenia or the worried, nervous, immature maternalism of a Mother Felicita might not be more helpful now than her too gingerly concern for every twist of the young, waiting soul.

"That is good—such improvement in your sleep," she said. "And it shows that bad sleeping, nightmares and waking up too much and so on, are only very temporary things. They happen—for big and for little reasons—quite often in life. But by facing them and checking them we know that they can be faced and checked. So you see—if you did begin again to sleep badly, which I don't think you will, you would know how to deal with it, and that it would certainly pass."

"I *couldn't*," Anna said, very low. "I'm frightened."

Reverend Mother turned her chair a little away from her desk, so as to face Anna.

"But why?" she asked earnestly.

There was a pause in which Reverend Mother counted twelve ticks of the clock.

"It's always the same dream," Anna said. "He's under the water and everything is extraordinarily quiet. There are no waves or noise or anything. But his eyes are wide open— they were very blue, you know—and they seem to be like blue glass in the dream. I can see straight through them, into his brain and into what he's thinking. Oh, oh!" she cried on a sharp note. "I can't say any more!"

Silence fell deeply round her sudden cry. She stared ahead at nothing visible to others. Her eyes were large, full of helpless pain.

"I can't explain it," she said. "You'd think I was hysterical. But when I have that dream I *know* about—about his last minutes. I have his thoughts, and I know that it was—that it was *horrible*. I know."

A shiver ran through her.

Reverend Mother did not speak at once.

"Have you ever thought of discussing this dream with Father Quinn?" she asked at last.

"You mean—in confession?"

"Well, yes—if in confession was the best opportunity for talking of it."

"I've never talked to anyone. It isn't a sin—to dream like that—is it?"

"No, of course not. But I thought that you might sometimes have had to ask your confessor's help in lessening your resistance to God's Will."

"I haven't resisted God's Will. How could I? Charlie is dead."

"You acknowledge God's ordinance in that fact of his death?"

Anna nodded, in surprise.

"Then you acknowledge the same ordinance in his birth and his life? If God took away his human life, God also gave it. And if you say that you don't know why God took his life away, you must equally admit that you don't know why He bestowed it. Of course, as a Catholic you should, and you do, know both these 'whys'—the only point I'm stressing is that you either know both or neither. You cannot accept the mystery of life and refuse that of death."

"I'm not refusing the mystery of death! How can I?"

"You refuse it Christian acceptance, by making it into an abnormal, unnatural horror which contradicts everything else you know of Charlie. It is natural for us all to imagine that the moment of death is frightening and lonely, if we are fully aware of it, which few are, perhaps. But so may be—if we could exercise our imaginations more extensively— the moment of birth. We know nothing, remember nothing, of the conditions of sensibility of the newly born, except that the immortal soul is present. But whatever the ordeal of entrance into life, it was brief, and most of us are glad to have been born. So, too, with the moment of death. Whatever it holds, it is brief—and you and I know that, for those who have tried to be good, it is a gateway to perfect happiness."

She knew that she was being trite, but she saw that only two things, both vague, should be attempted at present against Anna's confused desolation—to appear non-inquisitive, and simultaneously to ensure that the ice of reserve did not harden again.

"He was only thirteen," Anna said.

"Long lives and short ones, all are tiny in eternity, Anna. While we are here our wills and faculties are free, but 'Men must endure their going hence, Even as their coming hither: Ripeness is all.' "

"Who said that?"

"It's in *King Lear*. Listen—I'm going to say something that may sound hard. Charlie's life was not just a thing you valued which has been taken from you. It was *his* life— an absolutely private thing, marked off by itself in eternity, as yours is, and mine. That it was given its particular shape— as it happens, a lovely, untarnishable, poetic shape, unlike the outward shapes of most lives—is a part of this privacy, on which your love actually has no claim, Anna. Can't you detach yourself enough, for a minute, to see that?"

"I do see it. I'm not thinking of myself. Always, always I think of *him*. He should have lived! He wasn't the sort of person to die. He was so good, he was so sweet! He should have lived! He deserved to! Oh, the cruelty—the *meanness* of his death!"

"You say that because you are *in* this life, and obsessed with it. That is natural, at your age. But also you are an immortal soul, and that means that at times you must attempt the longer view. Imaginatively even, leaving Christian faith out of it, it is a good thing to detach yourself now and then from personal feeling, and face the beauty, the simplicity and goodness of Charlie's life and death."

"I can't do that. I think of him terrified and alone, wanting to live——"

She covered her face with her hands.

Reverend Mother looked at her with sad eyes. She loved her for this long-controlled agony of pity, so awkwardly revealed, and which no one who had watched her in these months could have accused her of dramatising or of using as any kind of outlet for her own heart. For the change which was remarked in her this term had been to silence, which she had always found difficult, and to an absent-minded docility which again was uncharacteristic. Moreover, from being a good worker at her lessons she had become an avid, almost a brutal one—and all these new defences of reserve, with her tearlessness, her silence about Charlie, and her refusal to go home on Sundays, made people say that his death had "hardened" her, made her selfish. That she underwent insomnia in the first months had not been discovered by any complaint she made, but by her drawn face, and by the observations which Reverend Mother had secretly commanded; and sleep-walking was a dramatisation which was out of her control. This suffering was true, and the suffering of a good kind of love. And though it was pitiful Reverend Mother did not find it alarming. Neither, however, did she foresee easy release. But she believed in the sanity of Anna.

Meantime there was nothing for an outsider to do more than protect her from interferers, see from afar that she got a sufficiency of sleep—and if, as now, she attempted to speak, answer in such a way as would neither bring false comfort nor freeze her against another attempt. There was prayer too —and that was all, Reverend Mother decided.

"I am going to say now to you what everyone must have said many times, Anna—about Charlie's death: that he cannot have known, at any rate for more than a fraction of a second, that he would drown. He was a brave and good swimmer, and you know better than anyone that when he slipped into the water he would not have been frightened;

he would have taken the accident as an exciting challenge to his swimming. He could not know that his head was going to strike that hidden rock. And when it did, there was no room for fear—he was unconscious. You know that. You know that there was no long struggle—because the fisherman said they saw him slip from the rock, and rowed to him at once. Were it not for that blow on his head, they could easily have saved him, or he could have saved himself, they said. It was that which made him go under—and he was *unconscious* then."

"I know, Reverend Mother. I *try* to make myself see how short it all was."

The patience in so young a voice was hard to bear; Reverend Mother decided that no more preaching or insisting was possible.

"You have been brave this term, Anna. Brave in coming back to it—and brave getting through it."

"Oh no. I had to come back. That wasn't brave."

Reverend Mother waited. She wanted Anna to return to her request about the Christmas vacation.

"When I said I don't think of myself, but only of him—that wasn't true! Sometimes I think of nothing else but myself! And that's why I can't go home for Christmas. I can't. They must have mercy on me over this—and let me stay here! It's the only thing I've asked for—since he died. I've given no other trouble, I think. But I—can't go home! I can't go to Castle Tory yet!"

"I understand that. Believe me, Anna. And if you go on feeling as you do now, you *shall* stay here for Christmas. I promise you. You need have no further fear about it."

Anna gave her a look of desperate and almost incredulous gratitude.

"Oh thank you!" she said. And then, in tones of deeper wonder: "You are extraordinarily good to me."

"That is what I should like to be at present—but there is no 'extraordinary goodness' of any human kind that can be of much use at present. Still, the will is there, Anna—and you have only to ask me for any help you think I could give."

# IN REVEREND MOTHER'S STUDY

The forlornness of the girl's aspect had been poignant to Reverend Mother all through the term, and was not less so in this interview. Clearly in losing Charlie she had not merely undergone a violent shock of the obvious kind but had suffered a particular loss—the loss of a chief source of love. Expressive affection, its security and reassurance, went with Charlie. For Anna's parents had become so increasingly inimical to each other with the years and so much involved in the tussle of enmity, that they had no time or instinct left for more than perfunctory intimations of parental feeling. Her elder brothers seemed hardly to know Anna, and her grandmother was a hard over-pious woman. But Anna had drawn the warmth of life from Charlie, and so peaceably and surely that she had not even sought especial friendship at school. Now he was gone, and she was not only outraged by the manner of his going, and horrified by her first close brush with death—but she was cold in the lonely winds of mourning; she was isolated in grief, and the one warm love that could have comforted her was the love of the brother for whom she grieved. Charlie alone, thought Reverend Mother wearily, could have made her feel sufficiently loved to weather this unlooked-for poverty and winter.

She folded her nervous hands together and spoke diffidently.

"Anything I can do to help you now, or at any time, Anna, is nothing. It is what I am here for, and why I am Reverend Mother of this school. I am at your disposition—because we are both, you for the time being and I for life, members of *Sainte Famille*. But—you came here when you were a very little girl; you have been our child for a long time. Moreover, you have been a very dear and very good child—and I, for my part, have always been fonder of you than of other pupils. Perhaps because you were such a baby when you came—I don't know." The nun paused, and looked uncertainly into Anna's hungry, attentive eyes. She formed a resolution and went on: "You said a poem to me when you were only a week or two at school, I think. Quite by accident

—and the first of many. Do you remember?" Anna nodded. "Well, I liked you that night. And liked your poem. Do you remember it, Anna? 'My soul, there is a country Afar beyond the stars, where stands the wingèd sentry . . .'"

Tears rained along Anna's cheeks.

"Oh yes! Oh yes—I remember."

"Say it to yourself to-night—in Chapel. Say it instead of prayers, if you like. Do you remember it all?"

"I think so." Anna could hardly speak for tears.

"And now I won't preach at you any more. Only I want you to understand that—if you really cannot face it—you will not go home for Christmas. But—would it be *very* painful, Anna?"

Anna nodded.

"Why—particularly?"

"He and I were together always there. I have no one else. And I know by Mother when she comes here that Father's—drinking. Oh, I think he's drinking terribly now. And the way Granny goes on, and all the talk about money, and about me, and how unfeeling I am—oh—please! You don't know what it'll be like! Truly, truly—I don't think I could face it!"

Reverend Mother looked at her gravely.

"I see. I think I'd feel as you do. It certainly will be a hard and terrible Christmas—for you all." Anna looked surprised. "You don't have to decide anything until the last minute—but think it over, Anna. There's your father, who's been made so very unhappy about Charlie. Perhaps your being there would be of some use to him—I don't know. And anyway, you're your mother's only daughter, and if she's having a particularly hard time, perhaps you ought to let her feel that you see she's not happy. Charlie was very fond of both your parents, I believe, and I don't think he'd want them to feel estranged from *you* just now. Anyway, I think you might afterwards think yourself that it was a mistake to funk going home this Christmas. I can't judge for you—and I know I'd feel afraid in very much the way you do. Well,

240

child—think it out. And let me know, any time you like, what you're going to do. Just come and knock at my door, as you did this evening. I'll arrange things with your parents, if you *do* decide to stay here."

Anna stood up.

"You see. I'm afraid. I—can't think about them, or anyone, except myself. And Charlie. I can't help it. I'm a coward."

"You're not a coward, Anna. I think you're brave. Ah, there's your Chapel bell."

"Thank you, Reverend Mother. I'm sorry I cried."

Reverend Mother laid a hand on her head.

"God bless you," she said. "Run quickly; you'll be late for Chapel."

That was six months ago.

Anna had decided to go home for Christmas. And the holidays, Reverend Mother understood, had not only been unhappy but unpleasant—punctuated by angry scenes about money, about the future, about selfishness and unselfishness. Granny came on a visit—and Anna was made to understand, with little said, that a girl with a drunken, insolvent father and a grief-stricken mother was extraordinarily lucky still to be receiving education—through the noble kindness of a grandmother—when her sixteenth birthday was in sight. She saw clouds rising already, as she listened to Granny, on the far, wide sky of liberty, more important, if less beautiful, in its immaculate vastness, now that Charlie was gone and the hedged-in present was empty.

Much of this Reverend Mother apprehended, from one conversation with Anna—and also from the frenzy with which she applied herself to work. For she obtained permission from Mother Mary Andrew to take matriculation in this summer, being almost two years younger than the usual age of entrants. It was, however, a very easy examination. What Anna was really applying herself to was the winning in May of that County Scholarship which, in his time, her brother

Harry had won. Her mother had consented almost absent-mindedly to her sitting for this—merely saying that she might as well, that it might come in handy—you never know; only, of course, she wouldn't get it, so why bother?

Reverend Mother had felt that, on the contrary, Anna almost certainly would get it, seeing her mood. And to some extent she welcomed the crude external conflicts which Christmas at home and with Granny had set up—as counter-irritants to grief.

Also, softer, more blessed, there had been talks with Joe—in the harness-room. Joe talked to her of Charlie. And he talked of her father, and of drunkenness, and the temptations and troubles of life. She told Reverend Mother some of Joe's views about people, sin and the hereafter.

"He is a very thoughtful man," she said. "Charlie loved him. I'm glad you made me go home, Reverend Mother. I told Joe about that—and he said you were right."

"But I didn't make you, Anna. You decided it yourself."

Now Reverend Mother sat in the sunlight of a June morning, and while she grieved for the beloved old friend and counsellor who was gone, and prayed that, if she were chosen for high office she would not be too unworthy of it—and even while she dreamt with nostalgic, bitter pleasure of return to *Place des Ormes*—her heart was heavy too, for Anna, whom within a month she would not see again, and whose griefs and conflicts were but beginning.

There was a knock at the door and Mother Mary Andrew entered the study. She had some opened letters in her hand.

"I'm sorry to interrupt you, Reverend Mother; I know you must be busy to-day—but Mother Eugenia has just gone through the post, and there is some good news. Anna Murphy has won the County Scholarship."

Reverend Mother smiled in great pleasure.

"Good news indeed, Mother Mary Andrew! Has she been told?"

The other nun looked shocked.

"Not yet, Reverend Mother. I wish to show the notification to you first, naturally."

She placed an official-looking document on the desk, and Reverend Mother read it dutifully.

"I was in little doubt that Anna deserved to win this scholarship," she said, as she read, "but examinations are dangerous things—and she was so determined to win that one could not help feeling anxious. Apart from everything else, this victory should help her psychologically."

She knew that her last observation was of a kind to gall Mother Mary Andrew; she waited with curiosity for the reaction.

"I wonder! I should have thought that defeat might have had more psychological value—for Anna. However, from the practical point of view it is satisfactory. Do you wish her to be told this morning?"

"Why, of course! I wish the whole school to be told. It is very pleasant news, and will brighten up this mournful day. And please give Anna my especial congratulations. I should like her to come and see me here this evening before Chapel." Reverend Mother saw the mulish, grudging look in the other nun's eyes, and felt disgusted. "She really is brainy that child. I hope she gets all the opportunities she is worth."

"Well, I doubt if she will get many," said Mother Mary Andrew with covert malice. "And that brings me to my second point, Reverend Mother. I have here a letter from Mrs. Condon, Anna's grandmother. Mother Eugenia tells me you left all the post to her to open this morning? Well, in this letter, addressed to me, Mrs. Condon says that she is visiting the convent, with Mrs. Murphy, this afternoon, and wishes to see me, or you, Reverend Mother. It appears she has only just heard from her daughter that Anna sat for the scholarship, and she is angry. She says she has other views for the girl's future, and that in any case she should have been consulted. She is, however, confident that Anna won't have won it."

Reverend Mother smiled.

"May I read the letter, Mother Mary Andrew?"

She read it and handed it back.

"Anna is determined to go to the University, is she not?"

"Yes, quite determined. But if one could see an aim in her determination it would be easier to sympathise."

Reverend Mother wondered if indeed anything could make it easy for Mother Mary Andrew to sympathise with Anna.

"What kind of aim?"

"Well, to be a teacher, or a professor, or a doctor—or to get some kind of good post afterwards. Not that there would be money for her to be a doctor, of course—but she denies interest in all sensible suggestions. She just has nothing to say for herself, except that she wants to go to the University. Very childish, I call it."

Reverend Mother made no comment. She saw some further communicativeness in Mother Mary Andrew's eye, and did not wish to deflect her.

"Of course, it has occurred to me lately that—*perhaps*—Anna may yet think of joining the Order. She is at present a rather hard and selfish girl, and not, in my opinion, a religious type. But undoubtedly she must have suffered over her brother's death—and she seems to have no other human affections, almost. She may be developing a vocation. And if that *is* so, her having a University degree would, of course, enhance her value to us. Particularly as she is very good at Irish."

Reverend Mother was looking out of the window, towards the cemetery, during this speech, and did not answer at once.

Mother Mary Andrew studied her with exasperation. Doesn't agree with that, of course, she thought. Never does think anyone wants to be a nun, it seems to me. It's a miracle we ever get a postulant here. I suppose she'd really like to be the entire Order herself. Of all the conceited, cold faces. Well, perhaps there'll be some changes when we have a new general. They always said the old one had a soft spot for her. But she's quite unsuited to an Irish convent. We want someone of *national* feeling, someone progressive. I wonder what moves there'll be? You'd think that she'd at least welcome the idea of her darling Anna as a novice——

Reverend Mother turned her head.

"The religious vocation is an unusual thing, Mother Mary Andrew," she said coldly. "It is always best to remember that."

"I know that is your view, Reverend Mother," said the other unyieldingly.

Mother Eugenia entered. Her eyes were red. *Mère Générale* and she were contemporaries and friends at the old novitiate of Chartres, and later had worked together in Austria and at Rouen. She felt this death in her affections and as a signal to be ready herself.

"I didn't know you were engaged, Reverend Mother," she said.

"We have finished our discussion, Mother Eugenia. You will see Mrs. Condon and Mrs. Murphy this afternoon, Mother Mary Andrew?"

"Yes, Reverend Mother."

"I shall tell the portress to tell me when they are in the parlour, as I wish to see them too. That is all, I think."

"Thank you, Reverend Mother."

"Do not forget to give my congratulations to Anna." Mother Mary Andrew nodded as politely as she could and left the room.

Mother Eugenia put a sheaf of telegrams on the desk.

"I'm pleased for the Murphy child—indeed she deserves it. But I find it hard to be pleased about anything to-day." She sat down, looking weary. Her eyes filled with fresh tears. "Poor *Mère Catherine!* She was a great woman, God rest her! And she and I were almost the last left now of our year at Chartres. She was a few months younger than me, I believe."

"You're quite ready, just as she was."

"Yes—I suppose I'm as ready as a weak old sinner can hope to be. And if this means a lot of changes here, I hope He takes me quickly. Who do you think we'll get for General, child?"

"I have no idea."

"There's that bustling one in Chicago—a very common

woman, I believe—God help us all! Well, if she gets in, I wouldn't be surprised if she deposed you, my child, and put the linen-draper over us. Farewell, '*la pudeur et la politesse!*' "

Reverend Mother laughed.

"You're an uncharitable old snob, and a gossip," she said.

"You're right, faith. And may God forgive me. But here's another bit of gossip for you. It wouldn't surprise me at all to hear that *Mère Catherine* had commended yourself for the generalship. What do you think of that?"

"We are not expected to indulge in surmises, Mother Eugenia."

"Aren't we? Nevertheless, if Catherine really has done that to me, I can only hope that I'll be joining her soon, Lord have mercy on her!"

*The Second Chapter*

# THE SCHOLARSHIP

EARLY that afternoon Sister Maria told Reverend Mother that Mrs. Condon and Mrs. Murphy were in the parlour, and was instructed to summon Anna to her relations and to inform Mother Mary Andrew of the ladies' arrival.

In a very few minutes the portress returned to announce that his Lordship the Bishop was in the Long Parlour.

Reverend Mother rose and went to meet him at once. The Bishop's visits were always brief, and to-day's was only a formality, to express his condolence with the Order in its loss. He would detain her exactly long enough for Mrs. Condon to have warmed to her theme of Anna's future.

Throughout the years the Bishop and Reverend Mother had stood on the boundaries of a reciprocal regard, almost a friendship, which a too arrogant authoritarianism in the one and a cool dislike of this attitude in the other had kept untilled. They respected each other; time and again each tacitly admitted the other's character, or spiritual distinction. But the Bishop did not very much favour those religious Orders which functioned within his diocese yet were not officially under his jurisdiction; moreover, he disliked the English voice, and believed that he hated the English race; and he knew that he must never assume that he knew what Mother Mary Helen Archer was thinking. Reverend Mother, for her part, disliked illicit, politic attempts by outsiders to manage the convent's business; she disliked to have nationalism intruded on religion, or on education; and she grew bored by the somewhat *naïve* condescension with which this arrogant man made allowance for her Englishness. So at mutual respect they let their acquaintance stand—in spite of moments of true appreciation of each other. And they counted themselves lucky that in thirteen years they had not quarrelled. This felicity was not of the Bishop's making; he was free with his quarrels, all over his diocese. But Reverend Mother was not a quarreller.

"Good afternoon, Reverend Mother. I received your telegram at midday. This is mournful news for your Order, and I sympathise most sincerely."

"Thank you, my Lord. It is good of you to call on us so quickly. The community will be very much touched to receive your sympathy. We have lost a very wise leader, and some of us mourn for a dear personal friend."

"I am quite sure of that. She was a long time at the helm, was she not?"

"Thirty-four years, my Lord. She was elected to office in 1880. The Mother House was still at Rouen then, and she was Reverend Mother of our Paris convent. I was in my first year of novitiate at *Sainte Fontaine* at the time, I remember."

"Thirty-four years! Then she must have been a very old woman at her death, surely?"

"She would have been eighty in November, my Lord."

"Oh, not more? But do you mean to say she was made General at forty-five?"

She could see his mind racing interferingly towards the question of the succession. She was amused beneath her gravity.

"Yes, my Lord. It was the first time in our history that a General had been elected under fifty-nine. I remember hearing some astonishment and grumbling from one or two old nuns at *Sainte Fontaine*. They objected to being governed by a mere chit of forty-five! I remember how that amused me, because I was nineteen then, and forty-five seemed ripe old age to me!"

They laughed—but she knew he was doing the sum which, for mischief's sake, she had offered to him. Nineteen in 1880, now she is fifty-three. I wonder?

"You were brought up at Brussels, at *Place des Ormes*, were you not, Reverend Mother?"

"Yes, my Lord. Brussels is the first place I really remember, although my parents had lived in Cambridge and in Paris and Bonn before we settled there. Of course, *Place des Ormes* was only a very humble foundation then."

"But you worked there later, as a nun, I believe? As Assistant to the General?"

"Yes, my Lord. I worked with *Mère Générale* before she appointed me to this house."

"Now I wonder why she did that? Was she thinking only of this house, do you think—or of the whole Order, on a longer view?"

Reverend Mother assumed a faintly puzzled air.

"I do not quite follow you, my Lord."

He is a quick thinker, she conceded, as often before. Moreover, he has the Irish advantage of absurdly quick intuition.

He smiled at her.

"Well, from this and that I have gathered over the years that *Mère Catherine Mandel* did nothing for superficial reasons—. and on the face of it you would not have been an obvious choice to govern this house. You must pardon my interest in someone else's technique in what is after all very much my own *métier*, Reverend Mother."

"Why, of course. But surmise about such long-buried motives is perhaps somewhat sterile, my Lord."

" 'Long-buried?' That's just what I'm wondering?"

Reverend Mother let him wonder, and turned the talk to the late *Mère Générale*.

"She was a very remarkable woman," she said. "Few people can have so honourably combined holiness with shrewdness. But that was, I suppose, simply because her shrewdness was devoted to the glory of God. She sometimes spoke of her father, who was a very successful merchant in Lille, and she used to say, with an amusing twinkle of vanity, that she believed she had most of his capabilities but, happily, none of his tastes. I think that must have been true. She might have been a very successful business woman—if she hadn't happened to be something of a saint."

The Bishop smiled appreciatively.

"I wish I had known her," he said.

"You would have liked her, my Lord. You and she would have appreciated each other, I believe."

"You were particularly fond of her, were you not, Reverend Mother?"

"Yes, my Lord. I had the happiness of working with her intimately, and I have never known anyone who was at once so wise and so kind."

Tears suddenly brightened in her eyes.

The Bishop was touched.

"Naturally then you grieve particularly, my child. And as I believe she held you in especial regard, she will be humanly glad to-day of your grief. No one is so saintly as not to wish friends to mourn them at death."

"I believe that is true," said Reverend Mother.

The Bishop turned back to the practical issue.

"When and how is the successor appointed?" he asked.

Reverend Mother told him the method of election. He listened attentively.

"I see," he said. "And the General's wish is usually fulfilled?"

"Hitherto always, I believe. But times are changing fast nowadays, and our western provinces may very likely enforce a break with tradition. Our late *Mère Générale* was an inflexible traditionalist, but now she is gone, new forces will get to work in the Order, I believe."

"And I believe that she foresaw that. Why did she send you westward—a very promising lieutenant?"

Reverend Mother looked at him very innocently.

"By 'western' I really meant our American provinces, my Lord."

"I see. Well, well, you'll be busy to-day, and I mustn't tire you. You will be having a Requiem Service, of course?"

"Yes, my Lord. On Tuesday, at eleven o'clock. This morning I sent an invitation to you. It will be a very great favour to the community if you are able to be present."

"Certainly I'll be present, Reverend Mother. Who's to preach the memorial?"

"We are in some doubt as to whom to invite."

"Well, get someone clear-minded, and with freshness in him, if possible. It's an inspiring theme—and if we aren't afflicted with someone like that poor windy Jesuit, O'Halloran, I'll be obliged to you."

They both laughed.

She knew by the alert light in his eyes that he was stimulated by the sudden conviction that she would be the next General of the Order, and removed therefore from a position where she impeded a cause he had at heart; but also she guessed that it excited him to debate whether her accession to supreme authority might not, even from far-away Brussels, militate against such specifically Irish improvements as he would skilfully seek to impose through her successor. She felt no resentment at this; indeed in an amused way she was almost sympathetic, and he thought she looked unusually amiable.

"We'll do our best about it, my Lord. But you know the difficulties!"

"I do indeed, my child."

They stood up.

"We have also had a piece of good news this morning, my Lord," Reverend Mother said, as they crossed the Long Parlour under the tinkling chandeliers. "Anna Murphy has won the County Scholarship to the University."

The Bishop beamed.

He liked intellectual competence and he liked Anna Murphy; he was a vigorous supporter of the National University and always eager that the scholarships awarded by his county should fall to worthy candidates; and he believed in education—up to a point, or when they seemed worth it— of women. He said that, when they had brains, which was seldom, these tended to be fresher and more independent than the brains of men.

"Good child, very good indeed! That's a bit of sense from the County Council, praise be! And it'll be needed, I should think—from what I hear of Harry Murphy's goings on?"

"Very much needed, my Lord. Her whole future depends now on Anna's own efforts, I imagine. She is also going to take the University Entrance Scholarship in September, and if she wins that, she should be well launched on paying for her own career."

"Ah! good girl—I hope she gets it. And I really think she ought to. She's no fool at all, that child." They were standing on the steps in the sun, and the Bishop's carriage-horses jingled their harness impatiently. "Is she anywhere at hand? I'd like to congratulate her."

This was what Reverend Mother had wanted.

"She is quite near, my Lord—in St. Anthony's Parlour. I'll fetch her to you."

When she opened the door of this parlour she merely bowed coldly to the ladies, and beckoned to Anna, without entering the room. There was a surprised silence for the seconds of her interruption, but all the faces were variously agitated. Anna looked white and hopeless.

Reverend Mother closed the door, and taking Anna's hand led her through the hall to the steps.

"I have just told the Bishop of your great success, and he wishes to congratulate you."

There was no time to say more, nor did Reverend Mother want to yet, although she was wrung by the effort Anna made to check the expression of despair which came to her face.

The girl took the Bishop's hand, dropped on her knee and kissed his ring. Before she rose again he laid his hand lightly on her head and said softly:

"*Benedicat te omnipotens Deus, Pater et Filius et Spiritus Sanctus.* Amen." And then: "Well done, my child! That's very good work indeed. And I wish you every further success that you can lay hold of, so long as it is pleasing to God, and keeps you faithful to His Will. I expect your parents are very pleased with you to-day—as indeed they ought to be. Reverend Mother here is almost being vainglorious about it,

I may say! Well, well, *Sainte Famille* has always been a bit extra fond of its oldest inhabitant, and now you're going to do it much credit up there in Dublin."

"Thank you very much, my Lord," Anna said, with a smile which Reverend Mother admired for its bravery and reserve.

"I hear you're going to try to get the Entrance too," the Bishop went on. "And I believe you'll get it. They say it's not so stiff as the County—as our County, that is. Ours is one of the stiffest in Ireland, I'm proud to say. Well, I must be off now. I'll see you again before University term, Anna. Try to enjoy your holidays. You're looking overworked. Good-bye, Reverend Mother. You'll convey my sympathy to the community. And I'll be here on Tuesday for the Requiem."

He got into his carriage and drove away. Reverend Mother had kept her hand on Anna's arm during his last remarks, and she did not wish her to return to her relatives alone.

"I also want to congratulate you very much, Anna," she said. "But you and I will talk about it later. Just now I want to see your mother and grandmother."

"Thank you, Reverend Mother. They'll be delighted to see you," said Anna tonelessly, and she opened the door of St. Anthony's parlour and stood aside for the nun to enter.

Mrs. Murphy and Mother Mary Andrew rose quickly upon her entrance, and the former came forward to shake hands politely.

Mrs. Condon half rose invalidishly and was motioned back into her chair by Reverend Mother. Although approaching seventy she still flaunted much of the prettiness she had transmitted to her daughter, but there were highly marked intelligence and arrogance in her face which the latter's lacked. She dressed in the manner of a pretty woman, but with becoming dignity, and she had altogether an air of breeding which Mother Eugenia considered "excessive" in the widow of a county town ironmonger and timber merchant. However, Bartholomew Condon had been an ironmonger with a difference—the difference of success; otherwise, it was uncharitably safe to assume, Maud Hegarty would not for an instant have contemplated the immense condescension of her "love-match," as she called it. For the Hegartys were a very respectable legal family, though at the time of Batt Condon's courtship of Miss Hegarty they were financially embarrassed. They had risen again however through the years, assisted by the ironmonger's money. A brother of Mrs. Condon had taken silk at the English Bar; a younger sister had married into an English County family; and the youngest brother was now a proud and successful parish priest in the diocese, eagerly on the watch for a canonry. Mrs. Condon was proud of all this, and was always particularly devoted to her youngest brother, who was a paragon of that kind of priestly fanaticism and snobbery which she admired. She intended that he should be a Canon. And Reverend Mother happened to know of this determination.

Reverend Mother was very little disposed towards going to the parlour, and she had managed within the ten years of Anna's schoolings to have no more than two encounters with this formidable "old girl," Anna's grandmother, who indeed, living some distance away, was an infrequent visitor.

The two eyed each other with new appraisal now therefore, knowing themselves set for conflict.

"Forgive me for not rising with the correct *Sainte Famille* bow, Reverend Mother—but these old bones——"

"You suggest very little indeed of old age, Mrs. Condon," said Reverend Mother, seating herself at some distance from the old lady, and with the faces of the company well in focus. "We are glad to see you here, and I hope that it gives you pleasure to return to the old place—even on a day of mourning. You will have been told of our great loss?"

As she deliberately spun this badinage and took up the polite replies it evoked, she was studying the rich old lady with interest. If Anna ever achieves elegance, which she might do and I hope she does do—her mother has somehow missed it—she might superficially look like this woman in old age. But only superficially, I hope. I cannot see how she would ever have that watchful, quarrelsome eye, or that self-important pull about the mouth. But she does get some attributes from Granny, the practical side of her intelligence, I think, her trick of detailed observation, and her reserve—her ability to keep quiet and play her own game. But mercifully the child is not all legal-minded and calculating Hegarty. There is the robustious, generous Condon too in her blood, to say nothing of the drinking Murphys. However, at this moment Granny herself in her own person is more formidable than Granny the transmitting ancestress—and I have to tackle her. The end must justify the means. *Ad majorem Dei gloriam*, she added self-mockingly.

"I believe that you were annoyed, Mrs. Condon, at not having been told earlier that Anna was taking the County University Scholarship examination; but I assume that Mother Mary Andrew has explained to you that, having obtained the permission of Anna's parents, we had done our duty. We naturally imagined that you would then have been informed."

"Well yes, Reverend Mother. I have of course reprimanded the scatter-brained Maud, who says that in fact she forgot the whole matter. Still, since I pay the bills here, clearly I should have been consulted."

"No doubt, Mrs. Condon. But the whole thing was settled verbally, in one conversation—you remember, Mrs. Murphy? —in this parlour, and I confess it did not occur to me that anything more was necessary, for such a natural and sensible decision—in view of Anna's circumstances."

"That may be—and I am now quite prepared to forgive and forget."

"Yes, I know that, of course. Anything else would be—well, more than a little ungracious, since Anna has won her scholarship!"

Mother Mary Andrew bent forward to speak, but Mrs. Condon raised a hand.

"That is, I admit, a surprising accident—and I certainly hope that the child's work won't have been wasted, or have done her any harm, but I have explained to Mother Mary Andrew that there is, of course, no question of Anna's taking up the scholarship—no question whatever, Reverend Mother! And that being so, I still deplore the fuss and the wasting of time."

"I do not understand you, Mrs. Condon. How can there be 'no question' of Anna's using her scholarship?"

Anna had been sitting very still, as if deadly tired, but now Reverend Mother saw her move and lift her head to look in her direction.

Mrs. Condon gave a pretty but rather insolent shrug of weariness.

"Usually I only say things once," she said, half laughing to cover her rudeness.

Reverend Mother smiled innocently.

"Naturally," she said, and only Anna, alive and watchful now, understood her contempt. "But if you'd be so good, in a few words perhaps——?"

"If you insist, Reverend Mother, and in a nutshell, I have other grandchildren besides the Murphys; I have done, or almost done, all that I propose to do for Anna; and her brother Harry is a considerable expense to me; although he justifies it all indeed, and wins exhibitions and prizes which we have no reason to believe Anna could possibly win——"

"So far, Anna has outshone her brother. He was eighteen when he won his scholarship. She is barely sixteen."

"That doesn't interest me. I disapprove of money wasted on the academic education of girls. And in this particular case, in view of recent family sorrows and misfortunes, and since her mother has so little peace or happiness, I wish Anna to stay near at hand and also to become of practical usefulness. To earn money, Reverend Mother. A very great deal has been spent on her. I am now going to arrange for her to be able to show that my generosity has not been wasted."

"How are you going to arrange that, Mrs. Condon?"

"I am putting her into the Bank next autumn," said Mrs. Condon. "I have obtained a written promise from the chairman of my bank—a very old friend of mine—that on receipt of Anna's application she will be appointed to a clerkship at once. Further, he has promised that she will be posted for her first year or two to Magherbeg; this means that she will be able to live in my house, and also that she will only be twenty miles from Castle Tory. The manager of the Magherbeg branch is a nice, gentlemanly man, and for my sake will be particularly kind to her. And of course she will be safe under my roof. I shall not charge her anything for her keep, but, in order to teach her responsibility and unselfishness, I shall require her to send half of her salary to her mother—now that times are so bad at Castle Tory. Out of the balance she should be able to save up against the day when she will have to pay for lodgings. Of course, if they do soon open a branch in Lissanmoher village, which they think of, I could have her moved there and she could live at home, and contribute to the housekeeping."

"What salary would she receive?"

"I believe she will begin at approximately seventy pounds a year. Which for sixteen years old, and a girl, is quite good, don't you think? Another advantage is that the Four Provinces Bank is extremely careful only to accept *ladies* for clerkships. The chairman said in his letter that she being a *Sainte Famille* girl—like her grandmother—would count very much indeed in her favour. So you see, there'll be no trouble at all about her future, Reverend Mother, and the poor child could have been spared all the strain of the scholarship work!"

"When did you tell Anna of this idea of yours, Mrs. Condon?"

"Well, just now; that is, she was present when I was telling Mother Mary Andrew. I didn't wish to moot it while it was only an 'idea,' as you call it, Reverend Mother! I preferred to produce it as a fixed plan."

"It isn't anything like a fixed plan yet," Reverend Mother said coolly, and turned without pausing to Anna. "Does it attract you—just as an idea, Anna?"

Anna looked at her out of desperate eyes. It was not an

easy moment for her. However the issue fell out, she had to live a long time yet in contact with this arrogant, dangerous Granny, and indeed would very soon be her puppet, in her house and in the Four Provinces Bank. To speak honestly therefore, the first time in the whole course of Granny's visit that she was invited to speak at all was to invite years of cruelty and unforgiveness. Yet, if someone came to fight for her, even someone so used herself to power that she did not see when a cause was as good as lost and outside her reach, she must certainly have enough graciousness to be true, and to fight on the side of her rash champion.

Reverend Mother saw the conflict of dilemma.

"No, Reverend Mother," Anna said steadily. "No—I hate it."

"I thought you would," said Reverend Mother. "So should I."

Mrs. Condon used a lorgnette. She peered through it now—first at Anna, in outraged contempt; but then, in sheer incredulous amazement, at Reverend Mother.

"Really, Reverend Mother!" she said. "I am hardly troubled about the opinion of a foolish child in a matter she cannot possibly judge, but when a religious, a superior of a convent I have known and loved from childhood, speaks with such extraordinary flippancy of a matter in no way her concern—well, I assure you I am flabbergasted, and I protest——"

Reverend Mother lifted her right hand in an authoritative gesture.

"No, Mrs. Condon—it is I who am about to protest—and to interfere. By what authority do you dispose of the life and talents of another?"

Mrs. Condon's lorgnette slid to the ground. In her almost seventy years of life no one had ever spoken to her thus. It took her a few seconds to understand the insolent manœuvre. Her daughter bent and rescued the lorgnette, which she accepted from her without pause of acknowledgment.

"By what authority, Reverend Mother? By what authority do *I* arrange my penniless grandchild's future?"

"That is what I asked you, Mrs. Condon."

"I do not know that you have any particular right to an answer—and therefore you will pardon me if it is crude. I arrange what Anna is to do because I pay for her, and because I have always been interested—I think you will admit generously interested—in her."

Reverend Mother smiled at Mrs. Condon's addiction to the word "generous" in description of herself.

"It is difficult to believe that you are truly interested in Anna if you think that she would be happy or using herself to the best advantage as a bank clerk in Magherbeg. However, you are no longer being asked to pay for her, so you may allow your interest to become more detached, Mrs. Condon."

"I am not being asked! Then who is, if you please?"

"The County Scholarship which Anna has won is worth seventy pounds a year for three years. A little more than her bank clerk salary, and more seriously earned. The University Entrance Scholarship for which she will sit in September, and which she has a very good chance of winning, is worth forty pounds, I believe."

"I know all this, Reverend Mother. Her brother has won these things—and the Entrance is only for one year. Harry has made about one hundred and thirty pounds already in his first year, in scholarships and prizes, yet I assure you that he is still a very great drain on me. I will not contemplate Anna's being the same. Harry is, after all, a man."

"Yes. That is why he is so expensive, Mrs. Condon. I know, through old pupils, much about the cost of living for students at University College. Men students find it more expensive than women do, I believe. For one thing their lodgings are dearer. But Anna's County Scholarship will, if she takes a liberal degree, pay for her keep in one or other of the women students' hostels, and will also pay her very modest university fees. If she wins the Entrance and re-wins it on the yearly examinations, she will be self-supporting—provided"

—Reverend Mother smiled at Mrs. Murphy—"provided her parents allow her board and lodging at Castle Tory in the vacations."

"Nonsense, absolute nonsense!" said Mrs. Condon. "I tell you I know the way this Dublin life eats up money!"

"It can do so. But if Anna goes to the University she will go as a poor student—and will simply have no money for Dublin to eat up. But so long as she has food, sleep, work and companionship, the severest austerity will do her no harm at all, but only great good. And since in the major thing she will be happy, in having secured time—earned time, Mrs. Condon—in which to work and think and get a glimpse here and there over the great vistas of knowledge—I think that she will manage all right without new hats and cream buns and so on. I am quite certain that Anna has enough character to be very poor and retain her sense of proportion."

"Your theories and ideals are quite interesting, Reverend Mother. But would it not be better to air them in Anna's absence? Your high opinion of her is very flattering to us all, of course, but as the child is already quite sufficiently conceited—is she not, Mother Mary Andrew?"

"That is a failing of Anna's undoubtedly, Mrs. Condon."

"I prefer Anna to hear this discussion in full," said Reverend Mother, "if she can bear to hear us all bandying her about, that is! I speak indeed without her authority, but simply because I know, from conversations during the year and from the passion with which she worked for her scholarship, that she desires to go through the University before choosing a career. And I wholeheartedly approve of that desire, and believe it to be the right thing for her to do. Therefore I think she will forgive me for what seems like interference. But so far as I know, Mrs. Condon, you have no authority, from Anna, for the things you have been saying."

"I should think not indeed!" Mrs. Condon gave a cold, exhausted laugh, then proceeded to fold her lorgnette and gather herself as for departure. "I am sorry that we should have had this painful difference of opinion, Reverend Mother

260

—but there is no hope of our reaching understanding, so I had better leave. All I wish to make clear is that Anna will politely decline the scholarship in this evening's post—and that ends the whole foolish matter."

"Then you have misunderstood me from beginning to end, Mrs. Condon. Unless Anna herself tells me that it is her true wish and desire to decline her scholarship, she will not do so."

"I pay for Anna's education. She is bound therefore to do what I direct about it."

"She did you credit in her ten years here. When she takes up her scholarship her duty to you ceases."

"May I hint, Reverend Mother, that I have not yet paid this term's bill?"

Reverend Mother laughed.

"It's an unladylike hint—but happily Anna has had her term. Do exactly as you please about the bill. We have very good lawyers."

Mrs. Condon winced. She was purse-proud, and could not bear the idea of light flung from without upon her meannesses.

"In any case," she said, "Anna is a minor—and therefore must obey me."

"Not *you*, Mrs. Condon. You are not her guardian."

"I know I'm not, Reverend Mother—but her parents will do as I say. Her wretched father knows better than to oppose any will he may have against mine."

Reverend Mother had been waiting for this—the one real difficulty in her case. But she believed that she had been provided with a probable means of removing it. Now was the moment of trial.

She bowed her head acquiescently to Mrs. Condon.

"Naturally," she said, "if you are able to compel Anna's parents to do her this mean and petty injury, I have nothing further to say. But I shall be bound to lay the whole matter before the Bishop, setting out the facts—and seeking his advice."

Mrs. Condon moved uneasily.

"The Bishop?"

"Yes, Mrs. Condon. That, by the way, was why I called Anna out of the parlour just now—the Bishop wanted to see her and give her his blessing. I had told him of her winning the scholarship, and he was delighted. He congratulated her most warmly, and said he would like to see her again before university term began. You see, he does believe in wasting money on the academic education of women. And he was very pleased that Anna had the courage to try for the scholarship at her age. He often visits her Latin class, and he thinks very well of her general work."

"Do you mean that the Bishop *expects* Anna to go to the University, on this scholarship?"

"But naturally he does. She has *won* it, Mrs. Condon. However, now I shall have to tell him of your very extraordinary views, and your intention to compel—or is it blackmail?—Anna's parents into cheating her of her legitimate future."

"You will tell him nothing of the sort, Reverend Mother! And how dare you use the word 'blackmail'?"

"I will dare use any word which I believe to be just, Mrs. Condon. And I shall use those terms which seem to me accurate when I explain your attitude to the Bishop. Meantime and in conclusion let me say that, in opposition to you in this affair, you will not merely have his Lordship, but the entire strength of the Order of *Sainte Famille*. Which means that you will not put Anna into the Four Provinces Bank. The Bishop will feel as strongly as I do that that is a purposeless and deadly injustice, and between us, whatever powers we invoke against you, we shall avert it from Anna. Our Order is world-wide and powerful, Mrs. Condon, and it takes care of its children. That is its *raison d'être*. And Anna is very particularly our child. We shall look after her, and she can rest assured that, between us and the Bishop, means will be found to prevent her becoming a clerk in the Four Provinces Bank."

Mrs. Condon had had time to think—which was exactly

what Reverend Mother was giving her as she span out her threatening and not very safely founded speech.

"But really, Reverend Mother," she said in quite humorous tones, "if I may be very disrespectful, you are now being a little—melodramatic. It seems to me that you have misunderstood me—my, my character, I mean. I am—I think naturally—unwilling to commit myself to any unnecessary expenses. I have a great many grandchildren, and I must be just in my favours. But if you had told me, months ago, that so excellent a judge of merit as the Bishop particularly desired Anna to take this scholarship! Well, you see, I am growing old, and I haven't kept pace with intellectual things—and Anna *is* conceited, and so one inclines to think that very probably her brains are no more than any other child's. But the Bishop is, we all know, a hard man to please, and if he thinks well of her work—that alters everything, of course. I think I shall call on him, to discuss the question. That would be a good plan, don't you think?"

Thank God, I have won, thought Reverend Mother. By my mean understanding of meanness. But still, thank God.

"I think that would be an excellent idea, Mrs. Condon. And I am sorry that I did not tell you of the Bishop's great interest in Anna and the scholarship. But you see, I thought you knew all this."

"Indeed I did not. Really, Maud, you have been very remiss about the whole affair. I am glad we have got it clear at last however. I shall write to the Bishop to-morrow. It is quite a long time since I last had a talk with him. Brilliant man, undoubtedly. Don't you think so, Reverend Mother?"

"He is very gifted, and very saintly too, I think, Mrs. Condon. And now you must be tired—and I have much to do."

The nun rose, and so did Mother Mary Andrew. Anna and her relatives also rose politely. Hands were shaken; voices and smiles were cordial. As Reverend Mother left the room, she paused by Anna, who was holding the door open for her, and laid a hand on her shoulder.

Anna's eyes were burning, all their blue lost in the widened blackness of the pupils. Reverend Mother could feel the excited shaking of her thin body. She smiled at her and the girl smiled back tremulously, on the brink of wild tears.

"This child will need a very good rest this summer," she said, "before she tackles the Entrance Scholarship."

"Indeed she will," said Mrs. Condon. "We'll see that she gets it, Reverend Mother. Never you fear."

As the two nuns went along the corridor Mother Mary Andrew spoke grudgingly.

"If I may say so, Reverend Mother, you managed that well. I could get no good at all of the woman before you came in."

"You hadn't my weapon. The Bishop."

"But why did the mention of him have that effect, do you know?"

"Alas, I do. Mrs. Condon is rich because she never quarrels with power, particularly hierarchical power. And she has a brother in this diocese, Father Hegarty, whose career lies near her heart."

Mother Mary Andrew smiled.

"I see."

"I am not proud of the method, Mother Mary Andrew. But I had to use it. I hope God will forgive me."

They entered the community room. Mother Mary Andrew was convinced now that Reverend Mother had private reason to believe that Anna Murphy intended eventually to become a nun. For there was no other reason why she should fight so tenaciously for something which after all was *not* of great importance to *Sainte Famille*.

*The Third Chapter*

## "IVY NEVER SERE"

ANNA had the bench under the chestnut tree to herself. Books lay beside her, but she sat in idleness. To-morrow was the day of the English and History papers; the following morning there was Latin; then Sunday and Monday, half holiday and half preparation for Prize Day Concert. Tuesday was Prize Day, and on Tuesday evening she would go home from *Sainte Famille* for the last time; she would have left school.

She was in no mood to cram, as she saw others doing, solitarily or in groups, about the lawns and playgrounds. To-morrow was important for everyone, since to fail in English in the Intermediate Examinations meant total failure. But Anna felt fatalistic; either she was ready to answer to-morrow's papers, or if she were not there was nothing she could do at this late hour to help herself. She always felt thus on the eve of examination—incapable of last-minute efforts. She knew this state in her exasperated others, but she could not help it. So she sat alone now so as not to annoy the frenzied with her idleness; she liked to sit alone.

Because of the standard of work required for the County Scholarship Anna had last September moved from Junior to Senior, skipping Middle Grade. This had meant extra private work, so as to catch up in mathematics and history, but no industry would have been too much for her during the sped year, because of the reality of her dual purpose—escape from grief, and direction, in some sense, of her own future. During the first week of July she would take Matriculation at the Magherbeg centre, staying at Granny's house for the week; in September she would go to Dublin for the University Entrance Scholarship. That meant that between May and October she would have sat for four public examinations.

She felt herself already to be the confirmed examinee, and she saw realistically that her only way out of life lay over many of these somewhat foolishly designed, formal barriers. But she was content at being allowed to run this obstacle race to the unknown. It was the only track she could see, and it had one great point—it ended in emptiness, on a wide horizon. That was all she asked.

The battle for it still startled Anna to remember. All lost in one pronouncement of Granny's—and then, after a useless-seeming struggle, all won again by a trick of Reverend Mother's guile. Anna thought that on her deathbed she would still be grateful for that agonising conflict in Saint Anthony's parlour, and the sudden moment of victory.

Victory almost comically complete—for Granny, from being her enemy, had become somewhat menacingly ambitious now on her behalf. The visit to the Bishop had apparently been a triumph, because Granny seemed to have impressed his Lordship with her generous, progressive understanding of the need for higher education among Irishwomen. "A remarkably clear-sighted old lady," the Bishop had said to Mother Mary Andrew.

Reverend Mother. Anna stirred uneasily, and pressed herself back against the tree-trunk. She would never be able to make head or tail of the mystery of Reverend Mother. But it embarrassed her in these last nostalgic days, it oppressed her to realise how much she owed to Reverend Mother. Even the obvious great services of the last year, the slow, unhurrying help about Charlie, and the magical battle suddenly waged for her right to go to Dublin—even these obvious things had been done, Anna reflected, as other people could not have done them, and so that their full value took long in revealing itself. But they, for which she would never be able to explain or even really know her own gratitude, were after all only sudden strong lights, flashed and gone, on something that was always there, and might never be seen fully, or appreciated.

The school's conventional phrases for Reverend Mother were "cold fish" and "dark horse," and "queer one" and

"Sassenach." Anna had acceded to them and used them, in spite of remembering that to her, in her innocent, unconventional days, the days of the poems, Reverend Mother had never seemed to be any of those things. But at least it was true that, for ordinary purposes of designation, she fitted closer to those descriptions than she would have done to their antitheses. And, annoyed at being known as her pet, when there were no signs whatever of favouritism, Anna had been all the more free with this common coinage. But she had noticed originalities which were more interesting than queer, as she grew up; though, determined not to be "Reverend Mother's pet," she kept them to herself. She noticed, for instance, the singular, mezzo-soprano beauty of her voice, as it rang alone, very clear and holy, at Vespers on Sunday afternoon, or in the grave Lenten prayers of the Stations of the Cross—"Christ was made obedient unto death." Even as a little girl, Anna used to wait enraptured for the lift of the light, sad voice, before the confused response of the whole dark chapel broke on it.

She noticed too that whereas what were called "snubs" were common form from nuns to pupils—being any trick of authority to deflate or humiliate—Reverend Mother, almost alone, never "snubbed"; she never "lectured" an individual at length in public either, which most nuns delighted to do; and she never—oddly enough—meted out punishment. Anna had pondered these things increasingly as she grew up, and had mentioned them, with caution, to Norrie O'Dowd, who had reflected on them and had agreed that they were true observations.

She noticed that the austere Reverend Mother was indulgent too, when other nuns were relentless. She always took breakfast with the school, at Foundress's Table, and was generally waiting there, with the milk already in the cups, when the children took their places. Thus it was that on many mornings of Lent or Advent, girls who had given up sugar in tea or coffee for the season of abstinence, found sugar in their cups when they tasted them. "The Holy Ghost suggested to

me that you should have some sugar to-day," Reverend
Mother would say to the protestor. Anna often wondered
if this playfulness surprised or touched other girls as much
as it did her. Sometimes also if a girl had had "a sleep"
instead of getting up for early Mass, and announced this at
breakfast, Reverend Mother would say: "It's done you so
much good you'd better have another sleep to-morrow."

Anna, observing these things with great attention during
her last year, wondered why the chief description always was
"cold fish." And yet she was cold. You could use the word
"warmth" about a nun like Mother Eugenia or Mother
Felicita; you could indeed freely use the word "heat" about
the tempers and blastings of Mother Mary Andrew; but
Reverend Mother was cold. The word described her—
beautifully, Anna thought. And even in those moments when
you saw her most brilliantly, in fullest light—as when she
said that night in her study: "My soul, there is a country,"
or when she said to Granny: "By what authority do you
dispose of the life and talents of others?"—then, too, her
word was "cold." She was like someone, Anna thought,
who has made a lifelong, personal study of the impersonal.
Like a scientist perhaps, or a scholar—except that her
problems were just ordinary human situations.

Certainly, it was one way of being a nun—which could
be, Anna conceded, an enigmatic business.

She had thought very much in past months of the religious
vocation. Charlie's death had chilled and frosted the whole
measurable sum of life, and sometimes, kneeling in chapel,
she had felt herself so alone, so detached and empty of human
direction or love that it seemed to her in her fear not merely
easy but necessary to give her life to God.

It was not, she became able to argue with herself, that she
had loved Charlie in the way of proposing only to love him
among human beings, but that through his eyes, through
his temperament, softer, dreamier, gentler than her own, she
had seen life as he saw it, flowing, easy and to be loved. He
had been to her at once a protection and a touchstone, and

when he was gone it was not simply that he was gone, but that alone she felt too angular, too inept and too soon forsaken to go on in search of all that she believed existed, as he also had believed.

So she thought of the escape into religion, and although she knew that her facile thinking, her cold willingness, was not a vocation and had no vestige of sacrifice in it, yet she found distraction from loneliness sometimes in pursuit of the idea.

Loneliness. That seemed to be the black dog on her shoulder always now. She had been lonely in this school, more lonely than it would be possible to measure in this sped year—yet now, in three weeks of hurrying farewell, her sense of loss was very deep. She knew that her thoughts of vocation were false, a kind of game she played, a kind of hypnotism she used—and that she would not come back to take the holy habit of *Sainte Famille;* she knew that one great certainty had vanished last summer at Doon Point, and that now another, all this scene and frame and idiom of the remembered years, was dying too; that childhood indeed was over, that infinite lifetime, and that she was going out from it with no lessons learnt and no preparations made.

She looked at the shining lake, and thought suddenly with a twist of her heart of *Mère Martine*—her mind gone at last, and her poor fingers unable to pluck the guitar. "*Vogue, mon beau navire . . .*"

"Anna Murphy! Be a saint and have pity on me!"

Pilar O'Farrell was calling her. She sat with a book in her lap on the stone steps that led to Second Rec.'s playground.

"What's the matter, Pilar?"

"This most nonsensical poem, my dear! Oh, please explain it to me, Anna! Be an angel!"

Anna rose and went across. She sat on the step.

"What's the matter?" she said.

Pilar pushed the Middle Grade English Literature text book into her lap.

"This poem!" she said. "Will you explain to me two consecutive words of it, if there is any explanation! Oh, have a caramel!"

The poem was "Lycidas."

Pilar was seventeen, and was not returning to *Sainte Famille*. She was going to a finishing school in Lausanne. She had taken school life easily, but now desired to please her parents by passing an examination—for a surprise. So with much comedy and to the delight of her giggling friends, she was taking Middle Grade Intermediate.

"Why, what don't you understand in it?" Anna asked her.

"My dear—I don't understand *any* of it!"

Anna stared at her.

"How do you mean, that you don't understand *any* of it?"

"But what I say! Oh, I know he's lamenting about his friend—but I just don't understand the words he uses, Anna! The way he uses them! All this old bosh at the beginning—look! About 'bitter constraint and sad occasion dear' and 'forced fingers rude' and the something or other of a melodious tear! What's *up* with the man, *anyway?*"

"He's gathering stuff for a wreath for Lycidas. Surely that's plain?"

"Anything but! Anyway, talk of making ten words do the work of one! And he's just funny most of the time without knowing it, poor ass!"

"Ah no, Pilar. That's an idiotic thing to say."

"Oh, I know you're clever. But do you really mean that you don't feel giggly at 'Begin, and somewhat loudly sweep the string,' somewhat loudly!"

Anna's eyes ran on over the lines.

She knew the poem, but during this year if ever by accident her eyes fell on it from a Middle Grade girl's open book, or if she heard any bored or hilarious chanting of it by a memoriser, she winced. Now, however, on this lovely summer evening, with the sense of farewell making her breast seem empty, cavernous, receptive and still, she felt, almost as if she herself imposed it, the elegiac composure of the lines. "So may some gentle Muse with lucky words . . ." she read dreamily.

She let the book slide and leant her head back against the stone urn at the top of the step. Geraniums streamed from it and pressed about her; she inhaled their smell with careful delight. She looked at Pilar, seated a little below her at the other side of the steps. The landscape fell away through ilex-trees beyond the playground to the still lake and the evening sky, where Venus shone.

Pilar was still laughing obstinately.

"It is no good, Anna! He uses too many words for me, that old Milton."

Anna had always agreed with the general school opinion that Pilar was very pretty; but she did so without particular consideration, for the South American, girlish and silly, lacked the heroic, dominating elements of beauty which Anna thought important and which Molly Redmond had possessed. Also Anna tended to keep out of the way of Pilar's set, which was too rich and frivolous for her, and by its perpetual insistence on mockery and hilarity made her feel her lack of humour as a deformnity. Not that Pilar or her great friend Colette was ever anything other than kind—still, Anna felt an intruder in their world, and in the last three terms was simply too sad for their relentless gaiety.

Now, however, she saw Pilar in a new way. She became aware of her and of the moment on a plane of perception which was strange to her, and which during its visitation she did not understand but could only receive—delightedly, but without surprise in fact, and as if she had been waiting for the lead it was to give. She saw her, it seemed, in isolation and in a new sphere, yet one made up of broken symbols from their common life and which took its light from the simplicity of shared associations. A foolish school-girl, smiling at poetic verbiage—yet herself a symbol as complicated as any imaginative struggle in verse; a common piece of creation, an exquisite challenge to creativeness; she saw Pilar as a glimpse, as if she were a line from a lost immortal; she saw her ironically, delightedly, as a motive in art.

She did not understand this translation of the ordinary; she could only accept it and wait; but her heart leapt pre-monitorily. She knew little of pictures, save from battered volumes of old master reproductions in the reference library; yet memories from these books floated upon the acutely visual moment; for the marmoreal gravity of "Lycidas" recalled Mantegna, and in the light and the ilex-trees she felt a bright memory of Giorgione—but Pilar herself was something else, though Anna's racing responsiveness might not pause to find it—she was a girl of *La Vida Española*, a young girl in Goya, who dances and gathers grapes, and plays blind-man's-buff; a small-waisted girl with shining eyes, eternally lifted off in joy from other Goya worlds.

So Anna beheld her; something that life can be about, something with power to make life compose around it. She stared at her in wonder, hardly seeing her any more, but realising her lustrous potentiality, and feeling that for her, the watcher, this moment was a long-awaited, blessed gift; that in seeing this transience, this grace, this volatility, flung in a sweet summer hour against great ilex-trees, against the evening star, she was encountering, alone and in terms of her secret need, a passage of beauty as revelatory and true as any verse of the great elegy.

"Where will you live, Pilar—after Lausanne?"

"In Lima. Why?"

"What's Lima like?"

"It's lovely. Very white, and full of gardens. They say it is like Sevilla."

Colette's voice rang across the tennis courts.

"Pilar! Where on earth have you got to?"

Pilar sprang up.

"Oh, my dear, the thing is, where were you?"

She flew over the grass to join her friend.

## "IVY NEVER SERE"

Anna's eyes fell back to the forgotten book on her lap.

"For we were nursed upon the self-same hill . . ." she read, and went on slowly to the end. She felt peaceful, emptied of grief.

## The Fourth Chapter

### TE DEUM

REVEREND MOTHER had always had a particular affection for Bishop's Walk. When she walked with the community at summer-evening recreation they usually lured her from it to the wilder path by the lake—and for recreation hour she welcomed that, for the antics of wildfowl, the variations of scene and the fresh, water-whipped air were good for the gaiety she liked to induce among her nuns; when she took exercise, talking convent business, with Mother Eugenia, the latter liked to stroll, alert and practically critical, about the kitchen garden; if she had to entertain the Bishop, who was a botanist and a gardener, he chose to stride among the azaleas and rose-bushes, the arbutus, fuchsia and eucalyptus trees of the lower lawns, about St. Joseph's Grotto. But for herself, to the nuns' polite surprise, she liked the formal, shaded quiet of Bishop's Walk.

"I hate elm-trees anyway," Mother Eugenia said. "They're untidy-looking—even our beauties."

Reverend Mother conceded their untidy trunks.

"But they are very tall," she said, "and they meet overhead like arches of a church. Like *Sainte Gudule*," she said once.

She liked the limited, urban formality of Bishop's Walk; she liked its lack of aspect, its peaceful dissociation from the scenic splendours around; and she liked it because its trees were elms, trees of childhood and home.

Often through the years she had escaped in a lull of afternoon to walk there alone in brief meditation. And in moments of self-examination arising there from consideration of the ideal of prayer and before the intractability of her human substance, she sometimes wondered why, in embracing religion, she had not had the courage to seek its

274

completeness, the full contemplative life. And then she would remind herself sadly that in fact she had not chosen this life of service of God, that she had not thought, weighed and given up in the desire for perfection—but merely had fled in outrage and blind hurt from one collapsed house of her spirit to another standing by, intact.

She had heard her father say sometimes that one of Herbert's epithets for prayer, "the soul in paraphrase," was so felicitous, so *witty* as to be, he believed, unmatchable, on its own ground. And in later years, pacing under the elms, she often turned it to and fro in her mind, in envious, lonely appreciation. Whether or not it was witty she hardly cared, but she felt in the phrase a mystical exactitude upon which her soul had hardly courage to encroach.

But this afternoon she had come out to the shade of the trees not to pray or to wrestle with reflections on prayer— but simply for some minutes of rest.

It was a busy tense day. To-morrow was Prize Day, and all through the house there was the exhausting composite excitement which always characterised its eve. Loneliness, excitement, nervousness, relief, regret, delight and desolation —all these were quick through school and community in varying measures, and all had to be subdued within and without to manifold urgent duties. Reverend Mother carried a load of mixed emotion through these days, and feared the morrow's break-up, and the news from Brussels which any hour might bring. So she came alone to Bishop's Walk, seeking nothing save its beneficent quiet, and, perhaps unconsciously, from evocations of the elm-trees, the spirit of *Mère Générale*.

"Softness, and peace, and joy, and love, and bliss . . ."— the words from the sonnet surprised her, flowing unsought across her mind—

". . . Exalted manna, gladness of the best,
Heaven in ordinary, man well drest,
The milky way, the bird of Paradise,

Church bells beyond the stars heard, the soul's blood,
The land of spices, something understood."

It occurred to her as the words refreshed her that *Mère
Générale*, most cautious and least lyrical of holy women,
would accept each one of these images for prayer, weighing
it as it came and assenting with a shrewd drop of her head.
But "Heaven in ordinary, man well drest"—Reverend Mother
smiled outright as she thought of the practical appreciation
with which the old Frenchwoman might greet those ideas.
She might even find a motto in them for the active religious
life, a standard for the *Compagnie de la Sainte Famille*.

Reverend Mother enjoyed this light surmise, and did not
rebuke her own smiles, for she needed the visitation of her
old friend.

She turned at the end of the walk, where brightness
began above the fields with the view of the lake. As she
retraced her steps Sister Maria came towards her. Faithful,
good Sister Maria, the portress. As she approached
Reverend Mother saw an orange-coloured envelope in her
hand.

She stood quiet then, unable to go forward to meet it.
She received it from the lay-sister with a smile of thanks.

"No, do not wait, Sister Maria. If there is an answer I
shall deal with it later."

"Very well so, Reverend Mother. I'll tell the boy to be
off with himself."

"Thank you very much."

Sister Maria waddled away.

Reverend Mother opened the envelope slowly and unfolded the message. It was from Mother Assistant General
at Brussels.

"*Ma Mère, vous avez été appelée à la dignité de Mère Générale
de la Compagnie de la Sainte Famille. Précisions suivent par
courrier. Au nom de maison mère et de Compagnie entière me
permets de vous présenter nos plus humbles félicitations et de vous*

*assurer de la joie profonde avec laquelle nous recevons cette heureuse
nouvelle. Le Te Deum sera chanté dans toutes nos maisons ce soir.
Respects profonds et pieux. Votre fille obéissante, Marie-Sophie
Renaud.*"

So it had come.

She folded the telegram neatly, resisting a nervous inclina-
tion to refold it and fold it again. It must look tidy and
orthodox for Mother Eugenia.

Presently she must go to the house and give it to the
latter, whose duty it would be to announce its contents to
the community and afterwards to the school.

Everyone, except possibly shrewd old Mother Eugenia,
everyone would be astounded. Clearly there was no idea at
all in the air that she, their own Reverend Mother, was a
possible Mother General. Yet to-night at evening chapel
the whole house would sing *Te Deum* because she had been
placed in final human authority above them. By tradition
*Te Deum* would be sung to-night in every house of *Sainte
Famille* throughout the world.

Reverend Mother remembered the singing of it—to cele-
brate the election to Generalship of an unknown nun in
Paris, *Mère Catherine Mandel*—in the chapel at *Sainte Fontaine*,
on a November night in 1880. Certainly no guess would
have seemed more silly to the nineteen-year-old novice of
that night than that the next general *Te Deum* of the Order
would be sung to welcome her to its highest place of
government.

She folded her hands very tightly together and with bent
head resumed her meditative walk.

She should pray, she felt, under the intimidating command
of this news. And in a sense she did pray, but only quickly,
evasively, to ask for time, to ask for a minute in which to
adjust her soul to the awaited fact. She had prayed very
much in this month for wisdom and guidance, and would
pray, would need to pray she assured herself, incomparably
more. But in this moment of climax she was aware that all

the doubts, regrets, emotions, fears and anxieties of the month were forming themselves into one cold and leaden amalgam—sadness. And she felt a need to reason against that, to lift it somewhat, if she could, by her own agency, and so turn a polite and willing face towards her new ordeal, so full of traps and dangers.

Pride, she had been compelled to notice, ordinary professional pride, was one of these traps. It was alarming but true that she found consolation in reflecting that so wise a woman as her own *Mère Générale* regarded her as wise enough to hold high office in her turn. And it was true, and even more shocking and alarming that, apart from the compliment of *Mère Générale's* posthumous trust, she took pleasure in the idea of going as far as it was possible to go in the life she had chosen. Struggling with the warmth of this vanity, accusing herself and praying against it, she had thought of her father, and almost laughed at the state of shouting disgust which such an admission as the latter of these would have induced in him. "But 'to go as far as possible,' in terms of power and elections and so on, proves *nothing*, Helen! Proves nothing ever about anyone! In any case, don't you know that nothing can be settled about us while we live? Oh, my poor child, I'm ashamed of you!" She laughed and reflected that her offending, vulgar sentiment would also have been reproved, more ironically, by her mother, but that nevertheless the latter would have understood and even felt it, as her father never could. I am, after all, the child of both, she thought. And mother was a much frustrated woman, and would have taken vicarious pleasure in this news.

Pride—ah yes, most difficult—ignoble emotion; though extenuated more than she allowed herself to see by the sense of failure which had dogged her in Ireland. She might feel too much its foolish stir because here for long she had felt humiliated. Here she had been "a cold fish," "a queer one," "English"; now she was going back, perilously rewarded by the proud confidence of a good judge, to a place where she had mostly learnt to be whatever she now was, and where the love which had chosen and believed in her waited, she felt sure, in every memory, every shadow, to bestow its ghostly kindness, its haunting, blessed reassurances.

She thought of *Mère Générale's* dim, white-walled study; the brass Crucifix on the wall and the wire screens on the windows, darkening the view of the square. It would be a happy thing to return to work in so good a place, and to grow old striving with duties she believed in. She could pray for courage and for judgment; she could remember and call upon the quick, familiar wisdom of her predecessor. Shadows of evil and danger were indeed gathering, as *Mère Générale* had said. Germany, Austria, the Balkans, all were seething—and in Ireland too there were fear and passion in the air. No one could guess how war would come to Europe, but only that it was visibly on its way. When it came old faiths would be tested, and indeed all human hopes and dreams might have to undergo an ordeal impossible to imagine, and which might outspan lives of watchers younger than she. But things to come would bring with them each its complementary duty, and beyond accomplishing that one could do no more than pray for the troubled world. And whatever *was* to come, the Church was One, Holy, Catholic and Apostolical, and must ride, with its militant faithful, above mere temporal storms. The training of the Christian mind would go on, Reverend Mother reflected, however many wars barbarians wage. And indeed *Place des Ormes* seemed as peaceful a corner as any other in Europe now from which to promote the glory of God.

The trend of her thought surprised her, for it showed that she had slipped at once into acceptance of her new responsibility, and that she was not for the moment more than decently afraid of it.

No. What she *was* afraid of, what she was evading in these serpentine thoughts, was the ordinary sensation of sadness: the double sadness that lay for her in return and in departure. Perhaps she liked power, she conceded to herself; perhaps such power as she had wielded here had been more compensation than she knew for day-to-day frustrations; and perhaps she was even so conceited as to let herself hope that, always trusting in God's grace, she had learnt with the years to understand power a little, and to use it with care. God must help her in the dangerous pride of these thoughts, and she must hope that at least there was some safety in facing them; but it was true, for better or worse, that now it was here she was not afraid of a destiny she had long seen approaching. For she never had been seriously afraid, at any moment of her life, of the spaces over which her mind had full command—and this was so, not because of arrogance or presumption but, contrarily, because she could assess the limitations of her intellect, and so ensure it against darkness. But the planes of memory, attachment, sensibility—these were beyond survey, and she had once been driven in horror from their boundaries. For ever since she had been afraid of the most innocent or tender movements of her heart. And it was only because he, who had so mortally injured her, had told her in his curious, ironic wisdom that she was growing "merciless" and thus unfit for her work; because he had said that he feared for "the young and the weak and the senti-mental" who would fall into her charge, and because reason and good will had seen the truth of his warning, that she had forgone the coward's armour of obduracy, and tried to compromise with human feeling.

And now human feeling lay in recognisable weight upon this hour. Her heart was sad. Sad that a return often dreamt of would be at last to graves and empty places; sad that a departure which once she had most bitterly desired should seem at its coming so inconsistently a sacrifice. And indeed, twisting about in her soul against her undisciplined pain, she marvelled how emotionalists endured their lives at all, since she who hardly tolerated feeling found its touch intolerable.

However, let sadness come, let it be. Her years in this house were over, and whatever their general content of usefulness or error, she believed that her being here, her sentinelship—for it was no more—had been of good to the one creature whom by accident she had allowed herself a little to love.

She had loved the child Anna in sheer playful pleasure at first—for a questioning, pure quality she found in her face, and because the little voice speaking old verses rang a happy echo from the past; she loved her then because she felt her father would have loved her, and perhaps have been reminded of the same past. But as the child grew, and in some ways grew less lovable, Reverend Mother saw that the pleasures of affection sow responsibilities—and these she was glad to harvest. And as love grew anxious it grew deep. But there is little that love can do—the best of its goodness often being to keep still. And this Reverend Mother learnt.

And now all was done that age may do for childhood. Anna's schooldays were closed, and there was no appeal against the advance of life and the flight of innocence. She had been taught to be good and to understand the law of God. Also, she had been set free to be herself. Her wings were grown and she was for the world. In poverty, in struggle, in indecisiveness—but for some these were good beginnings. Good for Anna, Reverend Mother thought, and was glad to know that it was forward to them that she was going. Prayer would follow her; prayer always could. It would have been happy to have been at hand a little longer, to have heard something of the first flights and first returns. But such a wish was nothing. All that could be done was done. Anna was for life now, to make what she could of it. Prayer could go with her, making no weight—and whether or not she remembered "the days of the poems," an ageing nun would remember them. How sweet is the shepherd's sweet lot, from the morn to the evening he strays. Reverend Mother passed by the bright opening of the elm-trees and looked over the lawns to the blue lake.

A girl came out of St. Joseph's Grotto, carrying two flower-pot stands. She crossed the lawns diagonally upwards, coming towards Bishop's Walk. It was Anna.

"Oh—Reverend Mother! May I take this short cut?"

The children did not frequent Bishop's Walk, which was reserved for the community and for distinguished visitors.

Reverend Mother smiled. Anna had clearly been going to use it—without permission.

"You may, Anna."

"Mother Mary Andrew sent me for these, for the *salle*." She indicated the flower-pot stands of plaited wire.

"Ah! You are decorating for to-morrow. Do you know your part, Anna?"

Anna was playing Cassius to-morrow, in the quarrel scene from *Julius Cæsar*, to Norrie O'Dowd's Brutus.

"I think so, Reverend Mother."

"Well, you certainly have the lean and hungry look! I hope you are going to have a good holiday."

A shadow crossed Anna's face.

"Granny has taken a house near Dungarvan," she said. "I—I'm going to try to get over to Ring sometimes—you know, the Irish-speaking district where there's an Irish summer school. It's near there, I think. I—I don't want the —usual sort of holiday."

"But it will be different at Dungarvan—an entirely different kind of coast."

"I expect so," Anna said politely.

They were walking under the elm-trees.

"I helped to choose some of your prize books last evening, Anna. You have done very well indeed this year, and will be receiving an astonishing number of prizes to-morrow."

Anna smiled with shyness.

"Oh, thank you, Reverend Mother. And thank you for choosing them."

"I don't care for their bindings. The prize-book convention is ugly—and I hope you won't think I have loaded you with too much verse."

"Oh, I don't think I could!"

"Among others I have chosen Henry Vaughan for you— for old time's sake. Do you remember, Anna?"

"I won't ever forget that poem, now. I had sort of

forgotten it—but you reminded me about Charlie; you told me to say it instead of prayers. And now often, when I think of him, it comes into my head."

Silence fell. They were standing again at the open end of the walk, and they paused to look about them. The air was fragrant; the lake shone like a blue jewel below the dark trees; the hills lay softly against the brilliant sky.

Reverend Mother smiled.

"I admit that this is very beautiful," she said.

Anna looked surprised.

"Haven't you always thought so, Reverend Mother?"

"Yes, in a way. But I have sometimes thought it too easy— like Irish conversational charm. However occasionally the light does something to this unaccountable landscape, and really makes it seem holy for a minute—an island *for* if not *of* saints, Anna!"

She knew that the girl was too shy, too much in awe of "Reverend Mother" to venture a response. But her face had the pure, attentive look that had made her endearing in little girlhood, and her eyes, searching the scene they discussed, were as blue as the blue lake.

But suddenly they filled with tears, and the lids, the lashes, came down in defence of secrecy. Anna turned her head away, and Reverend Mother said nothing. Presently in a controlled, soft voice the girl spoke.

"I didn't know it would be like this—leaving school. I didn't know things mattered so much—that I depended so much on—on everything here. I feel frightened—and yet, not altogether frightened. Oh, I don't know!"

They turned away from the view and walked back under the trees.

"I suppose I ought to have advice for you," Reverend Mother said. "But I have none. *Sainte Famille* has given you whatever it has to give, and you have understood its lessons. I am confident of that. You will make what you must of the life for which we have tried to prepare you. And you have gifts for life. Spend your gifts, and try to be good.

And be the judge of your own soul; but never for a second, I implore you, set up as judge of another. Commentator, annotator, if you like, but never judge."

Her voice vibrated as Anna remembered to have heard it when—so long ago it seemed—she spoke with passion to Ursula de la Pole, while Molly Redmond stood in woe against the beech-tree. It had the music Anna had so often listened for in the stations of the Cross. Christ was made obedient unto death.

I shall never hear that again, Anna thought. I shall never know anything about her.

"It is a very hard thing, I suppose," she said impulsively. "It is a very hard thing—to be a nun."

"I think so," Reverend Mother said.

"I—I thought of it sometimes this year—but not properly. Not for holy reasons. Only because I was frightened."

"I know. Holy reasons are the only ones—and they are hard to be sure about, and hard to sustain."

"I don't think I could possibly be a nun!"

"You are young, Anna."

They came to the top of Bishop's Walk, near the house.

"I must go in," Anna said. "Mother Mary Andrew will be frantic for these."

"Yes, you'd better hurry."

"I've—I've never tried to thank you, Reverend Mother, for all the things you've done for me—but then, I never could."

"Anna, there are no thanks to be said. Since you came to us you have been my very dear child, and you always will be that, to the end of my life. Run on now, and God bless you."

Anna ran across the scuffling gravel, towards the playground entrance to the house. She ran with her head down, and Reverend Mother guessed that what she had said to her had brought new tears.

The nun stood a moment at the foot of the sweep of Georgian steps that led to the convent's main doorway.

She admired the terraced flower-beds, by God's grace and Sister Jerome's labour brought to the climax of their summer pride in honour of tomorrow; she looked over the empty tennis courts; she listened to the hum of life within the house —clash of pianos, footsteps hurrying, a handbell sharply rung; far off she saw Sister Simeon trudging in peace with buckets, to feed her hens.

All had poignancy now, the poignancy of farewell against which Anna too was struggling; all had henceforward the poise of things remembered. *"Que la volonté de Dieu, si juste, si aimable . . ."* Reverend Mother smiled. There would be *Marie-Jeanne* at least to find again.

The telegram still waited in her hands. She went indoors to give it to Mother Eugenia.

*Oxford, September,* 1940.

**THE END**

# VIRAGO MODERN CLASSICS
## &
## CLASSIC NON-FICTION

The first Virago Modern Classic, *Frost in May* by Antonia White, was published in 1978. It launched a list dedicated to the celebration of women writers and to the rediscovery and reprinting of their works. Its aim was, and is, to demonstrate the existence of a female tradition in fiction, and to broaden the sometimes narrow definition of a 'classic' which has often led to the neglect of interesting novels and short stories. Published with new introductions by some of today's best writers, the books are chosen for many reasons: they may be great works of fiction; they may be wonderful period pieces; they may reveal particular aspects of women's lives; they may be classics of comedy or storytelling.

The companion series, Virago Classic Non-Fiction, includes diaries, letters, literary criticism, and biographies – often by and about authors published in the Virago Modern Classics.

'A continuingly magnificent imprint' – *Joanna Trollope*

'The Virago Modern Classics have reshaped literary history and enriched the reading of us all. No library is complete without them' – *Margaret Drabble*

'The writers are formidable, the production handsome. The whole enterprise is thoroughly grand' – *Louise Erdrich*

'The Virago Modern Classics are one of the best things in Britain today' – *Alison Lurie*

'Good news for everyone writing and reading today' – *Hilary Mantel*

'Masterful works' – *Vogue*

# VIRAGO MODERN CLASSICS
&
## CLASSIC NON-FICTION

Some of the authors included in these two series –

Lisa Alther, Elizabeth von Arnim, Dorothy Baker, Pat Barker,
Nina Bawden, Nicola Beauman, Isabel Bolton, Kay Boyle,
Vera Brittain, Leonora Carrington, Angela Carter, Willa Cather,
Colette, Ivy Compton-Burnett, Barbara Comyns, E.M. Delafield,
Maureen Duffy, Elaine Dundy, Nell Dunn, Emily Eden, George Eliot,
Miles Franklin, Mrs Gaskell, Charlotte Perkins Gilman,
Victoria Glendinning, Elizabeth Forsythe Hailey, Radclyffe Hall,
Shirley Hazzard, Dorothy Hewett, Mary Hocking, Alice Hoffman,
Winifred Holtby, Janette Turner Hospital, Zora Neale Hurston,
Elizabeth Jenkins, F. Tennyson Jesse, Molly Keane,
Margaret Laurence, Maura Laverty, Rosamond Lehmann,
Rose Macaulay, Shena Mackay, Olivia Manning, Paule Marshall,
F.M. Mayor, Anaïs Nin, Mary Norton, Kate O'Brien, Olivia,
Grace Paley, Mollie Panter-Downes, Dawn Powell,
Dorothy Richardson, E. Arnot Robertson, Jacqueline Rose,
Vita Sackville-West, Elaine Showalter, May Sinclair,
Agnes Smedley, Dodie Smith, Stevie Smith, Christina Stead,
Carolyn Steedman, Gertrude Stein, Jan Struther, Han Suyin,
Elizabeth Taylor, Sylvia Townsend Warner, Mary Webb,
Eudora Welty, Mae West, Rebecca West, Edith Wharton,
Antonia White, Christa Wolf, Virginia Woolf, E.H. Young

'Found on all the best bookshelves' – *Penny Vincenzi*

'Their huge success is solid proof of the fact that literary fashion is
a snare and a delusion – people like a good old-fashioned read' –
*Good Housekeeping*

*Also by Kate O'Brien*

# THE LAST OF SUMMER

It is 1939, the last summer before the outbreak of war. Travelling through Ireland, French actress Angèle Maury abandons her group of friends and takes herself instead to picturesque Drumaninch, the birthplace of her dead father. She has come to make sense of her past, and is soon absorbed into the strange, idiosyncratic world of her cousins, the Kernahans. Self-conscious with her pale, exotic beauty, Angèle finds herself seduced first by the beauty of Ireland and then by the love of two men, as history threatens to repeat itself in a perfectly structured psychological love story.

**'Rush out for the works of Kate O'Brien. You are in for a treat'** – *Val Hennessy*

# THE ANTE-ROOM

Ireland, 1880, and Teresa Mulqueen lies dying. Beneath the gloom of her household, though, is a spark which threatens to destroy the composure of this prosperous, provincial family. Unmarried Agnes anxiously awaits the arrival of her sister Marie-Rose and brother-in-law Vincent. She adores her sister but secretly, passionately loves Vincent – and she knows their marriage is foundering. Ahead lies a terrible battle between her uncompromising faith and the intensity of her love.

'A grave and beautiful story, exquisitely composed and cut to a jewel-like fineness' – *Daily Telegraph*

# MARY LAVELLE

*With a new Introduction by Michèle Roberts*

It is 1922 and Mary Lavelle, young and beautiful, leaves her family and fiancé in Ireland to become a governess in a Spanish fishing village. She goes to seek a small space, a hiatus between her life's two accepted phases – as daughter and as wife. But despite the impressive surroundings and her three charming charges, she finds life as governess to the Areavaga family lonely. And with the arrival of the family's brilliant but married son, Juanito, Mary finds her loyalties and beliefs challenged by his fiery politics and passion.

With characteristic elegance and subtlety, Kate O'Brien, one of Ireland's most beloved writers, illuminates the anguish and ecstasies of a young woman at the heart of a family and a nation divided.

'A superior type of romantic novel . . . colourful and unorthodox' – *TLS*

# Now you can order superb titles directly from Virago

| | | | |
|---|---|---|---|
| ☐ | Mary Lavelle | Kate O'Brien | £6.99 |
| ☐ | Without My Cloak | Kate O'Brien | £7.99 |
| ☐ | The Ante-Room | Kate O'Brien | £7.99 |
| ☐ | The Last of Summer | Kate O'Brien | £6.99 |
| ☐ | Full House | Molly Keane | £6.99 |
| ☐ | Devoted Ladies | Molly Keane | £7.99 |

Please allow for postage and packing: **Free UK delivery.**
Europe; add 25% of retail price; Rest of World; 45% of retail price.

To order any of the above or any other Virago titles, please call our credit card orderline or fill in this coupon and send/fax it to:

**Virago, P.O. Box 121, Kettering, Northants NN14 4ZQ**
**Tel: 01832 737526   Fax: 01832 733076**
**Email: aspenhouse@FSBDial.co.uk**

☐ I enclose a UK bank cheque made payable to Virago for £ ...........

☐ Please charge £.............. to my Access, Visa, Delta, Switch Card No.

Expiry Date ☐☐☐☐   Switch Issue No. ☐☐

NAME (Block letters please) ...................................................................

ADDRESS ...........................................................................................

..........................................................................................................

..........................................................................................................

Postcode ................................Telephone ...........................................

Signature ...........................................................................................

Please allow 28 days for delivery within the UK. Offer subject to price and availability.

Please do not send any further mailings from companies carefully selected by Virago ☐